S0-AGF-121

WITHDRAWN

THE CANOPY

This Large Print Book carries the
Seal of Approval of N.A.V.H.

THE CANOPY

ANGELA HUNT

THORNDIKE PRESS

An imprint of Thomson Gale, a part of The Thomson Corporation

HUNTINGTON CITY-TOWNSHIP
PUBLIC LIBRARY
200 W. Market Street
Huntington, IN 46750

THOMSON

™

GALE

Detroit • New York • San Francisco • New Haven, Conn. • Waterville, Maine • London

Copyright © 2003 by Angela Elwell Hunt.
Scripture quotations are taken from the *Holy Bible*, New Living Translation, copyright © 1996. Used by permission of Tyndale House Publishers, Inc. Wheaton, Illinois 30189. All rights reserved.
Thorndike Press, an imprint of The Gale Group.
Thomson and Star Logo and Thorndike are trademarks and Gale is a registered trademark used herein under license.

ALL RIGHTS RESERVED
This is a work of fiction. Names, characters, places, and incidents either are the product of the author's imagination or are used fictitiously.
Thorndike Press® Large Print Christian Romance.
The text of this Large Print edition is unabridged.
Other aspects of the book may vary from the original edition.
Set in 16 pt. Plantin.

LIBRARY OF CONGRESS CATALOGING-IN-PUBLICATION DATA

Hunt, Angela Elwell, 1957–
   The canopy / by Angela Hunt.
     p. cm.
   ISBN-13: 978-0-7862-9590-6 (hardcover : alk. paper)
   ISBN-10: 0-7862-9590-2 (hardcover : alk. paper)
   1. Large type books. I. Title.
PS3558.U46747C36 2007
813'.54—dc22   2007014953

Published in 2007 by arrangement with Thomas Nelson, Inc.

Printed in the United States of America on permanent paper
10 9 8 7 6 5 4 3 2 1

Do not be afraid of
the terrors of the night,
nor fear the dangers of the day,
nor dread the plague that stalks in
darkness . . .
If you make the LORD your refuge,
if you make the Most High
your shelter,
no evil will conquer you;
no plague will come near
your dwelling . . .

He will not let you stumble and fall;
the one who watches over you
will not sleep.

— Psalms 91:5–6, 9–10; 121:3

1 April 2003
6:12 a.m.

Though his body sang with pain, the native kept running.

Struggling to move through thickened air that pressed upon his skin, he held one hand over the gaping wound in his gut and loped toward the spangled light dancing over the crude path gleaming in the jungle shadows.

His pursuers had come close last night. One of their spears had pierced him, pinning him to a tree, but he had found the strength to pull the weapon out and fling it away. After that, his blood left a trail even a child could follow, but the Spirit of keyba had blinded their eyes while sending a beacon for him to follow.

He paused, intensifying the pressure on his abdomen, and squinted at the dazzling light hovering twenty paces away. Despite the pain that ripped at his insides like a piranha, his feet had carried him far from his pursuers.

The fiery ball had led him through the deepest part of the jungle under black night, and the man knew his enemies would not follow.

Though darkness filled their hearts, still the night frightened them. The jaguar's snarl, the anaconda's hiss, the carnivore ant's silent march . . . these things had frightened him, too, before he began to follow the Spirit of keyba.

The native leaned forward, bracing his free hand against his trembling knee. Air moved through his nostrils with a faint whistling sound as his jaws clamped against a spasm that sent a shaft of pure white pain ripping through his body. When he pried the stiff fingers of his right hand from the yawning hole in his gut, the brown skin parted like a pair of bloody lips.

He felt his mouth twist. He had seen wounds like this in other men, and not even the shaman could save them.

In the forest canopy, hundreds of macaws screamed and whistled as they fought each other for precious perches in the dappled rays of the rising sun. The man winced at the noise, then lifted his head and studied the trail ahead. How much farther would he have to go? He had traveled for two days before encountering warriors from the Angry People. The Spirit of keyba had not left him, but his strength would not last forever. And the barbed thorns, spiked leaves, and sharp-

8

edged grasses of this brutal forest had sapped his power.

Blinking, he lifted his head and saw the light, still beckoning. Pressing his hand back over the wound, he straightened and stepped forward, moving with a slower gait. Breathing deeply, he inhaled the scents of orchids and mangoes, decaying vegetation, and the unmistakable acrid odor of snake.

Without pausing to investigate, he staggered toward the light, his chest burning with each breath. He had not gone far when a new sound reached his ears — the happy squeals of children. Another series of steps brought him to a fringe of forest overlooking the river. Three young ones played in the shallows, splashing and laughing while their mother bent at the water's edge.

Looking up, he saw that the light had disappeared. Apparently he had reached his destination.

Calling on the last reserves of his strength, the native left the concealing jungle and stepped into a clearing. Lifting his left hand, he called out a greeting.

The children turned to look at him with dark forest eyes. The woman whirled, one hand extended toward her young, the other reaching for a shiny object that might serve as a weapon.

He took another step forward, lifting both hands this time, and to his greeting he added

9

a plea for help. The boy's eyes went wide at the sight of the bloody wound, and the little girl screamed. Snatching the smallest child out of the water, the woman bared her teeth and yelled in a language he could not understand.

The native waved his hands to demonstrate that he had not come to make war. He took another step forward, then realized that the muscles of his legs had become as stiff as wood. Wasps of agony buzzed along the length of his arms and swarmed in his belly. Gray pain roared behind his eyes and in his ears, drowning out the frantic woman's voice and blocking the bright sun on the river.

He took another step, saw the woman screech and lift her weapon, then his legs crumpled and the soft shoulder of the riverbank rose up to meet him.

1 April 2003
8:43 a.m.

"You are doing fine, Dr. Pace. Keep going, but whatever you do, do not look down!"

Alexandra Pace gritted her teeth as Milos Olsson's patient voice floated up from the rainforest floor. The stocky Swedish botanist had probably been climbing trees and mountains since he was old enough to wear lederhosen, but the act of traveling upward via muscle and rope was still new to Alex . . . and more than a little unnerving.

"Just clip and pull." The new voice belonged to Deborah Simons, the American entomologist who was clambering up the rope ten yards above Alex. The outdoorsy Texan had taken to the sport of tree climbing like a monkey. "Hey, if this gal can get the hang of it, anybody can."

Clip and pull? Closing her eyes, Alex dangled in space as the words brought back memories of hot Saturday afternoons sipping a Diet Coke beneath the hair dryer in her favorite salon. Now the nearest hair dryer was probably two hundred miles away, and few people in the Amazon jungle had even *seen* a Diet Coke . . .

"Dr. Pace, you awake up there?" Someone beneath her jiggled the rope, snapping her out of her daydream even as the motion sent adrenaline spurting into her bloodstream.

"I'm moving!" She slipped her foot into the prusik loop attached to the main line, then stood, the prusik holding her weight while her right hand nudged the mechanical ascender another twelve inches upward. The metal Jumar slid easily along the purple rope, its surface cool beneath her damp palm.

"One," she whispered, reciting the count she'd rehearsed a hundred times the day before. Olsson had the entire team practice climbing a tree in front of the lodge, and Alex had been surprised when most of her teammates took to climbing as enthusiastically as teenage boys took to driving. She had scaled the thirty-foot tree three times, gaining confidence in the technique, but today her muscles were stiff and complaining.

She squinted as she tipped her head back to see the purple line disappearing in a ceiling of green leaves. *This* was no thirty-foot tree. The strangler fig's uppermost branches filled the forest canopy over one hundred thirty feet above the ferns carpeting the jungle floor.

"Two." She sat back, leaning her weight on the carabiner linking her pelvic harness to the guide rope, then tugged the lower prusik upward with the toe of her sneaker.

"Consider *Eupithecia orichloris*," Deborah had explained yesterday. "Think of yourself as an inchworm moving steadily up the tree."

Alex was certain no worm had ever inched his way up this particular specimen of *Ficus Americana.* Too many hazards lay along the path of the trunk — ants and birds and wasps and snakes and even plants that would delight in snacking on any worm that happened by. The odds of an unperturbed passage weren't much better for human climbers, so she and her teammates were climbing this tree as if it were a mountain, with ropes, carabiners, and harnesses.

"It's simple, really," she muttered under her breath. "Just part of a day's work. And necessary for your research."

"Move along, will you, madame?"

Alex glanced down in time to see Louis Fortier, the French perfumer, jiggle the rope beneath her. "We are eager to climb, too."

"I'm moving!" Blowing out a breath, she stepped on the prusik again and slid the Jumar upward. Leaning back on the carabiner, she was about to lift the loop around her sneaker when her fingers spasmed, making her lose her grip on the line. The weight of

13

her backpack pulled her backward, her unattached left leg flew upward, and for a horrifying instant fear froze her scalp to her skull. Then the carabiner snapped against her harness, preventing her fall, and the rope around her right shoe tightened.

Gasping, with both arms helplessly beating the air, she hung upside down like a pinioned parrot.

"You are all right, yes?" Olsson called.

Alex forced herself to draw a deep breath and calm her pounding heart. She was *not* all right. She was as far from all right as she had ever been in her life. But no one could know her secret.

Summoning what she hoped was a measure of dignity, she directed her gaze down to the place where a knot of researchers huddled around the rope. "I'm fine. My hand slipped." With an effort, she folded her arms around her head as an inquisitive wasp investigated her face. "I seem to be stuck, however."

"You are not stuck." Olsson's no-nonsense tone told her she would have to get herself out of this predicament. "Reach up from the waist, Dr. Pace, and catch the rope with your fingers."

She closed her eyes. Olsson spoke with the confidence of an athletic man who could still run and jump and bend without pain. He had never lived inside the body of a thirty-something-year-old woman for whom regular

14

exercise consisted of frequent trips to the coffeemaker.

And he had no idea her central nervous system had begun to short-circuit.

Drawing in a breath, she lifted her head, then urged her arms and fingers to reach toward her toes.

She couldn't do it.

She fell back, squinching her eyes into knots while her brain railed against her situation. This was the result of a simple slip, perhaps one more related to exhaustion than to her condition. And though panic attacks were one of the symptoms of her illness, she would *not* panic here, not now, not today . . .

"Twinkle, twinkle, little star." She sang the old nursery rhyme under her breath. She'd loved the song as a child, and in medical school she'd discovered that singing it brought peace to her jittery nerves. The reason probably had something to do with the security of childhood and the resilience of embedded memories, but psychology had never particularly interested her.

Struggling against tears, she was calmly whispering the rest of the song when Valerik Baklanov, her research partner for this expedition, stepped up to the rope. "Momentum will help you counteract the gravity," he called, compassion streaming through his Russian accent. "Swing, Alex, like a child. Then you can reach the rope."

She nodded, not trusting her voice, and began to rock from side to side. While Deborah Simons squealed overhead, Alex swung herself forward, finally building enough momentum to reach upward, catch the rope, and pull herself upright.

Thank the stars, this time her fingers had obeyed. She clung to the guideline, closing her eyes as the walls of the jungle swayed around her, then forced herself to look up.

"Sorry," she called to Deborah, who had vanished into the canopy.

"Dr. Pace," Olsson called again. "We are waiting for you to ascend."

Of course they were. And while they waited, they were probably thinking she was the most uncoordinated American woman ever to step foot in the jungle, but that was okay. She'd rather they think her uncoordinated than know that her body had begun to weaken.

Determined to make up for lost time, Alex drew a deep breath and stood in the prusik, then slipped the ascender upward.

1 April 2003
9:20 a.m.

Dr. Michael Kenway removed the tongue depressor from his small patient's mouth, then patted the boy's cheek with two fingertips. *"Bien."* Yielding to the deficiencies of his Spanish, he gave the boy a wide smile, hoping it would say what he could not. *"Es muy bien."*

The little boy's eyes darted to his mother's face, then he scrambled into her arms. Michael picked up the child's chart and scribbled a note to himself, then glanced at his nurse, Fortuna.

"Please tell the mother that she must continue giving him the antibiotics until they are all gone. His throat is better, but it's quite important that her son finish all the medication. If he gets sick again, she must bring him back to the hospital immediately."

Fortuna nodded, then turned to address the mother. While she translated his instructions in a geyser of Spanish, Michael flipped the page and studied the boy's chart.

The folder contained far too little information on the lad, and the available data was incredibly unhelpful. Four-year-old Rudolfo Lopez had been born in the village of Puerto Miguel, his mother had received no prenatal care, and the child had received no vaccinations — at least none were recorded. Michael suspected the boy may have received immunizations for measles or DPT when missionary doctors passed through the village, but since no one kept records, how could he be sure?

Aside from the raging case of strep throat that had compelled Rudolfo's mother to bring her son to the hospital last week, the boy seemed in good health. Surprising, really, that the mother brought him in at all — for anyone who traveled by canoe, Puerto Miguel lay a good five hours away from the hospital and the journey would be exhausting. Furthermore, since prescription drugs were available in Peru for anyone who could pay for them, most people self-medicated first and talked to a physician only if their medicines of choice had no effect.

He lifted his hand, interrupting Fortuna. "Does Puerto Miguel have a chemist?"

She frowned.

"You know, a place to buy medicine — *una farmacia.*"

Her frown deepened. "Why, Doctor, do you ask about Puerto Miguel?"

"Doesn't this woman live in Puerto Miguel?"

Fortuna looked at him as if he'd just suggested the lady lived on the moon. "No, Doctor! She lives here in Iquitos, by the Belen Market."

"Ah. Has she lived here long?"

Fortuna put the question to the patient, then returned the answer. "Two years."

"Good." Grateful to have one mystery solved, Michael jotted this information on the chart.

The mother, a dark-haired woman whose face had been prematurely etched with lines of weariness, thanked him as she stood and settled the child onto her hip. *"Muchas gracias, el doctor."*

Michael reached out to ruffle the boy's hair. *"De nada, Señora Lopez. Adiós, Rudolfo."*

Fortuna led them out, then lingered outside the doorway. "Do I need to clean the room this time, *el doctor?*"

"Si." Michael gestured toward the can of spray disinfectant on the counter. "Every surface and the mattress, please."

Leaving his nurse to clean up, he shook his head as he left the exam room. Peruvian medicine was not backward, but supplies were hard to obtain in this city. Hemmed in by the forest and accessible only by river or air, Iquitos was home to half a million people, most of whom lived in poverty. In addition to serving the residents of Iquitos, Regional Hospital also provided medical care to untold numbers of people who still preferred to live in the vast jungle along the Amazon.

When he first arrived, he had instructed Fortuna to clean the room after every patient, but soon he realized that New World standards of cleanliness were inappropriate in the jungle. Spray disinfectant was difficult to obtain, and when it was not available, Fortuna had to scrub the room with soap and standing water from a pail — not exactly a sterile solution.

Now she disinfected the room only after treating infectious patients. Michael's British colleagues would be horrified by his revised office procedures, but three years in the jungle had taught him to reorder his priorities.

He was moving toward the waiting area to summon his next patient when an orderly rounded the corner. "Dr. Kenway! *¡Prisa! ¡Emergencia!*"

Leaving his patients in their chairs, Michael broke into a jog and followed the orderly through the serpentine hallways that led to the casualty ward. He saw no patients in the narrow receiving area, but the double doors beyond stood open to a brick-walled courtyard. There, under the blinding tropical sun, two men were carrying an inert body on a stretcher.

Michael pulled a pair of latex gloves from the pocket of his lab coat as he hurried forward. The patient wore no clothing apart from a string of twine around his waist, but someone else might have stripped him as they tried to assess his condition. The patient's problem, however, was obvious — a ten-centimeter wound in his lower abdomen had coated half of the man's groin with blood.

Signaling the stretcher-bearers to halt, Michael lifted the man's wrist even as he scanned the body. Judging by the bowl haircut and the facial markings, the fellow appeared to be Indian, but Michael had never seen a native so covered with tattoos. The patient was emaciated, suffering chills and dehydrated, for despite the intense heat he was not perspiring.

"Lucky bloke," Michael murmured, studying the injury. If whatever had penetrated the abdomen had struck the abdominal aorta, this fellow wouldn't have made it out of the jungle.

He bent to check the native's respiration. As he pressed his stethoscope to the man's chest, he noted there were no visible indications of chest trauma or signs of bruising. The man's heart, however, was racing, probably the result of the body's demand for oxygen because of dehydration or a septic state resulting from his injury. Michael realized he might be looking at a bowel perforation . . . always a critical situation.

The only other obvious indication of injury was a bloody right hand, but after a quick examination Michael realized the skin had not been lacerated — the man had used his hand to apply pressure to the injury.

Clicking his tongue against his teeth, Michael pointed the stretcher-bearers inside. This patient, whoever he was, was probably more than half dead already, but perhaps the infection could be halted. Indigenous individuals who had not been exposed to antibiotics often responded with amazing swiftness if the proper drugs were administered in time.

Following his casualty patient, Michael called for help, then hurried to the exam room where the stretcher-bearers had clumsily transferred their burden to a gurney. Michael thanked them, then bit the inside of his lip as he bent over the Indian. The man was unconscious, which was probably a mercy, but he'd have to go into surgery almost immediately.

A pair of orderlies strode into the room. Michael was about to issue instructions for IV fluids when one of them threw up his hands and stepped away from the table.

"What's wrong?" When the orderly didn't answer, Michael looked at the second man, a fellow he had worked with on several occasions. "Rico, what's bothering your friend?"

A shadow of annoyance crossed Rico's face as he questioned his coworker. In a torrent of Spanish they argued across the exam table until Michael interrupted. "Hold it!" He held up his gloved hands. "Stop! In English, please."

Rico cast a look of derision at his companion. "Hector will not touch this man. I told him he is an ignorant fool, but still he refuses."

Michael glanced at the patient on the table. "Why not? Does he know this fellow?"

Rico shook his head. "He knows nothing about him. But Hector is Yagua, and superstitious. He is only one generation removed from the jungle, and he will not let go of the old ideas."

With no time for further questions, Michael jerked his thumb over his shoulder. "If Hector won't work, get him out of here and find someone who will. But we haven't time to argue the point."

Hector left immediately, with Rico hounding his heels. Snorting at the inefficiency of jungle medicine, Michael pulled an IV bag from a cart and glanced up at the two good Samaritans who had delivered the patient. They had remained in the room and were now leaning against the wall in the relaxed attitude of men who had finished their work and were happy to watch someone else hustle for a while.

"Do either of you speak English? *¿Habla inglés?*"

The first fellow shook his head, but the second, a burly man in shirtsleeves, nodded. "I am Paco. I speak English."

Michael forced a smile. "Good. Where did you find this fellow?"

The man scratched his head, then pointed toward the east-facing window. "Some of the river people brought him to us this morning. They say he came out of the jungle and started shouting in a language they had never heard."

Michael frowned as he tapped the patient's inner arm. He could feel the heat of fever even through his gloves. Due to dehydration, the veins had totally collapsed. "He came out of the jungle? Where?"

Paco shook his head. "I don't know. The people who brought him in were eager to be rid of him. They kept saying something about a *maldición.*"

"A what?"

"A curse, *el doctor.*"

Michael groaned inwardly as he splashed the patient's neck with Betadine in preparation for a right IJ triple lumen. Though Peru was a modern nation, primitive practices persisted in many parts of the country. "Curses do not cause wounds like this, Paco. A weapon injured this man."

24

"I do not think they meant a curse made him sick — they said he *was* a *maldición*."

With an ease born of practice, Michael inserted the large-bore catheter into the patient's jugular vein. "I think it's rather apparent this fellow might have been a victim of bad luck, but I doubt he was the cause of it." As he reached for a syringe, Michael tipped his chin toward the wound. "Do you have any idea what caused this?"

"No, Doctor. No idea."

Michael filled the syringe with five ccs of heparin, then slid the needle into each of the three ports of the triple lumen to test for blood return. When he was certain there were no clogs, he injected the drug, then reached for a curved needle on the cart behind him.

The first tug of silk through flesh must have undone Paco's friend, for by the time Michael tied off the sutures securing the catheter, both men had inched toward the doorway. Their faces, which had been open and curious a moment before, now gleamed pale with perspiration. Experience told Michael that if they did not leave, soon *they* might be lying on a gurney.

"*Gracias, amigos,* for bringing this bloke in. You may have saved his life."

Both men nodded in mute acknowledgment, then slipped out of the room. A moment later, Rico returned and took his place beside the gurney.

"What do you need, *el doctor?*"

Michael inserted an IV line into the first port, then stepped back to allow Rico room to work. "Cefoxitin, two-gm slow IV push. At least two liters of fluids. As soon as we get some fluids in him, call for an operating room; this patient is headed to surgery."

As Rico worked at the native's head, Michael tenderly probed the tissue around the abdominal wound. The skin was swollen and warm to the touch. After injecting a bit of local anesthesia into the matted tissue, Michael debrided the area with a scalpel and noted that the peritoneum had been violated. Only the pressure of the man's hand had kept his intestines from spilling through the opening.

As Michael probed the flesh, he noticed fecal staining on the edges of the wound — obvious evidence of a bowel perforation. Small wonder the patient had passed out. The pain of the abdominal wound, coupled with severe dehydration and septic shock resulting from bacteria-laden fecal material . . . amazing that he had made it out of the jungle at all.

Undoubtedly, massive peritonitis caused by the infection in the abdomen had already led to bacteremia, the result of bacteria invading the bloodstream, and possibly septicemia, in which the entire body began to experience the effects of poison. Unless Michael could infuse his patient with fluids, repair the colon,

26

and administer effective antibiotics, septic shock would be followed by multisystem organ failure, beginning with the kidneys.

Looking up, Rico caught Michael's eye. "What do you think, *el doctor?*"

Michael dropped a sterile dressing over the wound. "We're probably looking at massive peritonitis," he answered, "bacteremia, and septicemia. Septic shock, probable kidney failure. We'll be facing multisystem organ failure within a few hours . . . unless the Almighty sends us a bloomin' miracle."

He snapped off his gloves. "I'm going to scrub up, Rico. Take this man to whatever operating room is available and wake the anesthetist from his midmorning siesta. We've no time to waste."

Suspended eighteen stories over the rainforest floor, Alex crawled on her hands and
knees over the canopy platform. A French
invention, the canopy raft served as a treetop
station for researchers who wished to sample
flora and fauna at the uppermost reaches of
the rainforest canopy. Dropped onto the
emergent layer by a rainbow-colored dirigible, the platform consisted of six triangular
sections that had been lashed together to
form a hexagon. Inflatable red pontoons
bordered the edges of each triangle, and mesh
surfaces between the pontoons provided
ample space for researchers to maneuver.

The plan, expedition organizer Kenneth
Carlton explained to the group, involved the
study of a different tree at a different location
each day. Each morning at sunrise the French
dirigible pilot would fly in from a clearing
upriver and drop the platform at prearranged

coordinates. The researchers would have several hours to explore the canopy at this site, then they'd climb down and make their way back to the lodge. Before sunset, the dirigible would float back in, remove the raft, and return to the launching site upriver.

Reaching the platform once it had been lowered onto the canopy was the challenge Alex dreaded. Researchers climbed the entire distance on a rope, then entered the raft through a porthole in the center. After snapping a carabiner on her safety harness to a guy wire on the raft, Alexandra released the climbing line . . . and shivered in a brief instant of terror when she realized she was sitting on top of the world.

"Kinda strange, isn't it?" Deborah Simons tossed a grin over her shoulder as she crawled away from the porthole. "Sort of a loosely strung trampoline."

Perhaps . . . but no gymnast Alex knew had ever dreamed of ascending this height.

Knowing she had to clear the area to make way for the next climber, Alex sat on her rear and pushed her way over one of the cylindrical pontoons. Scorched by the equatorial sun, the slick vinyl radiated heat even through her cotton trousers. As the wind rippled across the green sea around her, jostling the supporting branches beneath the platform, she clutched at the guy wire and lay back upon the pontoon, ignoring the swaying of her stomach.

She would not panic. She refused to give in to her unstable emotions. No mere breeze could dislodge this ventilated raft, nor could it blow her off balance. She had affixed her safety harness to a rope running the length of the pontoon, so even if by some freak chance she happened to lose her mind and launch herself off the edge, she wouldn't drop more than six feet before the rope caught her.

She would not panic — not today, not here, not now.

"Twinkle, twinkle, little star."

With one gloved hand firmly wrapped around the rope, Alex stared up at the open sky. No one would think it odd if she took a moment to catch her breath. The effort had winded her; even the thought of climbing such a distance drained her. But a cool breeze seemed to be rising from beneath the raft, a hint of moisture in its breath.

"Having trouble, Madame Doctor?" Louis Fortier abruptly appeared in her field of vision, his grinning face hanging over hers like a French jack-o'-lantern.

"No trouble, Louis." She forced a smile. "Just enjoying the view while I wait for my partner."

"The Russian is on his way. He was climbing right behind me." Louis snapped his safety harness to an adjacent guy wire, then strode toward the edge of the raft with a bouncy, confident step. Gaping, Alex lifted her head — she wouldn't have been surprised if the lithe Frenchman had executed a back-flip on the springy surface. Then again, this wasn't his first canopy expedition. Last night over dinner he had regaled her table with stories of his adventures in Cameroon and Belize.

She let her head fall back to the surface. Of course Fortier was accustomed to life amid the treetops — the French had invented the canopy platform.

She had managed to sit up and assume a reasonably relaxed position by the time Baklanov crawled through the porthole. She greeted him with a weak smile, then discreetly turned away while the red-faced, perspiring Russian went about the awkward business of releasing himself from the climbing line and snapping his harness to the safety ropes.

Baklanov didn't seem the type to suffer from acrophobia, and he'd handled yesterday's climbing exercise with aplomb. But a thirty-foot climb was nothing compared to this.

She heard the sounds of his raspy breathing as he maneuvered behind her. Like every other Russian researcher she had known, the man was a chain smoker. The thought of going without a smoke for a period of several hours probably bothered him more than the realization he could die up here from sunstroke, heart attack, a fall due to a frayed rope —

No. She wouldn't think of those things. No panic allowed, not today. She would not allow her brain to focus on anything negative. She would find something else to think about.

"Baklanov," she called over her shoulder, "how many others are still climbing?"

He coughed, then cleared his throat. "Carlton and his woman. Olsson, of course."

"Of course." The botanist had promised to bring up the rear.

Carlton had assembled an international team, whose members were subsidized by several organizations for varying reasons. The World Health Organization had sponsored Baklanov, a leading researcher in Russia, in order to expand the international library of bacteriophages, an area of study that held great promise for Alex's own research. During correspondence exchanged prior to the trip, she and the Russian researcher had agreed to work together during this expedition.

Alex met Valerik Baklanov for the first time at the airport in Lima. Tall and broad, he had moved through the crowd with the awkward gait of a man who has been sitting for too long. His clothing smelled of tobacco and sweat, but his eyes softened with kindness when she introduced herself, and the smile he had offered her ten-year-old daughter,

Caitlyn, had been genuine.

Yes, she had been immediately impressed with the serious scholar. Like her, he had given his life to his work.

On the hourlong flight from Lima to Iquitos, he gave her a brief history of his science. Alex knew the Russians had been utilizing microscopic viruses to fight bacterial infections for generations. The tiny disease killers had been discovered during World War I, but phage research came to a screeching halt in the United States with the arrival of penicillin. Why would a patient want to swallow a spoonful of live viruses when a tiny white pill could accomplish the same purpose?

All living things, however, struggle to survive, and deadly bacteria had adapted to the threat of antibiotics. Resistant bacteria strains were forcing scientists to find new methods of fighting illness, and some bright doctor at the World Health Organization had remembered a drab Russian research center where the doctors were so poor they treated patients with live viruses instead of antibiotics.

Baklanov had laughed when he explained how phages had come to Russia. Canadian biologist Felix d'Herelle, who had discovered bacteriophages along with Englishman Frederick Twort, happened to be a Communist and an ardent admirer of Stalin. After the war, d'Herelle moved to Russia and established what would later be known as the Eliava Institute. When the Western world abandoned Stalin — and phage research — d'Herelle and his team kept culturing bacteria and feeding them to phages in an effort to determine which phage devoured which bacteria.

"We have had many setbacks over the years," Baklanov said, the hand in his lap twitching for a cigarette. "The city is poor, especially now that the Soviet system has been dismantled. The refrigerators where we keep our cultures fail when the power often goes out, and sometimes we lose years of work. But it is simple research, really." He winked at Caitlyn. "This little girl could do it."

"I think I could." Caitlyn looked at him with the expression of a diva presented with an insultingly simple song. "I would need an EM, though."

One of Baklanov's bushy brows rose. "She has an electron microscope?"

Alex laughed. "Of course not. But she is familiar with the lingo, and she's seen an EM at our lab."

A wry half-smile twisted the corner of Baklanov's mouth as he went on with his explanation. He had come to the rain forest in search of new bacteriophages, for the little bacteria-assassins seemed to have one-track minds. Though hundreds of phages existed, each virus killed only one variety of bacteria. Predator and prey had to be perfectly matched for a cure to be effective.

Phages lived everywhere, Baklanov assured Alex. Though they were only one-fortieth the size of the average bacterium, they swarmed in almost every conceivable medium, busily eating germs.

"Under the electron microscope," Baklanov explained, leaning toward Caitlyn, "they show up as translucent spiderlike creatures with box-shaped heads, rigid tails, and a tangle of legs for gripping their prey. They are so tiny that a single drop of purified H_2O —" he reached out and tapped the water bottle on the airline tray — "may contain a billion of them."

Caitlyn, who had been most impressed by Baklanov's quest, announced that she would begin a study of bacteriophages as soon as they returned to Atlanta. Alex had been more dubious — phage research might provide the key she had been seeking, or it might prove to be another blind alley. Only time would tell.

Except for Fortier and Olsson, who had become partners because of their mutual interest in plants, the other team members were working independently. Emma Whitmore, an anthropologist from the University of Southern California, had come along to study indigenous people groups — and had

HUNTINGTON CITY-TOWNSHIP
PUBLIC LIBRARY
200 W. Market Street
Huntington, IN 46750

wisely decided to keep both feet on the ground and work at the lodge while the others, as she put it, "played Tarzan and Jane."

The only people actually *playing* on this trip appeared in the porthole opening moments after Baklanov. First came Kenneth Carlton, CEO of Horizon Biotherapies and Alex's employer, followed by his administrative assistant, Lauren Hayworth.

Alex resisted the impulse to roll her eyes when the pair crawled through the canvas opening. She could understand why Carlton had organized this expedition — with antibiotic resistance on the rise in Western countries, every savvy health company in the world had trained appraising eyes on Baklanov's work with bacteriophages. Carlton had shown considerable ingenuity, in fact, by allowing other researchers to join the team, thereby disguising his primary motivation.

Alex wouldn't have been at all surprised if Louis Fortier or Emma Whitmore had no idea what Carlton had up his sleeve, but anyone in the medical research field would have caught on in a heartbeat. Bacteriophages appeared to be the definitive answer to antibiotic resistance, so if Carlton and Baklanov came to some sort of agreement on this jungle journey, Horizon Biotherapies would soon be miles ahead of the competition.

Alex had no trouble admiring Carlton's business acumen. She could even respect the

HUNTINGTON CITY-TOWNSHIP
PUBLIC LIBRARY
200 W. Market Street
Huntington, IN 46750

chutzpah required to assume Baklanov would warm to Carlton's generous support. But how Kenneth Carlton could leave his wife and two teenage sons at home in order to escort a nubile twenty-something faux assistant to a remote jungle lodge — well, it didn't take a degree in cellular technologies to deduce that Carlton's marital fidelity had suffered a malignant mutation.

She didn't think much of his moral standards, but as an employer he paid well and granted Alex the freedom to conduct her research. His womanizing didn't affect her, so she had no complaints.

She pushed herself up to her hands and knees, then glanced at Baklanov. "Want to start at the south edge?"

The Russian pushed a hand through his uncombed gray hair and regarded the southern horizon with blue eyes set in shadowed circles. After a moment, he shrugged. "Why not?"

Alex started forward, her stomach tightening, but a moaning noise made her hesitate. Behind her, Lauren Hayworth had crawled onto the raft and was lying prone on the mesh. "I don't think I can do this," she whimpered, clawing at the fabric as if she wanted to sink her nails into it for security. "I want to go down, Ken."

Shading her eyes, Alex glanced up in time to see a look of frustration flit across Carlton's face. "We can't go down now, Lauren. You came all the way up — rest for a while, then we'll go down."

"I won't move." Lauren kept her head down, speaking to the canopy's surface. "I can't even look around. I'll be miserable the entire time —"

"Then keep your misery to yourself, chérie." Louis Fortier, who was still bounding over the raft as if he'd been born on a trampoline, dared to answer the woman's complaints without even looking to see if Carlton minded his bluntness. "We do not mind you taking up space so long as you do not make us all miserable in the process."

"Hear, hear!" From the spot where he was spreading out his tools, Baklanov voiced hearty agreement.

Watching the prostrate younger woman, Alex realized she hadn't been the only one affected by the height and the sensation of instability. Olsson had warned them that the raft took some getting used to, but nothing could ever really prepare a person for this experience.

Pausing on her knees, Alex looked around. Several of the others had untethered their harnesses in order to move freely around the raft; only when they knelt at the edge did they snap them to the outermost safety lines. She could remain attached — the six-foot extension rope gave her room to walk around —

or she could take a bold step toward battling the panic that sat like a lead weight in her chest, ready to batter her heart at the least provocation . . .

Feeling like a paratrooper about to jump without a parachute, Alex curled her fingers around the metal carabiner, pressed on the clasp, and pulled it free. Gulping back her fear, she crawled over the pontoon to Baklanov, who had settled at the southern edge of the platform.

Sighing in relief, she hooked her elbow around the security of a support wire, then clipped the carabiner of her safety harness to the line that ran along the edge. Baklanov, she saw, had secured his line, too, so she didn't feel like a complete wimp.

Shrugging her way out of her backpack, she met the Russian's gaze. "Sorry it took me a while to get here."

A smile flitted through the man's gray beard. "The sensation is a little like being at sea, so you should not be surprised by a touch of seasickness. This is your first time aboard the raft?"

Nodding, she pulled a box of empty test tubes from her pack.

"You will become accustomed to the feeling in no time." Leaning out over the pontoon, Baklanov lifted a branch from the strangler fig's emergent layer, then extended his free hand toward Alex. Fumbling among the tools he had spread on the mesh, she found a slender glass pipette and placed it in his hand.

The Russian placed the pad of his fingertip over the end of the delicate tube, then lowered the pipette vertically until the suction end rested within a few water droplets that had collected in the center of a leaf cluster. Baklanov quickly lifted his fingertip and lowered it again, allowing the sudden change in pressure to draw a few drops of the liquid into the pipette.

Moving cautiously to avoid breaking the seal, he swiveled the pipette to Alex, who offered him a sterile test tube filled with agar, a solution for growing cultures. After punching through the paper seal with the pipette, Baklanov released the liquid and withdrew the slender glass straw. Alex immediately plugged the tube with a rubber cap.

She smiled as she slipped the test tube back into its padded container. Some of her more laboratory-oriented colleagues would frown at this less-than-sterile working environment, but when in the field, a scientist had to do whatever was necessary to gather specimens. Refinements could wait until the specimens had reached the lab.

Using a fresh pipette for each effort, Baklanov took samples of moisture wherever he could find them — on the leaves of vines, within open flowers, even from within a broken stem. With every specimen he drew, Alex recorded the time and location in a small notebook.

"Interesting, how the water collects up here," Baklanov said as he used a pipette to probe a slurry of bird droppings. "One would think it is raining *up,* not down."

Intent upon watching him, Alex nodded. She had read about this particular phenomenon — due to the respiration of such a vast amount of foliage, water did rise through the canopy, to be collected in rain clouds that would return the liquid to the earth. At that moment she felt nothing but gratitude for the mist that kept them from being broiled alive beneath the hot sun.

She lifted a brow as Baklanov offered a specimen from the bird droppings for a test tube. Though distasteful, this specimen might be particularly valuable. D'Herelle had first discovered bacteriophages in the diarrhea of locusts.

"Your phages," she said, watching the Russian work, "have you discovered any that might have the ability to mutate proteins?"

The Russian did not answer for a moment, then his lips pursed. "There is one we call T4 — it is nothing, really, but a string of DNA wrapped in a protein. When it encounters a bacterial host, it docks and injects its entire DNA payload into the cell, leaving its protein shell empty and useless. The shell then drifts away as cellular debris." He shrugged. "But that does not answer your question, does it? A discarded protein is not the same as a mutated protein."

She capped the test tube. "I suppose you know why I'm asking."

One corner of his mouth twitched in what might have been a smile. "I am a little familiar with your work in neurology. Our research has much in common, but still . . . proteins are not bacteria. I am not sure your prions have anything to do with my phages—"

"I'm hoping there's a link."

She handed the last sterile pipette to Baklanov, then watched as he reached toward a spider web from which several water droplets hung like crystals.

"There has to be some enzyme or virus that will stop the reproduction of malformed proteins," she continued. "The brain damage in encephalopathy is cumulative, so if we can stop the process early, we can halt the disease."

Unable to lower the pipette without breaking the spider web, Baklanov brought the end of the tube to his lips, then gently inhaled. Alex squinted, then spied a single shining drop in the pipette stem.

"You are good." She held out a clean test tube. "I'd have swallowed that one."

Baklanov laughed. "Once you have seen

these things under a microscope, my doctor friend, you develop a rather strong aversion to the notion of swallowing unknown substances."

"I can imagine. I've the same aversion to eating red meat."

She looked up as Fortier released a shout of jubilation. Kneeling on one of the open triangles, the perfumer was pulling a white flower through a reinforced cutout in the mesh. *"C'est magnifique!"* he exclaimed, tenderly bringing the blossom to his face. "It exudes a scent of raspberry with notes of vanilla."

Milos Olsson, who had been the last to come through the porthole, crawled toward the Frenchman. "May I?" Taking the flower into his hands, he sniffed, then daintily plucked a petal and dropped it onto his tongue.

"Good," he announced a moment later. "It might make an excellent raspberry flavoring. Where did you find it? On a vine or in the tree?"

As Olsson and Fortier discussed the miracle properties of the flower, Alex wished her assignment were as simple as seek and sniff. Olsson had come to the rainforest in search of new plant species, but his work had a decidedly commercial bent. Last night at dinner he had confessed to being commissioned by a corporation that wanted him to find plants that could be grown cheaply and used as food flavorings. Last year his company had netted over two billion dollars selling botanical ingredients to national food corporations.

Louis Fortier, on the other hand, cared more for the aroma of plants than their taste. An independent perfumer with a degree in chemistry, he made his living selling scents to top fashion houses like Armani, Estée Lauder, and Christian Dior.

Alex couldn't help but be fascinated by the stories Fortier and Olsson told. Last year they had gone together on a raft expedition in the African rainforest. In Cameroon, Fortier had found a plant whose leaves, if rubbed on a person's foot, produced an astringent sensation in the mouth. Olsson had returned to the States with a piece of bark that produced a strong aroma of garlic and onion — perfect for seasoning potato chips — and a green fruit whose flesh smelled and tasted like beef bouillon.

"Last year I sold those two flavor products to a soybean company for three million dollars," Olsson had confided over a jungle dinner of fish, rice, and fried plantains. "They plan to use both plants in vegetarian frozen entrées."

Though astounded by her comrades' financial success, Alex had come to the Amazon to search for only one thing — a compound or process that could change the structure of proteinaceous infectious particles, commonly known as prions. Researchers had only begun to understand protein pathogens in the last decade; most scientists believed a cure for the neurological diseases they caused would not be discovered without years of continuing research.

Time, however, was a commodity she lacked.

While other researchers pinned their hopes on gene therapy, Alex had come to believe that even the so-called "inherited" brain diseases resulted from situations where one parent had unknowingly infected a child. Neurological diseases, or encephalopathies, could incubate for decades before a patient displayed any symptoms, so a fetus could conceivably absorb prions through his mother's placenta and not develop the disease for years.

Just as she had done . . . and most likely her daughter, too.

With all her heart, Alex believed a biological answer to prions existed . . . and, if all went well, Baklanov's expertise in virology might well point her to it. If one of the Russian's phages — or a substance from Fortier's flower, or Olsson's leaves — could instigate a chemical change in a single rod of a prion protein, all her work would be worth the sacrifices she'd made over the years.

Leaning back on the springy surface of the

raft, Alex held up one of the capped test tubes and stared at the drop of liquid shining like a diamond on the agar. These captured phages were unlikely to resemble anything Baklanov had cataloged in his Russian lab, for the canopy was an ecosystem unto itself, home to hundreds of plants, animals, insects, and organisms not found anywhere else on the planet.

If the canopy's visible world contained so much diversity, what must its invisible world contain?

1 April 2003
11:47 a.m.

Dripping like a wet sponge, Michael backed through the double doors of the surgery, then moved toward the sink to peel off his bloody gloves. After doffing the gloves and tugging the surgical mask from his face, he picked up a bottle of lukewarm water and gulped it down, then reached for a towel to mop his neck and forehead. His patient would probably not survive more than a few hours, but he had done his best.

Looping the damp towel around his neck, he carried another bottle of water through an adjoining corridor that led to a courtyard. Though the sun beat mercilessly upon the garishly painted concrete slab that passed for decorative pavement, the area was at least fifteen degrees cooler than his oven of an operating room. His operating theater, if one could call it that, was a windowless room with an operating table at the center, a single light

47

overhead, and not even a fan to move the stultifying air. Michael had perspired profusely during the entire procedure, soaking his scrub suit, surgical gown, and cap.

He had scrubbed up under conditions that would horrify his colleagues in Britain (a bucket of water served as a sink because no water flowed into the hospital after 7 a.m.) and operated in a sauna that would compel less demanding surgeons to resign in protest. He had been assisted by one unsuperstitious orderly, two surgical nurses, and one anesthesiologist. He had cut with a scalpel that had obviously seen sharper days, and he was certain the cloth covering the operating table had not been changed since the previous procedure that morning.

Most surprising had been the conclusion he'd reached after opening the wound — his patient's abdomen had been pierced by some type of spear, most likely a sharpened stone, for Michael had pulled flakes of chipped rock from the peritoneal cavity.

The presence of rock fragments made him lift a brow. There was no rock in this part of the Amazon. The stones used by the Indians for cultivating crops, sharpening machetes, and grinding food were purchased from a "stone man" who gathered his stones near his home in the foothills of the Andes, then traveled downriver selling his wares. So this man had either been injured by a weapon carved of relatively rare rock . . . or he had come from some part of the jungle far away from Iquitos.

He'd wager a decent shepherd's pie that none of his mates at St. George's Hospital in London would treat a stone-spear wound in the entire length of the coming year.

Michael pulled off his cap, then shook his head and ran his fingers through his wet hair. A medical practice at the jungle's edge kept life interesting . . . and kept his thoughts occupied. Which was the entire point of his being in this godforsaken place.

He flinched when Fortuna interrupted his reverie by slamming the exit door against the concrete wall. "*El doctor!* The patient is awake."

Michael glanced at his watch. The man had recovered from the anesthetic rather quickly, but the anesthesiologist might not have administered the proper dosage.

He stood and walked toward his nurse. "Is he in pain?"

"*No se,* Doctor. He is talking, but I cannot understand him."

Michael frowned. "He does not speak Spanish?"

"I believe he is speaking an Indian dialect. I do not recognize it."

Michael exhaled as he led the way to the postoperative ward. The man could be babbling nonsense in his pain, but if he could communicate at all, they needed to ask for his name and the name of his nearest relative. As the anesthesia wore off, perhaps one of the hospital staff could find a way to communicate with the unlucky fellow.

The patient lay on a gurney in the postoperative ward, his hands loosely bound by restraints to prevent him from disturbing the dressing. Michael leaned over the man and checked his breathing, then noted the blood pressure on the chart. An IV next to the bed dripped cefoxitin — the strongest antibiotic available in this place — into his veins.

Michael leaned over his patient when the man's eyelids fluttered. *"¿Senor? ¿Está usted en dolor?"*

The man's lids opened to reveal hazel eyes, a color Michael had never seen among the native peoples. For an instant the patient's body tensed in an atavistic flee-or-fight reflex, then he closed his eyes, relaxed against the restraints, and began to mumble in a low monotone.

Michael listened a moment, then turned to Fortuna. "Is he speaking Yagua?"

She shook her head. "I do not think so."

"Is anyone around here fluent in the native dialects? If this man has relatives, we'll need to find them as soon as possible."

"Un momento, el doctor. I will ask."

Fortuna spun on the sole of her sneakers, then disappeared behind the curtained divider. While she searched, Michael checked the man's vital signs and his urine output, then leaned over the bed railings to listen to the native's mumbling. Three years in Peru had improved Michael's Spanish to the point where he could usually follow the thread of a conversation, but these words bore no resemblance to the Spanish spoken in every Peruvian city and most of the Indian villages. This could be Yagua, Witotoan, or one of three hundred other Indian tongues, but those languages had nearly died out except in the native villages.

The man was definitely speaking *something*, though, and it didn't sound like gibberish. He seemed to be chanting, perhaps even singing . . .

Fortuna came around the curtain, followed by a dark-haired woman Michael had seen in the administrator's office. "This is Esma," Fortuna explained offhandedly. "She speaks Yagua and English."

The tip of Esma's nose went pink as she looked at the tattooed man in the bed. "I *did* speak Yagua," she said, meeting Michael's gaze. "When I lived with my parents. But that was a long time ago."

"Please." Michael gripped the side rails of the bed. "He came from out of the jungle, and his prognosis is not good. See if you can discover anything that will lead us to his family." Straightening, he turned to Fortuna and lowered his voice. "We'll need to watch him carefully for the next twelve hours."

Esma moved toward the head of the bed, then leaned on the railing and whispered a greeting in a tongue Michael had never heard. At the sound of her voice the patient's eyes flew open, bewilderment creasing his lined face.

Glancing up at Michael, Esma asked a question — presumably about his family. The patient stared at Esma a moment, shifted his eyes to Michael and Fortuna, then began to speak in abrupt, hoarse tones, his voice cracking with every word. When he paused to cough, frothy, blood-tinged sputum tinged his lips — a sign of adult respiratory distress syndrome. A patient who developed ARDS would not likely last the night.

"Has he a name?" Michael raised his voice to be heard above the man's coughing. "A wife? Someone we can call?"

Esma cut Michael off with an uplifted hand, then repeated the question. Confusion filled the patient's eyes, then he released a stream of flowing words that did not slow even when Esma turned to Michael.

"The language is not Yagua, but it may be related. I do not know all of the words, but I think I may be able to understand some of what he is saying."

Michael crossed his arms. "Has he family nearby? That is the crucial thing."

The translator showed her teeth in a humorless smile. "Patience, Doctor. He seems intent on telling me a story. Every time you interrupt, he begins again."

"That's lovely," Michael answered, his voice coagulating with sarcasm, "but I need to know about his next of kin *now.* We may have to send someone downriver."

Esma gave him the pointed look he always received when he inadvertently committed a cultural blunder. "He did not answer me, Doctor, and I think I know the reason why. You will not need to send for anyone."

Michael closed his fist around the bed railing. "And how, exactly, would you know this, seeing that he has not spoken a word that makes any sense?"

Lifting her chin, Esma spoke with quiet firmness. "He will not give me names, Doctor, because the jungle tribes consider it evil to speak the names of their loved ones . . . particularly those who are dead."

1 April 2003
2:20 p.m.

A headache had begun to hammer on Alex's optic nerves by the time the sun stood directly overhead. Not wanting to be the first to suggest it was time they descended, she sipped from her water bottle, ate the oily peanut butter sandwich in her backpack, and sweated away her sunblock. The wide-brimmed straw hat she wore provided some shade, but already she could feel her shoulders and arms burning.

Two more hours passed before Kenneth Carlton announced that it might be time to descend. Olsson, who had been hanging by a rope from the platform edge, climbed back onto the raft and seemed surprised to discover that his teammates had wilted in the blistering heat.

"We are ready to call it a day?" he asked, looking around.

"More than ready," Baklanov called, winking at Alex. "You have been in the shade for the last hour. We have been sizzling like — how do you say it? — eggs, sunnyside up."

"The lodge is supposed to send someone to pick us up," Carlton added. "I expect the man is down there waiting."

"All right, then." The Swede pulled a handkerchief from his pocket and wiped his neck. "Shall we let the ladies go first?"

Alex had assumed Lauren Hayworth would want to be the first to leave the platform, but that whimpering beauty developed a sudden interest in some odd berries her employer had collected. Deborah Simons probably wouldn't have minded leading the way, but she was trying to coax a recalcitrant grasshopper into a specimen jar.

Drawing a deep breath, Alex crawled toward the porthole. "I'm ready." She unsnapped the carabiner that held her to the safety rope. "Hook me up and send me down."

The descent from the canopy raft was less taxing than the climb, but easily twice as frightening. "Abseiling," Olsson had told them, "is as easy as falling out of a tree."

Battling the heat and her headache, Alex scooted to the porthole's edge and peered into the thicket below. This was not a tree from which she wanted to fall.

Olsson handed Alex a metal piece resembling a figure eight. "Remember how it's done?"

"Barely."

The corner of his mouth quirked in a grin. Apparently she wasn't the first researcher to experience blank-brain on the edge of a leafy precipice.

"Hook this whale's tail to the carabiner on your safety harness."

When Alex hesitated, he reached out and attached it for her.

"Hold on to this rope with both hands." He snapped a rope against her gloved palm. "Ease yourself into the opening, and release the rope slowly. If you let go, you will fall. Do not release the rope too quickly. But do not worry; you will get a feel for the proper pace. Let the rope slide between your fingers, and your body weight will carry you down." He paused to mop his neck, then gave her a lopsided smile. "You can do this, yes?"

"Of course I can." Moving with more confidence than she felt, Alex swung her legs into the porthole and gratefully eyed the thick green screen blocking her view of the forest floor. She could almost convince herself she was preparing to travel only a few feet . . .

Olsson wriggled his fingers in a farewell. "Away with you, then. The rest of us are ready for food and drink!"

Alex pushed off from the canvas, then caught her breath as the rope bobbed with her weight. Dangling in the center of the porthole, she moved her right hand below

56

her left, releasing about six inches of rope, and felt her stomach lurch as she slid a corresponding number of inches downward. Yesterday she had glided out of the practice tree, content to know solid ground lay only a few feet away.

"Twinkle, twinkle, little star, how I wonder what you are."

She would not panic. She had no reason to fear. She would calm her pounding heart with slow, steady breaths and clear thinking.

Besides, what difference did the distance make? She had only to move a few inches at a time. Gathering her confidence, she lowered herself through the canopy, moving through vines, branches, and leaves she had scarcely noticed on the ascent. A group of chattering marmosets scattered at her approach while a toucan watched with interest from only a few feet away. Holding her breath, Alex glided slowly past them.

She traveled by less attractive animal forms as well. A muddy wasp's nest stretched along one side of the tree's wide trunk, a monstrous formation over six feet tall and four feet wide. Alex's pulse quickened as she glided past the mound — one wrong sound or scent could agitate the insects.

"Up above the world so high, like a diamond in the sky . . ."

She heard herself gasping and paused to focus her thoughts. She would not panic. She could not panic, not here. She would think about the tree, about the strangler fig, which, according to Olsson, was a miracle of nature.

She removed her right hand from the rope, placed it below her left, and felt the rope slide beneath her gloves. Again, this time left hand under right.

Good. She was making progress. And her muscles were perfectly obedient.

She kept moving as Olsson's voice replayed in her brain. Just this morning he had told them they were about to climb one of the most amazing trees in the jungle. Stranglers did not grow from the ground up, but from seeds dropped by birds onto the branches of other trees. A seed that managed to sprout on the branches of a stronger tree would send out tendrils and roots that eventually surrounded the host tree's trunk and tapped into its water supply. As the host tree struggled to survive the invasion, the strangler kept growing, sending roots down to the earth while new branches and leaves shot toward the canopy and the life-giving sun. Eventually the old tree died, entombed by a parasite that had proven itself more adaptable to the climate.

"Nasty old tree," Deborah muttered.

"Do not think of the strangler fig as evil," Olsson had said, laughter in his voice. "It is only doing what it has evolved to do. And it benefits so many other life forms — its tangled roots and trunk offer shelter for an astounding variety of plant and animal life."

Alex could see several of those life forms now. With the wasp's nest safely overhead, her gaze fell upon a group of orchids and bromeliads scattered along a branch. Epiphytes flourished in the treetops, absorbing nutrients and water through fingerlike roots that stretched over limbs and sought out resting places in natural crevices. Brilliant blossoms of orange, white, and purple spangled the emerald canopy, and for an instant Alex felt the vague stirring of jealousy. If urgent personal concerns had not propelled her into neurology, she would have enjoyed botany.

Chalk it up as another of life's cosmic pranks.

Trying to think about anything but the fact that her life depended upon a rope and a safety harness, her mind flittered over other jokes the universe had deigned to play on her. Her genetic heritage, for one. Her fatherless childhood, for another. The orthodontia she'd been forced to wear for four years while all her girlfriends were out of braces within twenty-four months, and her penchant for books, which in high school had repelled every teenage American male within ten miles.

She tightened her grip as her memory drifted toward her college years. Oh, the men had come around then — but they'd only wanted sex and/or information. Could she type a paper . . . and spruce it up a little? Could she do a little extra research while she was at the library? Gee, baby, if you love me, you'll look up this one little thing . . .

One young man, however, had been quite capable of doing his own work . . . and little else. In medical school she had married teaching assistant Collin Wilt within days of finding out she carried his child and divorced him within weeks of discovering he cared more for his career than for her and the coming baby. She signed the no-fault divorce papers on Caitlyn's one-month birthday, then kissed her daughter's downy head and swore they would be okay. She'd reclaimed her maiden name, her room in her mother's house, and her lifelong dream of going into research, only to find her dream shadowed by a pressing urgency — the doctors had diagnosed her mother with fatal familial insomnia, a genetic and fatal brain disease.

During the eighteen months of her mother's illness, Alex read and researched and wrote countless letters to scores of other scientists working in the field, but whatever cosmic joker ruled the universe won the race against time. After her mother's death Alex mourned her loss, tried to care for Caitlyn, and went back to her work, this time for her daughter's sake.

Now she was convinced the infective agent

that caused her mother's disease was like a strangler fig — it had entered her mother's tissues and begun to grow, slowly and steadily. It had entered Alex's tissues, too, and probably Caitlyn's.

With every passing day she became more convinced that FFI was not inherited — at least, not in a genetic sense. Studies of several types of prion-induced diseases had demonstrated that the infective agent could be transmitted orally, surgically, or through other means of ingestion. Surgeons had unknowingly passed it from one patient to another by the use of metal probes in neurosurgery; the agent had also been transmitted by the injection of human growth hormone derived from biological sources. Kuru, a prion disease found in New Guinea, spread through cannibalism, and every scientist in Europe now understood that cattle afflicted with mad cow disease had spread prions to dogs, cats, pigs, sheep, and humans. Prions had probably infected chickens, too, but the birds didn't live long enough to show signs of the disease.

Prion diseases required time to develop . . . and the length of the incubation period depended upon the strain of disease being transmitted. For years researchers had assumed that fatal familial insomnia was the result of a genetic mutation among family members, but Alex believed the situation was

61

far simpler — the prion that caused FFI passed from mother to child through the placenta in utero. Children did not become symptomatic for thirty, forty, or fifty years because each person's metabolism functioned differently. Researchers had noted that stress seemed to hasten the onset of FFI, but perhaps the disease gained the upper hand because an individual's immune system weakened during trying times, allowing the prions greater freedom to multiply. And if stress was an accelerant, she shouldn't have been surprised a few weeks ago to find herself experiencing tingling limbs, panic attacks, and sleeplessness . . .

No. If Alex could help it, the cosmic joker would *not* have the last laugh this time.

"Twinkle, twinkle, little star . . ."

She had descended to within twenty feet of the forest floor when a strident scream broke the stillness. Deborah Simons hung on the rope about fifty feet above her, but above Deborah, Lauren was flailing about in a full-fledged panic. Alex felt an icy finger touch the base of her spine as the line vibrated in her hand. More worrisome than the fear of falling, though, was the thought of the wasps — what if Lauren's shrieking brought the pests out of their nest?

"How I wonder what you are."

Not particularly eager to linger in such a precarious position, Alex loosened her grip and let the rope slide over her palms. She hit the ground more forcefully than she had intended, then fell backward into a patch of soft dirt Olsson had thoughtfully arranged for a landing zone.

Lazaro Mendez, a native guide who worked for the lodge, stepped up and gallantly offered her a hand. Accepting it, Alex scrambled to her feet, then moved out of the way. Deborah Simons landed a moment later.

Deborah chuckled as she unhitched her safety harness. "I see you had the same thought I did. Carlton's going to have a time getting Lauren down."

"I'm sure he'll sweet-talk her through it." Alex winced at the sound of sarcasm in her voice, but not even Deborah, who seemed oblivious to everything but bugs, could have missed the undercurrents between Carlton and his girlfriend.

Deborah smiled a grim little grin as she peeled off her gloves. "How long do you think they've been together?"

"Not long — or he'd have known she wasn't up to a trip like this. I'm thinking Miss Hayworth is going to stay in her room tomorrow while Carlton hangs back and plays nursemaid."

Stepping out of her harness, Deborah shook her head. "I don't think Carlton is the nursemaid type. He's probably not above hiring one, though."

Alex glanced up, but she couldn't see anyone but Lauren on the rope. The young woman had stopped flailing, though, and that was progress.

She forced a laugh. "What do you think, Deb? Should we ask Lazaro to take us back to the lodge? It might be an hour before the others get down."

"It'll go fast once the princess arrives." Deborah bent her knees and sat in a squat, careful to keep the seat of her jeans off the muddy ground.

Imitating the entomologist, Alex stripped off her gear, then sat in the same fashion. "I'll bet Mr. CEO is thinking he should have brought his sons to the jungle instead of his mistress."

"All I'm thinking —" an impish grin lit Deborah's face — "is that I owe the good Lord a big thank-you. I almost asked Lauren to tuck a couple of my specimen bottles in her backpack, but something told me I should reconsider. I'm so glad I did — with all that screeching, she would have rattled my poor bugs to death." She took a deep, contented breath. "Yes sir, Jesus was really watching out for me."

Alex stared up at the climbing rope as a wave of disappointment engulfed her. Until that moment, she had thought she and Deborah Simons might actually become friends.

Too bad.

■ ■ ■ ■

Alex wanted nothing more than a speedy boat trip back to the lodge and a cold shower, but transportation in the Amazon was neither simple nor speedy. After regrouping on the ground, she and her teammates hiked twenty minutes to the place where Lazaro had left the boat. To her surprise, a jungle-style buffet waited in the clearing.

"I thought we'd be hungry for something more than sandwiches," Carlton said, slipping his backpack from his shoulders. "We'll have a snack here, rest a bit, then go on back to the lodge for a more substantial dinner."

Alex dropped her pack into the safety of the boat, then looked around with delight. Two young men from the lodge had built a table of sticks and logs, upon which rested palm leaves spread with cooked fish and a neat stack of fresh plantains. She eagerly accepted a plantain from one of the boys, then walked back to the boat where she could sit and eat.

Her companions quieted as they concentrated on food, and the chirping sounds of the jungle rushed in to fill the gaps between their conversations. Alex peeled her plantain and ate slowly, staring mindlessly at a rotting tree trunk jutting out from the riverbank. Terraces of toadstools lined the wood while a line of ants traipsed in single file from one end to the other.

She shuddered slightly. Nothing went to waste in the jungle. The moment something fell, be it animal or plant, scavengers moved in.

When they had finished and cleaned up the area, Lazaro offered to teach them how to fish for piranha. Alex groaned inwardly as Carlton and Olsson leaped at the opportunity. She wanted to get back to the lodge to check on Caitlyn, but she couldn't ask the entire team to accommodate her maternal impulses.

While the men accepted twigs, fishing line, and hooks from Lazaro, she stepped onto shore. Baklanov caught her eye as she moved toward a stand of trees. "Are you looking, excuse me, for a place to relieve yourself?"

She laughed. "If I am, do you think I'd announce it?"

His mouth tipped in a faint smile. "I am sorry, I forget about the modesty of some American women. I will leave you alone. But be careful, my friend, of the insects. They sting." He walked away, rubbing his backside. "Trust me, I know this from experience."

Though Alex would have given twenty bucks for the chance to use a porcelain toilet in a modern bathroom, her bladder couldn't wait. She sought solitude.

Taking care to keep the others in sight, she stepped carefully over the ground layer of the forest. Away from the river, the trees had reclaimed the sky, allowing only the faintest particles of sunlight to penetrate. The shade-loving plants, ferns, seedlings, and fungi grew here, and she recognized many of them — caladium and coleus, elephant's ear, and a spectacular *Heliconia,* dripping with red and yellow flowers that looked more like crab claws than blossoms.

She waded through a tangle of vines, then bent to study a moving train of leaf-cutting ants. The biology films she had watched in school came to life before her eyes as the ants moved in an unbroken line from some tree at her left to a mounded nest a few feet to her right. Each ant carried a scrap of leaf larger than his own body, yet they seemed to have no problem hoisting them like tiny sails and carrying them home.

Squatting down, she rested her chin in her hand and studied the amazing creatures. Science had yet to plumb the mechanics of the ants' collective consciousness. Though small and insignificant, they worked toward a common goal and cooperated not only with each other, but with nature itself. Leaf–cutting ants, she knew, did not actually eat the leaves they harvested, but offered them as food for a fungus in their nest. As the fungus consumed the leaves, it broke the plant material down into food for the ants.

She smiled against her palm. Such symbiotic relationships existed everywhere in the jungle, but they were rare in the civilized world. How many people would confidently help a stranger believing that the act would one day benefit them? She knew too many researchers who jealously guarded their research until they could publish the results, not thinking of the people they could help if they would only provide a clue to someone else in search of a cure for the same disease . . .

Sighing, she pressed her hands to her knees and stood. She would have to bring Caitlyn into the jungle and point out the leaf cutters. The lesson in cooperation would be good for her.

Her smile broadened at the thought of her daughter. Caitlyn had proved to be a precocious survivor, an uncomplaining traveler, and a brilliant student with a particular facility for language. Alex had worried that growing up in a single-parent family might cause Caitlyn to feel she was missing something, but over the years Collin's desertion proved to be more silver lining than cloud. When Alex walked away from the marriage with an infant and twenty thousand dollars in outstanding student loans, she'd thought they'd need a miracle to survive. But now, ten years later, the loans had been repaid, she had risen to the top of her profession, and her team had made remarkable strides in the field of prion research. Without a husband, she had been free to travel, and her daughter had been happy to journey with her.

Instead of a father's limited attention, Caitlyn had been schooled and spoiled by some of the world's most brilliant scientists, including some of the people on this expedition. Since their arrival in Peru, she'd had the opportunity to hear Russian folk tales from Dr. Baklanov, stories of mountaineering from Dr. Olsson, and the hottest gossip from the French fashion industry, courtesy of Louis Fortier.

Alex knew Caitlyn might one day want to settle into a more traditional educational experience, but until then . . .

After glancing over her shoulder to be sure no one watched, she thrust out her arm, splayed her fingers, and watched for any sign of tremor. None — not yet, anyway. Perhaps she would still be around by the time Caitlyn graduated high school.

She dropped her arm and turned toward the sound of her companions' voices. Before applying for this expedition, she had made certain her daughter could be safely entertained at the lodge while Alex worked in the field. Herman Myers, the American manager of Yarupapa Lodge, had assured her that Caitlyn could join the other lodge guests for the regular daily itinerary. Fortunately, this week the only other guests were two middle-aged sisters from Florida with extra time and money on their hands. Though they snapped photos of each other every ten minutes and squealed like tourists with a capital *T*, Caitlyn had warmed to them like a kid to a candy store.

Swatting at mosquitoes, Alex moved out of the forest and back into the clearing at the river's edge. Their guide, Lazaro, stood on the bank to demonstrate the fine art of piranha fishing to Lauren. Deborah, Carlton, and Baklanov dangled lines in the water while Lauren suppressed a yawn. Louis Fortier paid the fishermen no attention; he had buried his face in a crimson flower the size of a dinner plate.

"First you thrash your pole in the water," Lazaro said, whipping the brown water with a thin branch. "This tells the piranha that something has fallen into the river. Then you drop in the bait."

Crossing her arms, Alex grinned at Milos Olsson, who held a fish-filled bucket with one hand and swatted at mosquitoes with the other. Apparently he had caught his fill of the voracious fish and was happy to give the lovely *turista* a chance to snag her supper.

After throwing Carlton a frown, Lauren accepted the stick from Lazaro, then let the baited hook fall into the water. For a moment she stood stiffly, her arms locked and extended, while Carlton laughed softly.

70

"Don't think of them as man-eating fish," he said, one corner of his mouth dipping in a wry smile. "Think of them as members of the board of directors. You've already proven you can handle the most bloodthirsty of them."

As Alex felt a smirk lift her lips, Lauren squealed and jerked her pole away from the water. A razor-toothed fish with a decided underbite swung on the end of the line.

Lazaro laughed softly as he caught the flopping piranha by the tail. "Good job." With two fingers he grabbed the fish behind the gills, then extracted the hook and tossed the creature into Olsson's bucket.

Catching Alex's eye, the guide smiled. "Want to see something?" Bending down, he picked up another piranha. "One of the gentlemen caught this half an hour ago. But watch."

Carefully holding the piranha in his right hand, he scooped up a sardine and placed it near the piranha's mouth. Without hesitation, the carnivore worked its jaws, chomping away at the smaller fish until nothing of the tail remained but a bloody nub.

Olsson stared down into his bucket. "Good grief, how long does it take them to die?"

"Long time." Lazaro slipped the sardine's remains onto the hook, then picked up the rustic fishing pole and arched a brow at Alex. "Señora, you want to fish?"

She stared at the simple apparatus — a pole, a line, a hook — then threw a longing glance at the boat.

"Actually," she glanced at Carlton, "I was hoping we could head back to the lodge. I'm going to need a blood transfusion if these mosquitoes keep draining me."

"A good idea." Carlton placed his hand in Lauren's back and prodded his mistress toward the boat. "Thank you, Lazaro, for the demonstration, but I think we'll leave the other piranha alone. Perhaps tomorrow we'll fish some more."

"Thank you, Lord!" Deborah winked at Alex as she strode toward the boat. "God bless you, Dr. Pace."

Breathing out an exasperated sigh, Alex followed the others.

1 April 2003
4:05 p.m.

Sinking into the chair behind his desk, Michael propped his head in his hands, then tunneled his fingers through his hair. It had been a long and frustrating day. Since his casualty patient this morning, he'd examined twenty pediatric patients, two men with malaria, and four pregnant women. All four of the women had borne other children; one had an even dozen waiting at home.

In each obstetrical case he had gently tried to explain the advantages of tubal ligation. Since most of his patients were Catholic in name if not in practice, discretionary methods of birth control were considered taboo. But in a country where women as young as thirteen began to bear children and most continued to produce babies until menopause, tubal ligation could be a quiet blessing.

His explanation — or Fortuna's translation

73

— must not have been effective, for all four of his pregnant patients merely smiled shyly and slid off the exam table, content to go home and continue bearing children. Performing the ligation would be simple if they came to the hospital to have their babies, but he knew he would see few of his maternity patients again. Tribal women had been delivering babies in riverside villages for generations; they only sent for the doctor when things went dramatically wrong.

Lowering his hands, Michael glanced at a bagful of drugs Fortuna had collected from his last patient. The man, who had been clearly suffering from malaria, had visited an Iquitos *farmacia* and walked out with a collection of medicines including cough syrup, worm pills, and a bottle of drops for "cerebral circulation" — whatever that was. None of the medicines had helped, so the man had then visited a nearby *brujo,* or shaman, who declared that evil had been visited upon the patient and he could provide the cure.

The blending of old and new cultures constantly amazed Michael. While as a physician he recognized illness as a clearly definable condition within a physical body, he could not ignore the prevailing culture's view of sickness as the result of interactions between human bodies and spiritual forces. His patients thought nothing of visiting a *brujo* one day and a physician the next; what one did not cure, surely the other would. And their definition of illness surprised him — any upset, be it physical, mental, or emotional, caused *dis*-ease, so nearly as many patients consulted him for lovesickness as for parasites.

When faced with a lovesick patient, Michael frequently left the counsel and treatment to Fortuna, who knew far more about native spirits — and Peruvian marriage rites — than he did.

Peculiarities of the culture often frustrated Michael, yet one aspect of jungle customs pleased him — while in other societies a man might seek vengeance upon whomever had brought about an illness through spiritual means, the people with whom he worked made no effort to determine who the "bewitching" party might be. With surprising equanimity they accepted their illness and promptly sought cures from the brujo and physician.

Once he had asked Fortuna why this was so; she replied with a casual shrug. "There are too many people alive, too many dead, so how can you know who is responsible? You would go crazy if you tried to blame them all."

Thus far Michael had encountered only one exception to this rule: Early in his Iquitos practice, a little boy's father explained that his toddling lad's persistent diarrhea resulted from his deceased mother's efforts to persuade the boy to join her in the next world. After meeting the boy and the father's new wife, Michael privately suspected the stepmother had more to do with the child's illness than the spirit world, for the new wife had candidly told Fortuna she did not want to raise another woman's child. Native women knew their plants; the stepmother could have been giving the boy tea from a vine in the forget-me-not family or overdosing him with any of the many plants used to kill worms; all acted as purgatives. Both Michael and the village brujo attempted to treat the sickly lad; over time, they both failed.

Resting his head on his hand, Michael blinked the troubling images of the past away. This morning's fiasco in the casualty ward had vividly reminded him that superstition still thrived along the river. The orderly who fled at the sight of the tattooed patient never returned to the ward, and several of the nurses had shrunk from the sight of the unusual-looking native.

Michael glanced at his watch. That nameless patient was still fighting peritonitis and still losing the battle. His kidneys had begun to fail during the afternoon; death was only a few hours away. At midday, Fortuna had called for a priest to administer the last rites; she later reported that the patient resisted as the cleric approached, clearly wanting no part of the ritual. Michael had advised her to wait until later and then try again. While he doubted his patient was Catholic, Fortuna and the other nurses placed great emphasis on the ritual. The priest's efforts might not be worth two pence to the patient, but at least the nurses would be comforted.

Looking around his desk, Michael's eyes fell upon the English-language version of *El Tiempo,* Peru's largest newspaper. He had subscribed to this digest version several weeks ago, but thus far he'd done nothing with the paper but clutter his desk. On a day like this, though, it might be nice to have a gander at the English language, to read a phrase or two that evoked a memory of old Blighty and civilization.

After glancing up to be sure his door was closed (Fortuna had a habit of promising his attention to anyone who asked for it, even on his dinner break), Michael picked up the paper and shook it open. The editors of *El Tiempo* routinely translated the week's major stories, emphasizing those presumed to be of interest to travelers, students, or internationals.

A photograph on the front page immediately caught Michael's attention. At first glance he thought he was looking at a starfish on a grainy beach, then he read the caption: "This platform canopy, designed by French researchers, will be employed for the next three months at a site on the Yarapa River. A multinational team of researchers will pursue several scientific investigations while visiting Peru."

Reading the article, Michael learned that an international delegation had flown into Lima in late March. Many esteemed researchers would be staying at the Yarupapa Lodge and conducting various experiments throughout the months of April, May, and June.

"Among the American scientists are noted anthropologist Emma Whitmore and neurologist Alexandra Pace," the reporter wrote. "And while Dr. Pace's work is well known to medical researchers working in the field of brain diseases, few people realize why she has invested her life in this field of study."

Michael tensed as the soft popping sounds of flip-flops broke his concentration. He stared at the doorknob, willing it to remain closed, then slowly released his breath as the passerby continued down the hallway.

He returned to his reading.

Alexandra Pace, one of the world's leading neurologists, is employed by Horizon Biotherapies. She specializes in the quest for a cure or treatment for diseases caused by infectious proteins, more commonly known as prions. Few doctors have encountered prion diseases among their patients, but since the outbreak of mad cow disease in Europe, the threat of such illnesses hangs like a specter over mankind.

Prions — ordinary proteins that have somehow become misfolded — not only do not function properly in the body, but they cannot be eliminated or rendered harmless by enzymes. As they accumulate, they cause the patient to lose coordination, mental function, and speech. Often patients experience dementia or sleeplessness. Death usually occurs within two years after the onset of symptoms.

The quest for a cure brings Dr. Pace to Peru. When asked what she hopes to find within our country, the pretty American smiled and replied, "Nice people. Beautiful views. And hope."

She went on to cite the recent rainforest discovery of a substance that enhances the action of adenosine, a brain chemical that reduces the effects of strokes and may help combat Alzheimer's disease. She explains: "According to anthropologists, the Matses, a Peruvian tribe, use a particular frog to cure hunters of what we would call burnout. Whenever a weary hunter wishes to 'take frog,' another man finds the frog and harasses it, scrapes the defensively produced mucus off its skin, then burns the hunter with a hot twig. To the burn he then applies the frog mucus mixed with saliva. The hunter becomes violently ill for a few hours, but he awakens the next morning eager to hunt. And while I don't know much about hunters or Peruvian natives, I am vitally interested in chemical compounds that affect brain function."

When asked if she believes the frog mucus contains some bacteria or virus that will help her find a cure for prion diseases, she answers, "I have no idea, but at this point I'm open to any experiment. Researchers recently discovered a small molecule drug that can stop the misfolding of prions before they begin to malfunction. I'm looking for a molecule that can undo the damage caused by misfolded prions that result in brain disease. I am hoping to find that catalyst here in Peru."

The American researcher, who lives in Atlanta and is employed by the company sponsoring the expedition, went on to cite several pertinent statistics: "Seventy percent of all prescription drugs in the United States come from plants found only in the rainforest. More than 90 percent of all the world's plant and animal species live in the tropics. The rainforest contains the very biology of our planet, and if cures for our illnesses exist, I believe they can be found here."

Michael gripped the edges of the newspaper as a slight coldness settled around his bones.

He had never heard a local doctor speak of encephalopathies; few American physicians even knew what a prion was.

But his colleagues at London's St. George's Hospital knew all about prion-induced diseases. In their own wards they had treated variations of Creutzfeldt-Jakob disease, and under their microscopes they had peered at evidence of kuru and bovine spongiform encephalopathy, more commonly known as mad cow disease. BSE had frightened the country spitless in the late 1990s, resulting in the destruction of over half a million cattle . . . and the deaths of 107 people, including Michael's wife.

The empty air around him seemed to vibrate, the silence filling with remembered dread. Slowly, he lowered the newspaper.

"If you find a cure for prion diseases, Dr. Pace, I'll kiss your bloomin' feet."

By the time the sun had begun to drift toward the horizon, Lazaro had the crew of the canopy expedition back on the river highway that led to their jungle lodge. Leaning forward on her elbows, Alex stared at the water and tried to relax. The river flowed quietly here, eddying around the occasional log or fallen tree like melted chocolate pouring over Twix candy bars.

She smiled at the image — she must be hungrier than she realized, or maybe she was just craving chocolate. Out here, miles from a grocery store, she wasn't likely to satisfy a craving for anything but fish, rice, or plantains.

The Yarapa River, one of the many tributaries feeding the mighty Amazon, bore little resemblance to the wide thoroughfare they had traveled as they left Iquitos. The Amazon had been rough with waves and occasional whitecaps, and one of the guides told Alex it was not unusual for sudden rainstorms to swamp a small canoe and drown its occupants.

Studying the boat provided by the lodge, she could understand why the vessels swamped so easily. Even this boat, framed with benches around the sides and a wooden subfloor to keep the tourists' feet dry, rode with the gunwales only a few inches above the water. She could easily trail her fingertips in the brown liquid . . . and might have been tempted to if she hadn't known about the anacondas, caimans, and piranhas that lived in these waters.

The Indians, on the other hand, carved their boats from fallen trees. Their long, narrow, and extremely shallow canoes lacked benches or subfloors to provide comfort for passengers. After examining a native canoe at the lodge, Alex concluded that riding in it would not be much different from paddling on a rough-hewn plank.

The water swirled beside her now, quietly absorbing the passage of the boat. Lazaro sat in the bow, keeping an eye out for fallen logs, while one of the boys from the lodge steered from the stern. Her exhausted teammates had fallen silent, only an occasional camera click broke into the musical duet of the jungle and the outboard motor. Alex closed her eyes, relishing the breath of wind on her face. If her muscles hadn't ached, it would have been a truly magical moment.

She let her head fall back as the putt-putt of the outboard motor slowed and Yarupapa Lodge appeared through the jungle foliage. The motor died; the boat floated toward the dock.

One of the young men who worked at the lodge extended his hand as the boat nudged the tires against the wooden pilings. *"Gracias,"* Alex murmured, allowing him to pull her up. She clumped across the deck on legs that felt stumpy and uncoordinated, then laughed when she looked around and saw that the others were walking the same way.

"I thought I'd never put my feet on a proper floor again," Lauren moaned, one hand pressed to her forehead as Ken Carlton led her away.

Olsson peered at his arm as he walked; when he reached Alex, he pointed toward a pair of red welts on the back of his wrist. "Do you see this? There are cruel flies in these bushes. I did not even feel them biting, yet look at my arm —"

"It's the law of the jungle, Olsson." Deborah Simons good-naturedly patted Olsson on the shoulder as she passed by. "Don't take it personally. But I have some ointment in my room, and I'll bring it to you at dinner."

Dinner! Alex drew a deep breath and breathed in a wave of delicious scents. She didn't know what the lodge chef was preparing, but she was fully prepared to eat first and identify foods later. Caitlyn might not be so accepting, however.

Waving farewell to her teammates, Alex hurried to keep a long-overdue appointment with the rest room, then made her way to the cool shade of the screened walkway that led into the dining room. Herman Myers, the manager, sat at a round table playing cards with some of the lodge staff.

She nodded a greeting, then lifted her chin as Myers stood. "*Buenos tardes, señor.* Have you seen my daughter?"

Myers stared into the distance and tapped his chin with his index finger. "Your daughter . . . yes, I saw her in the hammock room a little while ago. We visited the village at Puerto Miguel today, and the ladies were tired. I believe you'll find your daughter and the other guests napping in the hammocks."

Alex thanked him, then forced her tired legs to traverse the long dining room. A chalkboard on an easel announced that dinner would be served at 6:00 p.m. — in just over an hour. Perhaps she could talk Caitlyn into a cold shower before dinner — Alex knew she had never felt more in need of one.

The hammock room lay just outside the dining hall. As she opened the screened door, for a fleeting instant Alex thought it should have been called a hammock *hut.* The lovely octagonal shelter featured eight hammocks attached to a stout center pole like the spokes of a giant wheel. A river breeze wafted through the screens while lizards rustled in the thatched roof overhead.

Alex entered quietly, then approached one of the gently creaking hammocks. One of the American tourists lay inside, her eyes closed and her manicured hands resting atop an open John Grisham novel.

Wrong hammock. Alex tiptoed to the next occupied hammock and immediately realized the body encased within was far too adult.

She had turned to leave when a drowsy voice broke the stillness: "Did you have a good day up in the trees?"

Turning, she greeted the brown-haired woman in the hammock. "Yes, thank you, we did. Ms. Somerville, isn't it?"

"Call me Gayla, please." The woman's lips parted in a bleached smile, dazzling against her tanned skin. "We had a good day, too. I brought several T-shirts to trade, and the villagers seemed happy to get them. I'll be taking home a purse, some baskets, and a piranha jaw necklace — the girls at my garden club will *love* that."

Though she yearned to find her daughter, Alex forced herself to make polite conversation. "I hope my little girl wasn't a bother. Did Caitlyn enjoy the trading?"

"She seemed to have a ball — except when

86

one little boy started crying because she ran out of candy. His mother couldn't get him to stop."

Rolling her eyes, Alex edged toward the door. "I told her not to take candy to the village. I doubt there's a dentist within fifty miles of this place, so the last thing those children need is sugar."

Gayla shrugged. "Whatever. The day was quite an experience, but I am absolutely exhausted." Straightening, she suddenly looked at Alex as if a cloud of weariness had evaporated from her brain. "By the way, that's one smart little girl you've got there. What is she, a genius?"

Alex took another step toward the screened door. "Pretty close."

The woman snorted a laugh. "Must be some kind of prodigy. One of the guides taught her a few words of Spanish, and before we left she was jabbering with those kids like she'd been born there." She frowned. "At least, I *think* she was making sense. But what do I know?"

"She has a gift for languages . . . among other things." Alex pushed the door open. "Well, I'd better find Caitlyn and try to talk her into cleaning up for dinner. Have you seen her lately? Mr. Myers thought she might be in here."

Gayla swung her legs out of the hammock, then looked around. "She was here, but she must have slipped out while I was napping. She said something about walking along the riverbank to look for fish. Mr. Myers was going to let her borrow his fishing spear."

Memories of the piranha sent a sudden chill up Alex's spine. The local residents probably thought nothing of sending their children out to hunt with spears and machetes, but Caitlyn was a sheltered American girl . . . and supremely overconfident of her abilities.

"She's probably in your room." The other woman, a heavier, older version of Gayla, sat up in her hammock. "You know how kids are. They always go home when they're tired."

"I'm sure you're right." Alex nodded at each of the sisters. "See you at dinner, then."

She hesitated on the elevated plank platform that led to the guest rooms. The bungalows lay deeper in the forest, away from the river and the common areas. Should she walk along the riverbank just to be sure she hadn't missed Caitlyn?

Jumping from the walkway, she walked over stubby grass and past a cluster of hibiscus bushes. She could see the river's edge to her left and right, but she saw no sign of her daughter. A group of the young men who served as lodge staff were laughing and smoking on the dock, while dozens of yellow butterflies danced around a rowboat half-filled with water.

Alex turned and moved over the wooden

sidewalk, humming to the rhythm of her steps on the wooden planks. Everything had been built above ground here; every building and permanent walkway rose from the ground on stilts. She had read that this part of the world did not experience four seasons. Because the lodge lay only three degrees south of the Equator, twelve-hour days were followed by twelve-hour nights and all seasons offered virtually the same climate. Rain fell two out of every three days at a rate of about 120 inches per year.

She came to a gap between the buildings and peered around a clump of shrubs. "Caitlyn?" The silence of the woods swallowed her voice.

Shaking her head, Alex moved on toward their bungalow. They were lucky, Myers had told them after their arrival, because they had come at the end of the flood season. Most of the areas they wanted to visit were still accessible by boat. The floodwaters did not come from rainfall, but from water accumulating in the distant Andes Mountains, where glaciers melted and runoff collected in scores of tributaries that poured their waters into the Amazon. The rivers began to rise in October; by November, the river would lap against the landing outside Yarupapa's dining hall and completely flood many Yagua villages. By mid-April, however, the waters would begin to subside as the mountain glaciers froze and precipitation in the Andes shifted from rain to snow. By July and August, the villagers and tourists would be traveling through the jungle on foot, and wide lakes that had provided fish and eel in November and December would be planted with rice, beans, and watermelon.

Turning left on the walkway, Alex glanced up at the sky, which was still bright and clear. Thankfully, it had not rained this morning on the canopy raft. She couldn't imagine how slippery the raft might become in the midst of a tropical rainstorm, but the experience wasn't at all appealing.

After reaching the bungalow she shared with Caitlyn, she studied the door and frowned. No doorknobs or locks secured these doors, only hook-and-eye latches on both sides — to block creatures while you were out and intruders while you were in. The outside latch had been secured, which meant Caitlyn had either found a way to latch the hook-and-eye from the inside . . . or she wasn't in the room.

To be certain, Alex flipped the hook and opened the door. "Caitlyn?"

The room lay silent and still amid the chirping of the cicadas. The lodge, while modern and pleasant, took pains to allow its guests to feel at home in the rainforest. Two screened walls opened to the jungle at the side and rear; the middle wall faced an adjoining bungalow; the solid front allowed a measure of privacy. Two wooden benches occupied the square room, matched by two beds, each securely enclosed by opaque mosquito netting. Two small ledges had been built into the wall; one of these supported an oil lamp and a packet of matches, while the other held a pitcher of purified drinking water and several plastic cups.

Caitlyn's suitcase lay open on the floor, her clothing scattered about. A pair of mud-spattered sneakers jutted from beneath a bench, which meant she was traipsing around the jungle in her rubber flip-flops . . . or her bare feet. A towel hung over the foot of her bed, and Alex's fingertips encountered dampness when she touched it. Either Caitlyn had already showered, or the cotton towel had soaked up humidity from the air.

After peeking into the mosquito netting over both beds, Alex whirled on the ball of her foot and left the room, letting the screen door slam behind her. Her naturally gregarious daughter was probably charming the kitchen staff with her gift for mimicry, or she might be sitting on the dock watching the swarming butterflies. No — she hadn't been there a moment ago, so she might be trying to attract butterflies down by the river. Dishwashing liquid would do it, one of the guides had explained. One squirt in standing water attracted butterflies like nothing else, and

Caitlyn found that sort of thing fascinating.

Alex pressed her hand to her chest as her lungs began to tighten. No — she would not freak out. The pounding of her heart resulted from a mother's natural concern, not a panic attack. She would find her daughter in a moment, and everything would be all right.

Breaking into a jog, Alex passed the women's bathrooms, then wheeled and barged through the swinging door. Of course! Caitlyn had to be in either the shower or one of the rustic toilet stalls. Being ten, she might be perched on a stepstool before the mirror, sneaking a peek at herself in a forbidden shade of lipstick. Maybe she'd raided one of the Somerville sisters' purses.

"Caitlyn?" Alex grimaced as the door slammed behind her, then moved farther into the Spartan facility. Every visible surface had been painted in a glossy gray enamel, the better, she guessed, to reveal the dark brown *cucarachas* that scurried for shelter every time sunlight pierced the shadowy room.

"Caitlyn? I'm not in the mood to play games."

A cockroach clung to the rim of the white enamel sink as Alex waited for an answer. Hearing no answer, she moved from stall to stall, opening doors and finding nothing but plumbing fixtures and termite trails.

Turning, she winced at the bite of an instinctive stab of fear. She had checked all

92

the obvious places and public areas. Surely Caitlyn knew she shouldn't be hanging around the kitchen while the staff worked to prepare dinner. She had always been good about obeying the rules when they traveled, but the Somerville sisters might not have been the most interesting companions . . . especially when they were snoozing in hammocks.

Caitlyn didn't like napping, never had. Even as a toddler, her active little brain had compelled her hands and feet to search out all kinds of mischief.

Alex left the rest room and jogged to the dining hall, then opened the screened door. She breezed by Lazaro and a couple of other staff members as she marched toward the kitchen area. Someone called out her name as she passed, but Alex had no time for anything but finding her daughter.

She pushed open another door, then found herself staring at two native women with wide brown eyes.

"My daughter," she said, wishing she remembered more of her high-school Spanish. *"Me hija.* Do you know — *donde esta . . . me hija?"*

The women glanced at each other, then shook their heads. One of them wiped her hands on an apron and began to chatter in Spanish, but Alex couldn't understand a word. She blinked away tears and turned, nearly bumping into Herman Myers.

"Your daughter?" he asked, clearly reading the distress on her face. "Was she not in a hammock?"

"No, she wasn't in a hammock." Alex bit her lip, trying to maintain control of her rebellious emotions. "She wasn't in our room or in the bathroom. Where else could she be, Mr. Myers?"

Propping one hand on his hip, Myers surveyed the dining hall as if he expected Caitlyn to pop up from beneath a table at any moment. Finally, he scratched his neck. "There are the gardens." Limply, he gestured toward the jungle. "And the river. You don't think she would go down one of the trails, do you?"

"She's not stupid." Alex bit down on her lower lip; she hadn't meant to speak with such animosity. "Will you check the gardens, Mr. Myers? I'm going to walk along the river."

She did not wait to hear his response, but set out with a long-legged stride any of the men might have envied. "I'll send Lazaro with you," Myers called, but Alex didn't wait. She exited the dining hall, jumped from the porch to the soft green grass, and began jogging toward the water's edge.

The late afternoon air was heavy, warm, and still, filled with a quiet malevolence that painted her frustration with fear. Caitlyn was a good kid; she wouldn't disobey. They were hundreds of miles from civilization, so she couldn't have been snatched by an insane serial killer. No drunken drivers whizzed by this lodge, so she wasn't lying in an emergency room somewhere. These people had never known the kind of fear that resulted from drive-by shootings and sniper attacks, so Alex had nothing to worry about —

Just jaguars and poisonous snakes and tarantulas.

"Twinkle, twinkle . . ."

Pausing, she leaned against a tree and forced herself to draw deep, steady breaths. She had to focus. Look around, study her surroundings, look for intelligent clues. If she panicked, she'd miss something.

Though an eel of fear still wriggled in her bowels, Alex lifted her chin and walked across the grass. Whoever maintained the landscaping had done a good job; the grounds could have vied with any resort in the world for flowers and plants. A colorful *Heliconia* in glorious bloom dangled from a tree beside the path; wild orchids festooned the limbs of sheltering trees and splashed the landscape with color. But after a moment of scanning the grounds, Alex turned her eyes to the river and concentrated on the soggy shoreline.

Spearfishing, one of the Somervilles had said. Caitlyn wanted to try spearfishing. So she would have walked this way, followed this shifting and watery boundary. Yet the grass was damp and slippery; with one misstep anyone could fall in. The water wasn't especially deep or dangerous, but caimans lived in this river, and those cousins of the crocodile had been known to drag dogs and wild pigs into the water.

Slapping at mosquitoes, Alex moved steadily along the shoreline, eyes alert for some evidence of her daughter's presence. Twenty yards from the dining hall, the grass ended abruptly, and in the mud she saw a footprint — a small indentation made by a rubber sandal. Caitlyn's flip-flop.

Alex caught her breath as she spied a round hole in the sand. She had never seen a fishing spear, but if it looked anything like a fireplace andiron, it might leave a mark like this if pressed into the mud.

She hurried on, following the footprints until they vanished in another patch of grass. Mosquitoes swarmed amid a tangle of hanging foliage, and in her determination to bat them away she walked face first into a spider web. Spitting and swatting, she stumbled up the embankment, then froze.

On the grass, barely ten feet away, coiled the largest snake she had ever seen. It undulated in loose curves over the earth, its powerful neck extended, its tongue flicking in her direction, tasting her scent.

Anaconda.

Terror lodged in her throat, making it impossible to speak or scream.

The snake hissed, its tongue darting toward her in quick strokes. Her brain screamed *run!* but fear paralyzed her legs. Helpless to flee, she recoiled even as her gaze swept over the gigantic body of the beast . . . and spied a suspicious bulge in the snake's midsection.

Alex's heart congealed into a small lump of terror. She stood motionless, staring at the bulge, while a single droplet of sweat traced the course of her spine.

How did anacondas kill? They suffocated their victims, squeezing the life-giving oxygen out of them. Often they attacked at the water's edge and held their victims underwater until drowned. Then they leisurely opened their jaws and swallowed their victims whole . . .

As a strangled sob rose from her chest, silver flashed at the corner of her eye. Trembling, she turned to see Lazaro standing beside her, his eyes dark and focused, a machete in his hand.

"Go back inside." He did not look at her, but kept his attention focused on the snake. "It has eaten. If we leave it alone, it will slide into the water and leave us."

Propelled by panic, Alex clawed at Lazaro's arm. "My daughter is missing. I saw her footprints here, by the river. And she is a very little girl."

He turned to her then, and she knew she would never forget the look of horror in his eyes.

1 April 2003
5:27 p.m.

Startled, Michael looked up as Fortuna rapped on his open door. His nurse had usually gone home by this hour.

"What is it, Fortuna?"

"The patient — the man with the stab wound. I checked on him for you. Esma is still with him, and she sent me to get you."

Michael swung his legs off the desk. "Is his condition deteriorating?"

"Yes, but it is the story that concerns Esma."

"His story? She understands him?"

"Enough. He is talking, she is picking up a few things, but she says he talks like a man out of his head."

"That's not surprising, really. I would expect some sort of delirium in his condition. What I find surprising is the fact he's able to talk at all."

Michael glanced at his watch — long past

time for dinner, and nearly sunset. He ought to go home himself. He snorted at the thought. What on earth for?

Nodding, he looked up at his nurse. "Thank you. I'll go tell Esma she can go home. We can't expect her to conduct a bedside vigil for every native who wanders out of the jungle."

Fortuna's eyes crinkled at the corners. "She does not mind, *el doctor.* But please, she wishes to speak to you."

Blowing out his cheeks, Michael pushed back from his desk. The day would never end unless he locked his office and went back to his flat. Sooner or later, he would.

Yet nothing waited for him there but impersonal furnishings and a television spewing out Spanish-language programs that only muddled his thoughts . . . and made him long for home.

Before Lazaro could act, the still air over the riverbank shivered into bits, a thunderlike blast scattering the birds that had flown in to roost for the night. The restless anaconda's head fell to the ground with a soft thud, and Alex fell with it. She sat down hard on the wet earth, feeling the grass beneath her fingers as she looked up and saw Herman Myers with a shotgun in his hand.

The blast had torn through the huge serpent's body and Lazaro wasted no time. With the expertise of a surgeon he sliced the still-shuddering carcass open, then stepped back, caught Myers' eye, and shook his head.

Alex closed her eyes as the world went black. She reached for something to cling to, felt the strong firmness of a human hand, and would have fainted if not for a childish voice that snapped her back to reality —

"Mom? What's going on?"

Energized by that voice, Alex opened her eyes and scrambled toward her daughter. Deborah Simons gripped Alex's arm, helping her to her feet, and she realized that the commotion had brought everyone from the dining hall, including her daughter. Mud-smeared and frizzy-haired, Caitlyn stood beside one of the staff boys, a bucket of fish in one hand and an iron spear in the other.

"Caitlyn!" Alex rushed forward and drew her daughter into her arms. "I thought you were . . . lost."

"I've been fishing." Caitlyn's muffled voice came from within their embrace. "Tito took me to a special place where it's quiet. Look what I caught."

Not quite willing to release her daughter, Alex peered over the top of Caitlyn's head. Half a dozen gaping piranha lay wide-eyed inside the bucket, yet Caitlyn didn't seem to have a scratch on her.

The situation was typical Caitlyn. The child learned best by doing, touching, and tasting, so she'd probably learned more about piranha in ten minutes with Tito than she would if she'd read a dozen articles on the subject.

Closing her eyes, Alex pressed her lips together. Part of her wanted to scream out her frustration, to scold Caitlyn for worrying her so, but if she vented those emotions now she might completely lose control. Besides, Caitlyn hadn't broken any rules. So it was better to be silent, to rein in her feelings . . . and brace herself for her daughter's next stunt.

Fortunately, Caitlyn didn't seem to realize the horror that had risen in Alex's imagination. Pulling out of Alex's embrace, she looked past Lazaro, then her jaw dropped at the sight of the huge serpent. An instant later her nose crinkled in disgust. "Ugh! Gotta be an anaconda, right, Mom?"

"I think so. Yes, I'm sure of it." Alex forced a laugh. "Ugly, isn't it?"

"Did it scare you or something? You're as white as chalk."

"Something like that."

With her arm firmly around her daughter's shoulders, Alex turned in time to see Lazaro peel back a thick flap of snakeskin to reveal the creature's last meal: a pig?

"It's a tapir," Caitlyn's voice warmed with recognition. "I wondered if we'd see one. Never thought we'd see one like *this*."

"What's a tapir?"

"An ungulate mammal with a bulky body, short legs, and a head characterized by a short, flexible proboscis, small eyes, and erect ears."

"And I suppose you know what *ungulate* means?"

Caitlyn snorted. "Hooves, Mom. Everybody knows that."

The Amazonian version of a wild pig, then.

Feeling weak-kneed, Alex turned and led her daughter toward the bungalow. "Why don't you and I get cleaned up for dinner?" she said, trying to keep her tone light. "I want to hear all about your fishing."

"It was great, Mom. Tito says you don't have to be afraid of piranha — he swims in the water all the time. They won't bite unless you're bleeding."

"All the same, I don't want you to go swimming unless there are lots of other people around. On second thought, stay out of the water all together, okay? I'll take you swimming when we get home — in a nice, clean pool. I'll take you anywhere you want to go."

As Alex ran her fingers through Caitlyn's tousled hair, profound gratitude washed over her, a feeling so intense and overwhelming that for an instant she almost wished God existed . . . just so she could say thank you.

1 April 2003
5:40 p.m.

Leaving Fortuna to close up his office, Michael walked with long strides to the postoperative ward. The hospital had grown quiet in the last hour; most people completed their business well before five o'clock. Except in the seediest parts of the city, the approach of sunset sent most of the locals scurrying to their homes. He suspected the habit had its roots in jungle life, where darkness and danger walked as one.

He found the injured native in a curtained cubicle. Esma sat in a chair, her head propped against the wall, her eyes closed. Not wanting to disturb her, Michael picked up the chart and skimmed the ward nurse's notations. The patient's kidneys had completely shut down. His respiratory rate had increased. His lungs would fail next, followed rapidly by his liver and brain.

He frowned as he read the man's temperature — thirty-nine degrees Celsius, so the patient was still febrile.

The chart clattered against the railing on the bed, startling Esma into wakefulness. She looked up and blushed when she saw Michael. "I am sorry to have stayed here so long." She glanced at the unconscious patient. "I think he is sleeping now. I would have gone, but I wanted to tell you what I learned."

Michael slipped his hands into his pockets. "I'm sorry, Esma, I should have come sooner. I hope you were able to get the name of a relative. I do not think he will live until morning."

A tremor touched the clerk's thin lips. "He knows he will die. He says the Spirit of keyba told him he would die soon after reaching the big naba village. But he is not afraid."

Michael crossed one arm over his chest. "Hold on a moment — what's a keyba?"

Esma wagged her head. "I do not know — the word is not Yagua. He said many things I could not understand — and I am not sure of the things I think I did understand. His story is *incredible* —"

"Why don't I grab a chair so we can discuss it? Tell me as much as you can."

As the patient stirred on the bed, Esma rose to wipe his forehead with a cool cloth. *A nice woman,* Michael thought, stepping across the hall to fetch an unused chair from another cubicle. A clerk with a nurse's compassion.

When the native had stilled, Esma sat down and consulted a notepad she had pulled from her pocket. "He would not say his name, of course, but I discovered it by asking incidental questions."

Michael sank into his chair. "How do you do that?"

Esma lifted one shoulder in a shrug. "I asked him who would be missing from his village if we were to journey there. The answer was Ya-ree."

Michael nodded, looking at his patient with new eyes. No longer was the man a nameless native, he was Ya-ree, from . . .

"The name of his village?"

"I'm not sure they have a proper name. But he says he was born into the tribe of the *feroz pueblo* — you would say the Angry People."

Michael frowned. "I've never heard of such a tribe."

Leaning forward, Esma lowered her voice to a confidential tone. "Neither have I, except in my grandmother's legends. They say the feroz pueblo are powerful cannibals who live deep in the jungle. They say the people of that tribe can move like spirits on the air without being seen."

Michael crossed his arms, not knowing whether to laugh aloud or pretend sincere interest. "Obviously," he began, taking care to speak slowly, "this man is visible, so your grandmother got the story wrong. But please, go on."

Esma glanced at her notes, then shot a guilty look toward the man on the bed. "He said he left the feroz pueblo when he realized he was dying of the shuddering disease like his mother and father before him. He had begun to tremble, and he knew it was only a matter of time before he could not walk. So he traveled four days to the village of his enemies, the people he had been taught to hate — the *árbol pueblo,* the Tree People who worshiped the Spirit of keyba and had the gift of healing."

Michael chuckled. "Now you've completely lost me . . . and I think our patient has lost his mental faculties. One of the signs of dementia is a reversion to childhood, and it sounds like Yar-pee here —"

"Ya-ree," Esma corrected.

"Ya-ree, then. It sounds like he is reciting every childhood myth the village shaman ever taught him. If he told you he ascended through the clouds and flew like an eagle over the jungle —"

"Actually," Esma lowered her notepad, "he said he walked to the top of the keyba and met the *luz* — the light — which cured him of the shuddering disease. He remained with the árbol people many seasons, until the shaman of that village sent him to find a naba."

Michael raked his hand through his hair.

"You've used that word before — what is a *naba?*"

"A non-Indian. Ya-ree set out, but on the journey he ran into a group of warriors from the Angry People. They chased him and stabbed him with the spear, but the Spirit of keyba sent lights to guide him to the river. The Spirit said he was not to worry, for his duty would be accomplished once he reached the big village where a naba would take care of him."

"Just curious — was I mentioned by name in any of this rambling?"

Esma's small smile faded. "Of course not, Doctor."

"Well, then. It's an interesting tale, but patently unbelievable." Michael drew a deep breath, then glanced over at his patient. "Why did his appearance frighten my orderly?"

Esma pressed her lips together. "The tattoos."

Against the stark whiteness of the covering bedsheet, the dark tattoos that marked the patient's face and chest stood out more than ever. "What about them? Are they some sort of symbols?"

"Apparently they are the tribal markings of the Angry People."

Michael lifted a brow. "You weren't frightened."

"I did not know what they were . . . until Ya-ree told me."

"He told you all of this — just as you related it to me?"

"*Si, el doctor.* He told me everything I have told you."

Michael sat silently for a moment, digesting the details of the dying man's story. For a patient exhibiting dementia, the tale had a surprising coherence. Most dementia patients had trouble recalling a progressive timeline. But if the story were even partly true . . .

He leaned back in his chair, folding his hands as he contemplated the possible significance of such a story. Supposedly "lost" Stone Age tribes had been discovered in Brazil; the Yanomani tribe of that nation now lived on thousands of protected acres. He had never heard of lost tribes in Peru, but the vast Amazon had never been fully explored. An unknown tribal group living deep in the jungle probably could remain undisturbed and undiscovered . . . for a while. Eventually, though, the civilized world would encroach upon their territory. In July 2002, Brazil had succeeded in installing radars and sensors to monitor every inch of its 1.9 million square miles of rainforest, so Peru would not be far behind.

He gave Esma an apologetic smile. "I'm sorry if I seem cynical. You warned me the story was incredible."

She acknowledged his confession with the smallest softening of her eyes. "But he spoke so clearly . . . I believed him. And I believe he does not fear death now. He cared nothing for the priest who came to anoint him. He is committed to this keyba."

"But what is it?" Standing, Michael moved to the edge of the bed and studied his patient. Apart from the tattoos dotting the man's face, neck, shoulders, and chest, his skin was nearly unlined, so he could not be much older than forty. Still, forty was a vast age in the jungle.

He glanced up at Esma. "Do you think *keyba* is a name for his god?"

She looked down, her lashes hiding her eyes. "I do not know. He certainly spoke of the keyba with — how do you say it? — *reverencia,* reverence."

"Does the word *keyba* mean anything in español?"

She shook her head. *"Nada."*

"Well, then. A question for an anthropologist . . . if we ever find one in these parts." Michael moved around the bed, then extended his hand to the clerk. "*Muchas gracias,* Esma. If the patient were conscious, I am sure Yar-pee would thank you for your kindness."

A half-smile tugged at the corners of her mouth. "Thank you, Doctor. And his name is *Ya-ree.*"

As she moved past him and exited the

cubicle, Michael stared at his patient and wondered what secrets lay behind his smooth face and hideous markings.

Alex twirled her fork in a heaping plate of vegetarian spaghetti and half-listened to the conversations swirling around the dining room table. To her right, Caitlyn was entertaining Dr. Baklanov with stories of their last trip to London, while to Alex's left, Louis Fortier was badgering Lazaro for information about fragrant plants with medicinal purposes. Directly across the table Emma Whitmore, the anthropologist with an avowed fear of heights, sipped from her glass in silence.

A small woman with clipped white hair and startling blue eyes, Emma caught Alex's eye and smiled. "I must confess, Dr. Pace, I was thrilled to discover Mr. Carlton didn't expect me to climb trees with the rest of you." She ran her fingertip around the edge of her glass of powdered *limonada.* "It's a real pleasure, though, to be with you on the ground. I rarely have the opportunity to mingle with other researchers when I'm in the field."

Alex leaned forward to be heard above the other conversations. "What does your work involve?"

The woman tapped her lips with a paper napkin, then tented her hands. "The Yagua, of course. I've been visiting the people of Puerto Miguel for fifteen years, working to complete a statistical study on education and children's health. The infants I weighed at the onset are now having babies of their own." Her voice grew wistful as her gaze shifted to Lazaro. "Some of them venture out into the larger world; others spend their entire lives in the village. A few of the lucky ones find employment at tourist lodges like this, where they can earn enough to support a household of fourteen or fifteen people. They are happy and usually healthy." Her eyes grew misty. "Still, though most of my colleagues would be horrified to hear me say so, I can't help wishing they had more."

Alex lifted her knife. "I think that's a very human response, Dr. Whitmore."

"Call me Emma, please."

"Only if you'll call me Alex. Why would your colleagues be horrified by your compassion?"

Emma tilted her head and half-smiled. "Because anthropology is the study of cultures as they are — our job is to study and record, not to effect change. In some ways we're like photojournalists — we are supposed to observe and report, not stage a scene. But sometimes, especially when I see those darling children, I want to help them. Is that wrong?"

Alex shook her head. "My field is so far removed from yours, I'm afraid all I can offer is simple opinion."

"And we all know what opinion is worth in science — nothing." Emma laughed softly. "Well, then. What are you learning in the treetops?"

Alex blew the bangs from her forehead. "How to sweat away ten pounds without getting dehydrated? Seriously — not much at the moment. I'm assisting Dr. Baklanov in his search for new bacteriophages. I'm hoping we can find something that will be able to attack infectious proteins. But it's like looking for a needle in a haystack."

The woman's fine brows flickered. "I can imagine."

"I've been watching the animals, though — particularly the primates." Alex kept talking as she cut her spaghetti. "Researchers around the globe have noticed scrapie turning up in several species. It's likely to appear in the jungle sooner or later."

She wasn't sure if the word *scrapie* or the mention of animals threw a wet blanket over the atmosphere, but while she spoke the other conversations at the table faded away. She looked up to find everyone watching her. "Sorry. Is scrapie not a suitable topic for the dinner table?"

Caitlyn shot her a reproving glance, but Baklanov laughed. "This is probably the best place in the world to talk about such things. This is not America, where you erect boundaries around dinner conversations. This is wilderness." He reached for the pitcher of lemonade. "More drink, anyone?"

Alex put down her knife. "How about the rest of you? Have you noticed animals behaving oddly? Lazaro? You're probably the best judge of jungle animal behavior."

The guide squinched his face into a question mark. "What do you mean, señora?"

Alex twirled her spaghetti, trying to keep her face composed in blank lines while she listed the symptoms she might soon be experiencing personally. "The indications I'm looking for would be a general loss of coordination, trembling, difficulty in feeding or swallowing. Some species begin to scrape away their fur — that's why they called the disease 'scrapie' when it first appeared in sheep."

"Wait a minute." With narrowed eyes, Louis Fortier waved his fork in her direction. "Are you saying a sheep disease is on its way into the jungle?"

"Could be." Alex lowered her fork, realizing that she may have inadvertently spoiled dinner for the entire table. She found it hard not to talk about her work, however, when the disease she studied was the disease she carried.

She looked at her Russian friend. "Why don't you explain cross-species contamination?"

The Russian cast her a "gee, thanks" look, then spread his hands. "It is simple, really. To use a meteorological metaphor, they say that a butterfly can fan its wings in West Africa and cause a momentary atmospheric disturbance that will send gradually increasing currents across the Atlantic until they hit the United States with hurricane force."

Caitlyn nodded as she reached for the bowl of fried plantains. "That's overstated, but probably true."

Baklanov grinned. "Thank you, little girl. Yes. Well, the same analogy applies to disease. Suppose a native hunter in west central Africa cuts himself while butchering a monkey. The monkey passes its virus to the hunter, who passes it to his wife, who passes it to their children. The AIDS virus probably began this way. Though it is not spread through casual contact, it can be transferred from one species to another through hunting and butchering."

"The people here eat monkeys all the time," Caitlyn announced. "Tito told me."

Alex looked from her daughter to the

anthropologist, whose face had paled in the dim light of the lantern.

"Scrapie has also been known to jump species," she said, gentling her tone. "Though it is not caused by a virus, but by infectious proteins called prions. Scrapie is actually an encephalopathy."

"Brain disease," Caitlyn inserted.

Alex frowned at her daughter. "Yes. There are many different strains of encephalopathy, but all are fatal. Once prions enter an organism, they cause normal proteins to mutate into the misfolded shape of the prion, and this mutation kills brain cells. As a result, the brain becomes spongiform."

"Like Swiss cheese," Caitlyn interrupted again, warming to her audience. "Full of holes."

Alex draped her arm over the back of her daughter's chair, then tapped on the girl's shoulder. "Let me tell it, will you?"

Caitlyn shrugged. "Just trying to help, Mom."

When Alex looked up, she noticed that Lazaro wore an alarmed expression. His hand had flown up to grip the gold crucifix he wore like a talisman around his neck.

"We have no evidence that prions have infected the monkey population here," she hastened to add, "or any population, for that matter. But in the last decade these diseases struck British cattle in what came to be called mad cow disease. Prions have also been found in cats, dogs, minks, goats, sheep, deer, elk, squirrels . . . and humans, of course."

Emma leaned forward, her blue eyes wide. "This disease you described — could it possibly be related to kuru?"

Alex nodded. "We know it is."

Louis Fortier waved his fork at the anthropologist. "If you would be so kind, madame, what is kuru?"

Emma blew out her cheeks. "I'm not sure you want to discuss this at dinner."

"I'm not squeamish." The perfumer looked around the table as if to dare anyone to contradict him. "You're all scientists — except, of course, for *la jeune* —"

"I'm not squeamish, either," Caitlyn interrupted. "You can talk about anything in front of me. My mom has never —"

Alex lightly clapped her palm over her daughter's mouth. "I wouldn't say you can talk about *anything* with a child at the table, but Caitlyn has heard of far worse things than kuru."

Taking Alex's comment as permission granted, Emma turned to the curious Frenchman. "Kuru is a disease with symptoms similar to those Alex has described. Until recently, the disease was endemic among the Fore tribe in New Guinea, particularly among the women and children. Typically, kuru struck without warning and with great force, causing unsteady movement in the first month, tremors and blurred speech in the second, and complete incapacitation in the third."

Fortier wagged his brows when she hesitated. "And what is so terrible we cannot discuss at dinner?"

Emma looked down at her half-empty plate. "Researchers found the source of the disease when they began to explore the reason women and children were infected more often than men. The Fore warriors, you see, were the hunters, and rarely shared meat with their wives and offspring. So the women and children found the protein they needed in what became an important ritual: the eating of their dead."

Fortier gasped in delighted horror. "*Quelle horreur!* Cannibals!"

Tipping her head back, Emma regarded the perfumer with a prim and forbidding expression. "Not anymore. Researchers convinced the Fore to abandon the practice after they realized the disease was transmitted orally. The women and children had been eating diseased brain tissues, contaminating themselves with the infective agent."

"Gross!" Caitlyn made a face and tossed her napkin onto the table, but Alex knew she was only playing to her audience. She'd heard all this before.

Alex glanced around the table. "The same

thing happened in the British animal industry — farmers had their downer cattle with mad cow disease hauled off to the knackers, who ground everything from the animals' hooves to bones and placed the resulting mix in products ranging from cattle feed to rose fertilizer. Britain eventually put a halt to the use of infected cattle for these purposes, but the damage had probably already been done. One of the women who died from a prion disease in 1996 had been a vegetarian for eleven years."

"How is that possible?" Baklanov lifted the question with bushy brows.

"Some strains have long incubation periods," Alex answered. "And the process of deterioration takes time. Which is why my work is so frustrating — I know someone will eventually find that needle in the haystack, but it's long, slow work . . . and people are unknowingly being infected with every passing day. I don't mean to sound like a doomsday prophet, but the little woman next door who breathes in dust from her rose fertilizer is probably just as susceptible as the Brit who eats steak three times a week."

She dropped her napkin with relief when one of the lodge busboys paused at her shoulder. "Finished, señora?"

"Yes, please." She waited until he removed her plate, then sent a weary smile around the table. "I don't know that prion diseases have

121

made their way to the tropics, but we have recorded sporadic cases that appear to occur without cause. Most of my colleagues believe they are the result of happenstance — a one-in-a-million quirk of genetics. I tend to think these patients were infected somewhere, somehow. So if you see any animals acting strangely, please alert me. It could be nothing, but it could also be something important."

It could save my life.

Emma leaned back as the busboy removed her plate, then she gave Alex a quick, gleaming look. "This is a myth, mind you, but the Indians have spoken of a tribe so isolated that no person living today has ever seen them. They call them the 'Angry People' and maintain that the spirits delight in tormenting these people with a shaking disease — an illness that has always sounded to me like kuru." She looked at Baklanov, who had pulled out his cigarettes, and lifted a brow. "May I?"

"Certainly." Without hesitation the Russian handed over a cigarette, then flicked his lighter into flame.

"There's no way to prove the story, of course," Emma continued, holding her cigarette to the lighter. "Though the implication of kuru interested me, I've always thought the Angry People were a Yagua version of the American boogeyman — something with which parents can intimidate misbehaving children."

"That's not right." Caitlyn folded her arms and spoke with authority. "Parents should not lie to their kids."

"Perhaps they weren't lying, dear." Alex shifted her attention back to the anthropologist. "Were the Angry People supposed to be cannibals?"

"Indubitably." Emma drew deeply on her cigarette, then exhaled twin streamers through her nose. "And kidnappers and woman-stealers and rapists. The other tribes credited the entire litany of jungle sins to this group; in time, they became the personification of every imaginable vice. They are said to be covered in fierce tattoos as a warning for others to stay away — a primitive 'mark of Cain,' as it were."

Alex looked to their native guide, who had listened to the story in silence. "Have you heard of this tribe, Lazaro?"

The native gave her a forced smile and a tense nod. "Yes."

"Do you believe they exist?"

"I have never seen them."

Exhaling with disappointment, Alex leaned back in her chair. Finding a tribal group afflicted with kuru would have been a coup, but if Lazaro had never heard of them . . .

"Lazaro." Dropping one arm to the table, Emma gave the guide a reproving smile. "You dodged the question. Alex asked if you *be-lieved* in them, not if you'd seen them."

The man's gaze dropped like a stone to the tabletop. "My father was a shaman," he said, a firmness in his voice that verged on the threatening, "and he spoke often of their evil. They live deep in the jungle, and we did not ever search for them. Why should we seek more evil than we already know?"

"You make a good point, Lazaro." Ever the convivial host, Louis Fortier patted the Indian guide's arm. "Why should we search for evil when we are surrounded with good food and good friends?"

He probably intended the question to be rhetorical, but Alex couldn't resist answering: "We search for evil in order to understand it . . . so we can defeat it."

Fortier snapped his fingers in her direction. "I see your point, madame, and I like the way you think. As for me, I live in France, where we have been importing English beef for years. I would like to know if I am going to die of this brain disease you talk about, and I will pray you find a cure."

"Thank you for the vote of confidence," Alex's voice went dry, "but you can forgo the prayers on my behalf. I'm a resolute agnostic."

Wariness and amusement mingled in Fortier's eyes. "Not an atheist?"

"An atheist," Caitlyn answered in a singsong

rhythm, "would have to know everything to know God does not exist. Mom says she can't know everything, but everything she does know leads her to believe people invented God to make themselves feel better about hard times."

Facing the giggles and guffaws Caitlyn's recitation had elicited, Alex shrugged. "When your work is focused on empirical evidence, you tend to long for concrete beliefs in your private life as well. I've never found any use for God."

"Not even as a child?" Emma smiled at the server who placed before her a dish of something that resembled custard. "Did you not believe in the tooth fairy or Santa Claus?"

"Sure." Alex pulled her napkin back onto her lap, then gestured for Caitlyn to do the same. "But then I grew up and realized that fanciful illusions do not make life any easier." She lifted a brow. "What about you? You study the role of religion in various cultures. What have you decided about God?"

Emma propped her cigarette on the edge of her dessert dish, then picked up her spoon. "I have decided that the creative spirit we call *god* is wrapped up in this bountiful planet that provides all we need to survive. Unfortunately, I also believe she has been appropriated by power-hungry males determined to oppress women and children. The god I see in nature has been reworked and reshaped to fit various political agendas in different parts of the world."

She turned to Fortier. "What about you, monsieur?"

"Me?" Louis hesitated, his spoon halfway to his mouth. "I am a Christian."

Alex grinned. "Really?"

"Oui." The Frenchman nodded as he swallowed a spoonful of his dessert. "I belong to the Universal Fellowship of Metropolitan Community Churches. We believe God is love, so we were created to love whomever we wish."

Glancing at her daughter, Alex wondered if this might be a good time to send Caitlyn from the table. She had trained her child to be tolerant of differing opinions, but she wasn't certain a ten-year-old needed to absorb a full-blown defense of a homosexual lifestyle.

Fortunately, Emma adroitly steered the conversation away from Louis's statement. "What about you, Lazaro? You were reared in a Yagua village, right?"

The guide inclined his head. "Everyone in my village is Catholic."

"But your father was a shaman. Doesn't that mean he talked to spirits?"

Lazaro shrugged. "*Claro*. But we still go to church when the priest comes."

"I think I'm going to be Jewish."

Alex nearly dropped her spoon when her

daughter piped up. "What did you say?"

Caitlyn stole a glance at Alex's face, then smiled at the others. "My mother has always said I should think for myself, and I have always wanted to study Hebrew. I also think it'd be fun to have a bat mitzvah."

Alex resisted the temptation to roll her eyes. "Eat your pudding. We'll talk about this later."

Baklanov, who had been silently eating his dessert, lifted his head. "I must join my friend Alex on the side of the agnostics. After the Soviet Union crumbled and we were granted freedom of religion, I watched to see what would happen. Many people went to church, read the Bible, and spoke in tongues, but I believe they overreacted to events around them. Now life has settled back into the old routine, and nothing is different about the way people live. If God exists, I have never seen him. I see people behaving in strange ways, but I do not see God doing anything in their lives."

"Touché." Alex gave Baklanov a look of gratitude. "In any case, whether I believe or not is immaterial. If I believed in God, what good would it do? I'd still be looking for the needle in the haystack."

"I hope you find it, señora." Finished with his dessert, Lazaro pushed away from the table. "And I hope you find God as well. It is easy to need him in the jungle."

127

1 April 2003
7:08 p.m.

Sitting at his desk, Michael sipped a luke-warm cup of coffee and reflected upon the story he'd heard earlier. The idea of a lost tribe was unbelievable, of course, but the tattooed native might be proof such a tribe existed . . . if he had told Esma the truth. If he had been babbling in the delirium of fever, it was far more likely he had merely recited stories from his childhood, tales as old as the Amazon itself.

Interesting, though, that he had spoken of a shuddering disease. Michael suspected he meant chills; the man had been febrile and dehydrated when admitted, so he had been experiencing chills. But they would have begun hours after the patient suffered the spear attack, and Ya-ree had told Esma he suffered from the shuddering disease some time ago.

Perhaps he was mistaken. Perhaps Esma

misunderstood. After all, she had been translating a language she did not speak.

Michael sat the cup on his desk and folded his hands, staring at nothing. The office around him was heavy with after-hours quiet, but the dark skies outside had opened up. The rataplan of rain on the roof usually soothed him, but tonight the pounding rain spoke of drums in faraway villages.

What about the man's odd tattoos? They had been significant enough to frighten one of the orderlies past the point of embarrassment. And though Esma was a kind woman with more than her fair share of compassion, Michael doubted she would have spent the entire day by the bedside of a tattooed Iquitos merchant with a strange tale to tell. Something about the native seemed to either entice or repel everyone he encountered.

Curious, Michael swiveled to face his computer, clicked away from the medical database he'd been using earlier, and navigated his way into a powerful search engine. When the search box opened, he typed *shuddering disease,* then clicked the enter key.

He tapped his nails on the desk until the results came up: nothing.

Rethinking his approach, he tried again with *trembling disease.*

After a long moment, a long list of links filled the screen. The first led to a listing from a medical dictionary: *kuru, the trembling disease.*

He read on to discover that kuru had been reported only among members of the Fore tribe in New Guinea. The disease involved a progressive degeneration of the central nervous system, particularly in the region of the brain responsible for control of the trunk, limbs, and head. Kuru affected mainly women and children and usually proved fatal within nine to twelve months. The condition was thought to be caused by prions and transmitted by cannibalism.

But Michael wasn't in New Guinea . . . and his patient had walked out of the jungle, which would be impossible with a disabled central nervous system.

Dismissing the idea of kuru, he clicked on the next entry in the list. The link brought up a personal experience essay by a man with Parkinson's. That disease also caused shivering and uncontrollable shuddering, so perhaps Ya-ree had suffered from Parkinson's . . .

No. Michael scratched his chin, acknowledging the obvious. He had not seen his patient twitch at all, and Parkinson's was incurable. Yet Ya-ree had said the shaman cured him.

He clicked back to the search results page and noted several other entries for kuru and another about a Chinese cure for a trembling disease often found in "hairy crabs."

He rolled his eyes as he closed out the screen. If Ya-ree had not had Parkinson's, he could have had some other weakness of the central nervous system . . . maybe some unknown condition, or something like dengue fever, which certainly left most patients longing for death. Perhaps the man had suffered from chills and fever many years before, and the shaman of the second village cured him — or the virus simply ran its course. A simpleminded native might have believed himself cured of a shuddering disease.

Impossible to know for certain, really . . . unless the man's tissues could be examined postmortem.

Michael pressed his lips together. The hospital did not usually perform autopsies on indigent patients who wandered out of the jungle, but it appeared there would be no family to protest. Burials in the tropics were usually accomplished with great haste, so he'd have to put a note in the patient's record if he wanted to examine the body after the man expired.

Sighing, he wrote up an autopsy order, then stood to walk down the hall and attach it to his patient's chart.

1 April 2003
11:45 p.m.

Caitlyn is asleep. I never thought I would envy my own child for anything, much less the simple ability to sleep through the night, but here I am, scratching this by the dim light of our kerosene lantern while she snores across the room.

And I envy her.

I have been trying to sleep since about ten o'clock, two hours after our party exited the dining hall and promised to meet at seven for breakfast. We will have another full day of climbing tomorrow; the dirigible pilot has already scouted another tree — a wonderful mahogany, he says, not more than two miles from the lodge. The mahogany is one of the giants of the jungle, rising above the canopy into the emergent layer . . . if I am not careful, I shall soon begin to write more like a botanist than a neurologist.

After dinner, Baklanov and I examined some of his samples under the portable microscope. My Micron is more advanced than the Russian model he carries, and he was thrilled to have the opportunity to use my little machine. But it is hard to know what we are seeing — the cultures will require time to grow, so perhaps in a few days we will have a better idea of what we have gathered. We did not spend too long in our study — the battery is rechargeable, but the people at the lodge are only willing to run the generator for short periods. Odd to think we are actually living without electricity for most of the day.

Let's see . . . this journal will become too long too quickly if I persist in writing every thought that crosses my brain, but it is the best way I know to take my mind off sleep — or, more accurately, my insomnia. (How I hate that word!)

Deborah Simons, a likable lady despite her religious ranting, told me that her official study will be called "Activity of Tabanids Attacking the Reptiles Caiman Crocodiles and Eunectes murinus in the Western Amazon, Peru." (Translation: Do horse flies bite crocodiles and snakes more often in the wet or dry seasons?)

She says she is merely taking specimens in the canopy, scouting for new ideas. The work for which she is paid occurs every morning and every night, when she goes out to sit by a caged anaconda and captured caiman, both of whom are treated as pets by the lodge staff. For thirty minutes she counts the number of horseflies landing on both animals, records her observations, then puts her work away in time to join us in the dining hall.

Something in me wants to scream about how silly her efforts are — who really cares how many times horseflies buzz around those reptiles? Yet I have spent my entire career around scientists, and I know that such seemingly insignificant grunt work can sometimes lead to great discoveries. So I say nothing negative. I congratulate Deborah on her brilliant scholarship and tell her I hope her efforts result in a better insect repellant . . . and millions of dollars for the chemical company that must produce it, of course.

I am almost embarrassed to be so cynical at the vast age of thirty-six. My mother would not like to hear me talk like this . . . but we don't always get what we want, do we? I wanted my mother to watch Caitlyn grow up. I wanted to find a cure for the curse that haunts our family before it took my mom.

But Life is a bitter jokester, and lately it seems intent on raising the stakes whenever I belly up to the table. Here I am, as close to pure biology as I have ever been in my life, and I can no longer deny that the family curse has begun to manifest itself in my body.

I could live with the occasional tremors, the moments of panic, and those occasions when words stick to a stuttering tongue. So far, I think I've managed to avoid those symptoms — or the exhaustion of travel has masked them.

What I fear most is nights like this one.

Insomnia.

Eternal alertness.

The inability to sleep.

A condition impervious even to my silly "Twinkle, Twinkle" song. The state in which the brain cannot shut off, REM cannot commence, and dreams do not come, thereby depriving the brain of an opportunity to work out the day's contradictions and process the day's events. Dreams, they say, deal with material that's more personally relevant than we have time to cope with during the day, so the process of dreaming is the very thing that keeps us sane and preserves the essence of who we are.

If tonight's insomnia does mark the onset of my disease, I suppose I am therefore likely to be a raving lunatic by the time we leave the rainforest.

Lazaro said I might need a god in the

jungle. If my disease progresses, I might actually agree with him.

Sitting up into the noisy chattering of tropical birds, Alex clutched a loose puddle of damp sheet to her chest and blinked. She stared up at the nearly opaque mosquito netting engulfing her bed, then pressed her palm to her forehead and groaned.

After writing in her journal, she had stretched out and stared at the soft weave of the beige netting for hours. Sleep had come, finally, but last night had been one of the longest she'd experienced in weeks.

She closed her eyes as the textbook prognosis scrolled across the blank screen provided by her memory: Stage one of fatal familial insomnia included increasing insomnia, panic attacks, and occasional failure of voluntary muscle movements. Duration was usually four months, but might be accelerated in cases where the onset of the disease occurred before age fifty.

Pressing the back of her hand against her brow, Alex bit back a moan. It wasn't fair. Her mother hadn't exhibited any signs of illness until age fifty-two, but apparently life intended to play another of its sick jokes on Alex.

She rolled onto her side, her anguish nearly overcoming her control, but Caitlyn must not hear the sounds of her suffering. She was a bright child, far too intuitive for her own good, yet she couldn't know how far — and how fast — the disease had approached Alex.

Clapping her hand over her mouth, Alex wept silently, hot tears running into her hair and dropping onto the pillowcase. When she heard the creak of Caitlyn's bed, she swiped her hand over her cheeks and steeled her emotions to obey her will.

"Mom?" Caitlyn's voice came through the heavy netting. "You awake?"

"Uh-huh." Alex didn't dare say more.

"I gotta run to the bathroom. Can I go in bare feet?"

Alex wanted to tell her to get her shoes, but she couldn't push the appropriate words over the lump in her throat. "Uh-huh."

She heard her daughter's footsteps on the planks, the metallic pop of the latch and the creak of the springs on the door. When Caitlyn's footsteps faded away, Alex swung her legs free of the netting and sat up, then pulled a tissue from her pack and blew her nose.

What a mess she must be.

Inhaling deeply, Alex lowered her feet to the floor, checking first to be sure no other living creatures occupied the space. She looked toward the open screens — day had dawned misty and pink over the jungle. In better spirits, she might have called it lovely.

She reached for her plastic sandals, picked them up, and gave each of them a solid shake before dropping them back to the floor. She stood and slipped her feet into the shoes, then glanced at herself in the small mirror Caitlyn had propped against her suitcase. She had slept in shorts and a tank top — not exactly modest by her mother's standards, but fine for the jungle heat. She ought to be able to slip out to the bathrooms without causing a scandal.

She pulled a clean towel and clothing from her suitcase, grabbed her toiletries case from the shelf, then stepped out of the bungalow. Caitlyn was approaching on the walkway, and at the sight of her mother she stopped.

Alex brought her hand up to hide her blotchy face, then looked away. "Hey there, cutie. I'm heading down to the shower, okay? You can go back to sleep if you want."

Caitlyn's gaze dropped to Alex's feet, then slowly lifted. A faint smile appeared at the corner of her mouth. "You wearing that to breakfast?"

"They aren't serving breakfast for another hour. If you sleep through breakfast, though, I expect you to stay in camp today. You don't go anywhere without one of the guides, okay? Stay away from the river . . . and the jungle. Just hang around the lodge and wait for me to get back."

"It's boring around here when you're gone." Caitlyn mumbled these words in a drowsy whisper, and Alex knew her daughter was still treading on the edge of sleep.

"Mr. Myers has something really special planned, I'm sure. And you can always talk to the Somerville sisters or Dr. Whitmore. Last night I got the impression she really likes you."

"Yeah, right."

"Hey." Alex reached out and gently squeezed Caitlyn's earlobe. "You've got studying to do, remember? When we get home, you have to take your tests."

Caitlyn mumbled again, but Alex knew her daughter had gotten the point. Homeschooling — or *field* schooling, to be more accurate — had never been a problem, for Caitlyn always scored far above her peers on the standardized tests the state required her to take each year. Occasionally some well-meaning educator murmured something about how much Caitlyn was missing by not socializing with her peers, but Alex had always believed adults provided better company for her child. Besides . . . she'd always found packs of children a little frightening.

"Go back to sleep, hon."

She took a step, but halted when Caitlyn called, "Mom?"

"Yeah?"

"You okay? Your eyes are all red."

"Allergies, I think." Turning, she forced a smile and twiddled her fingers. "Go back to bed. I'll see you later."

When Caitlyn had returned to the bungalow, Alex walked down to the bathroom, showered and dressed, then brushed her teeth using purified water from a pitcher. Herman Myers had explained that the showers and toilets dispensed chlorinated river water — clean, but still not safe for drinking. To avoid illness, tourists were advised to use purified water for anything that entered their mouths.

Leaving her nightclothes in a neat stack on a restroom bench, Alex walked down to the dining hall. Valerik Baklanov sat outside on a bench, a cigarette in his hand and a taciturn expression on his face. Alex quickly surmised he wasn't a morning person, but he returned her greeting with a flick of his cigarette and an abrupt nod.

Inside the hall, the Somerville sisters were sharing a table and a pot of coffee with Emma Whitmore. The anthropologist wore clothing suitable for the jungle: khaki trousers, a long-sleeved cotton shirt, and a wide-brimmed straw hat. The sisters, however, wore fluorescent orange pants, knee-high rubber boots, and matching T-shirts advertising Hooters restaurants —

Some things ought to be left at home.

Shaking her head, Alex went to look for a coffee mug. She found a row of them at a varnished bar against the wall, and a moment later she was joined by Deborah Simons and Lauren Hayworth. Kenneth Carlton stood behind Lauren, his cell phone pressed to his ear.

"Hello?" he shouted, as if screaming would somehow boost his reception. "Can you hear me?"

Lowering the phone, he punched in a series of numbers with his thumb, cursed softly, then knocked the phone against the counter.

"He's been doing that for the last half-hour," Lauren whispered, resting one elbow on the bar as she reached for a mug. "He's convinced he can call out of this place."

"Trouble at the office?" Alex asked.

Lauren shook her head. "Trouble at home, I think. His wife sent a radio message yesterday, but the help didn't deliver the note until last night when it was too dark to find the phone in our — in his — room."

Alex met Deborah Simons's knowing glance, then looked down to smother a smile. She followed Deborah to an empty table and took a seat, then summoned a smile as Milos Olsson dropped into the empty chair next to her.

"Good morning, all." The Swede flashed them an energetic grin that practically jumped through his wiry beard. "I've news from our dirigible pilot — he launched with the platform at sunrise and will drop it atop a lovely mahogany about three kilometers from here. Unfortunately, he and Lazaro couldn't agree on the shortest foot route to the tree, so we may have to do a bit of hiking before we find it." He slapped his thigh and grinned at the challenge. "So — eat a hearty breakfast and be sure to pack enough water. We'll be heading out at eight o'clock, more or less."

Deborah dropped her head onto her folded arms and grimaced at Alex. "How are your muscles? I'm aching all over."

"I'm not too bad." Alex tested her arms just to be certain. "My shoulders are a bit sore, though — all that resisting, I think, on the way down."

"It's going to be hot up in the canopy."

"It's always hot up in the canopy."

The women fell silent as one of the serving boys set a heaping plate in the center of the table.

Alex's jaw dropped. "Do those look like — ?"

"Yep," Deborah answered. "Good old

American Aunt Jemima pancakes. And surely they have syrup — with all the insect life around here, they should have honey by the bucketful."

Alex reached for the platter. "I'm hungry enough to eat them dry."

She had just taken a heaping bite of buttered pancake when Lazaro entered, his hands in his pockets and a wide grin on his face.

"Whassa matter, Lazaro?" Deborah called. "You never had pancakes before?"

The guide's smile deepened. "I have them every morning." He patted the soft paunch beneath his T-shirt. "I like them very much."

Alarmed by the mischievous glint in the guide's eye, Alex stopped chewing. "Um, Lazaro — these are made of flour, right?"

"Si." He nodded. "Manioc flour."

Alex hesitated, then swallowed. "I don't care what it is," she said, cutting off another bite. "It's good, and I'm hungry."

2 April 2003
7:14 a.m.
"El doctor?"

Michael swam up from the place between sleeping and waking, then opened his eyes into bright fluorescent light. One of the day nurses stood next to him with a clipboard in her hand.

"El doctor, el paciente es muerto."

For a moment her words didn't register, then the creak of vinyl reminded him where he was. He had gone to check on his peritonitis patient and fallen asleep in this uncomfortable visitor's chair.

Blushing, he brushed his hand across his jaw and felt the rasp of his morning stubble. The native had not moved since Michael checked him at three, but the nurse was correct: The patient had expired.

Michael stood and unwrapped his stethoscope from his neck, then did a perfunctory check for vital signs. There were none.

He lifted the sheet from the man's thin chest, then pulled it over his tattooed face.

"Um —" His Spanish had never been strong, and his tongue always seemed uncooperative upon waking — *"este paciente* needs, um, *requerir una autopsia."*

The nurse lowered her clipboard. *"Autopsia?"*

"Si." He gestured toward the hall. "The morgue — *el depósito de cadáveres. Entiende?"*

She nodded.

"Thank goodness."

Blowing out his cheeks, he moved past her and lumbered stiffly down the hall. He needed a shower, a cup of coffee, and about five more hours of sleep, but he couldn't afford those luxuries if he wanted to serve his patients. They would begin to fill his office by nine o'clock; they would test the capacity of his exam room and his nurse's patience by ten.

Furthermore, the hospital suffered from intermittent electrical as well as water outages, and the backup generators had been designated for life support, not refrigeration. So if this patient's autopsy were to count for anything, it had best be done quickly.

Bracing himself for another long day, Michael turned into a secluded hallway and went in search of a splash of cold water.

■ ■ ■ ■

Fortuna was not happy to hear about the autopsy. "You will have many patients today," she said, her tone sharpening to cut through the wail of a baby outside his locked office door. "The man is dead. Do you not know what killed him?"

"I know what killed him. If his story is true, I want to find out what kept him alive."

She dropped her purse into a desk drawer, then crossed her arms. "He was a crazy man, loco. You are wasting your time."

"I will never know, Fortuna, unless I do this. So keep the doors closed and see if that mother has milk for her baby. I'll do this as quickly as I can."

While Fortuna reluctantly held the early arrivals at bay, Michael found his deceased patient in the hallway outside the morgue. He checked the chart sitting atop the body, then wheeled the gurney through the double doors. "You're lucky you made it this far without mishap," he told the corpse. "I was half afraid I wouldn't find you within a reasonable length of time."

By eight o'clock he had transferred the deceased patient to the autopsy table, a waist-high aluminum fixture plumbed for running water (though there wouldn't be any at that hour). After positioning the thin corpse on

147

the block, Michael telephoned a second time for assistance and learned there was no one available to help him . . . and he had four patients waiting.

"I'll be up soon," he promised Fortuna.

He went to work. After making a Y incision from the shoulders to the pubic bone, Michael lifted the flaps of skin and let them fall to the left and right. He then cut and removed the pericardial sac and the sheath of abdominal muscle in the chest, exposing the internal organs.

Breathing heavily through his mask, he studied the arrangements of heart and lungs, spleen, liver, and intestines. He saw nothing unusual for a man who had died of multisystem organ failure resulting from acute peritonitis. The body had tried to wall off the infection in the colon by sealing it with omentum, part of a fatty apron that hung from the transverse colon, but fluid had oozed throughout the abdomen, sending bacteria into the bloodstream and eventually throughout the body.

Michael exhaled slowly. The examination revealed no surprises. The autopsy and the medical records would validate the cause of death.

The man's brain should not hold any surprises, either.

He moved quickly through standard autopsy procedures, lifting out the organs, weighing them, recording their weight and his observations. Curiously, the stomach was empty, so Ya-ree must not have eaten during his alleged flight through the jungle.

When he had finished with the organs, Michael turned to the head. He probed the eyes for hemorrhages, found none, then made an incision that would allow him to peel away the scalp. Using a high-speed oscillating power saw, he opened the skull, pried off the skullcap, then severed the connection that joined the base of the stem to the spinal cord. After lifting out the gray brain, he placed it in a glass jar filled with a 10 percent solution of formaldehyde.

Sinking onto a stool, he stared at the organ and wondered how — and if — he ought to proceed.

He had patients waiting — living people with pressing problems. He could do nothing more for the jungle man, and no relatives would appear to mourn him or question Michael's judgment. The hospital, desperate for doctors, would not care if the autopsy proceeded, and the government would cremate the remains with no questions asked.

He could easily walk away and never think about this fellow again. But the unanswered questions would linger, shimmering like reflections from the river every time Michael looked toward the surrounding jungle.

Despite his rational demeanor, Ya-ree had

probably been in the stages of a mild dementia when he related his story to Esma . . . or living alone in the jungle might have snapped his grip on reality. Esma's translation skills might not have been what they once were; she might have misunderstood several key phrases and twisted a logical story into an incredible one.

The man's story might have been true . . . and merely a reference to dengue fever or some other common jungle disease in his past. Depending upon the ailment, his body might or might not contain evidence of the previous disease, but only a fool would waste time looking for something that didn't matter to anyone. This man had died from complications stemming from a nasty wound, period.

The rational part of Michael's brain told him to sew up the body and set the brain on a shelf. If abnormalities existed within its folds, some medical student in Lima could have the honor of discovery and conjecture. He and his classmates could play "name that disease," but unless an extremely astute medical professor guided them, no one would guess that holes in the brain, if they existed, had been caused by prions.

Michael exhaled slowly. He ought to close the book on this case and move on. Still . . . if Ya-ree had spoken the truth, his body might have been invaded by a silent killer for which modern medicine had no cure. Brain encephalopathies like kuru and Creutzfeldt-Jakob had been claiming victims for years . . .

And Michael had watched many of them die.

Encephalopathy did not result in an easy death. Depending on the strain of disease, victims experienced trouble walking, eating, and swallowing. Some patients experienced the mercy of dementia while others remained bitterly aware of their physical and mental decline. And though Michael had never witnessed a case of fatal familial insomnia, he had read that those patients, for whom sleep became an impossibility, kept their wits about them until they finally lapsed into a coma that offered no rest until, like a raging oil fire, the brain finally consumed all its resources and died.

Lowering his head into his hand, Michael massaged his temple with his thumb and index finger, willing his tension away. Ashley would have laughed, seeing him like this. She always said he saw himself as a crusader out to save the world, but he'd never minded her teasing because it simply wasn't true.

And as for saving the world . . . he hadn't even been able to save his own wife. One day Ashley had stumbled into the room and joked about being drunk on Earl Grey, but he'd seen the fear in her eyes. Fearing a stroke, he had rushed her to the casualty at St. George's. When the diagnosis arrived weeks later, the neurologist said she was suffering from a variant of Creutzfeldt-Jakob disease . . . as were seven other British young people under the age of thirty.

The mad cow scare had begun . . . and Michael, who had specialized in pediatrics, found himself reading everything he could find on brain diseases. All the materials he read reinforced what the doctors told him — no cures for encephalopathy existed.

He had steeled himself to the reality of Ashley's illness, tried to comfort his wife in her final weeks, and kept their routine as normal as possible. While she lost her sight, her ability to speak, and even her ability to write, he begged heaven for healing. But like so many of the parents of his terminal patients, Michael discovered that while God granted strength and comfort and understanding, he gently insisted upon his will.

After Ashley's death in '96, Michael had tried to focus on his pediatric practice, but he couldn't enter the office without imagining his wife's presence at the desk in the reception room. After three years of struggling to function without her, he had taken a vacation in the heart of Amazonia . . . and found a second place to call home.

The simplicity of Peruvian life appealed to him. The average fellow got up every morning and spent the day providing food and shelter for his family. People set different priorities here, and they were not so quick to destroy values of the spirit when they had time for idle imaginings. In Iquitos there were no TV producers designing programs to mock religion, no screenwriters creating scripts intended to rob children of their innocence. Piety was expected, not ridiculed, and no one at the Regional Hospital laughed when he told them he'd come because God wanted him to help the people of the Amazon.

The Peruvian government had hoops to jump through, to be sure, but no one seemed to care if he jumped through them tomorrow or next year, so long as he worked at being part of the solution to their problems. So in the summer of the year 2000, Michael joined the hospital staff, became accredited by the Peruvian government, and established an open-door practice for anyone who came to the hospital seeking help. He still saw children, scores of them, but he also treated women who had never seen an automobile, wizened men with piranha-scarred calves, and the occasional shaman who wanted to see what sort of medicine the white doctor had to offer.

Days melted into weeks and weeks into months as the changeless seasons slid by. He had come to help, not to stay, but he had not yet found the time to consider leaving.

He had established a good and fulfilling life

in Peru. Until today he thought he had left London and its memories behind, but Ya-ree had proved otherwise. The biological agent that had infected and killed his wife might lie in Ya-ree's brain — or it might not.

He would never know the truth unless he proceeded.

He pressed his hand to the back of his neck and massaged the knotted muscles that had tensed his shoulders. This hospital did not have an electron microscope, but he wasn't certain he'd need one. If the patient's brain appeared normal, Ya-ree's penchant for inventing wild tales probably sprang from psychological causes. If, however, he was suffering from a prion-based disease, amyloid plaques would almost certainly show up in a microscopic examination.

Michael tugged a fresh pair of latex gloves from his pocket. If this were a hospital in the civilized world, he would send the brain off to a lab for analysis and simply wait for the result. But in Peru, one learned to do for oneself.

Sighing heavily, he pulled on his gloves, then thrust his hands into the specimen jar and removed the brain for dissection.

By midmorning a deep silence lay over the pathology lab, broken only by the squeak of the rusty ceiling fan overhead. Michael rubbed his nose — the smell of formaldehyde had always bothered him — then again lowered his eyes to the lens of the microscope. Since the autopsy he had created more than a dozen slides from each major area of his patient's brain — cerebrum, cerebellum, thalamus, and brain stem. The same strange images appeared in each slide.

He had immediately noticed that the brain tissue was not inflamed, nor did he see any signs of lesions within the brain itself, ruling out an amebic brain abscess. Under the microscope, however, certain sections definitely appeared spongiform, which supported his suspicion that the "shuddering disease" Ya-ree had mentioned might be neurological in origin.

Now, as he amplified the magnification on the microscope, he saw what looked like black, hairy disks floating among the smaller brain cells. The view pebbled the skin on his arms — he had seen these same shapes in London, in tissue samples from a teenage patient who had succumbed to a variant of Creutzfeldt-Jakob disease. VCJD, as it was commonly known, was a transmissible spongiform encephalopathy, or TSE.

Like fatal familial insomnia.

And kuru.

And mad cow disease.

In each of those diseases, prions killed millions of brain cells. When the cells died, the brain attempted to replace them with glial cells — the glue that literally bound neurons together — but the damage was irreparable.

Michael pulled a handkerchief from his pocket to swipe at his damp forehead. Hot as it was in the lab, he felt as though a sliver of ice had slid down his spine.

He had to be imagining things. He was tired, overheated, and haunted by the past. No TSE had been reported among the indigenous peoples of Peru or among their livestock, so this had to be something else.

This might not be the result of contamination at all. Sporadic cases of CJD had appeared in several countries around the world, and researchers had never been able to pin the cause on a single source. But it would be impossible, really, to trace every food, every product to which a patient had been exposed over a vast number of years.

Still . . . he closed his eyes as he considered another possibility. Argentina, with its profitable cattle industry, might have imported European feed laced with animal by-products. For all he knew, all of South America had been receiving contaminated products from Britain and other European countries, and it would take years for the disease to appear in the population. A pig exposed to contaminated feed would probably be butchered before it became symptomatic, and the people who ate bacon would be exposed to the infective prions without their knowledge . . .

His stomach dropped. He was certain of only one thing — Ya-ree had not been speaking of chills or palsy when he mentioned the shuddering disease, for a patient with this much spongiform tissue in so many quadrants should have been barely ambulatory.

Yet Ya-ree had allegedly walked out of the jungle. Even in great pain and suffering at the end, he had been coherent enough to relate a logical story.

Michael swiped at his forehead again, then returned his attention to the microscope. Across the decimated field of brain cells a network of swollen glia stretched like brown patches crowding an old woman's crazy quilt.

A patient in this condition should have been slurring his speech, stumbling, totally lacking motor coordination . . . and yet Ya-ree had allegedly managed to flee hostile pursuers in the forest, give his name and history to a hospital clerk, and expire in relative peace.

Michael's stool squeaked as he leaned back and stared at the water-stained ceiling. Perhaps, through some maneuvering of his subconscious, he had failed to recognize obvious symptoms of a neurological disorder. After all, Ya-ree had spoken to Esma about lights leading him through an uninhabited jungle. The lights could have been a hallucination produced by altered brain function. Just last month he'd read about new research proving the brain's ability to manufacture optical illusions . . .

He brought his hand to his chin. All his theories were conjecture, of course, and he couldn't prove anything with the rudimentary equipment available at this hospital. To discover the truth, he would require an electron microscope. He would need to find solid evidence of prions in the brain before he dared raise an alarm.

For a fleeting instant he thought about sending a message to Dr. Alexandra Pace at Yarupapa, but he'd be wasting her time if his suspicions proved groundless. If what he feared was true, however, she'd be the first person he'd contact.

Moving to the phone, he punched in Fortuna's extension, then asked her to arrange a flight to Lima.

"Lima!" she screeched, delivering a devastatingly good impression of a female Ricky Ricardo as a flood of Spanish followed. "You have patients!"

He glanced away, steeling himself to her objections. "They'll have to wait. See if one of the other doctors will come in to cover for a few hours."

"Lima!" She muttered a few choice words in her native tongue, then finished with, "What are you going to do there?"

"Going to visit the university," he told her. "I'm taking a brain to school."

The desk-sized electron microscope was one of two EMs in Lima; the other belonged to the leading hospital. Rather than stand in line to use the hospital equipment, Michael had decided to take his chances with Dr. Gustavo Mozombite, head of the new Structural Molecular Biology Center at the *Universidad de Lima.*

Thankfully, the learned doctor had a background in medicine and spoke excellent English. He had welcomed Michael with typical Latin generosity, listened to a brief history of the native patient, then lifted a brow when Michael pulled out his case of slides.

"You mean to examine the tissues now?"

"As soon as possible," Michael answered. "I must return to Iquitos this afternoon."

"Then let us not waste time."

Now Michael crossed his arms as Dr. Mozombite adjusted the transmission electron microscope to examine one of the specimens he had brought from Iquitos. They stood in a small, darkened room with the image projected onto a television screen. The EM used a beam of electrons rather than light to illuminate a specimen and magnified the image by focusing its beam with magnets rather than a glass lens. Because electrons have shorter wavelengths than visible light, the EM could achieve much higher magnification than a light microscope. The machine's spectacular capability meant that Michael and Dr. Mozombite could not only see brain cells, but small viruses, broken fragments of protein and DNA, even cell debris.

"It takes time to learn how to read and interpret what we will see here," Dr. Mozombite said, his face gray in the monitor's glow. "I had to learn the difference between a cell membrane, a discarded nucleus, and other building blocks of a cell. After you learn what is normal, you learn to identify what is not."

Michael stared at the screen, unable to believe he'd been staring at the same specimen only hours before. The EM had created a window to another world, a microscopic universe filled with good and evil, friends and foes . . .

With one hand expertly controlling the image, Dr. Mozombite pointed out cell walls, a cluster of cell debris, a cell with a broken wall.

"Here." With one hand Dr. Mozombite pointed to the screen, with the other he pressed a button that snapped a photograph of the image. "This is odd. These sticks — do you see them?"

Michael squinted, adjusting his perspective until he saw several sticklike objects among the microscopic cell debris. The sight sent a tide of goose flesh rippling up each arm. "I see them."

Mozombite cast him a shrewd glance. "I am guessing, but could they be amyloid plaques?"

"I know what they are." Michael's voice rasped against his throat. "They are scrapie-associated fibrils — now known as PrP, or prion proteins."

"Are these the cause of your patient's death?"

Michael shook his head. "The man died from acute sepsis resulting from a bowel perforation."

"The infection killed him first, then. But surely this encephalopathy would have proved fatal within a few months."

Michael let the silence stretch a moment, then looked directly at the professor. "The patient lived in an indigenous tribe — I doubt he had ever left the jungle until yesterday. Before he died, he told a clerk — perfectly lucidly — that he had been healed of the 'shuddering disease.' He had supposedly been

161

near death, but sought help from a shaman of another tribe. He said the shaman healed him."

Mozombite said nothing as he pulled other specimens from Michael's tray. Together they watched silently as the rodlike images appeared in slide after slide.

Finally Mozombite flipped the light switch. He sank onto a stool, rubbed his chin with two fingers, then folded his arms and lifted his chin.

"I have learned to curb my cynicism regarding native medicine," he said. "The Indian healers do offer amazing cures for jungle diseases. What they lack are cures for modern diseases, evidenced by the hundreds of unfortunate deaths in Brazil, where entire villages have been wiped out by malaria and measles." He closed his eyes and shook his head slightly. "I doubt your patient's story was true. Prion diseases are new; the natives would have no knowledge of how to treat them."

"How do we know for certain? If this tribe has truly been isolated, perhaps they do know of the disease. What if they've seen it in jungle animals? What if they ate the animals and became infected? While we were misidentifying prion diseases as Parkinson's and palsy, they might have identified it and found a cure."

Tilting his head to one side, Mozombite

gave Michael a slanted look. "A bold assumption, Dr. Kenway."

"It's a bold disease, Dr. Mozombite. So — if you were in my situation, with this evidence in hand, what would you do?"

"With the rise of BSE-infected cattle and the corresponding threat to our international food supply?" A muscle clenched along the man's jaw. "Neurology is not my field, but I've read enough to be alarmed for the planet's future. Plus . . . given the evidence in this man's brain, I think it's important to determine how he became infected. If prion-infected animals have reached this continent, we need to know." He rubbed his chin for another moment, then met Michael's gaze. "If your patient's story is true, Dr. Kenway, I'd risk everything I owned to find that healing tribe."

2 April 2003
4:52 p.m.

"What's that sound?" From under the wide brim of her straw hat, Alex peered out at Deborah Simons, who was photographing a parade of ants marching over one of the outermost canopy pontoons. "Do you hear it?"

Deborah lifted her head as the noise intensified. Rhythmic, quick, and low, the sound was unlike anything they'd heard since entering the jungle.

"Jungle drums?" Deborah guessed. "Lazaro showed us how they beat on the trunks of those hollow trees — "

"It's not the same. It's —" Alex groaned as the realization hit. "It's a helicopter."

A moment later, a chopper appeared on the green horizon, confirming her suspicions. Muttering an oath, Alex dropped to her knees and laced her fingers through the mesh surface. She had finally begun to feel at ease

164

on the raft, but she didn't relish the thought of being buffeted by the rotor wash of an intruding helicopter.

"What sort of idiot," she yelled as the chopper drew closer, "would approach us up here?"

Milos Olsson, who had been standing near the porthole, waved his arms in a desperate attempt to warn the helicopter away. But the pilot was either blind or stupid, for the craft kept coming, whipping the green sea beneath him into frenzied waves.

"Down, everybody," Olsson called, dropping to his knees. "Secure your equipment!"

Leaving one hand securely entwined in the mesh, Alex pulled her notebook from beneath her knee, then dropped it down her buttoned shirt. Her camera hung safely about her neck, her water bottle snuggled in the pocket of her backpack, and her mechanical pencil — well, by now it was probably resting in the well of a bromeliad or on the forest floor.

Amid a blizzard of curses flowing from her teammates, the pilot came nearer, then hovered above them for the space of about thirty seconds. Caught by the air currents, the platform rose and fell as the branches of the tree whipped to and fro, threatening the mesh fabric.

Tipping her head back to see beyond her hat's flapping brim, Alex caught a glimpse of two men behind the wide windshield — a grinning pilot in headphones and a white man wearing a baseball cap. The white man was emphatically gesturing to the east.

"That's right, Einstein," she muttered. "Please send him away. It's not like we're terribly secure up here."

A moment later, the helicopter turned and flew eastward, toward the river. Alex remained tucked into a ball until the loudest thumps had faded, then she lifted her head to survey the damage.

They'd survived with no serious casualties. Deborah was fussing because the windstorm had agitated her ants, and Louis was bewailing several lost specimens. But this tree was laden with flowers, so he'd be able to replace his samples with little effort. Flailing branches had torn a twelve-inch gash in the mesh near Baklanov, but after assessing the situation with a string of Russian curses, he announced that he would take care to avoid that spot until the fabric could be mended.

Olsson leaped around the raft, taking stock of the situation, then announced that they needed to descend if they wanted to be back at the lodge before dark.

They had spent a long morning on the platform and then had crawled into the shade provided by a towering teak for lunch and a shady siesta. After slathering on fresh applications of sunscreen and mosquito repellent, they had crawled out again to complete their investigations of the mahogany.

More accustomed to the raft now, Alex had finally been able to relax. She had spent part of the day helping Baklanov with his samples, then she had sat on the mesh with binoculars and studied wildlife in the treetops below, watching one particular troop of active marmosets for any sign of illness. She had observed nothing unusual, but still it had been a good day. Despite her weariness, she had managed to keep her emotions and her muscles under control.

After checking to be sure she and Baklanov had gathered all their supplies, she stood and moved over a pontoon toward the porthole. She halted when she saw a large gray object, no bigger than a football, a few inches from their exit. As she took another cautious step, she noticed that the object was . . . buzzing.

"Olsson?" she called, keeping her distance. "You wanna take a look at this?"

The sturdy Swede came closer, then grimaced and muttered a curse. "Stupid chopper dislodged part of a wasps' nest," he said, propping his hand on his hip. "Probably from that teak."

"Do we dare walk around it?"

Olsson turned to Deborah Simons, who was packing her bag. "Dr. Simons? This is your area of expertise, yes? What would you suggest we do?"

Deborah stood and came closer, then bent

with her hands on her knees. She studied the nest for a long moment, then the corner of her mouth drooped. "Yeah — I saw that species earlier today. A marmoset ventured close to one of those nests in the canopy below us."

Alex's mouth went dry. "What happened?"

"I didn't see the attack, but after a minute that monkey dropped like a stone. I'm not sure what species that nest houses, but right now I'm not especially eager to find out."

Olsson scratched at his beard. "Could we kick it away?"

The entomologist shook her head. "I wouldn't want to take a chance. What if it breaks when we kick it? Some insects will swarm if attacked, and if they do, we've nowhere to run."

"So how do we get down?" The question came from Carlton, who had ventured up without his lovely assistant.

Deborah straightened and slipped her hand into her pants pocket. "We find a way to fling the nest and hope like mad the wasps go with it."

Groaning, Alex slipped the kerchief from her neck and dabbed at her forehead and the back of her neck. The sun seemed to have become hotter in the last five minutes, the air thinner.

Baklanov came forward, one hand holding his backpack, the other pushing sweat from his brow. "So — how do we fling it away?"

Olsson pinched the bridge of his nose. "I am taking suggestions."

Alex glanced around the raft. Each researcher had brought only the minimum of equipment to the canopy — notebooks, cameras, specimen vials, water bottles, tubes of sunscreen. Though several of them carried insect repellant, nothing short of industrial-strength wasp spray would neutralize this threat.

"I have an idea." Louis Fortier's scrawny shoulders rose perceptibly as he stepped up to meet the challenge. He walked to within three feet of the nest, then bent and pulled a purple blossom from a plastic specimen container.

Deborah eyed the flower with narrowed eyes. "What is that?"

The bantam Frenchman grinned at her. "Tell me, Dr. Simons — have you observed that type of wasp on the forest floor?"

"Can't say that I have."

"In the understory, perhaps?"

She shook her head.

"I thought not. Well, I have not seen this flower below the canopy, either. I think the vine grows up here for a reason, and that reason may have something to do with your wasp."

After pulling a red kerchief from about his neck, Louis spread the fabric on the mesh surface of the raft, then crushed the blossom between his palms, squeezing the petals until his hands were shiny with wetness. He then wiped his hands on the kerchief.

"I only hope my human pheromones will not overpower the scent," he said, his expression serious as he took pains to wipe even the flesh between his fingers with the cotton cloth. "But I think we are in luck. The fragrance of this flower is strong, especially to a creature as small as a wasp."

He glanced around, then looked at Alex. "Madame Pace, if I may be so bold — would you donate your belt?"

Alex's hands flew to the plain leather belt strung through the loops of her khaki trousers. She couldn't imagine what the man had in mind, but if it would help them get out of this tree . . .

She unfastened the clasp and pulled the belt free. "Here," she said, tossing it to the Frenchman.

Grinning at Olsson and Baklanov, the perfumer poked the sharp tongue of the belt through a corner of the thin cotton kerchief. He then made a loop of the belt and locked the clasp, leaving the scented kerchief dangling from the metal prong of the hasp.

Holding the belt on his palm, in playful formality Fortier bowed to the Swedish botanist. "Monsieur Olsson, do you think you could cut a thin branch for me? I will need a fork at the end."

Grinning, Olsson retreated to a cutout in the raft. "How long?" he called.

Fortier eyed the wasp nest. "Two meters should suffice."

Olsson returned a moment later with a slender branch about six feet long. He handed it to Fortier. "I see what you're about to do. I hope it works."

"That makes two of us."

Gripping her pack, Alex took an involuntary step back as Fortier placed the belt in the forked end of the branch, then lowered it to within an inch of the wasp's nest. A moment later the buzzing sound increased as a veritable wave of insects swarmed out to settle onto the fragrance-soaked fabric.

"They don't understand what's happening," Simons explained, a smile in her voice. "But they are irresistibly drawn to the aroma."

"And that, my friends, is the power of perfume." Moving slowly, Fortier lifted the twig, drawing the kerchief away from the nest. Scores of wasps clung to it, while around it hundreds of others formed a living cloud. Stepping daintily over a pontoon, Fortier moved carefully, holding the kerchief aloft and away from his face. A sudden breath of wind fluttered the cloth for a moment, threatening to blow it back toward the group, but the clasp on the belt held it tight.

Creeping like a tardy husband sneaking into his wife's boudoir, Fortier proved himself the Pied Piper of wasps as he minced his way to the edge of the raft. He suspended the branch over the edge, waited for a lull between wind gusts, then smacked the base of the branch with his right hand, launching kerchief, belt, branch, and wasps over the edge of the platform.

"I hope those buzzing babies didn't land right by the rope," Alex called, moving toward the porthole.

Lifting his arms, Fortier danced his way to the center of the raft. "Do not worry, chérie — they will float around the kerchief for as long as the fragrance lasts. They will not bother you tonight."

As Alex hooked her safety harness to the line for the trip down, she realized the wasps had completely taken her mind off her dread of the descent.

For at least a few moments.

The sun had balanced atop the western horizon by the time the boat pulled within view of Yarupapa Lodge. Alex and her companions stared silently at the helicopter resting on its pontoons a few feet offshore. She knew she shouldn't have been surprised to find the helicopter at the lodge; this part of the jungle held few pockets of civilization.

Leaning forward on her knees, she propped

172

her chin on her fist and tried to disguise her annoyance in front of the others. So the man in the chopper had business at the lodge — fine, but why was he still here? Anyone in such an all-fired hurry should have completed his business and rushed off by now. If Mr. Baseball Cap were still around, she could only surmise that the pilot's mission had not been a matter of life and death . . . though it had nearly created a life-and-death situation for the canopy team.

Milos Olsson must have been thinking the same thoughts. "Stupid fool is still here," he muttered, tossing his gear onto the dock as the boat pulled alongside it. "If that's some millionaire dropping in for a nighttime caiman search, I'll —"

The sound of footsteps interrupted his threat. Alex looked up to see Herman Myers and another white man turn the corner. The stranger, a clear-eyed, stubble-cheeked thirty-something at least a foot taller than Myers, had lost the baseball cap. The pleated trousers and a polished cotton shirt he wore hinted at refinement, but his trousers were wrinkled and patches of perspiration marked the underarms of the shirt. Despite his disheveled state, he moved in an attitude of self-control and studied relaxation, his black hair falling over his collar and gleaming in the fading sunlight. One curl casually brushed his forehead, giving him the windblown look of a spoiled tourist who had just choppered in for a bit of sightseeing. As much as she wanted to be irritated at the intrusion, the sight of such an unexpectedly attractive visitor caught Alex off guard.

Lifting his hand, Myers pointed directly at Alex. "That's the woman you want."

To her annoyance, she felt herself blush.

The stranger came forward with long strides, offering his hand to help her out of the boat. "Dr. Pace? Mr. Myers said I might find you here."

She narrowed her eyes, trying to place his accent. He was not American — maybe English or Australian. Unless English was his second language; in that case, he could have come from anywhere.

"It's *Pah*-chay." She tossed her bag onto the dock. "I use the Italian pronunciation."

"I beg your pardon."

Ignoring his outstretched hand, she stepped onto the boat bench, then leaped onto the dock, rocking the boat. Behind her Olsson began to mutter in Swedish while Deborah Simons suffered a sudden fit of giggles.

The blasted man persisted with the outstretched hand. "Forgive the intrusion, Dr. Pace. I'm Michael Kenway, a physician practicing at the Regional Hospital in Iquitos."

He had to be English — his manners were too polished to be Australian. The few Aussies she'd met in her travels were more freewheeling and a thousand times more field-savvy than this guy.

Reluctantly, she shook the interloper's hand. "What brings you out to Yarupapa, Dr. Kenway? I certainly hope it was a medical emergency — snakebite, perhaps? Caiman attack?"

He released her hand. "Not an emergency, I'm afraid — unless you consider the term in a broad sense."

"Really?" Slinging her bag over her shoulder, she began to follow her departing teammates toward the dining hall. "I figured it would have to be something extremely important to make a helicopter pilot nearly knock a team of researchers off a canopy raft."

The doctor fell into step beside her. "I'm sorry. I tried to warn the fellow away, but he was curious."

"Well, that excuses it, then. Except that you weren't content to blast us with rotor wash or whatever you call it, but you also nearly inflicted another variety of violent and painful death upon us. Were you aware, Doctor, that your little buzzing of our work area kicked a wasps' nest onto our platform? And that nest of extremely large and terribly potent wasps landed only inches from the porthole through which we had to descend?"

A faint smile hovered about his lips as he slipped both hands into his pockets. "I'm sorry. I didn't know."

"Perhaps you didn't know that certain species of the Amazonian wasp can paralyze with one sting — and cause even more problems if a human is allergic to the venom. But, being the big-shot doctor you are, I suspect you were prepared to intubate anyone who stopped breathing —"

"That's quite enough." Turning in front of her, he blocked her path, halting the torrent of her words. "I'm trying to apologize, if you will only listen. I didn't know about the wasps, and I didn't know the helicopter would create such a problem. But when I rented the chopper, I happened to tell the pilot what sort of work you were doing, so the bloke was naturally curious. The moment I realized he'd spotted you and was descending, I tried to warn him off, but apparently I didn't speak forcefully — or accurately — enough. For my weak Spanish, I apologize. For causing you trouble, I apologize. For being here, I apologize. If there's anything else for which you'd like me to apologize, you had better tell me quickly because you, Dr. Pace, have taxed the limits of my patience."

She stared at him as a thought that she'd pushed aside resurfaced in her brain — this foolhardy doctor was an incredibly attractive guy.

In that lay a major problem.

She swallowed hard. "You're a man."

He blinked. "Am I supposed to apologize for that?"

"It might help. I've had bad experiences with men."

"Obviously."

He stood there, tall and irritated, and in that moment Alex realized he would not be intimidated.

She changed her tactics. "You told your idiot pilot what sort of work I was doing?"

"Yes."

"Me, personally? Or the entire team?"

"You, personally." Holding her stare, he crossed his arms. "If you would stop firing salvos in my direction, Dr. Pace, I think you'll be interested in what I've come to tell you."

"I fail to see how you could know anything that would interest me or —"

"I have information regarding a spongiform encephalopathy case in Iquitos."

Alex caught her breath. Mad cow disease had not yet been reported in South America. So this had to be either a genuine case of sporadic disease or . . .

She frowned as another thought occurred. "How did you know about my interest in prion diseases?"

"I read the article."

"What article?"

"In the Lima newspaper, *El Tiempo*. They even had a nice picture of you . . . though, I must say, I don't think it did you justice."

Good grief, was he *flirting* with her? She brought the meaty part of her palm to her forehead, wishing she could remember what she'd told the reporter. Probably nothing. After all, not even Carlton knew about her personal link to her work.

Lowering her hand, she focused her gaze on the doctor. "I'd like to know *why* you think your patient has spongiform encephalopathy."

"*Had* — he expired last night."

"You discovered spongiform tissue postmortem?"

"Yes."

"You did the autopsy?"

"This morning."

She shook her head. "I don't mean to disparage your methods, Dr. Kenway, but I doubt you have the proper equipment for a proper diagnosis."

"This afternoon I confirmed the results in Lima under an electron microscope. With my own eyes I observed spongiform brain tissue and scrapie-associated fibrils. I know what I saw, Dr. Pace. I saw prions."

Alex closed her eyes as surprise siphoned the blood from her head. Thirty seconds ago she would have thought it impossible to find a Peruvian prion patient *or* a physician who could discern a prion from a paramecium . . .

She studied the planks on the walkway.

"Did you train in neurology?"

"Pediatrics. But I worked with several BSE patients in London during the outbreaks."

"About your patient — any family history of the disease?"

"We couldn't take a family history. The man walked out of the jungle thirty-six hours ago. He spoke an odd Indian dialect — we were fortunate to find anyone who could understand him."

Abruptly, she lifted her head. "You say he *walked* out of the jungle? A patient in the last stages of a prion disease does not walk."

"That's why I came to see you. My patient died from acute sepsis due to bowel perforation — he'd been wounded with a stone spear."

She rubbed her forehead. Of course. The infection had ended his life before the disease could, perhaps the infection had been a mercy. Still . . .

She lifted her eyes to find him studying her. "Does your standard autopsy include a microscopic examination of brain tissue?"

His expression changed, some stray thought quirking the corner of his mouth. "Not when I have twenty patients waiting."

"Then why did you go the extra mile?"

His gaze shifted, his eyes momentarily darting up to the thatched roof as if he were appealing to a higher authority. "I looked because the patient told our interpreter that he had been stricken by the shuddering disease years earlier. Knowing he would soon weaken and die, he fled to a nearby tribe known as the Tree People and lived with them for years. He was searching for a white man's village when he encountered the spear-chucker."

"I fail to see —"

"The Tree People *healed* him, Dr. Pace. Though his brain tissue was riddled with prions, I observed no symptoms of encephalopathy in his body. He had good muscle tone, strong legs, and he was ambulatory even after his wounding."

For a moment Alex could do nothing but stammer while her head swarmed with words, then paralysis loosened its grip on her tongue. "I should warn you, Doctor, that I don't like games, particularly when the hour is late and I'm tired and hungry. The circumstances you've described cannot be accurate."

"Are you certain?" The setting sun gilded his face as he challenged her. "I, too, thought the story incredible until I saw prions under the EM. If his story is true, Dr. Pace, a cure for prion diseases exists . . . and it lies somewhere in the jungle."

Blank, amazed, and shaken, she could only stare at him as his words faded into the gathering shadows.

2 April 2003
6:30 p.m.

Watching Dr. Alexandra Pace from the corner of his eye, Michael sliced a piece of catfish with his fork as the researcher pushed the fringe of hair away from her eyes, then rested her cheek on her hand. For the last half-hour she had alternated between staring at her untouched plate and peppering him with questions about his deceased patient. His answers, he noted with relief, apparently intrigued her, for though she seemed to find him as irritating as a rash, she had not yet told him to bugger off.

The helicopter pilot seemed in no hurry to leave. He sat with the lodge staff at a table next to the kitchen, where beer and laughter flowed like water. Michael had tried to follow their conversation during one of Dr. Pace's lapses into silence, but their Spanish seemed more fluid than Fortuna's.

His nurse and the other hospital staff, he

decided after a few minutes, had been speaking a Spanish version of baby talk for his benefit.

Sighing, he returned his attention to his own dinner companions. Dr. Pace had offered quick, perfunctory introductions around the table, and Michael was still trying to match names and titles with faces.

The child obviously belonged to Alexandra Pace, for they shared the same petite build, light brown hair, and brown eyes. After taking the empty seat to Michael's right, Caitlyn had not hesitated to tell him she was ten years old and studying tenth-grade material. "It's our version of independent study," she had said, sitting on her hands and swinging her feet in wide arcs while she waited for the servers to bring their food. "I've learned Spanish since we came to Peru, and Tito has promised to teach me some Yagua tomorrow. I expect I will know five or six new languages by the time we get back to Atlanta."

Lifting a brow, Michael tried to look terribly impressed — not a difficult task. "Really?"

Caitlyn had begun to answer, but halted mid-syllable when Dr. Pace told her daughter to stop badgering their guest.

Milos Olsson, the Swedish botanist, sat to Michael's left, but he was primarily engaged in a conversation with the woman who sat next to him, a white-haired anthropologist named Emma Whitmore. The older woman had greeted Michael with a smile and a simple, "Call me Emma, please."

An Indian guide employed by the lodge sat next to Emma and directly across from Michael. He had merely nodded when Dr. Pace introduced him as Lazaro; now he seemed content to eat his dinner and smile whenever Emma tossed a comment in his direction.

Alexandra Pace sat next to the guide, and though she had cut her catfish into a dozen or so tiny pieces, Michael didn't think she had eaten a single bite. Her eyes were wide and unfocused, as though she were replaying their previous encounter and searching for some lapse in logic through which she could dismiss the entire conversation.

"Is it possible," she said as she propped her elbows on the table, "that the natives of this so-called healing village have access to a plant we know nothing of? You said they were called the Tree People — could they have access to a biological agent that grows in the canopy?"

Michael accepted a steaming bowl of rice from Olsson and passed it to the little girl. "Anything's possible, I suppose. But I'm not sure how much trust I'd place in Ya-ree's story. He seemed lucid while I observed him, but even my clerk found the story unbelievable."

"It's absolutely unbelievable." The poodle-haired anthropologist abruptly lifted her chin. "To my knowledge, none of the Amazon tribes have ever lived in trees. Virtually all of them have adopted the roundhouse style of timber dwelling commonly called a *shabono.* They lack the tools necessary for construction of a tree house."

Michael lifted his hands to show he had not intended to contradict common knowledge. "I didn't say they *lived* in trees, Emma; I am reporting only what my patient told our clerk. He said he lived with the Tree People — whether they lived *in* a tree or *near* a tree, I couldn't say. I was rather hoping you could shed some light on the subject."

"Perhaps they worshiped a tree." Milos Olsson injected his opinion into the mix. "That would be expected in a primitive culture, yes? After all, a tree can provide wood, shade, water, food, even medicine. I would not be at all surprised if a tribe decided to name a tree as its deity."

While Emma snorted, Michael lifted his glass and nodded at the botanist. "You may have something there. Ya-ree, my patient, spoke of the keyba before he died. I had never heard the word, and at the time I thought he was babbling in fever. But our clerk told me the patient spoke coherently and reverently of the keyba. He said it sent lights to guide him through the forest."

Emma's face brightened. "Ah, his people

184

were spiritualists, then. The shamans of many tribes have proven their ability to summon spirits to aid them in the jungle. I've heard some of them can call fire from the sky in order to frighten their enemies."

"I'm thinking fireflies." Olsson stroked his beard. "If these people worshiped a tree, or even lived in a tree, perhaps the tree housed a nest of fireflies. Your man might have come up with something that exuded a scent they found attractive, just as Fortier used that flower to entice the wasps this afternoon. It's possible the native literally escorted a swarm of fireflies away through the forest."

Alexandra laughed. "Really, Milos, be serious."

"I am being serious." The Swede tempered his smile. "Picture this — the man walked with a stick held out in front of him while the fireflies swarmed around some bit of fragrant material at the end of the stick. The bugs would have functioned as a lantern as he traveled through the forest."

Alexandra shifted in her chair. "I'm afraid I couldn't buy that one unless Deborah endorses your theory. I'm having a hard time believing that fireflies can create a light bright enough to illuminate a pathway."

"Don't forget, Mom, they would be *Amazonian* fireflies, which are actually bioluminescent beetles." Caitlyn looked up at her mother with an earnest smile. "Everything's

185

bigger down here."

"Not that big." Alexandra tented her hands, then pressed two steepled fingers to her chin. "Though the notion of fireflies may be doubtful, the timing could be right." She shifted her gaze to Michael. "When, exactly, did your patient leave the jungle?"

Michael counted backward. "Two nights ago."

She nodded. "Exactly. There was no moon that night, so your patient would have needed *something* to guide him." She looked around the table. "Have you stepped outside after sunset? The stars are as bright as new dimes, but without moonlight, it's completely black in the shadows. And the deep jungle, as you know, is nothing but shadows." She sighed. "So I'm thinking he carried a torch."

"A torch, fireflies . . ." Emma breathed the words softly, then shook her head. "I doubt he would have gotten far with a torch or a swarm of fireflies, particularly if he was moving quickly. I find it easier to believe your man was a shaman who summoned his guiding spirit — this keyba — to guide him through the jungle."

"Emma, if I may be so bold —" Michael gave her a smile — "may I inquire as to your own spiritual beliefs?"

She laughed, a husky, three-noted chuckle. "I have deep spiritual beliefs, strong convictions. I believe a spirit resides within each living thing — man, woman, child, animal, and yes, even trees. Our entire lives are spent searching for a way to commune with these spirits, but we civilized folk have forgotten the simple things nature once taught us. Native people like your patient are closer to the source of elemental things than we are." Her eyes grew large and wistful. "One day I hope to commune with the spirits of nature as easily as your Ya-ree."

Michael wavered, trying to comprehend what he was hearing. "So you believe he actually summoned fire from . . . where, heaven?"

She shrugged. "I don't know that it came from heaven — I doubt our definitions of heaven would mesh at all. I believe your patient probably knew how to persuade natural forces to accomplish his will."

"You speak as if these natural forces have personalities."

"They do, Doctor." A bit of a blush rose to the older woman's cheeks. "Trust me."

"What about you, Dr. Kenway?" When Alexandra looked at him, he was surprised to see a smile twinkling in her eyes. "Do you believe in spirits?"

"Of course I do." He returned her smile in full measure. "I believe in the Holy Spirit, part of the triune God. I'm sure you've heard of him — Jesus the Son, God the Father, the Holy Spirit? I hear they're very big in the United States."

An easy smile played at the corners of her mouth as she lifted her glass. "Indeed, they are — at least on those TV channels that play big-haired, hellfire-and-brimstone Bible-thumpers all day long."

Michael watched the muscles work in her long, slender throat as she brought the lemonade to her lips and swallowed. "What about you?" he asked when she had lowered her glass. "Are you a believer?"

She chuckled softly. "In hellfire and brimstone?"

"In God."

"I *do* love the way you Brits say that — *Gah-awed,* as if he deserves his own pronunciation. Sounds more holy that way, I suppose."

"You didn't answer my question."

"Didn't I?" She cast him a glinting glance, then picked up her fork and poked at the uneaten catfish. "I'm afraid I'll have to disappoint you, Dr. Kenway. I'm an agnostic on the verge of becoming an avowed atheist. Only a reasoned dose of humility keeps me from making a full declaration."

Folding his hands, he turned in his chair. "Was that so hard to confess?"

"It wasn't a confession; it was a simple statement of fact. If I seemed reluctant to share it, it's not because I'm ashamed. It's because now you'll feel you have to convert me."

188

"I can't convert anyone. I leave that sort of business to the Spirit — the one you dismiss so lightly."

"Sorry." She pressed her fingertips to her chest in a display of pretended modesty. "It's not easy, particularly in the Bible Belt, but someone has to represent logic and reason."

He lifted his glass, silently absorbing her comments, then tilted his head and addressed everyone at the table. "Did any of you study the Elizabethan period at university?"

Olsson grunted; Emma shook her head and smiled, obviously entertained by the ongoing debate.

Alexandra responded to his question by making a face. "Why do you ask?"

"Because the Elizabethans had a soundly Christocentric view of the planet. They believed that through God's revelation to Adam, human beings once understood everything about the natural world. This knowledge was lost in the intervening centuries due to the corruption of sin, but the Elizabethans believed it could be recovered as people listened to God and the Almighty revealed new fields to be researched."

"God and research." Emma smiled at Olsson. "Not often do we hear *those* words linked together."

Michael ignored her comment. "In keeping with this philosophy," he continued, "the Elizabethan explorers believed that since God knew sin would corrupt the planet, within nature he planted cures for every disease that would befall mankind."

"That's a lovely thought," Alexandra answered, "almost comforting. But weren't your Elizabethans the same people who believed the earth was flat?"

Michael smiled. "You're thinking fifteenth century. The Elizabethans lived in the sixteenth."

She shrugged. "Sorry. But while you were learning about your Elizabethans, we were studying Benjamin Franklin — you know, the American patriot who once said, 'He that lives upon hope will die fasting.' "

"And your point is?"

"Your Elizabethans died without finding every cure, didn't they? And as I recall, some of their so-called cures were fairly horrific. Bloodletting, for instance."

Resting one arm on the table, Michael bit back his rising frustration. "My point is this: The explorers of that age believed God loved the world so much that he provided remedies for sin, for loneliness, and for disease. Christ came to save the world from sin and restore mankind to fellowship with God, but to believers fell the task of thoroughly exploring the earth to find the cures for disease. That shared conviction fueled one of the greatest periods of discovery the world has ever known."

"How convenient." Emma's voice went dry. "They should have concentrated on discovering free love, painkillers, and hallucinogens — they would have solved the problems of disease and loneliness without getting into a lot of God-talk about salvation and sin."

"My point —" Michael repeated, but Olsson cut him off.

"You are trying to tell us that a cure for brain diseases might lie in the jungle. Fine. We are searching for it."

"But if a hidden tribe already knows of the cure?"

"How do you know they know?" Emma's bright blue eyes sharpened. "You cannot mount an entire expedition upon the word of one muttering Indian."

Looking around the table, Michael forced himself to speak in a calm and even tone. "I know Ya-ree came into the hospital suffering from sepsis, fever, and massive dehydration. Eyewitnesses saw him walk out of the jungle. Later I heard him speak to our clerk, and she found him coherent. Furthermore —" fumbling in his pocket, he pulled out one of the photos taken by the electron microscope — "I know my patient's brain looked like this."

He flipped the photo toward Alexandra, whose smile froze as she picked up the black-and-white image. Olsson and Emma continued to jibe in lowered tones until Alexandra looked at Michael, hope and confusion war-

191

ring in her eyes.

"We could save ourselves years of searching for the needle in the haystack," she said, tapping the edge of the Polaroid against the table.

Michael sat back as the woman dropped her defenses. Judging from her manner, he had assumed Alexandra Pace was as stubborn as Pharaoh's heart, but apparently she wasn't totally unyielding.

"I don't know about you all," she turned her smile upon the others, "but I don't want to waste a single moment looking at monkeys through binoculars if I could be investigating something with real promise."

Emma's jaw went slack.

Alexandra tapped the photo with her index finger. "Make no mistake, this is spongiform tissue, and those rods are infectious proteins. The odds of finding a case like this are astronomical, but if Kenway is right —" Her eyes suddenly swiveled to meet Michael's. "You're sure about all this?"

He met her gaze head-on. "I was with the man who took that photo this afternoon. And I hand-carried the slides from the autopsy room to the university in Lima."

"And you'd swear this man was ambulatory when he came out of the jungle?"

Michael considered. "My witnesses had no reason to lie."

"Then, friends," Alexandra looked at the

others, "I think we should investigate further."

"I don't suppose I should discount the opportunity to discover a lost tribe." Emma's spidery hand drummed the tabletop. "There are few uncontacted tribes remaining in Amazonia, and none I know of in Peru. If they exist . . . well, why not? I suppose I should welcome the opportunity to search for them."

Michael studied the expressions of those around the table, then settled on Alexandra's face. "I came here," he said, "because I believe my patient spoke the truth. Even if I'm wrong, can we afford to ignore the possibility that I might be right? Research is about testing theories and taking risks."

"You say *we*." Alexandra's voice went as cool as the smoke off dry ice. "Yet you are not a researcher."

"I'm interested in prion diseases."

"Why? Transmissible spongiform encephalopathies are not widespread in this part of the world. Every expert I know in the field of prion research would say your patient was an anomaly, the one-in-a-million case of sporadic Creutzfeldt-Jakob disease."

Michael felt memories stirring at the center of his gut, but fought them down. "TSEs caused a stir in London in the mid-1990s. I was caught up in . . . everything." He cleared his throat to push past the lump that rose whenever he thought of that troubled time.

"I've seen what damage variant Creutzfeldt-Jakob disease can do. I'd give my life to find a cure, even an effective treatment. If we could find something to stop prions from wreaking havoc in the brain, these patients would not have to die."

Alexandra's eyes seemed to weigh his sincerity and his motives, then she placed her hand on her daughter's head in a protective gesture. Lifting a brow, she flashed a smile around the table. "What do you say, friends? Should we move our fieldwork into the jungle?"

Emma leaned forward, her hands pressed together. "I'd love to." She tilted her head toward the next table. "But Kenneth Carlton's paying the bills."

She had no sooner spoken the pharmaceutical manufacturer's name than the American rose from his place at the next table.

"Count me in!" he called, walking to the empty space between Michael and Olsson. He dropped his arms to the backs of their chairs, then leaned into the gap like a coach intent on calling the next play. "We could send for a few additional team members and mount an expedition within a week. Any of you who want to come along would be welcome."

Alexandra gave the man a smooth smile. "I didn't realize you were listening, Mr. Carlton."

"Hard to ignore such a spirited conversation." Utterly unembarrassed by his eavesdropping, the man straightened and propped his hands on his hips. "My dinner companions were talking about dull topics like fishing and trading. But this —" He lifted a brow at Alexandra. "Horizon Biotherapies will finance the entire expedition. Give me three or four days to augment our team, then we'll set out to search for this mysterious tribe. Given the relatively small search area, how could we miss them?"

Michael parked his elbow on the table. "It may not be such a small search area. We don't know how far my patient had traveled before he was wounded."

Olsson looked up at Carlton. "Still . . . a wounded man could only run so far in twenty-four hours. We could probably do a thorough canvass of the area in a couple of weeks. A native tracker could help us find the tribe in even less time."

Emma snapped her fingers. "Sign me up. My work with the Yagua can wait."

Olsson hesitated, scratching at his beard, but the anthropologist placed her hand on his shoulder and spoke in a stage whisper. "The *Tree* People. Perhaps an undiscovered botanical species with unexplored medicinal benefits."

Olsson jerked his head in a nod. "All right. I am in."

Michael lifted his head to catch Carlton's eye. "I'd like to go along. If they survived years without me at the hospital, I'm certain they can cope if I'm gone a few days."

"That seems only fair, since you brought us this momentous news." Carlton looked at Alexandra, who had slipped her arm around her daughter's shoulders. "Will your daughter be joining us, Alex?"

"Mom?" The girl, who had been following the conversation with wide eyes, clasped her hands in a begging posture. "Please, can I go? It'll be so much fun."

Alexandra cast Carlton a "gee, thanks" look, then gave her daughter a rueful smile. "I don't know if you should go, hon. It's the jungle."

"*This* is the jungle!" Caitlyn waved her hand to indicate their surroundings. "Besides, how can I get into trouble if you're with me all day? I'd be safer in the jungle with you than hanging out here at the lodge with the Somerville sisters."

Alexandra did not look convinced, but her gaze shifted to the empty table where two tired-looking Americans had eaten dinner and slipped away.

"While Caitlyn would undoubtedly enjoy a trip through the jungle —" Alexandra met Michael's eye — "how can we guarantee her safety? After all, your patient suffered a spear wound."

196

"I'll bring in a security team," Carlton promised. "I know an ex–Navy SEAL who lives for this kind of gig. I'll have him on the next plane to Lima, but I need you, Alex, to give me 110 percent on this one. If that means we bring your kid along so you can keep an eye on her, then that's okay. Let her come."

For an instant Alexandra seemed to waver, then she gave Carlton a nod of assent. "All right. But we have to keep a reasonable pace. Caitlyn's strong, but I'm not going to risk her breaking a leg on some kind of jungle obstacle course."

"I'll tell the military warrior to go easy on us. You'll be safe — you have my word on it." Grinning, Kenneth Carlton went back to his table to share the news.

As the others at his table buzzed with the news, Michael noticed that Alexandra said nothing, but stared at her untouched dinner, her face a pale knot of apprehension. Her eyes flickered toward him. "What have I done?" she whispered.

"You have taken a step of faith." He lowered his voice to match her tone. "Congratulations."

"I'm trusting *you*." She pronounced the personal pronoun as if it were distasteful. "I can't believe I'm about to take my daughter into the jungle because you think I should."

"It's not me you're trusting." Michael set

his fork on the edge of his plate. "The photo convinced you, I think."

"It's crazy."

"It's probably the sanest decision you've ever made. You heard the facts and responded to them with logic and common sense."

One of the servers paused at Alexandra's elbow, his arm extended for her plate, but Michael put out a hand to stop him from taking it.

"You'd better eat." He turned to face her. "You'll need your strength in the jungle."

She looked at him, the corners of her mouth tight with distress and her eyes slightly shiny. He expected another sharp retort, but her reply startled him more than any comment he might have imagined.

"You may be right," she said, picking up her fork.

3 April 2003
11:52 p.m.

Almost midnight, and the Sandman and I are not on speaking terms. Caitlyn sleeps with her favorite stuffed monkey across the room: I can hear the reassuring slow sounds of her breathing even through the insect chatter that pours through our screen walls. Today I nearly convinced myself that my insomnia stemmed from my excitement over the upcoming excursion into the jungle . . . but I am no longer a child. It has been years since excitement kept me awake.

Still, I can't help but wonder how much of my insomnia is the result of my illness and how much may have been exacerbated by my knowledge of the disease. If I did not know about the symptom, if I did not recognize and prepare for it by supplying my bed with notebooks, flashlight, and other quiet entertainments, would I sleep easier? Or would I drive myself crazy with frustration and fear?

Impossible to tell — one of those "if a tree falls in the woods, does it make a sound?" types of questions.

(I can attest to the fact that a tree falling in the rainforest does in fact make quite a loud sound. Last night Caitlyn was awakened by what I thought was some sort of fireworks celebration — a long series of loud popping noises, rustling, then a tremendous crashing finale. I soothed Caitlyn and she went back to sleep; this morning Lazaro told us that a tree had fallen in the night. The popping sounds were snapping roots and vines that had staked their lives on the stability of the tree. Now the lodge staff will use the carcass — already Lazaro has planned to make two canoes from the mighty trunk. I hope I am as useful when I can no longer stand upright.)

Perhaps it is fear that hammers at my subconscious and keeps me awake. Perhaps it is complete exhaustion. My teammates have all gone to bed. Wiped out from the heat and a full day of canopy work, they have been silent and in their darkened bungalows for hours. I'm sure they think I am asleep, too, though this morning Deborah Simons did ask if my mattress was uncomfortable. Apparently I have dark circles under my eyes. I haven't really taken the time to look, and that small mirror in the bathroom does not tempt me to linger . . .

Night comes suddenly here, with the sun setting just before six and full dark settling in with a swiftness that astounds those of us who are used to a city's ambient lighting. If not for the stars, this would be the deepest darkness I have ever known.

My mother used to tell me to read the Bible when I couldn't sleep. While I wouldn't mind reading a Bible now — for completely different reasons than the ones she had in mind — I doubt there is a copy to be found in the lodge, unless Deborah Simons has packed one in her luggage. The lodge library, composed exclusively of books left behind by previous tourists — is heavy on Stephen King, Dean Koontz, and Nora Roberts. Not a volume of Holy Writ to be found.

Nothing dull enough to lull me to sleep except my own journal, which serves at least to stand in the place of dreams. Here I can sort through the day's events, record random thoughts, and — though I hate to admit it — record the progress of my deteriorating condition. If Life plays a winning hand before I hit my lucky streak, this journal may serve as the definitive record for another researcher.

Perhaps even my daughter.

Because if I am not successful, I do not doubt that she will be following my example, studying my journals, peering into every microscope until she finds the answer. If she does read this, I want her to know that I am allowing her to go with us into the jungle for only one reason — the simple need to cherish each remaining moment I have with her. When life has a foreseeable limit, every day becomes priceless.

One thought, oddly enough, comforts me. Dr. Michael Kenway, who dropped in on us yesterday, implied that he believed creation holds the answer to every disease on the planet — the almighty God apparently gave us the task of finding the cure and placing the proper key in the appropriate lock. In the same vein, Baklanov says that each bacterium requires a perfect match with the proper virus before it can be defeated. There are patterns in nature, designs I have not considered . . . but I find my mind opening to them now.

If there is a cure for encephalopathies in the jungle, I will either find it or go to my grave searching.

Perhaps the natives will speak of me — the skinny white woman who would not give up. Stranger things have happened. Who knows what odd things will happen when we enter the jungle? Already I feel we are operating in a world completely removed from everything I have ever known and trusted.

Alex paused, lifting her pen from the page. She could write more of her fears, but why dwell on thoughts that might one day terrify Caitlyn? Besides, fears had a way of turning into phobias and phobias into paranoia, all of which were symptoms of brain disease. She would have to guard her thoughts and not ramble only to pass the hours in which she should have been sleeping.

She closed her eyes, her fingers curling into a fist as she visualized the knotty little proteins that had amassed a microscopic army within her body. For years they had been accumulating, biding their time, waiting for her to enter the fullness of life —

I have never before thought that a microscopic protein could possess a moral value. Yet somehow I am convinced that just as Baklanov's bacteriophages are good, prions are evil. My colleagues would scoff at such a notion, but their brains are not playing host to the little devils.

She hated this disease, hated all encephalopathies because they struck at the core of a person's self. Take away a woman's arm or leg or stomach, and you still had a functioning human being. Take away a woman's mind, even a small but crucial part of her brain, and you had nothing.

Her mother, Geneva Pace, had been fifty-two when she developed the first symptoms of FFI. Alex and Caitlyn had been living with her at the time, so Geneva could care for the baby while Alex worked. She had experienced tremors, anxiety, and difficulty in falling asleep, but ignored these symptoms for months, chalking them up to the process of aging and the stress of caring for a young child.

Total insomnia, however, had been hard to ignore.

"It's the oddest thing," she'd said one morning at breakfast. "But I don't think I slept at all last night. I turned on one of those old movies to lull myself to sleep, but my mind just wouldn't turn off — I watched the entire movie, then two others."

Alex had looked up in alarm, but her beautiful mother smiled and shrugged. "I'll take a nap with Caitlyn this afternoon, dear, don't worry."

But she hadn't napped that afternoon, nor had she slept more than half an hour the next night. Within two weeks, her pupils had shrunk to pinpoints and her blood pressure had risen to alarming levels. Alex had taken her mother to the doctor, who had prescribed medication for blood pressure and sleeping pills, but the pills had only made her mother lethargic. He had asked for a family history; Alex had replied that her grandmother died from Parkinson's. Her death had been the reason Alex became a neurologist.

Undoubtedly, that diagnosis had been wrong.

For the next several months, Alex watched in horror as Geneva Pace withered to skin and bones. Her mother had never been a heavy woman, but every ounce of fat melted away as her body continually burned calories. She perspired constantly, which caused thirst and dehydration. Her attempts to sleep became desperate, and occasionally Alex would find her mother lying in bed, her mouth slack and her eyes wide. A light doze was the deepest sleep she could manage, no more than what other people would call a catnap. The sound of a footfall compressing the fibers of a carpet was enough to snap her back to wakefulness.

Geneva began to stumble and fall as her ability to balance slipped away. For a few weeks she could scrawl her thoughts on a notepad, but that ability disappeared as her motor skills deteriorated.

One of the last things she'd written for Alex was a warning: *Find a way to stop this. For you. For Cait.*

Alex had to put her mother in a nursing home, where the staff had a tendency to treat the sick woman as if she were unaware of her surroundings. She could not speak at the end, but her eyes told Alex she was cognizant of everything around her . . . and she was frightened.

Only in that last month did Geneva Pace enjoy anything resembling rest. After a long nightmare, she fell into a state of exhaustion that outwardly resembled a coma, though her EEG revealed a normal awake pattern.

Sitting by her mother's bed, Alex stared at the frail body and the EEG and wondered if her mother was, in fact, awake and a prisoner within her own physical shell. What sort of exquisite torture it must be to hear, feel, and think without any way of communicating. Sort of like being buried alive, but instead of being locked up inside a coffin, you were entombed within your own dying body . . .

Alex was present when her mother drew her last breath. A moment later, the EEG spiked, then went flat as the neurons of her brain finally stopped firing.

Alex moved through the burial and funeral like a shell-shocked soldier, but when the paralysis of grief wore off, she returned to work and asked for permission to spearhead a new project. Leaving the well-populated field of Parkinson's research, she began studying fatal familial insomnia and other prion diseases. When mad cow disease struck Britain in the last decade of the twentieth century, she realized that she had stumbled into the study of a disease as threatening as AIDS and as horrifying as Ebola. Agreeing with her vision, Kenneth Carlton of Horizon Biotherapies appointed Alex as head of the newly formed Neurological Research Department.

She had always heard that people found the death of a parent particularly sobering because it removed the so-called "buffer zone" between death and an individual . . . for Alex, her mother's death removed any doubt that she had inherited a fatal disease. If her mother and grandmother had died from FFI, odds were great that she and Caitlyn would suffer from it, too. The disease was active in their bodies even now, quietly persuading healthy proteins to join its traitorous army.

How did this disease come to be rooted in my family? And how far back does the chain stretch? More important, why do 50 percent of children in a family escape diagnosis? Are they not carriers, or do they not live long enough for the disease to manifest itself? Perhaps it has something to do with gender — an infected father would not pass blood to his offspring through a placenta, and in that case, none of the children should inherit the disease . . .

I am tired, for I am making no sense. Perhaps I am completely off base. If stress is a major accelerator, is it possible that some infected individuals lead such blissful lives that prions never amass enough strength to do real damage? Sometimes I think I'd give anything to experience that kind of bliss, then I realize that sort of innocence must be unattainable for a thinking person in today's world . . .

She lifted her pen as something rustled the leaves beyond the screen separating her from the rainforest. "Come in," she taunted, keeping her voice low. "Anaconda, caiman, poisonous snake. Come in and kill me, if you dare. But don't eat me, or you'll spread prions throughout the jungle."

She glanced up at the thatched roof as a random thought skittered through her mind — she should have told Dr. Kenway to soak his jungle man's corpse in bleach. The devilish prions had proven themselves capable of withstanding thirty minutes of boiling water, two months of freezing temperatures, as well as disinfection with formaldehyde, carbolic acid, and chloroform. The malevolent entities had successfully passed through filters designed to stop the smallest viruses; they were tiny enough to remain in a suspended state even when spun in a centrifuge at 400,000 revolutions per minute. Prions remained viable in dried brains for at least two years; they resisted doses of ultraviolet light that routinely killed phage viruses.

The only agent that had managed to destroy prions was chlorine bleach. "Good old Clorox," she murmured, capping her pen. "Wish we had a bottle with us."

The corner of her mouth curled. Kenway believed God had hidden a cure for every disease somewhere on the planet? God would have proven himself far more practical if he had buried a few bottles of bleach in the jungle.

"Mom?"

From out of the darkness, Caitlyn's voice startled her. "What is it, sweetheart? My flashlight keeping you awake?"

"Can't you sleep?" A note of alarm trembled in the girl's question, and Alex's heart sank at the sound of it. Caitlyn didn't remember anything about her grandmother's death, but through the years she'd overheard stories about Geneva's desperate insomnia.

Alex clenched her fist as her heart pumped fear and outrage through her veins. Life wasn't fair.

"I'm fine, precious. Just writing a few things in my journal." She reached for the flashlight and turned it off. "That better?"

The sound of silence hung in the darkness between them, followed by a sigh. "I can't sleep if you can't sleep, Mom."

"Okay . . . so do you want to play the word game?"

"Sure. Can I choose the topic?"

"Go for it."

Alex heard the rustle of sheets as Caitlyn

turned. "Okay. Words that other kids say about you behind your back."

An internal alarm rang in Alex's brain. "Like what?"

"Like . . . geek."

"Um . . . brilliant nonconformist?"

"They don't say that, Mom."

"But it's a synonym. It's just a matter of perspective."

"Nerd."

"Talented and unique personality."

"You're not playing by the rules."

Alex hesitated, wondering how much she could say without interfering. Caitlyn managed beautifully in the field but seemed to struggle with her peers in Atlanta. On more than one occasion she had run into the house in tears after attempting to speak to the neighborhood kids.

The other preadolescent girls in their subdivision pulled their chemically streaked hair in taut ponytails, wore polo shirts and khaki slacks to private school, and spent their spare time watching MTV. Caitlyn, who usually wore the first thing she could pull from the laundry hamper, had hair the approximate size and texture of a tumbleweed and spent her spare time memorizing entries from *Roget's Thesaurus.*

Geek. Nerd.

Sticks and stones could break your bones, but names hurt more than anything.

"Honey," she began, "have the kids back home —"

"Let's try another one: words you can say when you're angry. Without cussing, of course."

Alex looked away. So Caitlyn didn't want to talk about it. Maybe out here, miles from home, she could almost forget the snotty little girls back in Atlanta.

She pretended shock. "Oh, my."

"That's kinda mild, Mom."

"I wasn't playing — I was responding to your suggestion."

"Okay, so I'll go first. Jiminy Cricket."

Alex felt the corner of her mouth lift in a half-smile. "Rats."

"Blast — Dr. Kenway says that one. I heard him saying it when he got out of the helicopter."

Ignoring Cait's reference to the doctor's arrival, Alex pressed on. "Nuts."

"Confound it."

"Heck."

"Shoot."

"Dad-blamed, dad-burned, dad-gummit."

"Oh, my garden peas."

Alex stared into the darkness. "Who says *that?*"

Caitlyn giggled. "Dr. Simons. She said it tonight, right after spilling her lemonade on Lazaro's sleeve."

Alex heaved a sigh. "Good night, honey.

211

See you in the morning."

"Aren't we going to play any more?"

"You win. I'm too tired to think. And you need your rest."

She heard the thump of Caitlyn's slender frame on the boards supporting the narrow mattress, then . . . nothing.

Steeling her will, Alex lay down and stared into the blackness. "One," she whispered, summoning up the image of a khaki-clad preadolescent tormenter leaping over her net-draped bed. "Two . . ."

4 April 2003
4:37 p.m.

Standing behind his chair, Michael stared at the paraphernalia scattered over his desk: a portable battery-powered microscope, his medical kit, a six-inch hunting knife, a flashlight, and a bagful of bandages and an assortment of drugs, including penicillin, antihistamines, and snakebite antivenin.

He could never take all this — the others would laugh if he showed up with a duffle bag as big as a body. Alexandra and her crew were experienced field researchers; they would know how to travel light.

Sighing, he lifted the microscope and set it on a shelf. The wonderful little gadget was probably too weak to be of much use, anyway. While the device had proven invaluable for showing reluctant natives what chiggers and flea eggs looked like, the machine's magnification wasn't nearly great enough to penetrate the infinitesimal universe of viruses and prions.

Picking up an old canvas duffel he'd found in a storage room, he dropped in the medicines, medical kit, knife, flashlight, and the bag of drugs and bandages.

He looked up as Fortuna rapped on his door. "*El doctor,* there is someone to see you."

"A patient?"

"No. He says he has news about your tattooed man."

Instantly alert, Michael shoved the duffel out of the way. "Send him in, please."

Immediately after returning from Yarupapa Lodge, he had sought out Rico, the orderly who helped treat Ya-ree. After sharing the sad news that Ya-ree had died, Michael sent Rico into Iquitos to find the good Samaritans who had transported the Indian from the river to the hospital. After asking them who had brought the patient to Iquitos, Rico had been instructed to send messages downriver to discover exactly where Ya-ree had exited the jungle. Without that information, the expedition would not know where to begin its search for the healing tribe.

Rico came into the office, his eyes shining. *"Buenos tardes, el doctor."*

"Buenos tardes, Rico." Michael shook his hand. "I gather you learned something about our injured Indian."

Nodding, Rico pulled a slip of paper from

his pocket. "The family who found Ya-ree lives outside Libertad. It is a village of less than one hundred people, but it is only a few hours by boat. I have drawn a map."

Michael studied the diagram but could make no sense of the winding lines that doubtless represented several of the many tributaries feeding the Amazon. But someone who knew the area should be able to decipher it.

Smiling, he pulled a ten-sole note from his pocket and gave it to Rico. *"Gracias, amigo."*

When Rico had gone, Fortuna stepped into the room, her eyes shiny with distress. "How can I convince you not to go on this trip? We need you here."

"I've arranged for Dr. Aznar to fill in for me."

The nurse made a face. "That man is *anticuado* — he knows nothing of modern medicine. We need you to care for the little ones."

"That's very kind of you, Fortuna, but I won't be gone long. A week, two at the most."

"That is too long!"

He gave her what he hoped was a reassuring smile. "You managed very well before I arrived. I have every confidence you'll manage Dr. Aznar brilliantly."

He picked up the bag, intending to move past her, but she clutched his sleeve and stopped him just outside his door.

"Por favor, el doctor — do not do this thing!

You do not know the jungle. It is dangerous, especially for a white man."

"You mean for a white man from the city." He smiled with a confidence he did not quite feel. "I am traveling with a team of experts. I'm quite certain they're not about to let anyone get hurt."

"But you do not know the jungle! It is deep and dark. There are places even the most experienced hunters dare not go —"

"I'll be fine." Gently, he extracted her hand from his sleeve. "It is only a rainforest, Fortuna. Thousands of Peruvians have lived in it for generations, so I hardly think I'll have too much trouble in a fortnight."

Lowering her arm, she gave him a pouting look. If Dr. Garcia had not rounded the corner in that moment, Michael thought she might have whimpered.

Dr. Esteban Garcia, administrator of Regional Hospital, had visited the office only once before, a brief welcoming visit shortly after Michael's arrival in Iquitos. Michael wasn't sure what the man's duties included apart from riding in parades with city dignitaries and flying to Lima for political meetings. Hospital gossip held that Garcia hadn't examined a patient in years.

"Dr. Kenway." He reached out and shook Michael's hand. "I hear you are intending to leave us."

Michael let his duffel bag drop to the floor.

216

Apparently Garcia did pop into the hospital often enough to sift through rumors of staff defections.

"Only for a fortnight or so." Michael released the man's hand. "It's a rather critical research trip. A patient autopsy turned up evidence of a deadly infectious encephalopathy, so it's necessary we find the source of the disease."

Dr. Garcia slipped one hand into the pocket of his pristine lab coat. "I do not know that it is necessary at all. I reviewed the chart, and it is clear your man did not die from encephalopathy."

Crossing his arms, Michael searched for words that might penetrate the thickness of a stubborn skull. "Quite right. Which makes the case even more remarkable, considering that we found spongiform brain tissue in his autopsy. The man should have died years ago, but he claimed to have been cured by native medicine. If such a cure is possible, the necessity of this expedition becomes even more urgent. We must not only look for the source of contagion; we must also find the treatment that halted Ya-ree's disease. We will be serving our own people as well as the population of the entire —"

"If you leave your office unattended," Garcia interrupted as if he hadn't heard a word, "we will assign the space to someone else."

Michael choked back a hoot of laughter.

The hospital suffered from a chronic shortage of qualified physicians, and he doubted Dr. Garcia had a stack of applicants waiting to fill any spot. Only those with a genuine bent toward altruism would consider a position on the fringe of the jungle.

Still . . . the administrator had a responsibility to uphold. He probably felt duty required him to issue a perfunctory warning whenever the urge for jungle exploration struck his physicians.

"Dr. Garcia." Michael lowered his head in a respectful pose. "If a new physician needs this office, I will certainly understand if you must reassign it. Dr. Aznar, however, has agreed to oversee my chronic and casualty patients, and I will return as soon as I am able. But I fully understand your quandary, and I will not protest if this office is no longer available when I return."

This assurance seemed to satisfy the heavyset administrator, but apparently he could not resist one final warning. "Have you considered," he called as Michael picked up his duffel bag, "how many people may die because you have gone into the jungle?"

Michael met the older man's eye. "Have you considered how many may *not* die because I have gone?"

He moved past Garcia, gave Fortuna a brief wave, then strode out into the sweltering afternoon.

7 April 2003
6:40 a.m.

Alex pulled six pairs of clean socks from her suitcase, then tossed them into the shoulder bag she would carry on her foray into the jungle. She felt silly taking up valuable room for something as common as socks, but a week in the jungle had taught her that dry anklets were worth their weight in chocolate. Clean socks kept the feet dry, and wet socks did not stand a chance of drying in the equatorial humidity unless spread in the sun or hung in the dry heat of a wood fire. Better to take many pairs of clean socks and bury them at the end of the day than walk around with fungus factories producing mold between your toes.

She glanced across the bungalow, where Caitlyn had spread her belongings on her bed. "Don't forget the DEET," Alex warned. "Make sure you put your mosquito repellent in one of those side pockets. And don't forget

219

to spray the brim of your hat and the back of your neck before we set out. It won't stop all the mosquitoes, but it'll help."

Caitlyn screwed her face into the universal expression of preteen petulance. "You don't have to nag me."

"It's my job to nag you. Shoot, sometimes I wish I had someone to *nag* me."

Straightening, Alex mentally checked off the items on her list of things to pack: lots of socks, a water bottle with purification filters, her journal and two pens, a flashlight with extra batteries, matches sealed in a plastic bag, a camera also sealed in plastic, a rain poncho, insect repellent, a rain hat, sunglasses, a Swiss army knife, a compass, toilet paper, a mini toothbrush and toothpaste, a folded plastic tarp, a fresh pair of long pants, and an extra long-sleeved blouse, along with changes of rapid-dry underwear. What had she missed?

As she had anticipated, Kenneth Carlton had expertly risen to the challenge of mounting a deep jungle expedition. While the others continued their canopy work through the rest of the week, he and Lauren had remained at the lodge to send radio messages and assemble a team of support personnel for the mission to search for the healing tribe. Last night at dinner, Carlton had introduced the newcomers to the scientists, intending, Alex was certain, to put their minds at ease.

First Carlton introduced Michael Kenway, though most of the group had already met the physician from Iquitos. Caitlyn was thrilled to see the man again, and Alex felt the corner of her mouth droop when Kenway greeted her daughter with an affectionate hug. Tall, attractive, and affable, the man did have a way with children . . . but Alex wasn't completely certain she trusted him. Long experience with competitive researchers had taught her to be wary of other scientists, particularly if they were emotionally invested in an experiment's outcome. Kenway's personal history and his role in bringing the story to their attention almost guaranteed that he'd view any evidence they discovered from a biased perspective.

She couldn't deny her personal investment in the outcome of this venture, but she was too objective a researcher to be swayed by emotions, particularly as her time was growing short.

After Dr. Kenway, Carlton introduced Duke Bancroft and Raul Chavez, the two men in charge of security. Bancroft was an American, an ex–Navy SEAL, and he still wore the buzz cut Alex always associated with special-ops types. As burly and broad as a football player, Duke stood and greeted them with a cocky two-fingered salute. Alex frowned at the revolver at his belt. She was leery of all firearms, and who knew what sort of weapons the man carried beneath those baggy camouflage pants?

Bancroft's assistant, Raul Chavez, was Peruvian, and Alex was glad Carlton had the good sense to hire at least one national. Unlike Bancroft, who easily topped six feet, Chavez was compact and muscular. While Bancroft looked like he'd just stepped off a military base, Chavez wore a plain white T-shirt and green shorts. Glancing at his muscular legs, Alex saw no blades in ankle straps or guns in leather holsters, yet he still looked like a coiled snake ready to strike.

She made a mental note to position Caitlyn next to Chavez whenever possible.

The next newcomer stood with grave dignity when Carlton called his name. Alejandro Delmar, Carlton explained, was a professional Brazilian *sertanista,* or Indian tracker. "The Brazilians are trying to keep track of their indigenous population," Carlton added. "So they hire guys like Delmar to go into the jungle and search for lost tribes. Since that's what we're doing, I figured Delmar would be just the man we needed. Fortunately, he was able to clear his calendar and join us for a few days. Best of all —" Carlton's grin widened — "he speaks more languages than you can count, including Portuguese, English, Spanish, and several Indian dialects."

Delmar did not smile, but inclined his head, his grave eyes darting from face to face in the assembled group. He had dark hair and brown skin like the Peruvians Alex had met, yet a definite sense of otherness enveloped him. Perhaps it emanated from the leather pouch dangling from the belt around his waist. Though she had no idea what it contained, she could smell it from where she sat.

"That completes our team, then." Carlton rubbed his hands together. "The only people who will not be joining us on the expedition are the dirigible pilot, who will fly his blimp back to Iquitos, and Lazaro, who must remain at the lodge to play host to Mr. Myers's guests."

Alex glanced around the room — the Somerville sisters had departed on Saturday, replaced by two American father-and-son pairs who had arrived Sunday afternoon. The new guests, who were dining together at a table in the far corner of the room, sent occasional curious glances toward the expedition members.

Sighing, Alex shook her head. Though she desperately wanted her daughter nearby, the rational part of her brain had hoped that the incoming tour group would be chatty and female, women with whom Caitlyn would bond and feel comfortable. They would have offered Alex a second option for her daughter, but once again, life had dealt her a sour hand.

No way would Caitlyn want to hang out with two retired fathers and their middle-aged sons. Better all around, then, that she join the expedition.

Kenneth Carlton had looked around the group, his hands slightly upraised. "Any questions?" When no one answered, he had smiled again. "Good. Enjoy your dinner, and we'll see you on the dock at eight o'clock tomorrow morning. Breakfast, if you want it, will be served at seven."

Now Alex checked her watch — the sun had risen at five-forty. After sleeping maybe an hour, she had lain awake in the gloom and judged the day's advent by the gradual crescendo of birdcalls — every parrot in the forest seemed to sense the approaching sun and feel compelled to herald news of its arrival. Just as the noise became nearly deafening, the first rays of sunlight had appeared on the eastern horizon, pouring color back into the room where Caitlyn slept and Alex stared at the mosquito netting.

She shrugged away the frustrating reminder of her sleeplessness. Research had proven that FFI patients could carry a far greater sleep debt than ordinary people. If her symptoms were the result of early-stage FFI, she still had time to find a cure and begin its implementation. If she had to remain under the care of some village witch doctor until the protocol took effect, she would, and she'd make sure her daughter received treatment, too.

"Are you ready, Caitlyn?" She winced at the sharp edge of her voice. "Take your bag and run on down to the dining hall. I'll take a last look around and join you in a minute."

Caitlyn turned, her backpack dangling from her shoulders and her favorite stuffed monkey in her arms. "I'm ready."

Alex frowned at the stuffed animal. "I don't think it's a good idea to take Chester with us."

"But he's light! And I'll carry him the whole time, I promise. I won't ask you to take him, and I won't put him in your backpack —"

"He'll get wet, honey, and he won't dry properly in this humidity. Then he'll get moldy, and he'll start to stink. He might even get infested with lice or something, and then you won't be able to sleep with him."

"But —" Caitlyn's lower lip edged forward — "since I can't take a pillow, I thought I could take Chester. I've slept with him forever . . ."

Torn between reason and sentiment, Alex closed her eyes. It wasn't fair that her daughter had never known a father; it wasn't right that her grandmother had died such an awful and untimely death. Whoever wrote "God's in his heaven — all's right with the world" must have been verifiably insane.

"All right, take the monkey, but he's your responsibility. If you lose him, I don't want to see you cry."

Caitlyn clutched the monkey tighter. "Nothing bad will happen to him."

"Okay then." Alex jerked her thumb toward the door. "Scoot. Be sure to stop by the bathroom before you go to breakfast. We won't find any Porta-Pottis in the forest."

Caitlyn scurried out the door, letting it slam behind her. Alex took a last look around the room, bending to search under the bed. A cockroach scuttled into the shadows as she lifted her shoes. Shuddering, she carefully shook out each sneaker before putting it on to make sure no creepy crawlies had hidden themselves inside.

With her shoes laced tight, she placed her laptop into her suitcase. She would have loved to take it along, but she didn't want to subject it to damp and rough conditions.

After zipping her suitcase, she locked it and shoved it beneath her bed. The staff at Yarupapa had agreed to let the researchers leave their belongings in their rooms until their return — this was the slow season, Herman Myers explained, and they wouldn't need the space until June, when students descended in droves.

After a final survey of the bungalow, Alex slung her backpack over her shoulder then left the room and latched the door.

She found Caitlyn seated at a breakfast table next to Dr. Kenway. "Please," he called, spotting her. "Have a seat."

She hesitated when he pulled out the empty chair between himself and Kenneth Carlton. "What about Lauren?" She looked at her employer. "Will she be joining us?"

"Not for breakfast." He smiled, but a cynical tone underlined his causal reply. "When I woke she had four bags stacked by the door. When I told her she couldn't possibly carry four bags through the jungle, she laughed and said she figured I'd help her." He winked at Caitlyn. "She stopped laughing when I said each member of our party had to carry their own supplies. So now she's repacking in the bungalow. I expect she'll be ready just in time to join us on the dock."

As Alex slipped into the empty chair, one of the lodge's waiters lowered a steaming platter of waffles to the center of the table. Ignoring the food, Dr. Kenway gestured to the other men seated nearby. "Dr. Pace, have you met Raul and Duke?"

"Call me Alex, please." She smiled at the two newcomers, who had stood in her honor. "And please be seated. Though we didn't meet personally last night, I am glad to make your acquaintance. I'm feeling more at ease about this trip now that I know you've joined us."

"I'm sure there will be no cause for worry, Dr. Alex." Duke gave her a small salute as he settled back into his chair. "I've been on many a jungle expedition where we encountered nothing more dangerous than a three-toed sloth hanging from the trees — and he's only dangerous if he decides to urinate directly over your head."

"Really?" Not particularly eager to discuss treetop urination at breakfast, Alex gave him a bland smile.

"Maybe you did not see because you did not look." Raul grinned at his companion. "Me, I grew up in the jungle. I see everything, everywhere. But if I walk carefully, if I do not bother the jungle creatures, they do not bother me."

Alex speared a pair of waffles as Carlton passed the platter. "Do you live in Iquitos, Raul?"

"*Si, señora.* I have a wife and four children in the city."

"And you, Duke?"

The soldier grinned above a neck so thick that his head appeared to rest directly on his linebacker shoulders. "Shucks, ma'am, I couldn't live outside Texas if you paid me. Since retiring from active duty, I live in Dallas and take odd jobs like this just to fill my days."

"You have family in Texas?"

"A brother and sister. No wife, no kids, but I'd sure like to have them someday."

Alex looked away as she accepted a pitcher of syrup from Dr. Kenway, then caught him waggling his brows at her. *You heard it,* that waggle seemed to say. *The big guy's looking for a wife and kid.*

She scowled at him, then tipped the pitcher over her waffles and smiled at Duke. "You should get to know Deborah Simons, our team entomologist. She's from Texas, too. Your state seems to be brimming with pretty girls."

"I've seen a fair amount of pretty women here at the lodge, too."

Alex picked up her fork and studied her waffles. She was almost certain Kenway was chortling beside her.

Pretending an urgent need for private conversation, she leaned in to confront the doctor's merry expression. "Stop it. I'm sure he's not referring to me."

"How do you know?" His baritone lowered to a low rumble. "In case you haven't noticed, there are only four adult women on this expedition, and the anthropologist looks old enough to be Duke's grandmother. Carlton's mistress is obviously off-limits, so that leaves you and the insect expert."

She stared at him, then lowered her voice further. "How did you know Lauren was Carlton's mistress?"

He snorted softly. "Masculine body language transcends culture. I hadn't been here ten minutes before I realized Carlton would not be too keen on my spending time with

Miss Hayworth."

"Did you *want* to spend time with Miss Hayworth?"

He pulled back, regarding her with somber curiosity. "Dr. Pace, you astonish me. Is it ill-mannered Yankee curiosity that drives your question, or some desire on your part that I not spend time with the lady under discussion?"

Against her will, Alex felt rage rising in her cheeks. She wanted nothing more than to tell this man off, but too many people would freeze in mid-sentence to stare, including her daughter.

Grateful for the buzz of conversation around the table, she propped her head on her hand and met his gaze. "I really don't care where you spend your time. You may go to the devil for all I care, but it looks like we're going to be forced to travel in each other's company. So be nice, Dr. Kenway, and know this — I am not here to encourage any sort of masculine attention. I am here to find a cure for prion diseases."

His lips parted in what had to be pretended hurt. "I must apologize, Dr. Pace. Truthfully, I respect you as a serious researcher. The fact that our overly macho security guard finds you attractive is merely an entertaining diversion."

"You want entertaining?" Ignoring the stares of the others, she turned in her seat to face him directly. "I found some particularly interesting information on the Internet yesterday."

"The Internet? Here?" His blue eyes widened. "I didn't know they had power, let alone Internet access."

"I have a battery for my laptop and a satellite dish that can get me an uplink to a communications satellite during a two-hour window."

He shifted to face her. "Let me guess — those shadows under your eyes are the result of your tapping the computer keys at some godforsaken hour."

His words sent another tremor through her composure, but she kept a plastic smile on her face. "Thank you for noticing my less-than-perfect appearance, Dr. Kenway. And yes, last night I accessed the satellite."

"So what did your investigation turn up?"

She studied his face, trying to peer behind the pleasant smile he wore like a mask. Ordinarily she'd approach the topic with great discretion, but he had already lowered the bar of civil conversation.

She pressed her hands together. "I was curious as to why you knew so much about prions, so I typed your name into a search engine."

The smile flattened slightly. "And you discovered?"

"Your name linked with a vCJD patient —

Ashley Kenway, who died in 1996 at age twenty-seven. A vegetarian, the report said. A patient who hadn't eaten meat in eleven years."

Kenway turned to study his untouched plate. "My wife."

Alex looked away as the bitter gall of regret burned the back of her throat. Her barb had struck home; oddly, its effectiveness brought no pleasure.

"I'm sorry," she whispered. "I suspected the patient was a relative."

Kenway pulled his napkin from his lap and set it on the table. "Anything else you want to know, Dr. Pace?" he asked, keeping his voice low. "I have no secrets. As you have already discovered, my life and its heartbreaks are part of the public record."

Bracing herself to confront the pain in his eyes, the researcher in Alex pressed on. "How long was your wife symptomatic?"

"Less than a year. The strain was virulent and quick."

"Incubation time?"

"As you've surmised, at least eleven years. Unless, of course, prions passed through a chicken who ingested ground bone meal from an infected cow."

She quirked her brow. "So your wife ate poultry?"

"Never, but chicken droppings are used as fertilizer for vegetables. So Ashley either contracted the disease from prion-contaminated plant foods or she encountered a strain with an incubation span of more than eleven years."

Alex brought her hand up to push a hank of hair from her eyes, then checked to be sure Caitlyn was not eavesdropping. She wasn't — the girl was laughing with Duke Bancroft, who also seemed to have a soft spot for children.

"Long incubation times are not unusual for prion diseases." She pushed the words over her suddenly reluctant tongue. "The strain that causes fatal familial insomnia can incubate as long as sixty years."

He leaned back, frowning, then shook his head. "I've always heard that FFI and Gerstmann-Straussler-Scheinker disease are genetic."

"I don't think so. Why would one or two prion diseases be inherited when none of the others are? Consider the principle of Occam's razor — when two theories compete, the simpler is more likely to be correct."

Kenway propped his elbow on the table, then parked his chin in his hand. "Go on." His voice brimmed with interest.

Alex didn't hesitate. "Isn't it more likely that the supposedly genetic diseases are really long-incubating varieties? After all, incubation time and patterns of brain damage are the only observable differences in prion-based encephalopathies."

He did not answer, but his gaze shifted to his plate, then to Caitlyn, who had cupped her hand to whisper something in Duke's ear.

Alex felt a small, obscure twinge of unease. If she had discovered Kenway's secrets on the Internet, what might he have found out about her? Had she mentioned the cause of her mother's death in that long and rambling interview with the reporter from *El Tiempo*?

Of course, Kenway might not be thinking about Alex and Caitlyn at all. He might be staring off into space and Caitlyn's movement just happened to arrest his attention.

In a desperate attempt to direct his thoughts away from the hereditary aspects of prion diseases, Alex lightly tapped his arm. "Are you really a religious man, Doctor?"

He turned toward her. "I am."

"Then tell me this — did you pray for your wife when she was ill?"

He blinked, and she knew the question had struck at something deep within him.

"Do you always lob such personal queries at breakfast?"

"Anytime I can," she answered lightly. "It's the researcher in me. I've never believed in waffling around."

His eyes fell to her plate, where two soggy waffles sat in a pool of amber-colored syrup, then a soft smile curved his mouth.

"I begged," he said, his voice fainter than

air. "I entreated God every day, in every way I knew."

She crossed her arms. "Then I don't see how you can still call yourself religious. Your God failed you, Dr. Kenway."

"He didn't fail. He had another plan."

Shaking her head, she shifted to face the table. "To think I was worried about traveling with a religious zealot. Until you can prove that your almighty God is stronger than a minuscule prion, I'll trust you to keep the religious talk to a minimum."

He closed his eyes as his face rippled with anguish. "There are things you can't understand," he said after a long moment, "until you have a go at them yourself. I don't see Ashley's death as a defeat — in all important aspects, it was a victory."

"Sure it was." Hauling her gaze from his stricken face, Alex sliced a piece of her now-cold waffle with the edge of her fork. "I'm afraid I don't live in Bizzaro World, Dr. Kenway. I've 'had a go' at grief myself, and I will never be able to see a prion death as a victory. Not ever."

When he sighed and rubbed a hand across his face, she could hear the faint rasp of the stubble he had neglected to shave. "I will pray for you," he said finally, picking up his fork.

She thrust a forkful of waffle into her mouth, then forced it down in a hard swallow. "Save your prayers, Reverend Doctor.

235

Save everything. I appreciate all you've done so far, but at this point, I think it's best if you agree to come along and just observe. Be our team physician if you like. But leave the research and data collection to me."

A faint glint of humor filled his eyes. "You don't trust me?"

"I know how men are — since you've brought us this story, machismo honor will compel you to make us see a healing tribe even where one may not exist. I need a research partner who will be dispassionate and impartial — that's why I'm working with Dr. Baklanov."

Annoyance seemed to struggle with humor on his face as he picked up his knife and attacked his breakfast. "Whatever you say, Dr. Pace."

A fresh wave of guilt assaulted Michael as he watched Alexandra Pace help her daughter step from the dock into the boat that would carry them downstream. She'd caught him off guard at breakfast, disarming him with a couple of well-placed barbs and cutting his faith off at the knees.

Well, perhaps he was overstating the case a bit. His faith had proven itself strong enough to support him through the grief of Ashley's illness and death, so it could certainly withstand the stings of an American woman's acid tongue.

Still, he had felt woefully unprepared in the face of her ambush. But how could he explain faith to a woman who viewed her life through the unflinching eyes of reason? She'd spoken of grief — and he had no trouble believing she knew it well. Beneath that glib tongue and defensive posture, some sorrow had hardened her heart to everything but her daughter.

He ought to keep his distance, set a defensive perimeter around the woman and not venture closer than ten feet, but something about her piqued his interest. In less than five minutes' conversation she'd proven herself an expert on prion diseases in an era when few physicians knew much about them; in less than an hour she'd demonstrated her admirable devotion to her daughter. So she did have a soft side.

With luck, he might get better acquainted with it.

Blowing out his breath, he dropped his pack to the dock and looked around. Their traveling party of thirteen — an unlucky number, if one put stock in such things — was taking two boats downriver to Libertad, a small village near the spot where Ya-ree had stepped out of the jungle. From Libertad the team would set out on foot. They had no idea how long it would take to find Ya-ree's village, but a man with a perforated bowel could not have walked for more than twenty-four hours. After learning that information, Alejandro Delmar, the Brazilian tracker, estimated they would need five or six days to find the settlement they sought.

Just after the group finished breakfast, Delmar had spread a map of the area on a table and run his fingertip over a series of grids. "I have a GPS device," he said, pointing to a box hanging from his belt. "We will go into the jungle and move through the center of each square on this grid, looking for trails."

"What if there are no trails?" Deborah Simons interrupted.

Michael brought his hand up to cover a smile. The large-boned entomologist from Texas was as outspoken as Alexandra, but she lacked Dr. Pace's bite. He had liked her immediately.

"If there are people in the area," Emma answered, "we'll find trails. The jungle is impossible to penetrate without them."

Cocking his head to one side, Delmar tapped the map. "If we find nothing on the first pass, we will double back to a fixed location here, then press forward at a different angle, making a path through the jungle until we have completely covered the target area."

He tilted a brow at Carlton, who grunted in approval. "A good plan, Delmar. It shouldn't take long. If there are Indians living in the area, we'll find them. And if they have the cure we're looking for, well —" his grin widened — "we'll sweet talk it out of them, right?"

The anthropologist had groaned softly at that comment, but the group broke up and moved out to prepare for the journey.

Now Michael smiled in chagrin, mentally comparing the tiny compass in his bag with

Delmar's GPS, which could bounce a signal to a satellite in space, then reveal the latitude, longitude, and sometimes even the *altitude* of the device. Duke Bancroft and Raul Chavez also carried GPS devices, so the odds of anyone in their party becoming lost were virtually nonexistent, as long as they remained with the group.

He moved back as Louis Fortier, the effervescent French perfumer, stepped into the boat and took a seat on the bench next to Alexandra and Caitlyn. Duke Bancroft sat at the head of the boat, and Valerik Baklanov, the Russian, sat at the back with Milos Olsson and Tito, one of the young men from the lodge. Tito and Hector, regular "drivers" for Yarupapa, had agreed to take the group to Libertad and pick them up when summoned either by radio or messenger.

Michael hesitated on the dock. With a driver and six passengers each, both boats had been comfortably filled, so he was literally the odd man out. He glanced back at the second boat, then decided that given Caitlyn Pace's small size, logic dictated that he ride with the first group.

"Hope I'm not crowding anyone," he said, taking the single remaining seat on the right side of the boat. Settling his arms on the pack in his lap, he found himself almost knee-to-knee with Alexandra. She said nothing, but slipped one arm around her daughter while using the other to settle her straw hat more firmly upon her head.

Michael drew a deep breath. If the woman didn't defrost a little, this trip to Libertad would be very chilly indeed.

Propelled by Tito's oar, the boat moved away from the dock. When the young man started the outboard motor, Michael felt the vibration run through the boards beneath his feet. Scooping out two holes in the muddy brown water, the engine puttered steadily at the stern as they left the lodge behind.

For ten minutes they rode without speaking, each of them silently drinking in the sights of the river. Michael leaned back, propping an elbow on the gunwale, and marveled at the high-water marks on passing trees — amazing, that the river could rise and fall several meters within a matter of months.

Caitlyn Pace, imbued with a child's natural exuberance, quickly put an end to the silence. "Look, Mom — see those dots on that tree? They're fruit bats. They're sleeping now, but they'll fly away at sunset."

Michael suppressed a smile when Alexandra shivered dramatically at the thought.

Caitlyn turned on the bench, pointing out the distant gray rises of river dolphins, the calling macaw, and the occasional serpentine trail of a snake in the water. The girl was a virtual sponge, Michael decided, absorbing everything she saw and heard. While her mother had been bouncing around in the treetops, this girl had been learning from the guides at the lodge.

Caitlyn giggled when they passed an orchid-laden tree with marmosets scampering in its branches. As they slowed to maneuver around a submerged trunk in the river, Caitlyn reached out to pluck a green pod from an overhanging branch.

Alexandra put out a warning hand. "Be careful, honey."

"It's okay, Mom. Lazaro called this the medicine tree. And he showed me how to do this." With ease the girl cracked open the pod, then withdrew a yellow husk. "Lazaro said the boys use these for skipping stones — they count the number of skips, then tell each other that's how many wives they're going to have when they're thirty."

While Alexandra smiled indulgently, Caitlyn cracked the yellow husk, revealing a green seed shaped like a semicircle with scalloped edges. Grinning, she slipped her finger through a natural cleft in the seed, then clamped it on her earlobe.

Grinning at Michael, she lifted her hands to her head in a model's pose. "Neat, huh? Lazaro said the girls use these for earrings."

Michael nodded. "It's aces. A fetching color, actually."

"And totally free. Lazaro says the medicine tree grows everywhere."

"The medicine tree?" Alexandra bent to pick up one of the broken husks. "Did he say what else they use these for?"

Caitlyn shrugged. "He only talked about the stones and the earrings. I didn't ask about anything else."

"Hey, Olsson," Alexandra called. She held up the green seed. "Recognize this?"

The botanist grinned. "*Enterolobium cyclocarpum,* or elephant's ear tree. Very common in these parts."

Michael watched as Alexandra pulled one of the seeds from her daughter's earlobe, then sniffed at it. "They grow everywhere?"

"That's what he said. Look — they're all along the riverbank."

Michael turned. Caitlyn was right — apparently the tree was as plentiful as mosquitoes.

When he turned again, Alexandra's eyes were abstracted and distant. "If they're abundant . . ."

"They're probably not what we're looking for," Michael finished her thought. "But it wouldn't hurt to test a sample, would it?"

They rode in silence for a while. When Caitlyn hung one arm over the boat to trail her fingertips in the water, Michael asked, "Aren't you worried about piranha?"

She grinned. "Lazaro says they won't bite you unless you're bleeding. He's never been bitten and he swims in the water all the time."

"She's braver than I am." Alexandra met Michael's eye. "I cringe when I think about all the creatures living in this river. And when I remember that it also serves as a sewer for nearly every family in the jungle —" She shuddered again, and this time Michael did not think she was pretending.

Jerking her thumb over her shoulder, she gestured to Baklanov, who was puffing on a cigarette as if his life depended upon it. "Dr. Baklanov specializes in bacteriophages. He would have a grand time analyzing the bacteria and viruses populating this water."

Upon hearing his name, the Russian coughed, then leaned forward to join in the conversation. "I came here to look for new phages in the canopy." He gave Michael a conspiratorial smile. "But now that we have arranged to take a side trip, I will gather samples that might contain new phages wherever we find, um, interesting situations. It is not often that a Russian from Tbilisi has an opportunity to study in a tropical forest."

"It's not often that I do, either," Michael answered, glad to find someone willing to engage in relaxed conversation. "I spend most of my time in Iquitos — it's a nice city, but sometimes the workload drives me mad. We have too many patients and not enough doctors."

Baklanov rested his elbows on his knees. "I've been meaning to ask — what brought you to this place?"

Michael stretched one arm along the edge of the boat. "After my wife died, I took a brief sabbatical. One of my mates suggested a trip to the rainforest — at the time, he could have suggested the moon and I'd have signed on. Anyway, within a fortnight I found myself in Peru. I spent a week in the jungle doing tourist things, then made my way back to Iquitos. I was there, waiting for my flight to Lima, when I decided to see a bit of the city. I wandered around for a while, then stopped into a riverfront café and ordered a pizza and lemonade."

His voice softened with the memory. "I ate a few slices of pizza and left the rest sitting on the table — didn't have much of an appetite, I suppose, in the heat. Then the waitress came over and said something in Spanish — the only word I caught was *niño*."

"Little boy," Caitlyn supplied.

Michael smiled. "Indeed. In my confusion, I thought the waitress was asking if I wanted her to wrap up the remaining pizza to take back to my little boy. I tried to explain that I didn't have any *niños,* and somehow she realized her mistake. 'No,' she said, *'este niño'* — and she pointed to one of the street urchins who'd been trying like the dickens to polish my shoes.

"The truth hit me like a blow between the eyes — the boy was one of the many orphan children who live on the streets of Iquitos. She meant the food for him, and it might have been the only meal he'd receive that day."

He looked up to see Alexandra watching him, lines of concentration deepening along her brows. Caitlyn was listening with her mouth open in a perfect O, and Baklanov's eyes had gone damp.

He gave them a rueful smile. "I handed over my plate, and instantly regretted that I'd eaten as much as I did. I ordered a pitcher of lemonade, too, then called the boy over to sit with me while he drank and ate his dinner."

Shrugging, Michael let his gaze drift over the brown velvet river. "I knew I couldn't feed every street child, but I could do something to help this one. The poor boys wore old T-shirts and shorts; most had bare feet. They made a living washing tourists' shoes with river water they carried in empty pop bottles . . . and when they were sick, they had no one to care for them."

He shifted to meet Alexandra's eyes. "That's when I decided to spend a year or two in Iquitos. The people here are so desperate for help, no one protested when I arrived at the hospital and announced that I'd come to work. They found me an office, threw open the door, and suddenly I had more patients than I knew how to handle. Word got around, and soon everyone came to see me — children, old people, Indians, tourists. I've been in Peru three years now, and I can't say I've ever experienced what we'd call a routine day back in London."

Alexandra Pace cleared her throat and looked away.

"Wow." Admiration shone in Caitlyn's eyes. "I'll bet you speak excellent Spanish."

Michael laughed. "I'm afraid I'm not too keen on languages. My nurse speaks English, though, and translates for me when necessary. The others on staff take pity on me and speak slowly. Sometimes we resort to sign language."

"Dr. Kenway." Baklanov adjusted his cap to better shade his face as he turned toward Michael. "I'm interested in these prion diseases you and Alexandra are investigating. I have spent my life researching the invisible world, but I have never encountered these prions you speak of. I wasn't sure I believed in their existence until Alex showed me photographs."

Michael crossed his legs, resting one ankle on his knee. "I thought you were an expert on the subject, Dr. Baklanov. Dr. Pace has assured me that you and she are working together on this expedition —"

"Bah! I know nothing!" Baklanov sent Alexandra a look of bewildered incredulity. "Accept this man's help, my stubborn friend. Leave me to my phages; we will not get in

247

your way."

Michael stole a brief look at Alexandra — the woman's cheeks had flushed crimson, yet she continued to look out over the water as if she hadn't heard a word of the conversation.

Granting her mercy, Michael answered the Russian doctor's first question. "Unfortunately, Dr. Baklanov, I know about prions from firsthand experience. Still, I can understand your reluctance to accept them."

"Their structure makes no sense to me." The Russian knocked the glowing ashes of his cigarette into the river. "Every known living organism uses molecules of nucleic acid to carry information it needs to reproduce, yet these proteins do not contain nucleic acid. How can they reproduce at all?"

Caitlyn screwed her face into a question mark. "Remind me about nucleic acid, please?"

"DNA or RNA." Grinning, Michael lifted his eyes to meet her mother's. "How much do you know about how life begins?"

"She knows the truth." Alexandra waved in a deliberately casual movement. "We don't talk about birds and bees, for instance. She knows the proper terms."

"Right." Deciding to test the woman's assertion, Michael bent to Caitlyn's level. "Long ago, biologists used to think tiny little men lived inside human sperm. Using crude microscopes, they actually claimed to have seen these little fellows, or homunculi, as they called them. Supposedly, these little men settled in a female egg cell, ate the yolk, and grew big within the woman's womb."

Caitlyn giggled. "That's crazy. Everybody knows about chromosomes and the double helix."

Michael looked at her mother again. "How old is this child?"

"Ten," Alexandra answered, "going on thirty."

"Quite." Returning to Caitlyn's level, Michael continued his explanation. "In time, of course, biologists wised up and began setting things to rights. They finally figured out that cells — and chromosomes — contained DNA, the building blocks that could create a person. Obviously, you know about the double helix that separates when a cell divides."

Caitlyn shrugged. "I studied all that two years ago."

Baklanov gazed at the girl in rapt admiration. "Amazing."

"Well," Michael continued, "not every part of your body needs the entire DNA sequence — you are also composed of proteins, hundreds of different varieties. These proteins do the mechanical and chemical work of the body, and they are formed from RNA, which comes from DNA. These proteins do not contain nucleic acid, but they do have a proper structure. Imagine, if you will, one of those toy necklaces made of beads that snap together. The pattern in which they are joined affects how they perform in the body."

He had thought he'd lose her in the complicated explanation, but the girl nodded, thought working in her eyes.

Michael took a deep breath. "A protein, you see, doesn't reproduce like a virus or bacteria because it's nothing but bare beads, so to speak. Most of the time proteins are mass-produced by the body, and all of them are normal, snapped together in just the right formation. But occasionally the body will absorb a different protein — one composed of exactly the same materials, but snapped together in a different pattern. From that moment on, all the body's newly manufactured proteins begin to model themselves after the mutated one. We call the one that causes all the trouble a prion."

He squinted at Caitlyn. "I'm assuming you know what *mutated* means."

"Altered, transformed, transmuted." She frowned up at him. "But what caused it to be different?"

"I haven't the faintest idea."

"No one knows what triggers the mutation." Shooting Michael a glance of grudging respect, Alexandra entered the conversation. "Some have theorized that the process has something to do with crystals — like ice."

Baklanov's forehead crinkled. "Would you mind explaining that one?"

Caitlyn clapped her hands. "I get it! It's like water — two molecules of hydrogen, one of oxygen. At room temperature, H_2O is liquid. Above boiling, it becomes steam. Below freezing, it's ice. Three different forms of the same molecular composition."

"That's close, honey." Alexandra gave her daughter a smile. "But prions are a little more complicated. The process of crystallization occurs in our bodies all the time. It's through crystallization that our bodies turn the calcium in milk into teeth and bones. Because the process has been fine-tuned through evolution, our bodies know that teeth require one organic structure while bones need another. There's an atomic pattern, sort of like a blueprint, that these proteins follow in order to reproduce."

When Caitlyn blinked, Michael suspected that for the first time in a long time the girl had been handed information she couldn't instantly absorb.

He bent to peer into Caitlyn's eyes. "I wouldn't place much stock in that talk about evolution. I happen to believe it's blarney."

"Ignore him, dear." Leaning forward, Alexandra curved her upturned palm into a cup. "If you had a handful of marbles and you dropped them in my palm, how would they stack up?"

251

As Caitlyn stared at her mother's hand, Michael could almost see her mental computations — *three marbles across the fingers, perhaps four across the palm, the next row would stack in the concave spaces, a third row might fit before they began to spill over the edge of her mother's thumb . . .*

Caitlyn made a face at the imaginary marbles. "I figure you could stack thirty-three before they would begin to fall out of your hand."

Alexandra laughed. "That's good, honey, but I asked you *how* they would stack up. In order to figure the amount, you had to visualize how they would lie in my palm, right? So the answer is more oblique — the arrangement of the stack would depend upon the layout of the bottom layer."

Confusion clouded Caitlyn's eyes for a moment, then her face brightened. "Of course!"

Alexandra turned to Baklanov. "Crystals reproduce according to an atomic template. If that template is mutated, the resulting structures will pattern themselves after the mutation. We think that's how prions reproduce. One foreign template enters the body — probably from the ingestion or insertion of foreign prions — and every protein the brain produces from that point is also mutated. These proteins do not function properly, so brain cells begin to die. In time, the death of these cells creates holes in the brain.

And without a brain . . ." Her eyes darkened as her voice faded away.

Michael snapped his fingers as a thought occurred. "It's like *Cat's Cradle!*"

Three perplexed faces swiveled toward him.

"A Kurt Vonnegut novel — I read it during my adolescent science fiction phase. In the story, a scientist creates a new variety of ice that melts at 114.4 degrees Fahrenheit. Trouble is, whenever the stuff — he called it *ice-nine* — touched anything liquid, it turned the liquid into ice-nine."

Caitlyn grinned. "Cool."

Michael shook his head. "Not really. One character touched the ice-nine to his tongue, and his body — composed mainly of water, as all our bodies are — immediately froze solid. When the ice-nine encountered the ocean, all the seas and everything in them froze. Every river that ran to the ocean, every raindrop that touched the damp soil turned to ice-nine. That scientist's little invention spelled the end of life on earth."

Alexandra gave him a brief, distracted glance. "I haven't read that book, but I can appreciate the metaphor. Yes, prions might operate in the same way. Depending upon the pattern, they can clog the heart or the brain, and in time the living organism is . . . well, it's too diseased to function."

Two deep worry lines appeared between Caitlyn's brows, but she didn't look up at her mother. Instead she turned and studied the riverbank, signaling through body language that she had grown bored with the conversation.

Alexandra's eyes swept over her daughter's form, and for an instant Michael thought he saw a flicker of pain in those expressive depths. But then she looked toward the shore, too, her hand rising to adjust the brim on her straw hat.

Taking his cue from the women, Michael stared at the floor and surrendered to the silence that had settled over the boat. He couldn't help but wonder, though, why a woman as bright and competitive as Alexandra Pace would delve into a frantic study of diseases that until recently had struck fewer than one person in a million.

As the boat drew near the village of Libertad, Alex realized that the settlement had little in common with San Miguel, a village that had profited by its proximity to Yarupapa Lodge and a steady influx of tourists. While community buildings populated the outskirts of San Miguel, Libertad had no visible school, church, medical clinic, or jailhouse.

From her perspective, the community consisted of little more than a scattered collection of thatched structures on stilts. From the half-walls framing the fronts of the buildings, dark-eyed children peered at the approaching visitors and ducked shyly away when spotted.

The drivers from Yarupapa cut the engines as they entered the village, then propelled the boats through the flooded development with oars. The river did not recede here, Tito explained, until late May or early June. Until

255

dry land appeared, people traveled from house to house by canoe.

Alex's stomach shriveled when she realized they cleaned their floors, scrubbed their clothes, and fed their families with fish from the same river that served as their sewer.

As they drifted through the village, she saw a toddler playing at the edge of a floating dock, unsupervised except for a little girl who couldn't have been more than three or four.

She turned to face the young man handling the engine. "What if the baby falls in, Tito?"

Something in her must have expected him to reply that children were taught to swim during infancy, for his answer surprised her. "The girl will call for help," he said, his brown eyes sweeping the scene, "but many babies die."

What sort of mothers were these women? Alex drew a breath, about to ask where the child's mother was, then abruptly shut her mouth. After a week in this place, she *knew* where the mother was — in the house, cooking over an open fire banked on a mud-baked slab, caring for other children, or working feverishly to string grass seed beads into some little ornament a tourist might want to buy. No one could accuse the women of these villages of wasting time on the telephone or in front of a television.

Tito called out to a young girl who had stepped out to the front porch; the girl replied

256

in Spanish and pointed toward another structure at the edge of the settlement. After stopping at this house and asking more questions, Tito and Hector cranked the engines and reentered the main stream of the river, pointing the two boats to a lone building about half a mile away on the riverbank. This home, Tito told them, belonged to Julio and Maria, who had chosen to live outside the village.

The elevated building looked like all the others, except perhaps a bit larger. Bare spots yawned through the thatched roof and the half-wall along the front of the home, but dry grass covered the land between the supporting stilts. Squawking chickens raced under the floorboards, entertaining a quartet of children who squatted on the grass.

"So many children," Baklanov observed, smoothing his beard.

Tito shrugged. "Unlike you, our people have nothing to do after dark but make babies."

Rolling her eyes, Alex propped her chin on her fist and scanned the area for signs of an adult. These men would think twice about making babies if they had to carry them, nurse them, and bend over a bulging stomach to harvest meager crops.

As the boats pulled up to the muddy shoreline, she noticed that this family appeared to have a bounty of crops. A stand of banana trees grew at the side of the house, and another tree she didn't recognize sagged with heavy green fruit.

"Papaya," Tito said, following her gaze.

Of course.

They disembarked. As Duke Bancroft, Tito, and Alejandro Delmar went in search of the man who had first encountered Kenway's patient, Alex slipped her backpack over her shoulder, then helped Caitlyn with her bundle. They stepped onto the ground and walked along the shoreline, enjoying the opportunity to stretch their legs.

"Now begins the adventure," she whispered in her daughter's ear. "Are you ready?"

Caitlyn grinned, her bright brown eyes narrowing to slits above a sea of freckles. "You bet!"

The other boat's passengers disembarked as well. While most of the passengers paced in the grass, Kenneth Carlton and Raul Chavez hurried to the house. Alex watched them go with a wry smile — Julio and Maria might have to repeat the story for both sets of passengers. Men like Kenneth Carlton always wanted to hear things for themselves.

As the pair of men climbed the ladderlike steps into the house, Lauren stood quietly on the shore, her head lowered and her arms crossed over her chest. Alex noticed that the young woman wore suitable clothing for travel in the tropics — khaki trousers and a long-sleeved cotton shirt much like Alex's. Instead of a wide-brimmed hat, however, a Braves baseball cap hid most of her hair, leaving the sides of her face and neck vulnerable to mosquitoes.

Alex looked away, resisting the temptation to roll her eyes. Poor Lauren probably thought the baseball cap was cute — or maybe Carlton had given it to her. Either way, she'd be suffering from mosquito bites soon enough.

Several moments passed before the landing parties came out of the house. They exchanged polite farewells with Julio and his wife, both of whom kept looking toward the boats with wary eyes. Alex knew they'd be relieved to see the researchers go away.

Carlton assembled his team on the shore. "Our jungle man," he began, and for a fleeting instant Alex wondered when Ya-ree had become *their* jungle man, "exited the forest about twenty yards to the south. Julio says the fellow promptly passed out, so I'm afraid we will learn nothing new from these people. But that's okay. We have our starting position." He looked around, then winked at Lauren. "As they say, friends, it's time to make tracks. Let's move out."

"I suggest we walk two abreast," Duke Bancroft added, taking control as he appraised their group with a narrowed gaze. "Let Delmar and I take the point, while Chavez guards the rear. We'll be looking for tracks in the grass, and we don't want to risk anything being trampled until we've had time for a good look."

As the members of her group gathered their belongings, Alex paused to thank Tito and Hector for the ride to Libertad, then slipped an arm about Caitlyn's shoulder. Amazing, how exhaustion could make her arm feel as though it had become as heavy as lead.

"It's just like the Wild West, isn't it, Mom?" Caitlyn asked, grinning. "Indian tracks in the dust and all that?"

"Not quite the same, I don't think," Alex answered. "For one thing, nearly a week has passed since that poor man appeared. Things grow quickly here, and you've already seen how active the animals are. I'll be surprised if they find any tracks at all."

Struggling to stand upright against a tide of weariness, Alex followed Bancroft and Delmar into the jungle. With no visible breaks in the foliage, the men used machetes to cut a trail, the crack and rustle of their efforts disturbing the steady insect hum of the woods. The team would have made slow progress even if they had not had to clear a path, for a hiker had to be mindful of protruding roots, tangling vines, and threatening wildlife. In this edge habitat, where the river permitted abundant light, they would travel slowly through the thick and varied plant growth, a fact for which Alex felt deep and extreme gratitude. Once they left the river and entered areas crowned by dense canopy, hiking would become easier because only herbs, ferns, seedlings, and fungi grew in the shadows.

Moving slowly, however, proved as tiring as walking at a brisk pace. Once Alex stumbled and made the mistake of grasping an overhanging vine for support. Though she clung to the vine for only a moment, a line of ants filed onto her hand. She yelped as one of them stung her, then frantically swatted them away. "Ouch! Ants!"

A step ahead, Caitlyn turned to cast her mother a reproachful glance. "Lazaro warned us. There are all kinds of ants in the jungle, and most of them bite. Carnivore ants can strip a body down to the bone in a matter of hours."

"Thank you, Caitlyn, for the biology lesson." Holding her injured hand close to her side, Alex lowered her head and moved forward, deciding to walk closer to the leaders.

At the front of the line, Delmar and Bancroft pushed slowly and steadily forward, looking for openings that might indicate a trail. Alex realized Ya-ree would have looked for openings, too, especially if he were in danger. Though plants grew with amazing speed in the tropical environment, people and animals still managed to establish paths and canoe trails through the rainforest.

"Mom? You mind if I go talk to Mr. Fortier?"

Alex glanced up at the perfumer, who walked immediately behind Bancroft and Delmar. The little Frenchman had proven himself plucky and clever, yet his decision to shadow two men armed with machetes also attested to his common sense.

Alex nodded her permission. Better that Caitlyn should walk with Louis than notice her mother's increasing weariness. "Go ahead, kiddo."

Jogging ahead, Caitlyn caught up with Louis, who began to regal her with stories of where and when he had discovered famous fragrances. Their double lines shifted and relaxed, and a few moments later Alex found herself walking beside Deborah Simons.

She glanced down at Alex's arm. "I heard you got bit. You okay?"

"I think so." Alex held up her hand for Deborah's inspection. "Stung like the dickens, though."

Deborah caught Alex's wrist and studied the red welt. "Some ants can really pack a wallop. The bite of the tocandira, a giant about an inch long, results in twenty-four hours of pain and fever. But that ant is native to Venezuela, not Peru."

"I hope the ant who bit me wasn't a visiting tourist, then."

Deborah released Alex's wrist. "This welt should be gone by sundown. If you don't have Benadryl, ask me when we stop for a break. I know I have some in my kit."

Alex thanked her with a smile. "I never travel without it."

"That's good." Deborah peered toward the front of the line, then lowered her voice. "So? What do you think of our Mr. Bancroft?"

"The commando?" Though she wasn't in the mood for girl talk, Alex forced a laugh. "He's all right, I guess."

Deborah lifted a brow. "Don't tell me you didn't notice how he was flirting with you."

Alex would have stopped dead in her tracks if not for fear of being run over by Milos Olsson, who was panting heavily behind her. "You're kidding, right?"

"My dear Alex," Deborah said, grinning, "you've had your eye to a microscope far too long. Do you even remember how the game is played?"

Alex frowned. "I hardly think this is the time or place for games."

"Any time, any place is appropriate when the propagation of the species is a priority." Deborah smiled at Bancroft's broad back. "Even the Bible says we are to go forth and multiply."

"We've multiplied enough, I think. Last

time I checked, the planet had more hungry children than it needs."

Deborah heaved a sigh, then ducked beneath a spider web hanging like a silken parachute from a branch. "You're right about that, I suppose, but still . . . I hope to find a little romance before I'm too old to enjoy it." Her voice softened. "At least you have a child. My biological clock is rapidly winding down, and the Lord hasn't yet seen fit to bring a husband and children my way. Sometimes I wonder if a family is in his plan for me."

Beneath the brim of her sheltering hat, Alex cringed. Deborah Simons could spend her last breath blaming God for her lack of children, but Alex had a hunch the strait-laced entomologist had never even lost her virginity. "Wake up and join the twenty-first century," she muttered under her breath.

"Beg pardon?"

"I said you can have Mr. Bancroft if you want him. I'm not interested."

"Oh." A moment of thoughtful silence, then: "Maybe you have your eye on someone else? Dr. Kenway, for instance?"

"Good grief, we're not in high school." From beneath her hat, Alex shot her companion a black look. "I have no time for anything but my work and my daughter — can't you understand that?"

Deborah tilted her head back, her eyes narrowing. "You don't have to get riled up about

it. I was just trying to make conversation."
She shook her head. "Too bad. You're an
intelligent woman with a lot to offer. And
your kid deserves a father."

Alex snorted. "She has a father, a deadbeat
who doesn't deserve the title. And while I appreciate your interest in my emotional well-
being, I can assure you that I am content with
my life."

"Sorry — didn't mean to pry." Deborah
walked a while in silence, then lowered her
head to meet Alex's eye. "If you're not
interested in Duke, then you won't mind if I
talk to him a while?"

Alex wriggled her fingers in farewell.
"Knock yourself out."

As the entomologist pushed her way
through the line, Caitlyn slid back into step
beside her mother.

She grinned up at Alex. "I heard some of
that."

"Really? I wish you hadn't."

"She had a point, Mom. Your life shouldn't
be all work and no play."

"I play a lot."

"Like when?"

"Like . . . when you and I have fun together."

"We do word games and crossword puzzles.
Those don't rank very high in the field of
mindless entertainment."

"Mindless entertainment is vastly overrated. The world is filled with loads of more important things."

They walked without speaking while an oriole practiced his trills somewhere in the canopy overhead. As Alex bent to step under an overhanging branch, Caitlyn said, "Love is important, isn't it? I mean . . . man-woman love?"

Straightening, Alex found herself torn between maternal instincts and self-defensiveness. "Well," she waited until Caitlyn had passed under the branch, "sure it is, honey. And I've had that kind of love. I was in love with your father, and I gave that relationship all I could give. Then you came along and I adored you while your father . . . well, by that time he didn't want to love me anymore. He loved you, but he didn't have time for either of us. Our breakup wasn't your fault, and I don't think it was my fault, either. He just walked away and never looked back."

Shadows lurked in Caitlyn's brown eyes when she looked up again. "Do you miss him?"

"Not anymore, no. My heart is filled with you."

She reached out, intending to slip an arm around Caitlyn's shoulder, but the girl artfully dodged the gesture.

"I think Dr. Kenway must be a lot like my dad."

Feeling suddenly limp with weariness, Alex

266

made a face. "Why would you think that?"

"Well, Dad was intelligent, right? And Dr. Kenway's very intellectual."

Alex blew out her cheeks. "I suppose they are both smart men."

"And Dad was handsome, right? I think Dr. Kenway is very handsome. He could be on TV playing Tarzan or something."

Rolling her eyes, Alex thanked the stars above that Kenway walked at the back of the line, well out of hearing range. "Yes, they're both handsome in their way. But Kenway looks nothing like your dad. Your dad was medium height, with blond hair and blue eyes. Your doctor friend's eyes are blue, but they're darker . . . and sometimes they're a little scary. And all that hair?" She pretended to shudder.

Caitlyn tossed her head. "I don't think he's scary. I think he's the nicest man in this group. And I like his hair."

Alex pressed her lips together as a moment of understanding dawned. Caitlyn's sudden fixation on Michael Kenway had to be a preadolescent crush. After all, Alex had been about ten when emotional infatuation hit her for the first time. She had fallen in deep and desperate love with Johnny Quest, not even minding that he was only a cartoon character.

Softening her tone, she smiled down at her daughter. "You're right, honey, Dr. Kenway seems to be a nice man. A little too religious for my taste, but nice."

Her daughter's left brow rose a fraction. "Would you ever marry him?"

"Not in a million years. But that's okay — you can still be his friend. I think we can trust him with friendship, don't you?"

She had hoped this limited approval would lighten Caitlyn's heart, but though her daughter smiled in response, tiny worry lines remained in the center of her ten-year-old forehead.

"He'd make a good father," she said, her voice distracted. "And he likes kids."

"I'm sure he does, honey, but when a man and woman get married, it's important that they like each other more than anyone else in the world. And right now I'm pretty sure I'm not on Dr. Kenway's list of favorite people."

Caitlyn said nothing, but walked ahead, her eyes on the ground. Alex followed, her internal alarm systems on full alert. Something was not right with her daughter.

Caitlyn had never been good at keeping secrets, and behind her pasted smile a suggestion of melancholy radiated like some dark aura.

What could be bothering the child? Was it possible . . . no, Caitlyn was bright, but she could not have picked up any clues about Alex's threatening illness. She had been too young to remember her grandmother's symptoms, and Alex had been careful to hide every sign, every fear.

She swiped her damp bangs from her forehead, then saw her daughter glance back to the place where Kenway walked with the Peruvian soldier. So that was it, then. Caitlyn had developed a crush on the doctor, and Alex's lack of support had splashed those tender feelings with a cold dose of reality.

This would pass, surely. Unlike some diseases, adolescence was not terminal.

7 April 2003
4:12 p.m.

Michael groaned as he slid his pack from his back, then lifted his arms to stretch his tired muscles. They had traveled through several kilometers of canopy forest, then found themselves in another stretch of edge habitat. Knowing that water had to lie somewhere nearby, Delmar pressed through the thick foliage until an inky ribbon appeared. Pausing there, he decided to establish an overnight camp on a stretch of riverbank.

"Hang your hammocks in the surrounding trees, and secure the mosquito netting while light remains," Delmar had called, his grin revealing the gold surrounding his two front teeth. "We wouldn't want the bats or mosquitoes carrying you away tonight."

"Ken?" Lauren's whine carried across the clearing. "Is he serious?"

Grateful for the day's end, Michael opened his pack and pulled out the lightweight field hammock Carlton had given him earlier that morning. The ultramodern sleeper weighed only fifteen ounces, including support ropes, mosquito netting, and detachable rain fly.

As Bancroft and Chavez set about hacking away at the shrubby vegetation, Michael moved to a pair of trees and tied on his hammock. Once it was secure, he dropped his bag into the center of the fabric, then carefully lowered the mosquito netting over his bed and backpack. Though he was keen to learn about the jungle through firsthand experience, he wasn't particularly eager to share his bed with an assortment of insects and vermin.

Slipping his hands into his pockets, he looked around to see how he could help the others. Carlton was building a fire in a small clearing, while Delmar stood at the water's edge sharpening a narrow branch.

He walked toward Delmar, intending to offer his help, but he couldn't help but notice that Alexandra and her daughter were struggling to secure their hammocks. An inner voice warned him away, but the girl looked as though she would welcome his help.

Locking his hands behind his back, he changed direction and approached them. "Can I offer my assistance?"

"No, thanks. We'll manage." Alexandra's words came from behind clenched teeth, so he winked at Caitlyn and moved on to the river.

Delmar was tying a hook onto a length of monofilament as Michael approached. The Indian tracker glanced up, then held out the line. "Feel like fishing, Doctor?"

"I'd be happy to have a go at it if you'll tell me how it's done."

The man's mouth twisted in something not quite a smile. "The waters here are dark and still — perfect for piranha. Just tie the empty end of that line to a branch, then thrash it in the water. Bait it with a grub you've smeared with some blood from your finger; soon you'll have fresh meat to bait the hook."

Michael pulled his hunting knife from its leather sheaf, then cut a thin branch from one of the riverside shrubs. By the time he had securely tied the monofilament to the branch, Delmar and Bancroft already had lines dangling above the water.

The big Texan, however, looked a trifle nervous about approaching the water's edge.

"Watch, amigos." Delmar thrashed the tip of his stick in the water, then let the blood-smeared beetle on his hook drop into the water with a plop. Barely an instant later, the stick bent and the guide flipped his trophy onto the shore — a six-inch red-bellied piranha, whose razor teeth gleamed in the setting sunlight.

The guide grinned up at Michael. "He will

bite you if you do not kill him. Do you know how to do that?"

Michael fingered the handle of his knife. "With a blade?"

"No. Like this." While Michael and Bancroft watched, Delmar picked up the piranha by the tail, then tilted his head and sank his teeth into the spine just behind the gills. Within seconds, the toothy jaws stopped moving.

"Now I use my blade." After tossing the fish onto a broad leaf, the Brazilian picked up his machete and chopped the fish into several bloody pieces. He tossed one of the silvery bits to Michael. "Put that on the end of your hook, Doctor, and we will have dinner within minutes."

The guide's words proved prophetic. Michael baited his hook, beat the water with his stick, and lowered the meat into the inky blackness. A moment later a piranha jerked on the end of his line.

Conscious of the other men's eyes upon him, he swung the fish up, caught it by the flipping tail, and tilted his head. Though it unnerved him to breathe in the fishy scent and know that razor-sharp jaws were snapping only inches from his face, it would be far easier to kill the fish before removing his hook from its jaw.

The other men cheered as he bit down. Grinning in an acute combination of embarrassment and victory, he tossed the dead fish to Chavez, who had poured oil into a skillet.

Cheered on by Michael's accomplishment, Olsson, Baklanov, and even Fortier dropped lines into the water.

"The women aren't going to like this." Bancroft looked up at Michael and winked. "Should we tell 'em they're eating catfish or grouper?"

"You'd have to cut the heads off." Michael glanced dubiously at the growing pile of toothy corpses. "Without the head, we won't have much to cook."

"We eat them all," Delmar insisted. "Except the teeth, and our women save those for *tijeras*."

"I'm sorry — what?"

Delmar's forehead wrinkled as he sought the word. "Tijeras — you know, to cut things. Strings and yarn."

"Scissors." Michael supplied the word as he studied a piranha's jaw. "Hinged scissors. Brilliant."

As the sun sank over the treetops and the canopy began to flutter with nocturnal life, Carlton assembled the team around the campfire. He, Chavez, Delmar, and Bancroft were carrying a few bags of rice as emergency provisions, he explained, but these would not last more than a few days. In order to travel light, they would eat foods provided by the jungle. "Like piranha," he finished, pointing to the steaming skillet.

"I hate fish." Lauren Hayworth's voice cut through the rattle of insects in the hot air. "I'd rather starve."

"Stop complaining, Lauren," Carlton snapped. "Eat what you're given and be grateful for it."

Michael looked up in time to see Miss Hayworth's jaw drop, then he leaned back to let the women approach the fire. With the somber dignity of a chef at a four-star restaurant, Chavez served piranha to his companions. Delmar thoughtfully chopped the heads off a pair of fish for Caitlyn.

Aside from the whimpering Miss Hayworth, the other women seemed to be in good spirits. Alexandra nibbled at her fish with her eyes closed while Deborah Simons held hers aloft, staring at it as if it were a unique entomological specimen caught in one of her traps. Emma Whitmore ate stoically, with only an occasional disdainful glance in Lauren Hayworth's direction. She did, however, discreetly spit out the eyes.

He watched, amused, while Caitlyn Pace flipped her decapitated fish over several times, then touched it with her tongue. Seeing her grimace, he walked over and squatted before her.

"How is it?"

She rolled her eyes. "Tastes like sardines, I guess. Maybe anchovies. And I'd give anything for a pizza to put under this thing."

Michael tapped her on the shoulder. "I was rather hoping you'd be brave enough to have a go at it first. That way I'll know if it's edible."

Rising to the challenge, Caitlyn closed her eyes, pinched her nostrils with two fingers, and took a big bite. Her nose crinkled, then after a moment she removed her hand and began to chew.

"I was right." She looked at him, smiling as she swallowed. "We do need a pizza."

Michael laughed. Gripping his dinner behind the gills, he ate it as cautiously as he'd killed it. He found the fish bony, crunchy, and a wee bit salty, but his ravenous appetite appreciated the food.

"Tell you what," he told Caitlyn, who watched him with wide eyes. "When we make it back to civilization, the pizza's on me. Deal?"

Caitlyn laughed, then cast a guilty glance in her mother's direction. "Deal!"

After dinner, Alex watched in profound admiration as Duke Bancroft and Milos Olsson used a slingshot to propel a weighted rope over a high branch, then tied Chavez's pack of supplies and cooking gear to the end of the line.

When the line dangled four feet off the ground, Delmar opened the foul-smelling leather pouch at his waist and sprinkled the bundle with some sort of dried herb. "It won't be completely safe from predators," he said, retying his pouch. "The ants can get to anything. But at least we can make them work a little harder for our food."

Alex shook her head as she walked to the area where she and Caitlyn had hung their hammocks. She used to think the Indians spent their days pursuing food because a lack of education forced them to live hand-to-mouth. Now she understood that the jungle

277

itself forced the lifestyle — without electricity, food could not be refrigerated. Salting as a method of food preservation wouldn't even work here because none of the jungle structures she'd seen could effectively prevent ants or termites from getting at the food. She guessed nothing but pesticide could stop the insects that ruled the jungle, but poisoning them would affect the entire food chain.

Stepping out from behind a tree, Caitlyn tossed Alex a roll of toilet paper. "How embarrassing," she said, her cheeks glowing even in the deepening shadows. "I will never get used to going behind a tree."

"Just be glad you have toilet paper." Alex opened her pack and stuffed the roll inside. "The natives don't even have that. They use leaves, remember?"

Caitlyn backed up to her hammock, then gripped the edges and swung her legs up and into the curve of the fabric. "What if they get a poison leaf? Wouldn't that itch like the devil?"

"Another good reason for taking the time to study your jungle plants." Alex pulled the mosquito netting down over her daughter, then secured the Velcro strip along the hammock's edges. They'd received vaccinations for hepatitis A, yellow fever, and tetanus before leaving Atlanta, but they had skipped the malaria treatment, trusting the CDC's promise that malaria would not be a problem in the Peruvian Amazon. Still, one never knew what illnesses ticks, chiggers, and mosquitoes could carry. Dengue fever was common in these parts, and Alex had heard *that* ailment left patients wanting to die . . .

Leaning over the netting, she saw that Caitlyn had clutched her stuffed monkey to her chest. So the fearless adventurer needed a little comfort, after all.

"Good night, honey. Don't get out of bed after dark. If it's an emergency, call me."

"What if you're asleep?"

"I'll hear you." She kissed her fingertips, then lightly touched them to the screen above her daughter's face. "Sleep tight. And don't let the bedbugs bite."

"Or anything else, right?"

"Correct."

"Roger that."

"Affirmative."

"Okay."

Alex paused, searching her brain for another synonym. "As it should be," she whispered, moving away.

She halted at the soft sound of weeping in the woods. After a quick glance to be sure Caitlyn was okay, she moved through the brush and found Lauren squatting on the ground, her hands over her face.

Alex glanced around, hoping Emma or Deborah would step forward to handle the younger woman's emotional crisis. But neither of them was in sight.

Bending, she placed her hand upon Lauren's shoulder. "You okay?"

Lauren shook her head. "No." She lowered her hands, hiccupping a sob. "I shouldn't have come."

Alex straightened. "Well, the jungle isn't easy. But this isn't so bad, and you'll get used to it in time —"

"It's not the jungle, I can handle the jungle." Lauren spoke in a rush, her words tinged with exasperation. "It's . . . Ken. I shouldn't have come to Peru with him."

Alex folded her arms, stunned by the admission. "Well . . . it's a little late to turn back now."

The woman lifted her arm, wiping her damp nose on her sleeve. "The whole thing is wrong. He's got kids, for heaven's sake. I thought he would leave his wife and start over with me, but you should have seen how desperately he was trying to return her phone call back at the lodge. And did you see how he looked at me while we were eating? He hates me now, I know he does."

Alex slapped at another mosquito on her arm, then stomped her feet, wondering if a moving target would dissuade the insects hovering around her ankles.

"I'm . . . I'm not smart like the rest of you. And I can't do anything out here. I don't even know why Ken brought me . . . after tonight, I know he doesn't love me."

Alex resisted the urge to roll her eyes. "Listen, Lauren, I'd love to help, but I don't have much experience in this area. I've always found that life is a lot simpler if you don't try to bring your men home with you."

Lauren broke into fresh tears. Alex patted her shoulder for a moment, then jerked her thumb toward the circle of hammocks. "Um, we're going to get carried away by mosquitoes and who knows what else if we don't get to our beds. Come on, let me walk you back. I promise, things will look better in the morning."

Still weeping, Lauren stood. Alex escorted the woman to her hammock, pulled down the mosquito netting, then glared across the circle where Ken Carlton was talking to Bancroft, apparently oblivious to his girlfriend's distress.

Men. What sort of insanity possessed them?

Walking back to her own bed, Alex slapped at a fresh squadron of mosquitoes on the back of her hand. The smoke from the fire kept the nasty little bloodsuckers at bay, but the fire was guttering now, and insects seemed determined to invade the camp.

Blowing out her cheeks, she slid her pack to the foot of her hammock, then took a last look around the camp. Alejandro Delmar knelt by the fire, surrounding it with enough green branches to keep the flame alive and smoky through the night. Bancroft stood like a statue at the perimeter of their encampment, his bare forearms glistening with perspiration and crawling with mosquitoes. Alex lifted a brow, amazed by the man's stoicism, then shrugged. Maybe Deborah was right — the man was showing off. Or maybe deadpan cool was the usual demeanor for a Navy SEAL. Alex didn't know and didn't care.

She crawled into her hammock and secured the edges, then lay on her side with her palm under her chin. Her bones ached, having stumped over miles of jungle terrain, and her head buzzed with a dozen serious thoughts and hundreds of trivial ones.

Peering through the fine-mesh screen, she watched the men on the opposite side of the camp. Baklanov was having trouble with his hammock — the knot kept slipping down the tree he had chosen, so Kenway was helping him secure it to a more suitable tree. Louis Fortier had already gone to bed; Alex could see the outline of his form through the sheer netting over his hammock. Milos Olsson stood beside the smoky fire studying a broad leaf on his palm.

Her thoughts flitted back to a conversation she and the botanist had shared on the trail. "Leaves in the rainforest may live over twelve years," he had told her, his eyes brightening with the prospect of discussing a subject dear to his heart. "In Sweden, of course, the leaves of deciduous trees live only four to six months; they die when winter approaches. But trees do not drop their leaves in the rainforest. And a tree's leaves at the canopy are completely different from its leaves in the understory, did you notice? They are physically and physiologically different — they are smaller, for instance, tougher, and have a higher rate of photosynthesis." He had grinned at Alex like a child discovering a favorite toy at Christmas. "It is amazing, yes? That a tree can produce two different types of leaves?"

Gamely pretending to share his fascination, Alex had nodded. "The evolution of certain plants never ceases to surprise me."

She closed her eyes, forbidding her brain to replay the rest of the conversation. If she did not try to shut down her mental processes, she'd be reliving the entire day and forty or fifty different conversations.

She knew some sleep experts insisted that dreams were necessary for the brain to sift through the thousands of memories involved in a day fully lived. While dreaming, the brain reviewed the day's events, filing important information and tossing out the rubbish. Trouble was — Alex stretched out on her back, willing herself to relax — *her* brain kept replaying every memory of the day without sleep to numb the process.

"Like having dental work done," she murmured, "without the laughing gas."

"Twinkle, twinkle, little star." She drew a deep breath, conjuring up the mental image of a heavy blanket of weariness sliding over her legs, numbing her toes, her feet, her calves, her thighs. Eventually her brain would drop into a light doze, then she would sleep. Her heart rate and blood pressure would fall. The food in her digestive system would move more quickly, glucose consumption by her cells would slow as her muscles relaxed. Soon she would enter the evening's first REM cycle, and she would dream . . .

Perchance to dream . . . who said that, Shakespeare? *To sleep, perchance to dream: ay, there's the rub.* Yes, it was Shakespeare, and Hamlet in particular. Act 3, scene 1. From the "To be or not to be" soliloquy.

The heavy blanket image wasn't working. Neither was the song.

She rolled over, turning her face to the jungle in the hope of finding rest in the encroaching darkness. But her thoughts would not submit, they bounced from thoughts of dead poets to sleep stages, from biology to anthropology.

On the long hike she had also talked with Emma Whitmore about indigenous groups. The anthropologist had told her that over half the population of Peru was composed of what she called the "first people."

"There are many tribes," she had said, "and just when we think we have located them all, another group appears. A few years ago a petroleum consortium tried to develop a gas field in the Amazon, but they encountered several nomadic and previously uncontacted tribes. Fortunately, even though Shell and Mobil had invested over $250 million, they withdrew from the project." Her short white curls bobbed as she shook her head. "Contacting tribal groups is not without risk, and I'm not talking only about the financial side of things. In January 2002, scores of native people used arrows, machetes, and shotguns to clear out a group of men, women, and children who had invaded their land. They killed thirty-five people."

Startled by the statement, Alex missed a step and nearly stumbled.

Emma released a humorless laugh. "Some of the settlers' children were never found — experts think they may have been carried away to the villages. They'll grow up as Indians."

Alex turned to check on her daughter. "Is kidnapping a common practice in these parts?"

"Common enough. Over the years, more than five hundred white children have been taken by Indians in North and South America."

"But why?"

Emma lifted one shoulder in a shrug. "Sometimes the father takes a child to console a mother who has lost her own offspring. Sometimes a leader will lack a male heir. Rather than allow a rival's son to assume his authority, he will take an outsider's son and introduce him to the tribe as a compromise candidate."

"But these natives — the ones we're looking for. We have no reason to believe they would engage in this sort of thing, do we?"

"We know nothing at all about them, Alex. From what I can tell, Dr. Kenway's native might be distantly associated with the Yagua, a peaceful tribe that for the most part has been successfully integrated into Peruvian society. But others have had no contact with the white man and his civilization. The Korubo, for instance, live in the rainforest near Brazil — we know they exist, but no one wants to sully their way of life by foisting contact upon them. The Amahuaca live in the jungle near the border, too, in a valley that used to support the Machiguenga, Yine-Piro, Yaminahua, Amahuaca, Ashaninca, Nahua, and Kugapakori tribes. Most of those groups have suffered greatly from their contact with the whites, who tended to treat them unfairly and expose them to diseases for which they have no resistance or cure."

Guilt avalanched over Alex, pressing her down with its weight. Were they wrong to search for this healing tribe? She desperately needed what they might possess, but who could say what harm their expedition might do simply by entering an uncontacted village?

"I know the natives were often exploited during the Amazonian rubber boom." Thinking aloud, Alex stared past the trampled trail into her own thoughts. "I know some missionaries have tried to destroy the Indians' way of life. But we are not seeking their land, nor do we want to change their society. We only want knowledge — I want to know about a cure, you want to know about their people. Surely our little group will not harm them."

"I certainly hope we won't." Emma had walked on for several steps, then added, "But contact with an unreached group is like a stone thrown into a pond. The ripples spread far beyond our intent."

Alex clenched her fist as images of Emma and ponds and ripples pushed and jostled and competed for space in her brain. When the empty screen threatened to flicker with a new image, she opened her eyes to find rest.

Some nocturnal animal rattled the leaves of the palms near her hammock, but the sounds of human activity had faded. Alex rolled to her other side and studied the campfire. Everyone but Duke Bancroft had gone to bed. The muscled warrior sat alone by the smoking fire, his back ramrod straight, an impressive-looking black gun on his lap. His wide eyes were alert, his gaze flitted over each hammock as if he held himself personally responsible for the human treasure each contained. Alex smiled. Though she did not believe they would encounter the sort of danger for which Bancroft seemed to yearn, his vigilance was comforting.

She listened for steady breathing from Caitlyn's hammock, but the insects drowned out those soft sounds. Concentrating on the insect noises, she thought she could hear the rhythmic sounds of chewing, then she heard light thumping sounds on her mosquito netting and nearly laughed aloud. Deborah had warned her that the setting sun functioned as a dinner bell for most of the jungle's insect population. Shredded leaves and other bits of greenery would rain upon them all night as beetles and caterpillars munched their way to plumpness. To accompany the insect feeding frenzy, a pair of parrots in a nearby strangler fig crackled and cackled as they settled in for the night.

From studying her calendar, Alex knew that a quarter moon lit the canopy above, but just a few rays of moonlight penetrated this dark bower. Only in the clearing where Delmar had built the fire did shades of gray touch the gigantic tree trunks around her.

She lay silent for at least another hour, sitting up only when the solid sounds of snoring resonated from several points in the darkness. Bancroft had been relieved by Chavez, who sat in a black-and-white tableau, his chin resting on his chest, his hands curled around the weapon in his lap. Moving as silently as possible, Alex reached for the pack at her feet, dragged it to her belly, then pulled out her journal, a pen, and her flashlight. Crossing her legs, she hunched forward and opened the book, then began to write.

Monday, April 7th. Our first night under the stars, and even here I find it difficult to sleep. I tell myself this insomnia results from excitement, but Caitlyn, who was far more excited than I, is sleeping like a baby.

It is nearly completely dark here, and if not for my watch I would lose all track of time. My mind keeps rehashing the day's events, and if I do not force myself to write, to think, I'm afraid I'll soon start rehashing events from weeks and months ago. I'm beginning to feel like an Alzheimer's patient — I'm told that people suffering from that disease revert to their childhoods because the earliest memories are the most deeply imbedded. At least I have not yet begun to relive my days of making mud pies in my mom's garden.

The neurologist in me says I must stop the denial and face the hard truth — like it or not, I am 90 percent sure I have entered the early stages of FFI. Along with the increasing insomnia (accompanied by weariness, of course), I have observed an increasing tendency toward panic, ataxia, and dysarthria. Thus far I have been able to defeat panic attacks by anticipating them — and the simple fact that I am a female heading into uncharted jungle may disguise my anxiety, should an attack prove to be unstoppable.

The ataxia has not been severe — except for the one time my fingers spasmed on the climbing rope, I have not experienced any real difficulty. Tomorrow, though, if my legs suddenly refuse to obey my command to walk, I may find myself hard-pressed to explain my weakness.

I wonder if I could cite PMS as the cause for all my symptoms? Men certainly seem eager to blame female hormones for our perceived failures. Hmm . . . on second thought, I doubt anyone would buy that excuse, particularly Michael Kenway, M.D. A woman of my age should know her body well enough to have such things under control.

As far as dysarthria goes, despite my relative youth, I suppose I could attribute any stuttering or forgotten phrases to what my colleagues jokingly refer to as "senior moments." I could even develop a sudden case of Tourette's syndrome if the stuttering increases.

Fortunately, this trip will not outlast my disease. If I am right and I am well into the first stages, we are not planning to spend months in the jungle, only a few days. I am confident I can complete this trip with no major problems. What concerns me, though, is the research. If we do find a curative agent, the research and testing phase will take months . . . and by then my race against time will have become desperate.

Please, let us find the cure quickly. It frightens me to think how heavily I am depending upon Kenway's story of the jungle man.

I can't think about it. I'll go crazy if I do. The rational part of my brain says that if my mind will not shut down, I should put this excess mental energy to good use and spend these nighttime hours postulating. One would think I could come up with some illuminating hypothesis or insight while the others are sleeping . . . but my thoughts seem only to chase each other, like puppies nipping at their littermates' tails.

Is that, I wonder, a symptom of the disease or only overblown anxiety?

As confused as I am these days, I know one thing — we are closer to a cure than we have ever been, and each day finds me more desperate than the day before. If this is early-onset FFI, I have become symptomatic far earlier than my mother, but perhaps the reason is obvious. I have endured more stress than my mother at this age, and my immune system has to be considerably weaker. In this stressful place it will weaken further . . . just when I most need my strength, wits, and energy.

If I were a pessimistic person, I would tell Carlton the truth about my illness and ask to be evacuated and flown home. With rest and proper care, I might live another year. I could surround myself with friends before officially retiring to a nursing home, where I would finish my life in solitude, meeting death on my own terms.

But I must always consider Caitlyn. If she is to be free from the curse we carry in our bodies, I must press on. Though this journey is a gamble, I cannot withdraw now.

I cannot let this thing beat me. If it keeps me awake, I'll try to use my conscious hours wisely. If it steals my muscular coordination and my speech, I will express my thoughts with pen and paper. I will find a way to communicate what I am thinking even if I have to point out letters on a keyboard by the direction of my gaze.

I _will_ put the pieces together, and I will make others see the answer . . . as soon as we find it.

I feel like a stubborn player at a poker

table. I've gambled before and lost big time, but the dealer just slipped me an unexpected pair of aces, and I'll win if I can find another. Kenway is one ace — though the man arouses something in me for which I have no time or energy, I do value his expertise — and his story of Ya-ree is another. Now, if only we can find this healing tribe and make sense of their medical practices . . .

If only . . . if I could believe God did sit in heaven listening to our prayers, I would beg him to help me find the cure. But because I know heaven is a physical place containing solar systems, black holes, and a few zillion stars, I'll ask my traveling companions for help instead. I'm grateful Carlton knows how to assemble a team — I don't think I could have found better people to help in this quest had I auditioned the entire world.

At times like this I am tempted to pray — driven to pray, actually — but since I have disavowed the God worshiped by most of the civilized world, I shall have to invent my own. I believe I will call upon the God of Desperate Women in Tropical Straits: GODWITS, for short.

I'm a little out of practice with prayer — my mother never insisted on it, even at meals, and I've never been a member of an organized church. So here goes my first attempt:

May you help me, GODWITS, to maintain my sanity and preserve my strength. May you send sleep. And if you cannot do that, direct my steps so we find the cure we seek. May it be genuine, and available, and applicable to my situation.

For I have never been quite so desperate in my life.

Well, that's it. I don't know what else to do with prayer except offer an animal sacrifice, and it's too dark and dangerous to venture out in search of a willing creature. Besides, I think GODWITS frowns on such things. Sacrifices are so . . . messy.

Time to roll over and count . . . caterpillars. Not even my fevered imagination can envision a leaping lamb in this place.

After relieving himself in the darkness, Michael took two steps toward his hammock, then paused. Chavez dozed in the clearing, his face tinged a faint red by the low fire, but another light flashed across the circle of their camp. For an instant Michael recalled Yaree's words: *A light guided me through the forest.*

Hunching forward, he peered past his hammock and realized that the light came from near the women's hammocks. The glow was too concentrated to be fireflies, and too perfectly round to be a flame . . .

His stomach tightened as his fist closed around the knife sheathed at his belt. Should he alert Chavez? The weapon in the guard's hand would be far more effective against an enemy than Michael's hunting knife, but alerting Chavez might prove suicidal. Michael didn't know much about guns, but Bancroft had been more than willing to talk about the exceptional firepower of the H&K MP5 snuggled in Chavez's lap. Michael had come away from the discussion with respect for the gun and the quick reflexes of the men who carried it, even though Chavez now dozed in an upright position.

Keeping one wary eye on Chavez, whose finger rested entirely too close to the trigger on his weapon, Michael crept through the low underbrush, then halted, feeling suddenly silly.

The light did not shine near a hammock, but within it. One of the women had turned on her flashlight, but to do what? Read?

Spurred by curiosity, he moved toward the shining circle. In its reflected glow, he recognized Alexandra Pace, who was concentrating on something in her lap.

He crept forward until he stood a few paces from her hammock, then quietly asked, "Can't you sleep?"

She jumped with such force her hammock shivered. "Kenway?" Her voice sharpened as she shone the blinding light in his eyes. "Good grief, what are you doing out there? You scared me to death."

"Take that away, will you?" He waited until she had lowered the flashlight, then glanced toward Chavez, who had not stirred. "And lower your voice. You'll wake our sleeping sentinel."

"Fat chance. He's bone-tired; we all are."

"So why aren't you asleep?" He glanced at the glowing dial on his watch. "It's quarter to eleven."

She snorted. "That's early for me. The evening news hasn't even come on in Atlanta."

"But you're on jungle time now, and the sun's been down over four hours." He moved closer to avoid waking the others. "Everyone else is dead to the world."

She snapped shut the book in her lap, then stared up at him. "What are you getting at, Doc?"

"I — I'm not making a point. I merely thought to inquire about your well-being."

"I'm perfectly fine, thank you. And quite ready to sleep." To emphasize her point, she clicked off the flashlight, leaving them in total darkness.

After a moment, she laughed. "Better give yourself a second to let your eyes adjust before you go stumbling back to your hammock."

Michael blinked at the darkness, waiting for vague outlines to reappear. "Thank you, I will."

When she spoke again, a note of humor had entered her voice. "What brings you out of your snug little bed at this hour?"

He grinned, glad she couldn't see the blush that burned the skin beneath his incoming beard. "When nature calls, you know . . ."

She laughed, a surprisingly gentle sound in the warm night. "You should have planned ahead. Caitlyn and I made sure we took care of all that before we climbed into our hammocks. Then again, they say girls are easier to potty train than boys. Has your pediatric experience proven that true?"

"Indubitably." He stared into the darkness, wishing her face would appear so he could see if she was still teasing. Either this exasperating woman had found yet another way to twist his words into a miniature battle of the sexes, or she was making surprisingly pleasant conversation.

When she didn't launch another salvo, he relaxed. He was about to bid her good night and creep across the circle when a sudden thought occurred. "Alexandra?"

She groaned. "You still there?"

"You and I seem to have gotten off on the wrong foot, and I'd like to set things to rights if I can. Of all the people on this team, you and I are best suited to work together. I'd like to be your partner, not your adversary, but whenever I approach, you bare your fangs —"

"My what?"

"Pardon the unfortunate metaphor. But please." He lowered his voice. "If I have done something to offend you, tell me now so I can apologize."

Her flashlight gleamed and rose to shine in his face. He squinted and looked away, but after a moment she dropped the beam to his chest.

"You look sincere. A lot more sincere than Carlton."

"I am." He pressed his hands together in a penitent's posture. "And while I can't speak for Mr. Carlton's intentions, I want us to have a go at a partnership. What do you think?"

In the reflected light he could see her eyes shining like silver, but she did not answer.

"Was it the way I arrived? I've already apologized for the chopper's blowing your group about —"

"How like a man! You think the simple act of saying 'I'm sorry' will make everything all right?" Turning to face him, she pressed her hands to the mosquito netting like a caged lioness. "Have you considered the possibility that I simply don't like you?"

Michael blanched. "I suppose that's your prerogative. I'm sorry, I never imagined —"

"The thought never occurred to you, did it? Oh, I know how you doctors are. You think everyone should like you, respect you, admire you. You wear your white coats like you're some kind of divinity and strut around like you hold the power of life and death in your hands. Well, I'm a doctor, too, Kenway, but I don't work in a hospital and I don't treat patients."

He lifted his eyes to the dark canopy. "Thank God."

"What?"

He waved as if to ward her away. "Take care, Dr. Pace, I'm sorry to have bothered you. Go back to your reading or writing or whatever you were doing. If you should need me —"

"I won't."

"Fine, then. Good night."

Reeling from the encounter, Michael crossed the circle of darkness, calling out a chipper "Good night" to Chavez, too. The man jerked out of his sleep, clutched his weapon to his chest, then nodded slowly as Michael lifted the netting on his hammock and climbed inside.

Settling back into the embrace of his bed, he folded his hands under his head and took deep breaths, trying to exhale away the stress of his encounter with Alexandra Pace.

What on earth had made that woman so hostile? She had confessed to bad experiences with men, yet she didn't seem to have any problem getting on with Baklanov, Carlton, or Olsson. She seemed quite chummy with nearly everyone on the team, and she really did adore that little girl.

So . . . out of all the people in their expedition, why had she focused her hostility on him?

300

"Here is water." Signaling a halt, Alejandro Delmar held up one hand and pointed to a flooded area with the other. "We will take a break. Fill your water bottles now."

Groaning, Alex swung her backpack to the ground, then extracted the water bottle and filter. She put out a hand, about to rest her weight on a tree, then hastily withdrew her arm when she remembered the threat of ants and other stinging insects.

She was so tired her nerves throbbed. For five days they had trudged through the alternately rainy or steamy jungle without seeing a single sign of human life. For the first two days Alex had enjoyed talking to her companions — each expert on the team offered a different and interesting perspective on the wonders around them. By the third day, however, her body had grown weary and her tongue heavy. They ate little — mostly

301

fish, monkey, and grubs, supplemented by portions of rice from Chavez's pack of emergency provisions.

She did not need a scale to know she was rapidly losing weight — the lightweight slacks she had chosen for the trip now gaped at her waistline, and her pack rubbed against a bone at her hip that had not protruded when they left Yarupapa. Deprivation would affect everyone, but the others were not resisting a debilitating disease.

She tried to eat as much as possible at every meal, but she couldn't ask for more without alerting the others to her declining condition. Most of the team members joked about the benefits of eating fish and jungle roots for a few days; Deborah Simons declared she'd come out of the jungle as slender as she'd been when she graduated from college. Duke Bancroft, who had been spending a lot of time with Deborah, kept insisting that he should have been the Navy SEAL represented on the *Survivor* TV show.

Alex was beginning to wonder if she'd have the strength to walk out of the jungle under her own power. The first stage of fatal familial insomnia usually lasted about four months, but in her weakened condition, who knew how long she could continue with relatively mild symptoms?

She let her backpack fall to the ground, then squatted on it, bracing her elbows on her knees. A seam of fatigue opened in her mind as she tried to formulate a prognosis.

Second-stage FFI, which usually lasted about five months, would add hallucinations and profuse sweating to panic attacks, faltering muscle movements, and increasing insomnia. The third stage, which usually continued for about three months, would bring total insomnia and neuroemaciation, or extreme weight loss. Compounded with the scant diet she'd been eating since their advent into the jungle, she would quickly waste away. The fourth and final stage, which could last as long as six months, would involve a total lack of motor control. Like her mother, she would become mute, she would lapse into a coma, and she would die. If her illness followed the typical course, she'd be dead within eighteen months.

Unless they found a cure among the members of the healing tribe.

She pressed the back of her sweaty hand to her forehead, then jumped when Delmar shouted. She looked up to see him kneeling a few feet away by the water's edge. The others hurried forward; after a long moment, she summoned her energy and rose to join them.

Delmar had spread the grass from a patch of soft mud firmly stamped with a pair of footprints.

"Indian tracks," he said softly, brushing a

train of leaf-cutting ants away from the indentation.

Carlton shouldered his way to the front line of observers. "How can you tell?"

Tracing the mounded dirt with his fingertip, Delmar pointed to a gap between the first two toes. "There is a space here. This is a man who does not wear shoes."

Bancroft pulled the GPS from his belt and squinted at the display. "We're at 71.8 degrees longitude, 2.5 degrees latitude." He grinned at Alex. "Getting closer to the Equator all the time."

"And closer to Colombia," Emma Whitmore added. "The border is the river called Putumayo."

"This doesn't look like much of a river." Bancroft scanned the flooded land around them, then gave the group a sheepish grin. "As if I would know what constitutes a river in these parts."

Olsson stepped forward, one hand tucked into the waistband of his trousers. "How do we know this footprint belongs to one of our healing Indians? If there's a possibility this man belongs to some other tribe —"

"There are no other recorded tribes in this region." Emma lifted her head to meet Olsson's gaze. "Is it possible this is a hunter from a recognized tribe? Of course, but it's highly unlikely. We haven't seen a man-made trail in days."

"I agree." Delmar stood, one hand stroking his bare chin as he turned and stared into the underbrush. "This is a fresh footprint; the man who made it passed this way less than two hours ago. We will follow his trail, and I must ask you to walk single file behind me. Be quiet as you go, please, lest we frighten the others away."

"The others?" Carlton lifted a brow. "How do you know there are others?"

Delmar's square jaw tensed. "If there is one, there are others. And they will see us before we see them."

Reflexively, Alex turned to look for her daughter. Caitlyn had spent the day walking with Deborah Simons, who had entertained her with stories of insect oddities. Now Simons's face had gone sober. She caught Alex's eye and nodded, silently acknowledging the shift in the prevailing mood.

Moving quickly, Alex knelt to let water flow through the filter into her water bottle, then stood and added a couple of chlorine tablets for good measure. After calling Caitlyn to her side, she positioned her daughter behind her, then hoisted her pack and prepared to face what she hoped would be the last leg of their journey.

"Will it be long now, Mom?"

"I hope not, honey."

As Delmar led them out, Alex inhaled deep breaths, overcome by a mingling of hope and exhilaration.

They walked for twenty minutes through an area noisy with squawking parrots, then halted behind Delmar's uplifted hand. As the group shuffled forward, the guide pointed to a patch of greenery through which Alex could see something black shining in the sun.

"Water."

"Is it the Putumayo?" Carlton asked.

Delmar shook his head. "I think it is a lake. Our rivers are brown, not black."

Alex wasn't certain why black water had to be a lake, but she slipped an arm around Caitlyn's shoulder and followed the others as Delmar led them into a clearing. The terrain had changed since they found the footprint, the tall trees giving way to shorter cousins, the empty ground filling with sprawling shrubs and brush. Delmar's machete flashed rhythmically until the foliage bowed before him.

Upon reaching the water's edge, the guide turned to Carlton. "From this place our native launched his canoe and moved out. He was not alone." The guide pointed to the soft earth, where a series of footprints marked the sand. Alex could also see a smoothed trough that could have been made by the launching of a canoe.

Stepping into a patch of blazing sunlight, she gaped at an open expanse of black water filled with lily pads as big as beds. Delmar was right; they had reached a lake bordered by land on at least three sides. Directly across from where their group stood, however, a tree-covered knoll rose from the inky waters.

Emma Whitmore crossed one arm over her chest while her free hand absently plucked at a curl by her ear. "Is that an island?"

Delmar's forehead creased. "That would explain many things. These people have remained secluded because they do not live on the river."

Whitmore shook her head. "I don't buy it. They may live on an island, but this lake wouldn't have stopped them from reaching other tribes. Five days is not so great a distance."

Carlton crossed his arms. "I thought all the bodies of water in these parts drained toward the sea."

"Not all of them." Delmar picked up a stick and traced a serpentine path on the muddy ground. "Each year the rivers in the forest bend on their way to the sea. The water constantly moves against the riverbanks, wearing away the curves and moving soil. Sometimes a sharp turn becomes so narrow the water cuts through the earth and leaves a bend behind. The water that remains in that place becomes a black-water lake. No current moves there, and the land does not dry out like the flooded fields. Strange animals live in black water. Maybe strange people live here, too."

Squatting on the shore, Alex rested her chin on her closed hand and hoped the others would mistake her weariness for concentration.

"What sort of strange animals?" Deborah asked.

"Hoatzin birds," Delmar answered. "Electric eels, caimans, and many kinds of fish."

"I know about hoatzin birds." Caitlyn's voice sang over the adult rumbles like a piccolo in a brass band. "They have claws on their wings, so they can climb back into their nests if they fall into the water."

Kenway laughed. "That's fascinating, Cait."

Alex closed her eyes. Did the man genuinely like Caitlyn, or was he merely trying to annoy her mother? For the past five days she and Kenway had managed to avoid confrontation by avoiding each other. Caitlyn, though, had followed the man like a shadow, her stuffed monkey swinging from her arm as she and the doctor chattered almost nonstop.

"So — how do we cross this lake?" Carlton asked. "Can we build some sort of canoe?"

Delmar grunted. "One canoe takes one week to build. Two canoes take two weeks. We would need two canoes."

Bancroft stepped forward, a grin brightening his sweaty face. "I can build a raft out of logs and vines. Easy. If everyone pitches in, we can build two rafts tomorrow and cross to the island tomorrow night."

"We cross when the sun is up, not in darkness," Carlton insisted. "We will need to see what we are approaching. So let's make camp for now, get some rest, and tackle the project tomorrow."

Watching the black lake through narrowed eyes, Alex could only agree.

12 April 2003
7:03 p.m.

Moving through rain that fell in solid sheets, Michael decided that shelter was definitely a desirable thing. The gentle mist that routinely watered London's streets and soothed the parched leaves of her rose gardens bore no resemblance to the water pouring from a rip in the heavens above Amazonia.

They had finished the rafts. Now they just had to escape death by drowning in a sudden deluge.

Bancroft had risen early, pulling the men from their hammocks and leaving the women to fish for breakfast at the water's edge. While Chavez had prepared the skillet and Delmar used his hat to snag fresh water sardines for bait, Bancroft had walked through the forest, tagging trees that would be suitable for use in his construction project. They had only one ax — a lightweight tool from Olsson's field equipment, but they had put it to good use.

While Olsson chopped down slender trees, Michael and the others whacked at ropy liana vines with whatever blades they had on hand — the hunting knife he'd purchased in Iquitos soon proved its value.

The work was tedious, but Michael found it a nice change from the constant walking. The canopy of the deep forest provided shade from the broiling heat, but there was no escaping the sun when he neared the clearing at the lake.

He had been hacking his way through a particularly tangled vine when the sight of a banana tree stopped him in mid-swing. An armload of ripe bananas hung from a stalk, and the bounty fell into his arms with one well-placed cut. Enjoying a moment of unexpected bliss, he walked among his companions distributing the fruit. After such a haphazard diet, the potassium in the plantains would do them all a world of good.

As he handed bananas to Olsson and Baklanov, he saw Delmar look up, his forehead crinkled in thought. Puzzled by the man's attitude, he waited until Delmar was alone, then offered the man a piece of fruit.

"For you," he said, extending the banana. "I hope I'm not handing out poisonous plantains by mistake."

Delmar took the fruit. "No."

"Then . . . is something wrong? I caught your expression a moment ago. You looked like you weren't too keen on the idea of me passing these around."

The man jerked his head toward the spot where Michael had been working. "Look closely at the banana tree."

Michael turned, barely able to spot the long-leafed plant through the intervening growth. "I don't understand. They're just ordinary plantains, aren't they?"

"See the tree next to them? Papaya, and picked clean. You think you have found wild fruit, but someone planted those trees . . . probably the tribe you seek. You have just raided their crop."

Michael stared at the native guide as guilt rose like a geyser within him. "Blast, I'm sorry. I had no idea."

Delmar shrugged. "They wouldn't have come for the food with so many people about." A wry smile curled on his lips. "Take what you can find, eat it. Survival is all that matters here."

Michael exhaled deeply as he moved away. He supposed Delmar had a point, but it didn't feel right to take crops from people who had nothing but what the jungle could provide.

Still . . . the bananas would only rot if he left them on the ground. Someone had to eat them, and heaven knew they needed nourishment.

He found Caitlyn and Alexandra by the

lake and gave them two pieces of fruit. "Eat up," he said, injecting a stern note into his voice. Caitlyn seemed to be faring well, but the dark circles beneath her mother's eyes had deepened.

"Thanks, Doc!" Caitlyn peeled her banana like a kid ripping into a Christmas present.

Michael turned to the mother. Not wanting to disturb the chip on her shoulder, he had been trying his best to remain out of Alexandra's way. "How are you making out?" he asked, trying to keep his voice pleasant.

A wry smile tugged at her mouth. "That expression could use a bit of adjustment when you speak to Americans. But we are doing well, thank you."

"Really?" He slipped his hands into his pockets. "It may not be gallant to notice, but you look a little weary."

Her arched brows rose a trifle. "Who wouldn't? I've been sleeping in a hammock, hiking for days, and I've spent the morning slapping a lake in the hope of catching a few bites of food for breakfast, lunch, or dinner. The rustic life is not easy."

He smiled, grateful for her attempt at levity, then jerked his thumb toward the forest. "I'd better go back. The lads will be thinking I'm shirking my duties."

"I doubt anyone would think that, Doctor."

He lifted a brow, wondering what she meant, but she only lowered her makeshift fishing pole and began to thrash it in the water.

Lowering his head, he returned to the forest while thoughts of Alexandra Pace hovered around the edges of his mind. He had been thinking about her when the rain began to fall, and when some chivalrous impulse sent him running to see if the women had found shelter, he found the five of them huddled beneath a wide-leafed shrub, as wet as muskrats.

Caitlyn had pointed at him and laughed, humored, no doubt, by his own resemblance to a drowned rat. Alexandra had given him a smile, then wrapped her arms around her shoulders and shivered.

At that moment he'd had to resist walking forward to pull those two under the protection of his arms.

After sunset, as their soaked party sat on palm leaves and tried to dry out around a fire that spat sparks into a star-studded sky, he laughed as Caitlyn led the group in a rousing chorus of "Ninety-nine bottles of Inca cola on the wall."

They had worked hard, but two rafts, both sturdy and sea-worthy, waited on the shore, ready for sunrise. Buoyed by a sense of accomplishment, their spirits soared high enough to forget their growling stomachs, wet clothing, and aching muscles.

When the party broke up, Michael settled

into his hammock and lifted his eyes to the heavens. He had met many determined researchers in his lifetime, many of whom were quite ruthless in their efforts to best competitors in the field. The first to publish earned the honor of naming diseases, elements, even cells. Stanley Prusiner, the scientist who first coined the term *prion* for infectious proteins, had won the 1997 Nobel Prize in Medicine for his discovery. The news had brought little comfort to Michael; Prusiner only put a name on the entities responsible for Ashley's death.

Alexandra Pace, however, did not seem the type to seek personal recognition. She worked for Carlton, she seemed content to labor in relative obscurity, and she had not once mentioned publishing a paper on her work. Yet he had never met a more driven researcher.

What fire burned in her heart? What force drove her forward?

Was she simply obsessive? Or perhaps a bit mad?

He sighed as he laced his hands over his chest. She might well be out of her head, but she was a caring mother, a sharp wit, and a most interesting companion. A person altogether worth getting to know . . . once she sheathed her claws.

12 April 2003
7:30 p.m.

After settling Caitlyn into her hammock, Alex maneuvered her way into hers, then pulled the mosquito netting over her bed and secured its edges. She ached from head to toe; even her fingertips pulsed with weariness.

Stretching out on the damp hammock, she closed her eyes and tried to force herself to relax. Last night she had slept two or three hours, and she needed at least as much sleep tonight if she were to continue to function. Her muscles were still obeying, but on several occasions during the day she had tried to move one of her arms and discovered that it hung as limp as a noodle from its socket.

Ataxia — the inability to voluntarily coordinate muscles. Today, her arms, tomorrow, who knew?

Rest, Alex. Deep breaths. Think about the day, think about tomorrow, but relax as much as you can. Sleep will not come until your body

316

and mind are at rest.

As always, her thoughts turned to the day just passed. After spending half the morning uselessly beating the shallow waters with a fishing pole, she had handed the stick to Lauren in order to join Caitlyn, Emma, and Deborah at the clearing, where the men were building the rafts. After the guys laid out a group of appropriately sized logs, under Bancroft's direction the women took lengths of vine and wove them under and around each log, lashing each to its neighbor. The work had scraped and cut Alex's fingers, but she'd gladly suffer the pain if Bancroft's rafts carried them safely to Kenway's healing tribe.

"I feel like we're part of the Swiss Family Robinson," Caitlyn had chirped, her face red as they worked in the equatorial sun.

"Get the sunscreen from my bag," Alex interrupted. "Smear some on those freckles, will you? You're going to be in severe pain if you don't."

At the water's edge, Lauren squealed as something splashed in the shallows. "Help! Something's in there!"

Deborah rolled her eyes. "That's the point, Lauren. Whatever it is, we want it. Caiman, electric eel, fish, piranha — if it moves, spear it."

"I am not about to spear one of those crocodile things." Lauren marched toward them, then dropped her sharpened stick at

317

Caitlyn's bare feet. "Why don't you try your luck, kid?"

Alex turned to face Carlton's girlfriend. "She's busy. But if you need something to do, you might look for some fruit. Kenway found bananas. If you look around, you might get lucky."

The young woman raked her hand through her hair, then stalked off, but Alex knew she wouldn't wander far from the group. Women like Lauren were ornamental around the office but useless when thrust into the real world . . .

Or an Amazonian rain shower. Without warning, bruised and swollen clouds swept over the lake; a moment later, spits of rain filled the rising wind. The touch of a breeze was odd enough, for winds rarely penetrated the canopied rainforest, but these gusts whipped the lake, coaxing the black waters into whitecaps.

A wave of wet heat swamped over their camp, then the sky opened and rain came down, erasing the world.

The women had retreated into a natural arbor where they huddled under the leaves of a giant elephant's ear bush (*Alocasia odora,* Olsson later informed them) and resigned themselves to wetness. A few moments later, Kenway had come charging over like a lunatic, his dark hair turned into slick black ribbons by the rain, his eyes wide with something that might have been protective concern . . . and, unless her feminine instincts had completely atrophied, that concern had been directed particularly at her and Caitlyn.

Groaning, Alex turned onto her side in an attempt to derail *that* particular train of thought. Dealing with Caitlyn's infatuation with the noble doctor would be difficult enough when the expedition ended. She would not — *could* not — afford to make things harder by encouraging an unrealistic relationship.

She felt a smile twitch the muscles at her cheek. He had looked . . . interesting, though. Like Natty Bumppo from *The Last of the Mohicans,* rising out of the wilderness to rescue the woman who'd won his heart.

No — she knocked her fist against her forehead. What was she *thinking?* Better to worry about survival, about her health, about her daughter. Maybe these fantasies were an undocumented aspect of her illness, part of a mental weakness too embarrassing to be reported.

Blowing out her cheeks, she stretched along her hammock and felt the wetness of her socks against the fabric. Water could be hard to manage in the field. One of her colleagues had once gone on a jungle expedition and washed her clothing in a stream. Afterward, she made the mistake of hanging her wet clothes on a bush to dry. While she worked, flies landed on the wet cloth and deposited their tiny eggs amid the woven strands. Days later, the researcher had been wearing her shirt when the larvae hatched. The larvae then burrowed into folds of the researcher's skin, leaving her to later wonder how she had come to be intimately infested with maggots.

Alex rubbed her hand over her face in an effort to scrub the distasteful memory away. Such realities were inescapable in the tropics. Maggots and their ilk were probably one of the reasons natives found it easier to wear no clothing at all.

"Still awake, Alexandra?"

Kenway's deep voice startled her out of her reverie. When her eyes flew open, she saw him standing a few feet from her hammock, his form silhouetted by the dying campfire.

"Good grief, Kenway!" She pushed herself up onto an elbow. "If I was sleepy, I'm certainly not now. You almost scared me into adrenaline overload."

"Sorry." He stepped closer, daring to lean one hand on the tree supporting her hammock. "I saw your hammock moving and thought you might be awake."

She stared past him into the darkness. "What's the matter? Something wrong, or are you experiencing temporary insomnia?"

He laughed softly. "I think I could sleep standing up — which is why I'm walking around. I did lie down, but Bancroft came by to ask me to take the first watch. He's gone out to look for Chavez."

The confession strummed a shiver from Alex. Chavez had gone out to hunt for game about an hour before sunset. It was now an hour past.

Her heart began to thump almost painfully in her chest.

Don't panic.

With an effort, she turned her thousand-yard stare toward Kenway. "Are you worried about him?"

"I'm afraid I am. I treated Ya-ree, remember? Someone from some tribe in these parts speared the fellow. I don't think the natives around here take kindly to intruders." He gentled his tone. "But Chavez is an expert, right? While I wouldn't be too keen about roaming around in the dark, he knows the jungle. And he was carrying a very big gun."

Alex propped her head on her hand, her anxiety slipping away as she stared at Kenway through the mosquito netting. The rising moon was brighter tonight, very nearly full, and backlit his profile when he turned to survey the camp.

Caitlyn was right, the doctor was easy on the eyes . . . and, despite Alex's previous doubts, apparently genuinely concerned for her and her daughter.

Perhaps concern wasn't a bad thing.

"Thanks for the bananas today," she said,

intending her words as an olive branch. "I noticed you slipped Caitlyn an extra one when no one was looking. While that wasn't strictly fair, I appreciate your concern for a growing girl."

He turned, his smile shining through the darkness. "Maybe I was hoping she'd share it with her mother."

"Well." She looked away, grateful for the cloak of shadows about her hammock. His words roused feelings she had thought long dead, but she couldn't afford to entertain them.

"That's not exactly a compliment," she said, edging her voice lest he get the wrong idea. "You seem to be telling me I look tired and run down."

"You do." He paused to sip from the water bottle in his hand. "I think we all do, actually. In a few more days, I suspect we'll all begin to look as wild as the natives on those *National Geographic* television specials."

A moment of silence stretched between them, then he lifted his bottle, positioning it in a sliver of moonlight. "Have you noticed the water in this lake? It's not muddy like the Amazon. It's as dark as a good cup of tea."

She pretended to shudder. "I can't get used to drinking brown water. But perhaps if I think of it as coffee . . ."

She was about to ask if he'd packed any scones or clotted cream in his gear when a startled scream broke the stillness. Hammocks swung, mosquito nets lifted, and Bancroft spilled out of the shadows with his weapon ready.

Pushing the netting away from her bed, Alex looked to Caitlyn's hammock. Her daughter's eyes shone through the fine mesh.

"Caitlyn, stay in bed."

"What's happening, Mom?"

"I don't know, but we'll let Mr. Bancroft find out."

Immediately Bancroft, Carlton, and Kenway sprinted toward the source of the sound. Alex watched them go, a creeping uneasiness at the base of her spine.

"What's going on?" Lauren's voice had risen to a shrill pitch.

"We don't know," Deborah replied calmly. "I'm sure Bancroft will tell us everything in a few minutes."

They waited, the seconds stretching themselves thin, and Alex strained to listen through the night sounds. She heard the usual rustlings and chewings and the flutter of greenery on the screen above her head, followed by the rumble of men's voices and the swishing of tall grass.

She exhaled in relief a moment later when the three men returned with Louis Fortier between them.

The little perfumer was weeping.

"I didn't see him until I stepped on him,"

he cried between sobs. "And then — *quelle horreur,* what could have happened?"

Bancroft and Kenway looked at each other, some sort of unspoken agreement passing between them, then the doctor put his hand on Fortier's shoulder.

"I have medicine to help you calm down," he said, leading Louis toward his hammock. "What happened is a terrible thing, absolutely, but you must not lose your head. Not now."

Alex watched as Carlton and Bancroft retreated into the darkness, armed with flashlights and a length of rope. Straining to hear, she waited a few moments longer, then jumped when she heard a splash.

A few moments later, Bancroft, Carlton, and Kenway returned to the campfire. Standing by the flames, Bancroft dropped a gun onto a blanket, then turned to face the circle of hammocks.

In a moment of clarity, Alex realized that Bancroft had been carrying *two* guns — one in his hand, and one in his holster. That could only mean —

"We have found Raul Chavez," he announced, his face pale in the moonlight. "The carnivore ants got to him."

"How?" Deborah had rolled out of her bed and stood shivering in the moonlight. "How could carnivore ants attack a full-grown man?"

"He was unconscious on the ground."

The entomologist shook her head. "That's insane. Why would he lie down in the jungle when camp lay only a few meters away? Chavez knew better."

Bancroft looked at Carlton, who nodded almost imperceptibly. With some sort of permission granted, Bancroft pulled something from his pocket. "We found this lodged in his neck."

He powered on his flashlight, then held a slender object to the beam. Squinting, Alex could barely see something like a splinter between his fingers.

The security chief gave Alejandro Delmar a faintly accusing look. "Can you explain this, sir?"

"A poison dart." Delmar's voice had gone flat. "Made from a sliver of the inayuga palm and designed to immobilize an enemy. The paralysis is not permanent, but the ants must have gotten to Chavez . . . before he woke up."

Alex looked away as nausea roiled in her belly.

"Somebody's out there." Lauren stepped out of her hammock, her feet bare. "Good grief, Ken, somebody's *out there!*"

"Of course." Carlton shrugged. "They're probably the people we've come to find."

"Chavez would not have felt anything." Wrapping her arms around herself, Deborah moved into the dim glow of the fire. "The bite of the carnivore ant numbs the victim. His limbs would have been insentient long before he died."

Lauren moved toward the men, her eyes blazing. "You expect me to stay here with some crazy savages out there?"

"They didn't mean to kill him." Delmar's eyes had gone dark and unreadable in the firelight. "There is no honor in killing a man unless you are face to face with your enemy. They meant to paralyze him. I think they wanted to capture him, but something frightened them away."

"Mom?" Caitlyn's voice trembled.

Alex fumbled for the shoes she'd stashed at the end of her hammock. "I'm coming, honey. Stay put."

Bancroft pinned Delmar in a steely gaze. "Why Chavez?"

Delmar shrugged. "He is Indian. You are outsiders. Chavez was less intimidating."

Deborah pulled her flashlight from her pocket. "I'd like to see the ants, please."

Bancroft scraped his hand across his face. "Not possible. We disposed of the body."

"I understand, but I still want to see the ants. Will you take me to the spot where you found them feeding?"

"You threw him in the *lake?*" Lauren screeched like a starlet auditioning for a B movie. "Ken, I've had it. I want you to take me out of this godforsaken place *now!*"

As Alex hurried to her daughter's hammock, Emma Whitmore stepped free from her mosquito netting. "I know it's asking a lot, but could we possibly retrieve the body and carry it back to the lodge? His people will want to bury him properly."

"Dr. Whitmore." Delmar's dark face and direct eyes, which could intimidate most people even from a good distance, filled with exasperation. "You are in the tropics. Burial must take place quickly here, because decomposition —" he hesitated as Alex pointedly cleared her throat, reminding him of the child in their midst — "well, we could not wait. Chavez would understand; his family will understand."

"And you, sir, are a disgrace to your ancestors." Emma drew herself up to her full height of five feet, maybe two inches. "If you were living in the jungle with your forefathers, you would burn the body and then drink the ashes so a part of your brother, your heritage, would forever be a part of you."

"I do not follow the practices of my forefathers," Delmar interrupted. Though he had to be ticked off by Whitmore's sanctimonious sermonizing, his face remained locked in neutral. "I am an educated man, a product of a higher civilization. And Chavez was no brother of mine."

Leaving her teammates to squabble over

their differences, Alex crawled into Caitlyn's hammock and slipped her arms around her daughter. Holding Caitlyn's damp head against her pounding heart, she realized the full horror of what had happened. Raul Chavez had supported a wife and four young children in Iquitos. Now his wife would either have to find employment or depend upon the charity of relatives . . . not an easy thing when families routinely averaged ten or twelve members.

Would Chavez's children end up sleeping on the crowded sidewalks of that river city?

She pressed her hands over Caitlyn's ears as Emma's and Delmar's bickering combined with Lauren's hysterics. The younger woman might be worthless in the wilds, but she had a point. Someone was out there — and so far, contact with them had proven deadly.

12 April 2003
8:15 p.m.

Michael swiped his hand through his hair as Alexandra shielded her daughter from the sight of Lauren's mad flailings. The executive's woman was going off in a full-fledged tantrum, beating her man's chest and shrieking so loudly that even the insect chatter faded.

He flinched as something splashed in the lake. Bancroft must have heard the sound, too, for the arm holding his gun tensed. The guard stared toward the lake, then caught Michael's eye. Lifting his free hand, he pointed toward the outer rim of the camp and drew a circle in the air, signaling that Michael should walk around and check things out . . .

Armed with *what?* Michael's brain protested even as he turned to obey. He had a knife strapped to his belt, but it was only a six-inch blade, not a machete. Still, his hand

329

sought the reassuring solidity of the handle.

Moving quietly so as not to arouse the others, he crept toward the hammock where Louis Fortier lay with open, glassy eyes. The sedative had not yet had time to work, but perhaps he had quieted under a placebo effect . . . or the fellow had slipped into shock. Michael couldn't fault him if the latter were true. He'd be in shock, too, if he'd gone to relieve himself in the grass, tripped, and fallen on the half-devoured face of a friend.

Glancing over his shoulder, Michael saw Milos Olsson hand the Indian dart to Emma Whitmore. "What do you think about this?" The botanist's deep voice growled through the darkness. "You know about jungle people — what does this mean?"

Emma took one look at the dart, then dropped it back into the Swede's palm. "I think it's a warning, no more. We are uncomfortably close to their village, and this is a warning to stay away. Though many tribes are nomadic, they still consider the surrounding environs their own territory." Her eyes moved out into the dark, looking toward the lake and the island beyond. "Yet I doubt this tribe is nomadic. They have found security on that island, and they may have lived there for generations. If so, they will be determined to protect it."

Michael moved past Fortier's hammock, treading as silently as he could through the

330

tangling vines and broken shrubs. Holding tight to his knife with his left hand, he used his right to bounce the beam of his flashlight from tree to shrub, investigating the foliage along the edge of the camp.

"I say we establish a perimeter beyond the hammocks," Bancroft called, his voice strong and reassuring. "We station guards at the north, south, east, and west. Though we'll keep the fire blazing through the night, we're in luck because the moon is bright and right above —"

Michael froze in mid-step when the big man's voice broke. Glancing through the hammocks toward the fire, he saw Bancroft's eyes widen until they appeared to be in danger of falling out of his face.

Michael's feeling of uneasiness turned into a deeper and more immediate fear when Bancroft pitched forward. From the security of Carlton's arms, Lauren screamed as the executive folded gently at the knees and crumpled into a heap. Olsson, who had been reaching for Chavez's weapon, looked at Michael with wild eyes, then slapped at his neck, cursed, and tumbled into the fire.

Without pausing to think, Michael ran forward to yank the big Swede away from the flames. He grabbed the man's arms and pulled; when he looked up, Alexandra stood beside him, dragging Olsson by the boots.

"Take cover," he yelled. "We don't know

331

who —"

He flinched as the distinctive chatter of a machine gun shattered the night. Lauren had picked up Bancroft's weapon and was now shredding tender trees and foliage, ripping into anything that stirred the moonlit darkness.

"She's lost it!" Alexandra screamed, crouching as she ran toward her daughter's hammock.

Michael would have agreed, but necessity demanded that he hit the ground. Fortunately, Valerik Baklanov stood behind Lauren. Moving in from behind, he wrapped the hysterical young woman in a bear hug, lifting her from the ground until she dropped the weapon. After Emma darted forward to retrieve both guards' weapons, Michael turned to check on Alex and Caitlyn. The spunky girl had rolled out of her hammock and dropped to the ground at the sound of gunfire; now she and her mother lay amid a pile of tangled vines.

Rising to his knees, Michael noted that they were safe, then felt the hair at the back of his neck bristle with premonition.

From out of the darkness dense with trees and leaves and shadows, the jungle's soft breath carried the scents of sweat and aggression. Someone was close. And somehow — from some primal or extrasensory ability — he knew the enemy was dangerous.

He heard the quiet *pffft,* felt the stinging bite of the dart, and barely had time to fumble at his neck before his arms went limp and his legs gave way. He heard sharp cries and high-pitched screams, then his cheek slammed to the earth and he could not even summon the strength to blink the sand from his lashes.

Helpless, he lay on the ground and watched as ghosts of darkness entered the camp.

Mindless of ants, spiders, or anything else that might be crawling over the ground, Alex lay on top of her daughter, holding Caitlyn's shoulders tight. The last five minutes had passed in a blur, imprinting surreal images upon her mind. The men had fallen, one by one, and then the natives entered the camp, as fearless as eagles defending the sky. Emma Whitmore, who had captured both high-powered weapons, had kicked dirt over them as the Indians approached. Now she stood before the invaders in a posture of relaxed submission.

Alex blinked, then shook her head. She would never understand anthropologists.

"Mom?" Caitlyn's voice quavered.

"Shh, honey. We have to keep our heads."

At least two dozen natives had entered the camp — small brown men who had painted their faces and bodies in white lines and red patterns. Carrying clubs, bows, and spears, they scattered throughout the camp like ants exploring a picnic blanket.

When one of the men reached out to touch Lauren, she threw up her hands and ran screaming toward the lake. The warrior showed no expression, but nocked an arrow, then drew back the string and let the missile fly. Alex didn't see it strike, but by the sudden halt of Lauren's screaming, she surmised it had found its mark.

Twinkle, twinkle, little star.

She closed her eyes, her heart beating hard enough to be heard a yard away. Lauren might have been an affront to self-sufficient womanhood, but she didn't deserve to die like that.

"Rule number one," Alex whispered in her daughter's ear. "Whatever you do, don't run."

As she and Caitlyn lay motionless, the natives swarmed over the moonlit camp, poking at backpacks and prodding paralyzed men with the tips of their weapons. Alex's heart skipped a beat when one man pressed the sharpened edge of a spear to Michael Kenway's throat, but the native only screeched something in a language she couldn't understand, then scampered away.

A moment later a fiercely painted warrior stood directly before her, blocking her view of the others. He yelled, gestured toward the moonlit lake, and then stabbed at the earth with his spear.

Clearing her throat, Alex lifted her head as much as she dared. "My name is Alexandra." She lifted her hand to show she carried no weapon. "We mean you no harm."

When the warrior had the temerity to jab at the earth an inch from Caitlyn's head, Alex realized the futility of their situation. "All right," she snapped, determined not to show her fear. "We'll get up."

Moving with extreme caution, she helped Caitlyn to her feet, then surveyed their captor. The warrior before them was only an inch or two taller than Caitlyn — probably no more than five feet. But he was angry and armed, so they obeyed his prodding spear and walked toward the water.

Apparently content to leave the paralyzed men where they had fallen, the natives herded the women into canoes hidden among the grasses at the lake's edge.

Caitlyn balked at the sight of the shallow canoe. "I don't think this is such a good idea, Mom."

"It's all right, honey. Just follow me." Carefully, Alex crawled the length of the canoe, then sat back and gripped the narrow edges. "Remember all the natives we saw in canoes at Yarupapa? Just pretend we're with them, and we'll be fine."

Her temper spiked when she saw the anthropologist crawl into position behind Caitlyn. "Good grief, Emma, you had a gun. Why on earth did you put it down?"

The older woman gave her a disdainful look. "How are we supposed to learn anything from these people if we shoot them?"

"But they attacked us! Our guys were dropping like flies!"

"They subdued our men with more charity than we would have exhibited in the same situation. None of them have died."

"What about Chavez?"

"An unfortunate accident."

"What about Lauren Hayworth?"

The older woman's eyes closed. "That was regrettable. But she resisted, and with all that screaming she signaled she wouldn't cooperate. Remember this, Alex — they are more frightened of us than we are of them. That's what all this stomping and posturing is about — they're trying to convince us they are fearless."

"They're doing a remarkably good job."

Clinging tighter to the sides of the narrow canoe, Alex faced the darkness on the lake beyond. "I don't suppose, Emma, that you can guess what will happen next?"

The sound of a warrior splashing through the shallows prevented the woman's response. Apparently the sound of their conversation had displeased him, for he lifted his club and snarled out terse commands that must have had something to do with silence.

Alex hung her head in the same submissive posture she'd seen Emma adopt earlier. Her cowering seemed to please him, for he splashed away, leaving them alone.

"You speak the Indian language, don't you?" Alex whispered. "Can you understand anything of what they're saying?"

"Only a few passing words." Emma spoke in a stage whisper. "And I can't be certain what will happen next until we see the village. I suspect their community may be in need of women. Females are the lifeblood of a native community; they produce the children that make a people strong."

"Mom?" Honest fear threaded Caitlyn's voice. "I'd like to go home now."

As Alex turned to comfort her daughter, a warrior loomed out of the darkness and rapped her temple with the narrow edge of an oar. As a flashbulb went off behind her eyes, she leaned forward into the shallow bow, then pressed her hand to her throbbing head.

"It's okay, honey," she whispered, not daring to turn around again. "We're going to be okay."

"Fine?" Caitlyn's voice wavered.

"Great."

"Okey-dokey?"

"All right."

"Satisfactory?"

"Absolutely, irrefutably acceptable."

Back and forth they batted words of assurance as the natives launched the canoe into the deep.

12 April 2003
11:54 p.m.

Still groggy from the effects of whatever drug had been smeared on the dart, with difficulty Michael turned over and pulled himself into a sitting position. His captors had tied his hands behind his back with some sort of stinging vine, and testing the ropes only seemed to increase whatever botanical secretions irritated the skin.

Enveloped in a drugged blanket of exhaustion, Michael forced himself to focus on his surroundings. He could see none of the women; like phantoms they had vanished into the jungle. Their attackers had ripped every hammock from the trees; the contents of backpacks lay scattered over the ground.

Several of the painted warriors crouched around curiosities — one man peered into a mirror, another ran his thumb over the spines of a hairbrush. One fellow squatted on his haunches, staring wide-eyed as a breeze off the lake ruffled the pages of what appeared to be a handwritten journal . . .

Alex's notebook. Michael strained against his bonds, then felt the reproving bite of the malicious vines at his wrists. Taking a deep breath, he flexed his fingers until the urge to strangle the native had passed.

He had to collect his wits, evaluate the situation. At least, thank God, he was not alone.

All the men of their party had been tied up; several were scattered around the campfire, sitting where they had fallen. Taking a mental headcount, Michael came up short, then realized Louis Fortier was missing. He glanced toward the Frenchman's hammock to make sure the man was not hiding beneath the mosquito netting, but the slashed screen lay trampled on the ground, leaving the hammock empty. Realizing the little Frenchman must have slipped away in the confusion, for an instant Michael felt the stirring of hope — perhaps Fortier could reach civilization and get help.

His hope shriveled when he recalled Fortier's state of mind just before the attack. And how far could he run with heavy sedatives in his bloodstream?

Michael shuddered to think the perfumer might meet with Chavez's fate. On the other hand, there were worse ways to die in the jungle.

God, be merciful to him.

He shifted his gaze toward Alexandra's hammock, then felt a stab of memory. The women had been taken away over the lake — he had heard them calling reassurances to each other before he slipped into a drug-induced doze. Some of the invaders had undoubtedly gone with the women, yet several remained behind to bind the men and raid the camp.

The leader of the remaining group now seemed to be arguing with Alejandro Delmar. The Brazilian tracker was awake, angry, and defiant. Bancroft, who was tied as tight as a Scotsman's purse, kept demanding to know what the warrior was saying.

"I don't know," Delmar snapped. "I've never heard this language. It seems to be a cross of Yagua and Yanomamo."

"So? Can you speak those languages?"

"Shut up, Mr. Bancroft, and let me do my best."

Something in the tone of Delmar's voice, the natives' gestures, and Bancroft's frustrated expression told Michael that the guide was arguing for their lives. After one particularly impassioned exchange, in which Delmar repeated a series of words that only seemed to incense the warrior, the native planted his spear in the earth next to the fire, then stalked toward the lake, leaving his captives alone.

"They want the women," Delmar explained,

twisting to look around at the others. "They do not want or need us. But I've tried to convince him we are valuable people who could do much for their tribe." Looking past Bancroft, he caught Michael's eye. "I told him one of our men was a great healer."

Michael snorted. "In a hospital, maybe I could do some good. But out here?"

"You *are* a great healer," Delmar stressed. "If ever you believed that, you'd better believe it now. And Olsson —" he inclined his head toward the botanist — "is a great shaman who knows the secrets of jungle plants."

Olsson groaned. "If only."

A sneer of derision crossed Carlton's face. "You think you can negotiate with these heathens? You can't reason with unreasonable people —"

"I can reach them," Delmar said simply, his dark eyes gleaming in the light from the sputtering fire.

Michael considered the man's answer and found it credible. Alejandro Delmar was Indian, and he certainly had more experience in the jungle.

"I say we let Delmar do whatever he needs to do." Michael looked directly at the American. "This is no longer your expedition, Carlton. We must let Delmar take the lead."

Carlton snorted softly. "Fine. Just get us to the women, then get us out of here. Tell them whatever you need to tell them." His cold eyes sniped at Bancroft. "What did you tell them about *him?* That he's utterly worthless as a guard?"

"I said he is strong," Delmar answered. "He can lift a man with one hand. And Baklanov can see into the spirit of water and know when it will make people sick."

Carlton's mouth curved into a half-smile. "What'd you tell them about me?"

A sneer might have flitted into Delmar's shadowed eyes, but Michael couldn't be sure.

"I could say you were good at making money," the guide said, "but money means nothing here. So I said you are good for nothing."

Carlton's face twisted.

"They believed me, too," Delmar went on with killing calmness, "because only a fool would bring a stupid woman into the jungle — a woman not even his wife."

His face darkening, Carlton strained at his bonds for a full minute before dropping his shoulders in frustration.

He glared at Delmar. "You wait. When we get out of here, I'll have you blacklisted, blackballed, arrested, jailed, and whatever else occurs to me."

"I do not think so, Mr. Carlton." Delmar lifted his head like a cat calmly scenting the breeze. "This is the jungle, not America. These warriors will have to transport and feed the captives they take. Why should they carry a worthless man back to their village?"

At that moment the painted warrior returned to the fire circle. As the tattered fire cast its red light upon the conqueror, Michael felt a memory close around him.

Beneath his war paint, this native's skin was mottled with tattoos . . . exactly like Ya-ree's.

Calling to his companions, the warrior plucked his spear from the mud, then pointed toward the lake.

Almost immediately, another warrior's weapon pressed against Michael's rib cage.

Amid a chorus of shouting from the other natives, Michael groaned. "All right," he said, leaning forward to gain his footing. His legs still felt heavy and sluggish, but his stunned muscles worked well enough for him to stand and stumble through the lakeside vegetation. When he reached the shore, he saw that Delmar, Baklanov, Bancroft, and Olsson had preceded him into canoes.

Olsson's face had gone pale in the moonlight. As Michael settled behind him, he asked, "Did you see her lying there?"

Michael took a deep breath to quell the leaping pulse beneath his ribs. "Who?"

"Carlton's woman. Dead in the grass."

Michael closed his eyes as a bead of perspiration traced a cold path from his armpit to his rib. "I didn't see. Were there others?"

Olsson's jaw clenched. "I saw no others. But who knows?"

A few moments later they were floating over water the color of strong tea. Only when he twisted to look behind him did Michael realize Kenneth Carlton was not aboard either boat.

Alex's pulse quickened as the canoes slid onto a patch of soft sand. They had been traveling for hours, and her legs and feet were numb from crouching in the canoe. Subdued by the threat of their captor's club, Deborah and Emma had not spoken on the journey. Caitlyn had actually managed to sleep, her arms around Alex's waist and her head upon her mother's shoulder. Alex, however, had remained awake and shivering in the front of the boat, feeling like the point man on an incursion into unexplored and dangerous territory.

As soon as the bow touched earth, she heard a sudden splash and the sound of Caitlyn's gasp. One of the natives had jumped into thigh-deep water and was now urging the women to follow him.

"Mom," Caitlyn clung to Alex's shoulders, "there are *things* in that water."

Holding tight to the side of the canoe, Alex shuddered as fearful images rose in her mind. Caitlyn was right — anaconda lived in these black waters, and leeches, and piranha, electric eels, and who knew what else.

No. She could not panic now. She could not lose it here because these natives had no patience with women who dissolved into hysterics.

"So?" She injected an artificially bright note into her voice. "You said Lazaro swims in these waters all the time."

"But he's . . . used to them. I'm not."

Drawing deep breaths, Alex turned to look behind her. Emma had already jumped out of the boat, while Deborah scrambled to obey the warrior who kept jabbing her shoulder with the head of his club.

Alex focused on her daughter. "It's going to be okay, honey. If these people aren't afraid to walk through the water, we won't be afraid to wade only a couple of steps."

Gulping in a deep breath, she rose and extended her tingling legs into the lake. She had expected a shock, but the water felt surprisingly warm on her skin. Caitlyn followed, squeaking as her ankles disappeared into the brown liquid, then she took Alex's hand. Together they waded onto the shore.

With Deborah and Emma, they stood in silence for a moment while their captors ran around them in some sort of celebratory moonlight dance. They filled the air with warbling whoops until another contingent of natives arrived. Broad smiles shone from the faces of excited men and women, then the warriors prodded their captives forward.

Alex clung to Caitlyn's hand and followed Emma and Deborah, their wet sneakers squishing as they walked. A narrow trail had been trampled through the tall grasses, and they passed through it in a single line. The path ended in an open space before a round-house of timber and thatch. Two poles flanked the opening, each topped by a toothless, grinning skull.

Caitlyn tightened her arms around Alex's waist while Emma eyed the totems.

Alex stepped closer to whisper in the anthropologist's ear. "Do you think they are cannibals?"

Emma's eyes lowered, as did her voice. "Possibly. But I think these skulls are intended as a warning. Notice that they have no teeth — they probably came from people who died at an advanced age."

Alex frowned as a memory surfaced. "I thought most Indian tribes ground the bones of their dead and drank the dust."

"Many do. But there are always exceptions." Lifting her head, Emma met the bold gaze of one of the warriors, then inclined her head in a display of respect. "These skulls," she continued, keeping her voice low, "might belong to enemies. Or they might have done something to disgrace themselves in the eyes of the tribe. So the others would not want to drink their ashes."

Caitlyn tugged on Alex's arm. "Mom, what do they want from us?"

Alex glanced at Emma, who lifted her shoulders in a shrug, then followed the native who was gesturing toward the roundhouse.

Alex pasted on a nonchalant smile. "I hope, sweetie, that they're going to give us a night-time snack. I'm hungry enough to eat a tapir — how about you?"

Guiding Caitlyn, she followed Emma over a trail gnarly with roots, then heard Deborah's whispered comment as the entomologist brought up the rear: "I just hope they're not planning to put us on the menu."

The sun had begun to brighten the eastern horizon by the time the warriors' canoes reached what appeared to be a lakeside settlement. Michael had tried to follow their course as they paddled through the darkness, but even by the light of a full moon it was difficult to determine in which direction they were traveling. All their equipment — weapons, GPS systems, and even Michael's small compass — remained in the camp, where it would be ruined by rain and scattered by animals unless they could retrieve it quickly.

He glanced down, where the leather sheaf of his hunting knife still hung from his belt. The length of the scabbard had slipped into his pants pocket, obscuring all but the strap and hilt. The natives hadn't looked for a blade at his waist. Perhaps they had never seen a knife.

The thought of his weapon brought a dark

little pleasure. Though he couldn't reach it with his hands bound, it might prove useful in the hours ahead.

After an initial exchange of threats and grumbling, his companions and their captors settled into silence for the journey. The night whispered, chirped, and hissed as invisible things moved under the susurration of the wind. A circle of moon hung amid a jumble of stars above them, while around them black water held secrets Michael wasn't particularly keen to discover.

He had assumed these warriors lived on the island they had seen from the lakeshore, but though the natives initially paddled toward it, they skirted the island's edge and steered into a curve of the lake that lay hidden behind the elevated knoll. The lake turned out to be longer and larger than the explorers had imagined.

As the India ink sky brightened to deep purple and then to indigo, the natives quickened their pace and moved toward a clearing on a distant shore. As soon as the boats approached, several of the warriors leaped into the water and urged their captives to do the same.

Michael obeyed, stepping into bath-warm water, then splashed his way toward the others. He caught Olsson's eye, then shook his head, acknowledging a grudging respect for the well-planned raid. The warriors' weapons kept the captives in line, the savage vine kept their hands still, and the watchful eyes of warriors with blowguns kept them obedient. None of them wanted to suffer the effects of another paralyzing dart, for falling into the lake could easily prove fatal.

Once they were all ashore, the leading warrior pointed to a trail. The natives positioned themselves among the group, then they set out at a quick pace, following a flattened path cut through sharp-edged grasses.

As he strode forward, Michael couldn't help wondering what had happened to Carlton. Had the warriors cut his throat? Cracked his skull with a club? Immobilized him with another dart? Whatever they had done, they had accomplished their work quickly and efficiently, for Michael hadn't heard a sound from the executive. And even if the blow had not killed the American, he wouldn't last long in the jungle with his hands tied.

Michael glanced back at Olsson, trudging behind him. "What sort of vine would you say this is?"

The Swede shook his bushy head. "There is a giant stinging tree in Australia whose leaves inflict pain like a bee sting when touched . . . this might share the same chemical composition." He moved his arms, then winced. "A devilishly ingenious self-defense mechanism, no?"

Michael would have replied, but the warrior in front of him turned and lifted his spear while shouting an unintelligible phrase. Michael shrugged, then followed the warrior into a clearing where a grisly pair of skulls adorned wooden poles.

Snarling, Bancroft flexed his fists behind his back. "Who *are* these cold-blooded murderers?"

"Do not jump to conclusions, my friend." Baklanov tilted his head toward the skulls. "These bones are weathered, so they have been here for some time. And we do not know that they died anything but a natural death."

Bancroft growled deep in his throat. "Doesn't matter. People who use human skulls for decoration are seriously demented."

The painted warrior who had done the most shouting back at the camp walked to the head of their line, then waved toward a structure made of sticks and palm fronds. Michael closed his eyes. What had Emma called it? A roundhouse. A shabono.

Bancroft growled again. "He wants us to go in."

Delmar threw a warning look over his shoulder. "We should follow him. I do not think they intend to kill us — at least not without testing our abilities. Who knows?" His golden smile sparkled through the gloom. "If they find you useful, they might decide to keep you."

The former SEAL thrust his chin forward. "And you? You figure you're gonna get some special compensation just 'cause you can stutter enough of their language to make yourself understood?"

"I think I'm going to get out of here," Delmar answered, calmly turning toward the wooden structure. "If you're wise, you'll come with me."

With no other choice, Michael followed the others into the roundhouse. Once inside, he peered at the calm village scene, a bit astonished that such violent people could belong to such a peaceful place. He wasn't sure what he had expected, but he hadn't expected to see hammocks filled with sleeping children or women breast-feeding infants around the central fire.

The sleeping hammocks hung from poles supporting a roof that extended only along the outermost edges of the circular building. In an area open to the sky, banked coals glowed beneath the carcass of some pig-like animal, probably a tapir, which hung on a spit. A wizened older woman with short dark hair squatted by the fire, a green palm frond in her hand and a wary expression on her face.

He drew a deep breath, inhaling the scents of smoke, roasted flesh, and assorted odors associated with unwashed human bodies. Moving slowly as not to alarm anyone, Michael turned to survey the rest of the building. In the shadows under the roofed section, women cowered behind straw baskets while small-boned men stood alertly watching.

Like the warriors who had appeared in the night, these men wore nothing but strings around their waists. None of them wore beards, and all of them had short hair, shaped in what Michael thought his female teammates would call a bowl cut.

Taking a quick headcount, he estimated the building held at least fifty men and half as many women. Impossible to count the children, for most of them were hiding behind their elders.

"Dr. Kenway?" Starting at the sound of a familiar voice, he turned and saw Emma Whitmore and Deborah Simons seated behind a half-wall of palm leaves. A chill climbed the ladder of his spine until he walked forward and found Alexandra and Caitlyn huddled together and half-hidden by shadow.

Thank God their group had suffered no other casualties.

"Are you all right?" he called, careful not to raise his voice beyond the limit of their captives' tolerance.

Emma lowered her chin in a determined nod. "We're fine. We were herded here and left . . . to wait for you, I suppose."

He jerked his thumb toward Delmar. "I

wasn't so sure we were going to make it. But apparently our guide has convinced them that we blokes are extraordinarily gifted. Whether or not they'll buy that story is another matter."

He glanced at Alexandra. Weariness had carved merciless lines on her face, but determination still lay in the jut of her chin.

"How are you two getting on?" he asked.

"Fine." Caitlyn clapped her hands on her arms. "I've never had an adventure like this. It's invigorating, exhilarating, enervating, and stimulating!"

Alexandra's expression softened into one of affectionate patience. "We're good," she said, giving him a relieved smile. "And we're glad to see you. For a moment, I feared . . ." She blushed as her words trailed away. "It's good to see you, Kenway. All of you guys, I mean."

"Carlton didn't make it. Neither did Fortier." Their eyes met, and Michael knew he couldn't say anything more in front of the child.

Alexandra gave him a quick, denying glance, then lowered her eyes. "I'm so sorry."

"So am I."

He would have sat with her to offer further comfort, but at that moment the Indian men moved toward the central fire. The warriors who had raided the camp entered the alcove where Michael and the women waited.

Caitlyn's eyes widened as the natives began

to gesture toward the fire. "I think they want us."

"I think you're right."

After being jostled and shoved, he found himself wedged between Caitlyn and her mother as the expedition members were forced to sit on the sand around the fire. As they stared at each other through the wood smoke, two natives stepped forward and carried the tapir away, grunting with exertion as they removed the spit from its supports.

While the native women gathered to cut up the meat, an old man more tattooed and painted than any of the others emerged from the shadows with a long reed in his hand.

Michael searched his memory, but couldn't recall seeing the older man at their campsite. He was not a warrior, then . . . perhaps the village shaman?

A pair of young boys sat behind the captives with drums between their knees. They began to play, the rhythm of the drums increasing and growing stronger with the rising of the sun. The painted man accepted a gourd from one of the women, then dipped his fingers in it and knelt to smear a white streak across Olsson's nose. The Swede recoiled, but a curt command from Delmar stopped him.

"Let him paint you," the guide called, his voice firm and final. "Without paint, in their eyes you are shamefully naked." His voice lowered to a somber tone. "We are about to partake in some sort of ceremony. If you are not painted, you will be cast out of the shabono in disgrace. I think you know what can happen to outcasts."

Sighing in resignation, Olsson sat motionless as the shaman dabbed white streaks on his forehead. At the other side of the circle, the old woman dipped her fingers in a clay bowl and streaked the women's faces with blue mud.

The women, Michael noticed, seemed to be coping well with the strain. Emma watched the proceedings with the frank curiosity of a scientist at home in her field. Deborah wore an expression of bewilderment, but her hands did not shake and her voice did not tremble. Worry had etched fine lines between Alexandra's brows, and though Caitlyn squeaked when the old woman's fingers smeared paint over her cheeks, the girl did not cry out.

Michael closed his eyes when the paint pot approached. Though everything in him wanted to stand and beat a path back to civilization, he could do nothing but wait.

Looking up, he stared into the eyes of the old shaman and felt a shock of recognition — the man's eyes were hazel, as Ya-ree's had been. Another link.

The drums continued throughout the painting ritual. When the old man and woman had finished, the painted man handed his gourd to a child, then began to dance around the fire. The others joined in, following his example as he whirled and stomped and jerked to the pervasive rhythm of the drums.

As the men lost themselves in the dance, Bancroft leaned toward Michael. "Whaddaya say, Doc? You think those vines on your wrists are loosening?"

Michael flexed his arms, then winced as the stinging vine attacked his skin. "Sorry. The devilish thing is as nasty as ever."

"All right, then." Bancroft lowered his chin, his eyes following the dancing shaman. "We could still try to take some of them out. If I made like a human battering ram, I could probably lay the old guy flat and take out a couple of others. One of the women could untie your arms in the confusion, and —"

"Forget it." Delmar gave the chiseled guard a narrowed glinting glance. "You will make things worse. Wait and see what the shaman wants of us."

"You're a fool, Bancroft." This blunt observation came from Emma, who stopped smiling gamely at the dancers long enough to shoot daggers at the guard. "We came here in search of Kenway's tattooed patient's tribe. Look around — we have found it! Sometimes things don't go the way we planned once we enter the field."

Bancroft began to sputter. "You think this is a simple change of plans? Carlton is *dead,*

360

lady! Lauren is dead! We've lost Chavez and probably Fortier —"

"Hush!" Alexandra leaned forward, her eyes blazing. "May I remind you there's a child present?"

Bancroft cursed, then scrubbed his hand through his hair and muttered under his breath. Michael had to admit Delmar and Emma had a point. Though waiting undoubtedly went against Bancroft's gung-ho nature, they were not being tortured or otherwise mistreated. But it would be wise to remember that these natives had no compunctions against killing.

"Dr. Kenway?"

He looked down to see Caitlyn looking at him, her brown eyes wide. The enthusiasm she had exhibited earlier had disappeared.

"Are you okay, Cait?"

She nodded, then lowered her voice to a ragged whisper. "Do you think they're going to eat us?"

Michael forced a laugh. "I certainly hope not. I don't think a group as cheeky as this lot would be very digestible."

Her eyes widened farther, then a slow smile lit her face. "You're funny, Dr. Kenway."

"Hmm." Michael shifted his gaze back to the twirling medicine man. "Your mother wouldn't think so. She thinks I'm a little mad."

The girl leaned close enough to whisper in

361

his ear. "She thinks that about nearly every-body."

They fell silent as the day brightened. Shadows that had lingered in the western compartments of the shabono fled away as sunlight came pouring over the rim of the truncated roof. The drums raced, sending the dancers spiraling in faster, tighter steps, then the shaman dropped to the sand and knelt there, his chest heaving in exertion.

The other dancers quieted, the women and children crept closer. The drums continued, but in a softer, slower beat. Michael found himself holding his breath, anticipating whatever significant moment had to follow.

The painted shaman, who had appeared ut-terly spent only a moment before, rose to stand at the edge of the fire. From the sand he picked up a branch, then held it out and walked before their group like a salesman displaying his wares.

Michael could see that an iridescent green powder filled a bowl at the end of the stick. Comprehension seeped through his confu-sion — this was no ordinary branch. The sha-man held a *pipe.*

With great flair, the shaman inserted the hollow end of the pipe into his nostril, then closed his eyes as another warrior covered the bowl with his mouth, then blew the powder through the pipe with one powerful breath. The shaman stiffened, his face contorting into a painful grimace, and for a horrified moment Michael feared the man had overdosed on whatever substance filled the bowl. Then the native staggered two steps forward and sank to the earth, staring into nothingness.

"Delmar," Michael whispered as loudly as he dared, "care to explain any of this?"

"It is a trance," Delmar explained. "He has taken the ebene and called upon the spirit of his animal. Now he is roaming through the jungle, seeing everything the animal sees."

Bancroft snorted. "Hogwash."

"No, no, there is great truth in the traditions of spiritualism." Emma leaned into the conversation. "There are forces in the world far older than human civilization. What you are seeing is a practice reaching back to the beginning of human history."

"It's evil." Michael hadn't meant to speak so abruptly, but the words slipped from his lips. He glanced over to see Alexandra gaping at him — whatever for? Couldn't a man be politically incorrect when life and limb were at stake?

"I'd appreciate it if you'd keep your opinions to yourself," she hissed, glancing warily at the warriors who seemed to have forgotten their captives. "I think we're supposed to watch this — maybe even appreciate it."

"I'll never be able to appreciate what I'm seeing now." Steeling himself to her disapproval, Michael looked around the circle. "The world is full of spirits, good and evil, but you cannot acknowledge them without also acknowledging God, who is above all. Spirits either serve God, who is good, or Satan, who is evil. By binding these people to drugs and evil spirits, Satan has endeavored to be sure they will never know the truth."

"Do you *mind?*" Alexandra's weary voice dripped with sarcasm. "You're teaching a Sunday school lesson while Delmar is trying to prevent us from becoming hors d'oeuvres."

Emma pushed pearly beads of perspiration into the fringe of white hair on her forehead. "Dr. Kenway, I suggest you open your mind to reality. The mind-set you're exhibiting has caused the annihilation of countless tribal groups." A strong note of reproof underlined her voice. "When missionaries enter a village, they usually insist the people wear *their* clothing, worship *their* God, live according to *their* standards. Because they bring valuable tools and medicines, they are welcomed. But they also bring diseases for which the natives have no natural immunity. I happen to think that religion as you describe it is another ailment for which the natives have little resistance — and it destroys native life even more completely than disease."

Shifting her eyes from the transfixed shaman, Emma turned the full heat of her glare on Michael. "Where is your good and loving

God when tragedy strikes through the actions of Christian missionaries? Don't you find it ironic that the same religion you claim offers eternal life all too often brings death to these villages?"

Michael opened his mouth to reply, but the shaman, who had not stirred since kneeling in his trance, suddenly began to move in twitchy, epileptic jerks. Michael tensed, convinced the man needed medical attention, but when the pace of the drums picked up, the shaman responded in tempo. As the beat increased, the medicine man stood and danced, shuddering and twitching in an invisible world that reeked of demonic influence.

The old man swirled, jerking like a marionette on a string before Alexandra, then he bent at the waist and pitched forward, landing on his hands with his face only inches from Michael's. The man's eyes filled Michael's vision, his pupils dilated and skin flushed, then he opened his mouth in a scream so piercing Michael had to resist the urge to clap his hands over his ears. A torrent of words followed the scream, a fluid language completely unlike the guttural tongue the natives had spoken before. For a moment Michael wondered if he had descended into some sort of private hell, then the shaman's outburst ceased as abruptly as it had begun. The drums stopped. A churchlike stillness reigned over the shabono, with nothing but the morning cacophony of jungle birds to disturb it.

Michael glanced around, hoping to spy something that might help him make sense of the situation. Delmar provided the answer.

"He says," the guide whispered, his voice flat and faint, "that his wife is sick and you bewitched her."

Michael felt his jaw drop. "Tell him I did nothing of the sort. I am a doctor. I try to make people well."

Delmar lifted his head, about to translate, but the shaman danced away, screaming new words in a steady stream. The drums began to pound again, other warriors joined in the shaman's warbling and even the women wailed, their voices lifting to — what? The noise went on and on, lancing the silence, piercing the shabono and the jungle so that even the parrots in nearby trees took flight. The noise built to a deafening crescendo, then abruptly ceased as the shaman crumpled to the ground at Michael's feet.

Again, the drums stopped. Thick silence fell over the roundhouse; not even the babies cried.

After a long moment, the shaman lifted his head and turned to meet Delmar's gaze. The old man spoke, the sounds guttural and incomprehensible, yet Delmar replied, nodding occasionally to emphasize his halting words. On several occasions the two men seemed to shout at one another, and twice Michael thought he recognized the name Ya-ree.

Finally the shaman tilted back his head, stood, and walked toward an alcove built into the side of the roundhouse. The others watched him go, then the assembly broke up. The women returned to their work and their children; the men sharpened their spears and chipped stone to make spearheads.

Michael stared at the stone in one man's hand. Another proof! A stone spear had wounded Ya-ree, and those weapons did not exist in the jungle near Iquitos.

Behind Michael, Bancroft leaned toward Delmar. "Were you able to communicate with the old man?"

Delmar snorted softly. "We were both speaking baby talk, but yes, I think we understood each other."

"Then what in the world is he doing with us? And when is he going to cut these cursed vines from our arms?"

Delmar lifted his gaze to meet Michael's. "He asked your purpose in coming here. They do not often see white men — I don't think this generation has seen any."

"What did you tell him?"

"I said we came in peace, but we sought a tribe of healers. He cursed the name of the healers, he said his people ate the souls of the healers' children. But when he asked how we knew about the healing tribe, I told him about the man you treated in the hospital. He knew him; Kenway's patient was an outcast from this tribe. He then asked why we needed healers if we had a healer among us; I said you cured some diseases, the jungle cured others. We came in search of jungle medicine."

The guide's face clouded as he glanced toward the area where the shaman had retreated. "He knows of the healers — he says they are the people of the keyba."

Michael glanced at Alexandra, eager for her to hear this confirmation of his story. "That's right. My patient spoke of the keyba."

Delmar did not seem to share his enthusiasm. "This shaman will let us go to them only if we take his sick wife with us."

Michael glanced toward the compartment into which the shaman had disappeared. "What's wrong with her?" he asked, though he suspected he already knew the answer.

"He said she has been taken by shuddering disease. It is widespread among their people."

Michael met Alexandra's eye. This might be a prion case . . . or it might not. But Yaree's "shuddering disease" had definitely involved prions as an infective agent.

"Why doesn't *he* take his wife to the healing tribe?" Alexandra asked. "He might discover a cure for his entire village."

"The old man would not admit it," Delmar

answered, "but I suspect he is too proud to beg the healers for help."

"He loves his wife." Michael searched Alexandra's face, wishing he could reach into her thoughts. "The power of love leads people to do unusual things."

He waited, looking for some softening of her eyes or mouth, but she remained focused on the matter at hand.

"There are others with the same illness," she whispered, lifting her hand to discreetly point into the crowd of natives. "See that man with the herky-jerky gait? And the woman sitting near the entrance — some sort of palsy is affecting her arms."

Michael studied the villagers in question, then nodded, silently agreeing with her tentative diagnosis. "Impossible to know for sure, but if the shaman's wife is infected, others could be."

"The shaman cares most for his woman," Delmar continued. "If the people of the keyba heal her and she returns, they will release —" He glanced around the circle.

Alexandra reached for her daughter's hand. *"Who?"*

"Whichever one of us stays behind as a hostage." The guide's heavily lidded eyes flickered for a moment. "It must be a woman, the shaman says, for if they lose a woman, someone else must take her place."

"That's ridiculous." Bancroft strained at his

bonds again, then winced as the vicious fibers stung his skin. Red-faced, he gave Delmar a look of pure menace. "Give me five minutes out of this spiteful string, and I'll beat the desire to bargain out of all of them."

"If we don't agree," Delmar's voice was grave, "they will kill all our men and keep the women." His mouth curled in a slight smile as he shifted toward Alexandra. "As capable as you ladies are, I do not think any of you could find your way out of the jungle alone. All our equipment is lost, along with our weapons."

"I still have a knife." Michael spoke in a hoarse whisper, almost afraid to reveal the ace in his hand. "It slipped into my pocket, and they must not have seen it in the shadows."

Alexandra's eyes widened as she stared at his belt. "For once, the reverend doctor is making sense."

"That's all we need." Bancroft jutted his jaw. "Alex can take the knife and quietly cut us loose. We'll sit still, waiting until they're distracted —"

"There are more than fifty men here," Olsson interrupted. "There are only nine of us. And they have weapons."

A swift shadow of anger swept across the burly guard's face. "They are Stone Age primitives! And they're only five feet tall!"

His face brightening, Baklanov entered the

argument. "Olsson makes a strong point. They had no trouble bringing us down at the camp, did they? Fighting makes no sense. Even if we broke free, how do we know we will not be speared through the back as we try to find our way out of this place?"

Bancroft's nostrils flared. "I am not going to sit here and let a group of pygmies terrorize me!" He looked around the circle. "How many of you agree?"

Michael watched as Bancroft searched for agreement among the men. Baklanov and Olsson lowered their heads, while Delmar lifted his gaze to the sky, refusing to meet Bancroft's eye.

The ex-SEAL licked his lower lip. "So we do nothing, then. You'd rather sit here and let that pint-sized medicine man tell you what to do —"

"I'll stay." Every eye turned when Deborah spoke. Hugging her knees, she turned her face from the fire. "Stop arguing. There's no reason for anyone to be hurt. I'll stay behind."

"Forget it." Bancroft stared at Deborah as if she'd suddenly sprouted another head. "We leave no one behind."

Alexandra reached out, placing her hand on the other woman's arm. "We can't leave you here."

"It's all right." Tears filled Deborah's eyes as she gripped Alex's hand. "Y'all have other commitments; I have no one waiting at home.

What will the world miss if I don't make it out? A horse-fly head count?"

"Deborah, no." Alexandra shook her head. "You can't mean that."

"I do. And who knows? Perhaps I can do some good here."

Emma scooted closer to the entomologist. "Deborah, you don't know what you're saying. These people consider women mere chattel; the men will try to claim you as their personal property as soon as we walk away. I have heard things about the hardships native women face —" She shuddered slightly. "The stories would curl your hair. You simply cannot remain here; it's too dangerous."

Tilting her head back, Deborah blinked up at the open sky. "I'm not afraid. I'm stronger than the native women, and I outweigh most of the men. Besides, I think I have a few tricks up my sleeve — enough to convince them to maintain a respectful distance for a few days."

"I do not recommend this." Delmar shook his head. "I cannot leave a white woman in a native village."

"You have no choice." Deborah's voice had gone soft. "If we resist them, some of you will die along with these people. I don't want anyone to die. Besides —" a tentative smile touched her mouth — "y'all are planning to come back, right?"

Michael looked at Bancroft, who wore an inward look of deep abstraction. When the

372

soldier did not answer, he turned to Deborah. "Of course we'll come back for you." He gave her what he hoped was a confident smile. "As soon as possible."

Emma held up a warning hand. "Hold a minute. What if this healing tribe does nothing for the shaman's wife? What if these stories of healing are only rumors? After all, we haven't even seen the sick woman; she could be suffering from anything."

Michael glanced to the thatched enclosure where the shaman had disappeared, but he could not see beyond the half-wall separating public and private space. Emma had raised an important point. He had spoken impulsively, but he'd only been trying to meet Deborah's boldness with a bold step of his own.

He looked at Alexandra, whose eyes radiated doubt and fear. Her faith in Ya-ree's healing tribe had to be wavering.

He shifted to face the anthropologist. "Are you a woman of faith, Emma?"

Her blue eyes narrowed and hardened. "You know I am. But the repositories of my faith are far different from yours."

"No matter. I was rather hoping you'd understand my reasons for accepting Deborah's brave offer. As I see it, we have a choice here — place faith in our own ability to stand and fight these well-armed people, or place faith in the stories we have now heard from two separate sources. As for me,

I've more faith in the people of the keyba than in Bancroft's plan." He cast the military man a quick glance. "No offense, mate."

Bancroft's brows pulled into a distracted frown, but for the moment he seemed too stunned to speak.

Emma lifted her hands in a gesture of surrender. "Fine. If you and Deborah want to risk her life on a rumor, so be it. If nothing else, the gesture will buy us time."

Olsson's mouth had gone tight and grim. "We are coming back for her, yes?"

Bancroft jerked his head. "Affirmative. Absolutely. With weapons, if necessary." He gave the entomologist a smile that was 90 percent bravado and 10 percent affection. "We won't leave you here, Deb. You have my word on it."

Conversation ceased as a pair of Indian women approached with dripping gourds, offering water to the thirsty captives. Michael took advantage of the distraction to lean over Alexandra and speak directly to Deborah.

"Are you absolutely certain you want to do this? Bancroft is dying to bash some heads together. We could let him have a go at it."

She smiled, but her expression held only a trace of its former warmth. "I'm sure. I'll live here for a while and teach these people everything I know about insects . . . and life. If the Lord wills, y'all will be back for me before too long." Her chin trembled. "If it's not the Lord's will, well, at least you will know I didn't come here with an agenda. I'm only doing what the Lord would want me to do."

Michael looked away as his heart swelled with admiration. In his lifetime he had known many people who claimed the name of Christ, but none had ever demonstrated that allegiance so powerfully.

Dawn came up in streaks and slashes over the rough edge of the thatched roof. Lying with the others near the communal fire, Michael kept his head low so as not to attract attention from the warriors who had been milling about since sunrise.

His companions lay scattered around the fire like rag dolls. Several of the men had groaned and moaned in the night, helpless to ease the pain of blisters left by the stinging vines, but the women hadn't slept much better. Michael had awakened several times when Caitlyn cried out in a nightmare, but the sound of Alexandra's patient shushing eased both Caitlyn and Michael back to sleep.

The tension of the previous day had eased when Delmar told the shaman they would agree to leave one of their women in his village while they transported his wife to the people of the Keyba, also known as the Tree

People. They would then bring the shaman's woman back, and they expected to receive their woman in return.

Michael had studied the shaman while Delmar labored to stitch words together and convey his message. Something brutal creased the shaman's mouth; something feral lurked in his eyes. When Delmar asked why the shaman and his men did not transport the sick woman themselves, the medicine man replied that too much blood had flowed in wars between the two villages. His people hated the people of Keyba Village, and the people of that village had reason to fear the Angry People. So they could not approach on their own, but the people of the keyba would surely accept the nabas . . .

Michael had no trouble believing that the two tribes had been involved in bloody and brutal skirmishes; after all, Ya-ree had died from such an encounter. What surprised him was the discovery that they did not reserve their cruelty for outsiders. The warriors, most of whom came only to Michael's upper arm, thought nothing of clubbing anyone whose attitude they did not like, including their own wives. This morning one of the native women had paused by the fire to stare at the prisoners and a moment later her husband clubbed her on the side of the head. Bleeding from the ear, she huddled like a mouse in the small enclosure where her children slept.

No wonder they were experiencing a shortage of women. They treated their wives like dogs.

Since their arrival, however, no one had struck the captives. After Delmar spoke to the shaman, a pair of warriors stepped forward to cut away the stinging vines that bound the men. Women brought gourds of murky, warm water to ease their thirst.

With the expert eyes of a physician, Michael realized that most of the people were starving. Though they had eaten meat last night, he wondered how often they met with success in the hunt. Most disturbing was the way they ate — the men partook of the kill first, leaving the leftover portions for their women. Only after the prisoners had been fed (grudging handfuls, but food nonetheless) did the women offer their children a few morsels of meat.

A few of the little ones cried almost incessantly. Most had the bloated belly Michael recognized as a symptom of malnutrition. And the tribe's population — probably not more than one hundred, with only a dozen or so children — indicated a high infant mortality rate.

He managed a little wave as Emma, who'd been dozing on the ground next to him, pushed herself upright.

Slowly, she opened her eyes. "Are we still here?"

He released a sour laugh. "Sorry, but it wasn't a bad dream."

Sighing, she exhaled loudly, then began to roll up her shirtsleeves. "Can you believe this blouse was white when we left?" She pushed a rolled sleeve past her elbow. "Makes you wonder how they can survive in all this dirt, doesn't it?"

"I wonder how they survive at all." Michael kept his voice low, not wanting to attract unwanted attention. "The children are malnourished, and the women don't look at all healthy. Last night they had meat, but I'm wondering how often they have that sort of success in their hunting."

"Probably not often at all, though the natives are resourceful. If it moves, they'll eat it. Life in a primitive village is hard, especially one as isolated as this. Look around, Doctor — do you see one knife, even a bit of metal?"

"None."

"I've seen nothing, either. One of the most effective ways to lure a hidden tribe out into the open is to offer them mirrors, knives, machetes. Since these natives have nothing, I'd be surprised if they've had any previous contact with civilized people."

Michael glanced at his belt, thinking of the knife in his pocket.

The anthropologist must have followed his thought. "Keep it hidden, Doctor. Tribal wars have been fought over lesser things." She glanced across the fire, where Delmar sat with his back to them, attempting to talk to the shaman.

Emma inclined her head toward the guide. "What's *he* up to?"

Michael shrugged. "I have no idea. But he's been murmuring to the shaman since sunrise."

"I wish I could understand this language better. It's similar to Yagua, but not close enough for me to pick up more than the odd word or two. I would love to learn more about them." Emma's voice held a wistful note, and at the sound of it, Alexandra lifted her head. Her wrinkled cheek bore the imprint of her hand, but the eyes flashing toward the anthropologist weren't at all sleepy.

"Don't tell me you admire these people."

"Of course I do." Emma waved toward a mother nursing her child. "They lead such simple lives, and they are in touch with nature in a way you and I will never be."

Flames lit Alexandra's brown eyes. "Don't give me that noble savage claptrap. You can't seriously believe these people are better off here than in a civilized settlement."

Emma's jaw lifted defensively. "Your prejudices are showing, Alex. That shaman over there can probably list ten medicinal uses for every plant within fifty miles of this dwelling. Isn't that why you're here? To discover what he already knows?"

"If these people are so clever," Alexandra countered, sitting up, "then why have they not bettered themselves beyond this stage? Why did they stop learning?"

The anthropologist's graceful brows lifted, then she stood and brushed dirt from her trousers. "Excuse me." She turned toward the entrance of the shabono. "I feel a sudden need for fresh air."

14 April 2003
7:05 a.m.

Alex shifted to look at Kenway, who wore a twisted grin as he watched Emma's exit.

"Why are you smirking? It was a perfectly valid question."

"Indeed it was," he agreed, "and I enjoyed watching Emma try to wriggle out of it. Quite truthfully, I have my own theory about why these people stopped learning . . . but I'm not sure you'd be too keen on it."

"I'm all ears."

Smiling, he traced a diagonal line in the dirt. "I believe God created man for one purpose: fellowship. As long as man remained in fellowship with God, he was able to fully exercise his brain, his physical strength, and his spirit. When sin separated man from God, however, man began to atrophy in all those areas. We now use less than 10 percent of our mental faculties, age and disease corrupt our bodies, and our spirits have become withered shadows of what God intended them to be. We physicians treat only the body, often neglecting the mind and paying only the slightest attention to the spirit."

Alex was on the verge of agreeing with him out of sheer weariness when a small dose of reason shocked her back to her senses. "You think we're . . . withering."

"An apt metaphor, yes."

"And these people — what? Are they more withered than the rest of the civilized world?"

"They are held in bondage . . . to sin, to darkness. Bondage holds them back."

She closed her eyes as a tide of irritation began to flow through her. Just when she thought she might like the man, he began to spout utter nonsense. "Let me get this straight — despite all the advances of the twenty-first century, you think we are getting more and more stupid."

He nodded. "We have more toys, more gadgets, yes. But we're building on what previous generations have accomplished."

"So you believe we're atrophying."

Grinning, he snapped his fingers. "By George, I think you've got it. The second law of thermodynamics, the law of entropy: In a closed system, energy disperses. All things deteriorate over time. Why should mankind be excluded?"

"Thanks for the lesson, Reverend Doctor, but I think you're positively loopy." Alex leaned forward and pushed herself up, then closed her eyes as the world swayed around her. Though she'd pretended to sleep with the others, she'd spent most of the night listening to the sounds of the jungle, her restless companions, and her frightened daughter. Caitlyn behaved like a trooper during daylight hours, but suppressed fears reigned over her nightmares.

The loss of her beloved stuffed monkey hadn't helped matters.

She squinted into the slanting morning light. "Where's my daughter?"

"With Deborah, out looking for fruit." His voice deepened. "Are you all right?"

"I think you're driving me a little nuts." Alex forced her eyes open, then gave him what she hoped was a sarcastic smile. "If you keep it up, I'm afraid I'm going to have to go find fresh air, too."

The corner of Kenway's mouth drooped as he rested his hands on his folded knees. "I thought scientific research required an open mind."

She swiped a layer of sand from her forehead, wishing she could still the pounding in her head as easily. "I'm not the one with the closed mind. I'm not clinging to creation myths when every credible scientist on the planet accepts that evolution shaped the earth and everything in it —"

The doctor cut her off with an uplifted

hand. "We're not going to argue that one."

"Scared, huh?"

"Not likely. But Jesus once said something about being careful not to cast pearls before . . . people who wouldn't appreciate them."

She hesitated, certain that his comment contained some sort of insult, but movement from the shaman distracted her attention. He had risen and gestured to his men; some of his warriors were gathering weapons.

"Uh-oh." She winced, dreading the day ahead. "I think it's showtime."

Delmar walked to Olsson and Baklanov, who were sleeping on their backs, as oblivious as dead men. They awoke with groaning and shuffling, then squinted at the squadron of tattooed warriors around the fire.

"Good morning," Olsson said, idly smoothing his beard as he sat up. "Does this mean our escorts are ready to go?"

"Do you think," Baklanov acknowledged them with bleary eyes, "they might have anything like a cigarette in this place?"

A few moments later the shaman's intentions became clear. A group of six warriors would accompany the expedition to the healing village while one white woman remained behind. The natives would carry spears, bows, and arrows; the white men would carry the shaman's sick wife.

As a group of men brought the sick woman forward, Alex was able to get her first look at her patient. Unable to walk, in the shabono the woman could do nothing but lie in her hammock; on the trail she would have to be transported by one of the men.

As she examined the woman, Alex found herself looking for the telltale signs of a prion disease. Though it was impossible to tell which variant the patient might have contracted — if this were, in fact, a prion case and not some tropical fever or infection — the woman exhibited several symptoms that could be attributed to kuru or CJD. Her body was emaciated, her arms limp, her mouth lax. If this were kuru, this patient had to be in the latter stage. Without proper care, she would die within days.

Kenway agreed with her observations. While Alex didn't need his opinion to form what amounted to a shaky diagnosis, his support sent a flood of warmth rushing through her. With Carlton gone, she was now working for only herself and Caitlyn . . . but at least she wasn't working alone.

As she stood from her patient's side, she saw Bancroft talking to Deborah, one of his meaty hands around her arm. Apparently he was trying to talk her out of staying, for she kept shaking her head even as her hands pressed against his chest.

Overcome by the feeling that she was intruding, Alex looked away.

She would have liked to make a few preparations before setting out, but apparently these tribesmen didn't put much stock in pre-planning. Brandishing their spears, they prodded the expedition members toward the opening in the wall of the shabono, halting only long enough for Bancroft to enter the shaman's enclosure and lift the sick woman into his arms.

Before they left the village, Alex turned to say one last farewell. Standing with a group of women who had come out to observe their departure, Deborah Simons wore a calm expression, but a look of unutterable distance filled her eyes.

"We'll be back," Alex called. "We won't leave you behind."

As Deborah nodded silently, Alex gathered her strength, then gripped her daughter's hand and followed the others out into the tall grass.

They had walked only fifteen minutes when Olsson halted in mid-step and lifted his hands in outright mutiny. Alex came to an abrupt stop, her heart jumping in her chest, as one of the taller warriors stepped forward and lifted his blowgun to his lips. A single dart would paralyze Olsson, and the man was too heavy to carry through the dense foliage . . .

Delmar rushed forward, lifting his hands before the warrior. As two of the natives jabbed at Olsson's midsection with the tips of their spears, Delmar waved and babbled in the native language. After a moment, the warrior lowered his weapon.

Kenway turned to stare at the botanist. "What are you doing?"

The big Swede pointed to the woman in Bancroft's arms. "We cannot carry that woman like this. We will be exhausted and she will suffer needlessly. But if they'll give us a few minutes, I think I can make a travois from that specimen." Bracing his hands on his hips, he inclined his head toward a wide tree with yellow flowers. "The journey will be a bit rough as the back end drags on the ground, but it'll be no harder on her than the rest of us."

Delmar pressed his lips together, then nodded. "I'll explain it to them." He jerked his thumb toward their guards. "You do what you must."

While the natives watched with suspicion, Olsson demonstrated what he had in mind. Using odd bits of vine and leaves, he created a miniature version of a travois, then gestured toward the jungle and spread his hands apart. "Like this, but bigger," he said, looking at their captors.

The light of understanding gleamed in one native's eye, but it took Delmar another ten minutes to convince the warrior to surrender the stone hatchet tucked into the belt at his waist. Within half an hour, though, Bancroft and Baklanov had chopped two long branches to serve as poles. Reaching high over his head, Olsson used the warrior's hatchet to slice the bark around the perimeter of the yellow-flowered tree. Then he made a vertical cut about five feet in length, followed by another slice around the perimeter of the base. As Alex and Caitlyn watched in wonder, he peeled the bark from the tree in one long piece, then flattened it on the ground. After piercing the edges and lashing it to the poles with narrow vines, Olsson held the two poles behind him while Bancroft gently lowered the native woman to the travois.

The woman made no sound, but stared up at them with wide, frightened eyes.

"Poor thing." Caitlyn's grip tightened on Alex's arm. "She doesn't even have a name."

"Of course she does," Emma answered, "but she would consider it bad luck for us to know it. Knowing her name would give us power over her."

"But we have to call her *something*," Caitlyn insisted. "Otherwise, she's just . . . something to drag along behind us."

Alex's thoughts drifted back to sunny afternoons in the nursing home, where nurses gaily gossiped around her helpless mother, surrendering to the all-too-common temptation to treat silent people as objects.

"You're absolutely right, honey." Feeling

the pressure of Kenway's gaze, she avoided his eyes for fear of betraying her memories. "We'll call her Shaman's Wife, okay?"

They moved at a quicker pace once the travois had been completed. The warriors, who positioned themselves at the front and rear of their party, led the way with less bravado, and something that might have been respect gleamed in their eyes.

Drawn by a feeling of responsibility for the woman she had named, Alex found herself walking by the motionless patient on the travois. Because the bearer could not handle the travois and clear the path, she took care to hold branches that might have snapped back to strike their patient or the man who pulled the travois. Joining in the effort, Caitlyn picked up a stick and pulled down spider webs overhanging the trail.

Alex knew part of her concern for the invalid sprang from memories of her mother. Despite the differences in time and location, the limp woman might have been Geneva Pace clothed in other flesh.

Alex wasn't alone in her concern for the woman's safety. Whenever they stopped to clear a path or drink from a stream, Kenway reached for the patient's wrist to take her pulse. Alex knew he couldn't do much without any sort of medicines or equipment, but the woman was now receiving better care than she had in the village.

Kenway's compassion, she guessed, sprang from his calling as a doctor . . . and because his encounter with Ya-ree had instigated this expedition. Bancroft, Olsson, and Baklanov cared for their patient because her life had become entwined with Deborah Simons's. If Shaman's Wife died before they reached the healing tribe, they would almost certainly have to fight to rescue Deborah from the Angry People.

As the hours wore on, Alex's mind drifted into a weary haze as she followed Olsson on the trail. Her arms itched from mosquito bites, her shirt clung to her damp chest, and her hair hung in ravels about her face. Trapped in what felt like an eternal day, she lost track of passing time. The few shafts of sunlight penetrating the canopy seemed locked in place, slanting neither east nor west. Sunset remained out of reach. Time had stopped, and the world where cars hummed on expressways and radios blared from clean kitchen countertops existed in another universe.

"So, Alexandra —"

She flinched as Kenway's voice sliced into her thoughts.

"What do you think about our patient?"

Mechanically, she replayed his words in her mind and forced herself to focus on the conversation. "Um, there's no fever at all," she said, resting the back of her hand on the woman's forehead. "So we can probably rule out a typical bacterial or viral infection."

Michael threw her a puzzled look. "The shaman said she had the shuddering disease. Do you doubt him?"

"I want to be certain, that's all. If we had the proper equipment we could test the cerebrospinal fluid for increased numbers of lymph cells to definitely rule out infection —"

"Did you look at her back? Bedsores, particularly bad ones. This woman has been immobile for some time."

Pressing her parched lips together, Alex studied her patient's mouth. "She's drooling, despite the heat. An inability to swallow is a late symptom of kuru. But while Creutzfeldt-Jakob patients show early signs of dementia and agitation, this woman is calm. I daresay she knows exactly what is happening around her."

"If so, she has to be terrified." Without losing a step, Kenway lowered his hand to stroke the woman's cheek. Something in the gesture seemed to affect Shaman's Wife, because an instant later the fingers of her right hand twitched.

"Look." Alex pointed toward the woman's trembling fingers. "Athetoid tremors."

Michael shook his head. "I don't think so. I think she was trying to respond."

"I certainly hope not." Alex looked away as

dark memories edged her teeth. "I know this may sound cruel, but I think Creutzfeldt-Jakob patients who experience dementia are fortunate — at least they are mostly unaware of what's happening to them. Kuru and FFI patients, on the other hand, are awake and cognizant until the bitter end."

Caitlyn, who'd been walking a few steps ahead, suddenly turned. "Like Grandmom, you mean."

Surprise whipped Alex's breath away. While she hadn't meant for Caitlyn to hear the conversation, she certainly hadn't meant for Kenway to know about her mother.

Swallowing hard, she lowered her eyes, hoping Kenway had been too engrossed in their patient to listen. They walked for several more steps, during which the living forest filled the silence with birdsong, screeches, and whirrs.

In a low voice, Kenway asked the question she'd been dreading. "Your mother died from a prion disease?"

Alex squinched her eyes shut to halt a sudden rise of tears.

"FFI," Caitlyn answered, speaking in a matter-of-fact voice as she swiped a monstrous spider web from a wild banana tree. "I was only a baby, but I've heard the stories. It was horrible."

Kenway caught Alex's eye. "She was alert until —"

"Until the final coma, yes." Forcing herself to speak in a professional tone, Alex bit back the pain that always accompanied thoughts of her mother's death. She brought her hand to her brow, wiping away beads of perspiration while she hoped he'd be too distracted to put the pieces together. Caitlyn didn't know that fatal familial insomnia was supposed to be inherited, but Kenway might know that and much more.

Her scampering thoughts veered toward a story she'd recently read. Alex dared to meet his eyes. "Have you heard the story of Joe Slowinski?"

He shook his head. "Can't say that I have."

"I read it in the *New York Times* magazine. Joe Slowinski was a young man who loved snakes and knew how to handle them. But on an expedition in the Himalayan foothills, he was bitten by a highly poisonous krait. At first he wasn't too alarmed — the snake was a juvenile, barely a foot long, and the wound so small none of his teammates could even see where the fangs had broken the skin."

She paused long enough to let Olsson maneuver around a huge termite mound, then she hurried to catch up.

Kenway matched her pace. "Go on."

Shifting the burden of the travois, Olsson grinned. "Do not keep us waiting for the end of the story."

Alex settled back into her place. "Slowinski

thought he might be okay, but he had to prepare for the worst. As he ate breakfast with his team, he joked about his thick skin and hoped the venom hadn't penetrated. But when he began to feel a tingling in his hand, he knew. After calling his team together, he explained what would happen to his body as the venom took effect. His brain would continue to function; he would remain awake and alert through everything, but the venom's neurotoxins would gradually paralyze his body, including his lungs. If he were to survive, team members would have to breathe for him for up to forty-eight hours."

Alex lifted her hand, warding off the memory of her mother struggling to breathe in the coma. In a slightly strangled voice, she continued: "After two days, Slowinski knew the effects of the venom would fade. His lungs would kick in, and he'd be all right.

"Everyone hoped for the best, but soon Slowinski's head began to droop, his eyes closed, and his lungs stopped working. Two women on the team began to give him mouth-to-mouth, and though he couldn't speak, he signaled his wishes by wiggling his fingers — one wiggle for yes, two for no. When a couple of the young men offered to relieve the women, Slowinski demonstrated his sense of humor — and his alertness — by protesting with two wriggling fingers.

"Eventually, though, the effort exhausted

the women. The men took over when Slowinski was no longer able to wriggle his fingers or toes. The team members tried to signal a helicopter rescue team, but bad weather prevented the chopper's landing.

"By the time help finally arrived, Slowinski had expired. But due to the nature of the poison, I think his brain lived until the last minute. It continued to function, so he knew time was passing . . . and help was not coming."

She looked up at Kenway, whose eyes had softened. "That's what Shaman's Wife is feeling; it's what FFI patients experience. We — they — know what is coming, and yet they are helpless and completely at the mercy of others."

The softness vanished from Kenway's face, replaced by a look of shrewd determination. "That's why you're here, isn't it? To find a cure . . . because of your mother?"

Cynicism warred with hope as she met his gaze. "Tell me, Doctor — you're absolutely convinced your Iquitos patient was healed of an encephalopathy?"

"We may have to qualify the word *healed*. Though Ya-ree walked and talked, he still bore evidence of the disease in his body. You saw the photograph."

"I saw proof of his disease. I never saw proof of his healing."

"I'm convinced he was healed from *this*."

Kenway gestured to the woman on the travois. "He must have gone to the healers for help when he first noticed symptoms. Whatever they did to him stopped the prions, perhaps neutralized them. I'm convinced the man I treated would have enjoyed a normal life span had he not been wounded."

She tilted her head, analyzing Shaman's Wife with a cool, appraising look. "You're sure this is the same ailment that affected your patient?"

"Ya-ree called it the 'shuddering disease,' and if we can trust Delmar's translation, the shaman used the same term. The source of their infection is no mystery. If they really do drink the ground-up bones of their dead, the entire village may be infected. It's only a matter of time before they all become symptomatic."

She lowered her eyes, moving gingerly through the mottled green carpet of ferns on the path. "Then, God help us, maybe we can find a cure."

"Do you mean that?" A smile lifted the corner of Kenway's mouth. "You want God's help?"

"I meant it in a colloquial sense," Alexandra answered, irritated by his mocking tone.

"Doesn't matter." Michael swished a fly from Shaman's Wife's face. "I'm sure he will help us . . . and I think he already has."

14 April 2003
5:30 p.m.

By the time the sun had climbed down the sky and filled the forest with inky shadows, Michael felt as lifeless as a wet tea towel. He breathed a silent sigh of relief as their native guides called a halt. True children of the jungle, they knew better than to sleep on the forest floor, so from their quivers they produced string-and-grass hammocks like those Michael had noticed in the shabono. They had not brought enough for all their captives, however, so Michael found himself sharing a hammock with Alejandro Delmar. Fortunately, the Indian tracker was only five foot two and lightweight.

In a tree across the path, Alexandra cuddled with her daughter, while the others hung hammocks in the vicinity and hurried to prepare for the shades of darkness. Though the moon was nearly full, only a residual silver glow penetrated the forest canopy.

Michael and Delmar had wordlessly agreed to sleep at opposite ends. Once in position, Michael clung to the edge of the thin hammock and tried to position his nostrils away from the jungle tracker's feet. Other than quick splashing at streams, none of them had bathed in the past week. Now the odors of human perspiration mingled with the stench of sweaty socks and the sweet scents of lilies and acacias.

As the black cowl of night settled over the jungle, the living sounds shifted from those of daylight animals to nocturnal creatures. Somewhere in the distance a jaguar screamed, startling even Delmar, whose wiry body tensed tight as a bowstring before eventually relaxing. Michael waited for him to offer a word of assurance, but the man remained silent.

No one spoke in the darkness, not even the two warriors who'd agreed to keep watch during the first part of the night. Every one of their party should have been fast asleep, but the green bananas they'd eaten on the trail did not agree with Michael's stomach, and its rumbling kept him awake.

His patient, Shaman's Wife, was faring as well as could be expected, but the remainder of her life could be measured in days, if not hours. He and Caitlyn had dribbled water down the woman's throat; Alexandra had smashed bananas in her hands and attempted to feed the invalid. Alexandra, in fact, had proven herself a compassionate nurse as she helped clean the woman and prepare her for the night.

As Michael helped Bancroft hang the sick woman's travois as a makeshift hammock, he'd been satisfied that they had done all they could for her. Shaman's Wife had closed her eyes, her breathing had slowed, and she seemed to be resting.

They were all bone-weary, yet if his eyes could be trusted in this darkness, Alexandra was not sleeping, either. She and Caitlyn had hung their bed from branches of a jacaranda tree that rained lacy purple blossoms over them as the wind stirred the canopy overhead. Alex's feet were visible at the edge of the hammock, two dirty sneakers crossed at the ankle, one foot rhythmically rocking the woven bed with a restless up-and-down motion.

The cold wings of shadowy foreboding brushed his spirit as his thoughts returned to an episode of the afternoon. Alexandra had glossed over Caitlyn's sudden comment about her grandmother's illness; perhaps she didn't think he'd notice. But in the moment after the girl's spontaneous remark Michael had experienced a spine-tingling revelation.

Alexandra Pace had not come to the jungle on a quest for fame or publication or to gain the admiration of her peers. She had come because she suffered from FFI. She was not risking her life for Horizon Biotherapies, but to save herself . . . and her daughter.

He closed his eyes, searching his memory for facts about the rare strain of prion disease. Researchers considered fatal familial insomnia genetic because it tended to run in families — he had read that one unfortunate Italian family was unable to get life insurance because it had lost so many members. Disease-carriers typically did not exhibit symptoms of the illness until well into their fifties, though exceptions had occurred.

Alexandra was Italian — and her mother had died from FFI, perhaps even her grandmother. She was probably no more than thirty-five or so, yet, judging from her gaunt appearance and the restless motion of her hammock, she had already become symptomatic.

He groaned as memories opened before him. With the curtain of her deception pulled aside, he recalled the many times he had found her awake, noticed her weariness, even commented upon the shadows under her eyes. No wonder she had been defensive! Time and again he had inadvertently stumbled across the secret she meant to keep from the world.

Now he saw the truth in the restless shimmy of her hammock, recognized an illness as evident as the sun at noon. None of the others had seen it, but they were not familiar with prion diseases. They had not watched one of their loved ones die from an affliction that riddled the brain while it robbed its host of the essence of life.

The snakebite story she told on the trail . . . she'd been thinking of herself as she told it. He had suffered as he watched Ashley die, but Alexandra was right, dementia could be a blessing as the disease gradually overtook a patient's cerebrum. But in FFI cases, prions attacked the thalamus, a completely different part of the brain, so Alex would not be granted that mercy, and neither would Caitlyn.

Oh, God. Rolling onto his back, Michael contemplated the noisy darkness above him. *Let us find the answer she seeks in this healing village. Clear her mind, banish her fears, and open her eyes to any truths we find there.*

She would be desperate to find a cure, but her strong streak of pragmatism might make it difficult for her to accept the cure if and when one was offered. Desperation might compel her to drink a brew or ingest a medicinal plant, but Alex would demand samples, tests, and hard evidence before she would commit to a treatment.

As the darkness deepened, Michael turned, then smiled as he recalled something Olsson had said during their tramp through the jungle. Because there was only so much available space in the uppermost layer of the canopy, the botanist had explained, saplings had to be the world's most patient life forms. As many as 150,000 seedlings might germinate annually in a hectare of rainforest, but less than 1 percent of those would ever grow to full height. The infant plants that survived germination and the early cotyledon stages would have to wait in shadows and shallow soil for as long as thirty-five years before an older tree fell and opened up space above. When that happened, all the saplings in the area would shoot upward, racing for that one available bit of sunlit sky. Eventually one — and only one — would emerge the victor.

Michael closed his eyes as the image of Alexandra filled the backs of his eyelids. Drowsing on the edge of sleep, he saw her racing across a finish line, her arms upraised in victory, her eyes glowing and her cheeks round with health. If God proved faithful to answer his prayers, she would win the race . . . because the healing tribe had been patiently waiting.

What had Ya-ree said? The tribe had sent him to find a naba. And he had died in peace, knowing he had done his duty.

For generations the healing tribe had been waiting for contact with the outside world. Now the world was approaching with Alexandra Pace, who sorely needed the people of the keyba to shed light upon her research.

14 April 2003
6:45 p.m.

Taking care not to disturb her sleeping daughter, Alex stretched in the cramped hammock designed to hold one small native, not two well-nourished American females. Suspended within the sight, sound, and smell of her companions, she slapped at another mosquito, then heard an answering slap from one of the other trees.

A rueful smile crossed her face. Tonight her friends might rest as fitfully as she. Without netting or a fire to drive the insects away, most of the humans would spend the night slapping and scratching.

She crossed her arms over her chest, mimicking the traditional pose of the dead in every horror flick she'd ever seen. Sometimes when she couldn't sleep, she could actually approach a dozing state by pretending to be dead, but not even that trick had worked last night. For the first time since her college all-nighters, Alex had passed an entire night without sleeping at all.

In the jungle she had been able to doze for one or two fifteen-minute intervals, but despite singing a dozen choruses of "Twinkle, Twinkle" in the village of the Angry People, she could not enter even the drowsy stage of sleep. Her heightened nerves might have had something to do with her condition, but the others, who were just as worried, had succumbed to the crackling fire and collapsed like the dead.

Alex had lain awake by Caitlyn's side, occasionally meeting the startled eyes of native children who wandered by for a closer look at the strangers in their midst. Alex tried to smile at them, but they retreated from her friendliness and scurried back to their sleeping mothers. Sighing, she had closed her eyes and pretended to sleep, wishing she had a decent piece of meat and bread to give each of them.

Even now her thoughts returned to those cherubic faces. How long would those children live, and how many would survive to old age? Would the little girls be given to men who clubbed them for the slightest provocation? Would the little boys grow up to become tattooed warriors like Michael's ill-fated Yaree?

Dangers lurked behind every shadow here

— poisonous snakes, piranha, the constant threat of animal attack or disease — yet the Angry People seemed determined to add to the violence. Men treated their women like slaves, and while the women seemed to cherish their children, that concern did not extend to self-sacrifice. Every woman Alex saw ate her fill before feeding her children, the only exception being the few babies who were still nursing.

What a sad day weaning must be!

Amazing, that people could live so close together and not feel more affection for one another. The shaman, fierce as he was, seemed to be an exception, for at least he had exhibited concern for his wife. But even as Alex cared for the helpless invalid, she couldn't help fearing for Deborah Simons. What would happen if Shaman's Wife died before they reached the healing village? What if the people of the Keyba Village had no healing powers at all? One of her greatest fears — a thought that might have kept her awake even without a malfunctioning brain — was that they would find the healing village and observe dozens of healthy people who could not account for their good fortune. Medical history was replete with patients who swore one substance cured them, when the cure actually stemmed from something else altogether. Given the state of Alex's own body, she had no time to waste exploring lunar moon cycles or investigating folk legends.

The worst thing would be stumbling over the cure and not recognizing it. If she were not careful, she could die the death she had feared for years while holding the cure within her hands.

No . . . the *absolute* worst thing that could happen would be learning that Michael Kenway was a complete crank, the prion photograph a forgery, and his patient Ya-ree certifiably insane. If they had risked their lives in search of a tribe that proved to be phantoms or folklore, she might be tempted to tie the good doctor to a tree occupied by a wasps' nest . . . a monstrous one. That fate would be far more merciful than what he deserved.

Yes, he could be charming. Yes, he knew how to handle children, and Caitlyn genuinely liked him. But Alex had met too many charming men to entrust her life to another one.

Hunching into the arc of the hammock, she pillowed her cheek on her hand and blew out her breath in a slow and steady stream. At times like this, she wished she could believe in a deity other than GODWITS. If a deity could hover above and listen to her prayers, she would beg for wisdom and supernatural vision so she would be sure to recognize what she needed when she found it.

If God could guarantee that . . . she could almost believe.

17 April 2003
3:35 p.m.

They had been traveling four days when Milos Olsson threw what Michael supposed was a Swedish temper tantrum. They were navigating a particularly dense stand of brush, swatting at mosquitoes and stinging vines, when Olsson abruptly lowered the travois and began storming in his native language. Lifting his fist, he looked at the green canopy overhead and shouted unintelligible epithets that startled both his teammates and their native guides.

Everyone halted and turned to stare at the broad-chested Swede. For an instant Michael feared the Indians would react in anger or fear, but they looked at Olsson with the curiosity they might have shown an unfamiliar animal. Moving cautiously, they padded toward the brawling botanist, their hands moving reflexively toward the shafts of their spears.

"It never ends," Olsson yelled, switching to English. "How do we know they are not leading us in circles? I'm hungry, I need a bath, and this poor woman needs a proper hospital. If we had taken her to the river instead of going deeper into the jungle, we might have been able to provide her with some genuine help."

"Milos." Emma stepped forward, lifting her dainty arm to the man's shoulder. "You are tired, we all are. But every step is one less we will have to take."

Looking around, Michael realized they had all neared the breaking point. Bancroft looked as if he would be happy to snap the necks of their native escorts, and the nicotine-deprived Russian grumbled beneath sweat-drenched brows. Emma, who had glibly chatted about various tribes during much of the first two days, had lately fallen silent as weariness sapped her strength.

Alexandra looked like walking death. Her cheekbones were like tent poles under stretched canvas, her lips shrunken to narrow lines of gray. For the last several hours she had walked with one arm tossed over her daughter's shoulders, vainly attempting to hide her frailty. Michael had already decided that tonight he would ask Bancroft to help him build another stretcher when they made camp.

Doctors, so the saying went, made the worst

patients, and he had a feeling Alexandra would be the most stubborn patient he had ever tried to help. But she weakened with each passing day, and at some point that stubborn pride would have to submit.

He gestured to Delmar. "Ask them how much farther we have to go."

The guide rubbed his smooth chin, then stepped toward the Indians and barked a question.

The leader held up his hand, all five fingers extended, then folded all his digits but the thumb. "I'm not certain," Delmar turned to face Michael, "but I think we're very close. If it is a five-day journey, we've covered four-fifths of the distance."

"We hope." Bancroft grunted as he assumed the burden of the travois. "We may not be traveling as fast as hunters who aren't carrying a load."

"My feet have blisters." Caitlyn, who had kept up without a word of complaint, looked at her mother. "I'm going to have to take my shoes off."

Alex lowered her gaze to the ground, and Michael knew she was weighing the risks of walking with bare feet versus the agony of canvas scraping against raw skin. "Okay," she finally said. "With all the noise we're making, it's not likely we'll encounter a snake on the trail. But watch where you're stepping. Your feet aren't tough like the Indians'."

Leaning on Alex's shoulder, Caitlyn slipped her foot out of a sneaker, then peeled off a soiled, bloody sock and held it before her mother's eyes.

Alex crinkled her nose. "Put it in your shoe, Cait. We'll clean it later."

Grimacing, Caitlyn stuffed the soiled sock into her sneaker. She was about to remove her other shoe when the leaves behind her rustled slightly. Michael's blood chilled when he glimpsed a painted face in the leaves — another native, this one painted in stripes of red, white, and black.

"Bancroft," he called, halting in mid-step. "We're not alone."

A sharp, lonely whistle echoed through the understory and vibrated in the silence.

"It's just a toucan," Caitlyn remarked, pulling off her second sneaker. She looked toward the canopy. "Do you see it anywhere?"

Michael drew a breath, about to call another warning, but his words fled away when the toucan sounded again and the forest began to bristle. Natives poured out of the woods from every direction, spears at the ready. Wearing nothing but strings around their waists, a score of diminutive men surrounded the traveling party.

Caitlyn stared with wide eyes as Alexandra drew her close.

"Down!" Bancroft yelled. "Get down now!"

Michael obeyed the order, covering his

head as he bent in the trail. The warriors from the Angry People lifted their spears in a desperate attempt at defense, but other natives still hidden in the greenery reacted with deadly precision. Each threatening spear was answered with an arrow, and each would-be defender fell before he could launch his weapon.

Michael waited until the last of their captors lay still. The visible natives said nothing as the trees became conspiratorial, plotting together in whispers.

"Mom?" Caitlyn's plaintive cry echoed in the stillness. "Are they going to kill us, too?"

"Doesn't look like it." As tense as a cat, Bancroft rose to his feet. He turned to study the circle of invaders, then slowly lifted his hands in the universal position for surrender.

Following Bancroft's example, Michael stood from his crouch and raised his arms. "I think we're going to be fine," he said, keeping his voice low. "If we are in Keyba territory, this attack was defensive, not aggressive."

Delmar stood as well. "The doctor is right." Walking to the front of the line with his arms extended, he stammered out a greeting in the tongue he'd spoken with the Angry People.

Slowly, arrows jutting through the greenery lowered. One of the natives, a small man with a sharp profile, came forward and jabbed the earth with his spear.

Holding both hands to his chest, Delmar addressed the man who had stepped out as leader. Though Michael couldn't understand what he said, the words proved effective. The unseen archers in the brush — at least a dozen, by Michael's count, moved onto the makeshift trail. One of them, an older man with grizzled white hair, approached the travois and looked at Shaman's Wife with pity in his hazel eyes.

Michael thought Delmar had asked a question of the man with the spear, but he did not answer. All of the natives shifted their attention to the older man, who knelt by the travois, then tenderly lifted the ailing woman's hand.

After studying the invalid for a moment, the old man shouted out a question.

Delmar answered in the same tongue.

"He asked what we are seeking, and Delmar told him we seek the Tree People," Emma whispered. She caught Michael's questioning glance, then shrugged. "At least, I think that's what he said. Hard to know for sure."

"You're right," Caitlyn answered. She grinned up at the anthropologist. "I've picked up a few words on the way."

The old man raised his eyes, then stood and turned slowly, his eyes acknowledging every member of their party. His brown gaze lingered on Alexandra, and Michael found himself wondering what had caught the old man's attention.

Apparently satisfied that none of them posed a threat, the old man gestured toward the left. The thirty or so natives led the expedition members through the tangled vines, then spread out on a well-trampled trail.

As they followed it into the depths of the jungle, for the first time in days Michael breathed deeply, reveling in pure and simple relief.

17 April 2003
4:02 p.m.

Holding tight to her daughter's hand, Alex followed the others toward a shabono that from the outside looked almost like the one they had left four days earlier. The structures were similar, yet she could see several striking differences. The natives here had cleared a circle of land immediately around the structure to grow fruit trees, including papaya, mangoes, and bananas. One towering tree dominated the field, casting a circle of shade upon the shabono, and fields of knee-high grass covered the open areas between the plants, rippling with the wind like a green sea.

Emma stared at the field with wide eyes. "It appears they've moved from a migrant to an agrarian society. These are orchards, not the sort of crops that are easily abandoned. Amazing."

Olsson narrowed his eyes as he studied the

crops. "These trees would make it harder for them to defend the shabono, though. They could see an enemy approaching through a flat field, but this?"

"That's probably why they had sentinels in the woods," Bancroft said. "They saw us coming long before we arrived. Obviously, they had time to raise an alarm and assemble a pretty efficient war party."

Olsson shrugged. "Still seems an inefficient way to defend a village."

Wordlessly, Alex lifted her free hand and pointed toward the fringe of the jungle, where a pair of natives had just stepped out of the dense greenery. Between them, draped over their shoulders, they carried an anaconda that had to be sixteen feet long.

Emma winked at Caitlyn. "We may be looking at our dinner. But don't worry — I hear it tastes just like chicken."

Caitlyn gulped, then returned Emma's smile. "I'm hungry enough to eat a snake. I think I'd eat anything anybody gave me."

The arrival of newcomers interrupted their discussion. Summoned by whoops from the war party, a band of women and children poured out of the shabono, their faces alert and curious. Careful to maintain their distance from the strangers, they welcomed the men with smiles and shouts.

Before greeting the women and children, however, each warrior walked toward a small hardwood tree growing outside the shabono. Without speaking, each man hung his bow, quiver, and spear from the tree's spindly branches, then turned to greet his loved ones.

Alex caught Emma's eye. "Aren't they afraid those things will be stolen?"

A gentle smile ruffled the anthropologist's mouth as she watched the odd ritual. "I've heard of this ceremony, but I've never seen it practiced."

"What ceremony?" Caitlyn asked. "Are they decorating the tree?"

"No — they are letting the tree take their shame. Because those weapons were used today for killing, the men are unclean and unable to touch their wives, their children, or even themselves. Yet when they place their weapons on the tree, the tree accepts their shame, leaving them clean." She bit her lip as a warrior bent to pick up a small child who had run to greet him. "Rather touching, isn't it?"

Alex followed the anthropologist's gaze. "The strong family structure?"

Emma shook her head. "The ritual. If Americans could set their guilt aside as easily, I've a feeling we could practically clear the appointment books of every therapist in the nation."

"These people do seem well-adjusted." Alex watched as another woman offered her baby to one of the returning warriors. "And healthy."

Alex squeezed her daughter's hand as she stooped to enter the wooden structure. Unlike the home of the Angry People, this shabono had been built much like a seashell — a narrow passageway led around the circular wall, forcing them to walk almost halfway around the shabono before encountering the actual entrance.

Bancroft grunted his approval. "This is clever."

Alex squinted at him. "What's so clever about making us walk another fifty yards?"

A grudging smile lifted the corner of his mouth. "An intruder would not only have to kill the sentry at the opening, but once the alarm was raised, he'd have to fight his way through every available man before reaching the women and children."

"Oh." Feeling stupid, Alex lowered her head. Her brain had not been functioning as it should, but whether her dullness resulted from fatigue or illness, she couldn't say.

But the others had noticed her increasing weakness. Several times she'd caught Kenway looking at her with concern, and soon he'd be prying even more deeply into her affairs.

Once they reached the inside, the warriors who had escorted them shed the last vestiges of their wariness. Leaving the foreigners in the center of the shabono, the women returned to their fires, the children to the small enclosures that afforded the families a bit of privacy. The men gathered in small groups, patting each other on the back as if congratulating themselves on a mission accomplished.

Alex and her companions sank to the sandy ground around the communal fire. The women who tended the flames seemed healthy enough — though they were thin, Alex could see no signs of malnutrition or skin disease. Many of the women in the tribe had lustrous hair cascading past their waistlines; several worked with chubby infants nursing in the crook of an arm.

"I don't know much about these things," Alex leaned toward Emma, "but I'd say this tribe's infant mortality rate is quite a bit lower than that of the Angry People. Have you noticed how many small children are scampering about?"

Emma bent her knees, then linked her arms around them. "The entire village is more balanced, but I'm not sure I understand why. Two groups separated by only a few miles and speaking the same language should share the same quality of life. Given the unique color of their eyes, I'm certain they sprang from the same tribe, but what made them split? Most of the native groups in this area are nomadic; they tend to splinter when food becomes scarce or an enemy threatens."

Caitlyn waved her hand. "But you said this

tribe doesn't move, on account of the fruit trees."

"Perhaps." Emma stared out at the natives, a watchful fixity in her face. "They could move seasonally and return to this spot."

"I don't think this group is nomadic." Brushing sweat-soaked hair from his temples, Michael Kenway entered the conversation. "Did you see the defensive structure outside the shabono? Do you appreciate how thoroughly we were ambushed on the trail? These people know how to defend this location. They have been here a while."

Emma opened her mouth as if she would object, then shrugged and cupped her chin in her hand. "We'll see."

"Look, Mom." Caitlyn jerked her chin toward a woman who carried food on a wooden platter. "I think it's dinnertime."

"Thank GODWITS."

"What?"

"Never mind."

Alex's stomach growled while the women fed their men and their children, then carried platters of food to the old man who had appeared in the jungle.

Delmar waved in a subtle gesture designed to capture their attention, then inclined his head toward the grizzled fellow. "Their shaman."

The old man accepted food from the women, uttered a flat phrase that might have indicated anything from gratitude to displeasure, then spread chunks of meat and fruit over several palm leaves. When each woman had brought a portion from her family's share, the shaman waved his hands over the food, then looked at Delmar and spoke in a voice that crackled with age.

Surprise blossomed on the guide's face. "It's for us," he said, turning to the team members. "He says it's all for us."

Alex couldn't recall when she'd been more grateful to be included in a meal. Drawing Caitlyn with her, she walked to the delicacies spread over the palm leaves, then knelt to gather a handful. Along with bananas and chunks of papaya, she picked up bits of brown meat that looked like tiny crab legs.

She winked at her daughter. "This does not look like an anaconda."

Delmar did not hesitate to scoop up a handful and drop them into his palm, then he threw a mischievous glance over his shoulder. "If Senorita Simons were here, she'd probably identify this with no trouble. It's tarantula."

Caitlyn's face blanched. "Mom, I don't think I can —"

"Eat it," Alex commanded, adopting her own mother's voice as memories of ancient food arguments floated to the top of her thoughts. Her mother had always insisted she eat lima beans, and Alex decided long ago that no food could possibly be as dreadful as mushy tree frog–colored beans.

"This other dish," Delmar continued, digging out a handful of soft gray mash from a gourd, "is monkey brain. These chunks are stewed monkey meat, but I don't think you'll find it very delicious. Monkeys are very skinny animals — no fat, no flavor."

Alex gave her daughter a stern look. "Eat a little bit of everything, but don't touch the brain."

She had good reasons for her warning, though this was not the time or place to share them. Research had proven that encephalopathies were transmitted more readily when people ate infected brain tissue. Though she'd heard nothing about mad monkeys, one couldn't be too careful in an area where humans were infected with anything resembling a "shuddering disease." She'd seen no signs of the disease among the people of Keyba Village, yet Shaman's Wife had contacted it from *something* in the area . . .

Without commenting further, Alex returned to her place by the fire and tried to savor the food in her palm. The fruit was delicious and the meat . . . interesting. At home she would have eaten more than this for an appetizer, but no one had taken a generous portion. The shaman, in fact, hadn't eaten a single bite. The palm leaves before him, once laden with food, were now shiny with fruit juice and nothing else.

Alex froze, her hand halfway to her mouth, when she realized she and her friends had literally stripped his plate. Looking up, she caught Delmar's eye. "The shaman — will he eat later?"

The guide glanced at the old man. "I doubt it. They seem to have enough for everyone, but not much extra for outsiders."

As her blood ran thick with guilt, Alex lowered her hand. "He shared with us — should we share with him, or would that be a breach of etiquette?"

"You'll need every bite to keep up your strength, señora." A wry glint appeared in the guide's eyes. "I suggest you save your pity and concentrate on survival. He is an old man, and you are starving."

While Alex's conscience wrestled with her raving appetite, Kenway approached the old man, then knelt respectfully and offered the food remaining in his hand — a banana and two long tarantula legs. The old shaman smiled, his face creasing in a toothless grin. Clapping Kenway on the shoulder, he accepted the food and began to eat.

"It's amazing we got anything at all," Emma murmured. "The law of the jungle does not usually encourage such generosity."

"Maybe this tribe has managed to advance beyond the law of the jungle." Alex looked around the circle. "Think about it — the other tribes know them as healers, and that signifies some sort of advanced learning. Maybe they have found more cures, or discovered some substance that provides nutrition and enables them to do more than live hand to mouth. Perhaps this tribe is an anomaly — when the others stopped learning, something enabled this group to keep adding to their store of knowledge."

Olsson stopped licking monkey grease from his fingers long enough to gesture at the crude wooden structure around them. "How advanced can they be, Alex? They haven't even discovered the wheel."

Spreading her hands in a gesture of appeal, Alex looked to Emma for an answer, but the anthropologist offered only one comment: "Time will tell us."

Michael finished his meager meal like the others — with a licking of his fingers and vigorous wiping of his hand upon his trousers. Several of his group stood to wander through the shabono after dinner, and no one made a move to stop them, not even when Bancroft walked to the exit and disappeared.

He frowned, not understanding their position. They were obviously not captives, and they had just been treated as the shaman's honored guests. Though the Keyba warriors had been quick to attack the natives who guarded them on the journey, they had not made a single threatening gesture toward the new arrivals.

He noticed something else, too — beneath the paint all the men wore, none of them were tattooed. Ya-ree must have been something of an oddity in this place.

Sitting with his legs crossed and his arms

426

folded, Michael watched the natives move through the routine of a dying day. A group of men gathered in an empty space, two of them playing drums while others danced in what must have been entertainment. One man played a reed instrument of some sort, but instead of producing a melody, the horn hooted a single note that served more as rhythmic punctuation than harmony. Mothers jiggled their babies on their knees and watched the cavorting men, their eyes glowing as the drums beat in a steady rhythm and the warriors shuffled in the circle. At one point the shaman pulled on a headdress of feathers and leaves and joined the dancers, but instead of shuffling, he stood with uplifted hands, chanting as he looked toward the sky that had gone pink in the long rays of sunset. A younger man joined him; they clasped arms and danced together in the light of the setting sun.

Emma recognized the significance almost immediately. "His son." She gestured to the younger man. "The heir apparent, as it were."

Michael glanced over at Alexandra, who sat a few feet away with her knees hugged to her chest. Her gaunt cheek rested upon a bony kneecap, and she had turned her face toward the fire, which deepened the shadows beneath her eyes.

"Are you all right?" He tossed the question

to her in as casual a voice as he could manage.

"Fine."

"Really?" Leaning back, he reclined on his elbows until his lips were only inches from her ear. "This won't sound very gallant, but you've been looking a bit knackered."

The thin line of her mouth clamped tight for a moment, and her thin throat bobbed once as she swallowed. "If that's Brit-speak for exhausted, well, who among us isn't?"

"It does mean exhausted, but I really meant to say you look ill."

Her eyelids came down swiftly. "I'm fine."

"I don't think so." He stared at her, willing her to open her eyes. "I may be a little slow, Alexandra, but I put the pieces together several days ago. I know you have FFI."

Her lashes flew up; her eyes flashed a warning. "Don't say a word."

"I wasn't planning on broadcasting it. But you're going to need help getting back to civilization."

"Maybe I'm n-n-not going back."

She lifted her head then, peered around the gathering, then dropped her chin to her knees when she spied Caitlyn playing with a little girl in her mother's lap.

Michael drew a deep breath. "Have you told Caitlyn?"

"I don't want her to know. I came out here to find an effective treatment. If I don't find it in time, I'll — well, maybe I'll stay and hope some of their good fortune rubs off on me."

"You're not serious."

"I may be. Look at these people — they're healthy."

"They may not be infected."

"Shaman's Wife is. And if they can help her, they can help me."

He stared at her, simultaneously alarmed and amazed at the echo of hope in her voice. He had doubted that Shaman's Wife would live until they reached Keyba Village, yet in her half-hysterical mood Alexandra was almost daring these people to do something for the poor woman. He believed this tribe knew how to halt the shuddering disease, but nothing short of a blooming miracle would restore health to the fragile native.

He looked up as Delmar insinuated himself into the space between Alexandra and the fire.

"Delmar," he said, knowing Alex would be grateful for the change of subject. "We need to ask the shaman about our patient. She'll not live more than a day or two, but perhaps he can show us some way to make her life easier? One of the women attempted to feed her, but I'd be surprised if she ingested more than a tablespoon of mashed banana. She will soon be completely unable to swallow."

Watching the warriors, Delmar nodded.

"When the dance is done, I'll speak to him. It is time we talked to him about why we have come."

Finally, the dance slowed. As it did, Michael noticed that none of the dancers had snorted any sort of hallucinogens during the ritual. Parents for a Drug-Free America could endorse this group. If not for the dancers' nudity, this performance would have been rated G.

When the warriors had dispersed, Delmar gestured to the shaman. The old man approached slowly, a pleasant smile on his face, then sank to the ground before Michael and Delmar. After giving Michael a look of frank curiosity, he turned his attention to the translator.

Gesturing broadly, Delmar spoke, then pointed to the sick woman on the travois. The old man listened, hesitated a moment as if to be sure Delmar had finished, then answered in the same rough language the guide had used.

When he had finished listening, the guide turned to Michael. "I told him we brought the woman to this place for healing while the Angry People hold one of our tribe for exchange. He understands this, but I'm not sure I understand his response. The language is like the Angry People's, a blend of other tribal tongues, but he uses words I've never heard before."

Interrupting, the shaman pressed his hand to Delmar's arm and began to speak again. Michael recognized the tone — his coworkers in Iquitos spoke Spanish to him in exactly the same way, as if they were talking to a slow-witted child.

"He says," Delmar translated, keeping one eye on the shaman as he spoke, "that the spirit of sickness lives in everyone from birth, and everyone knows this. It lives in the Angry People, and it lives in this people, too. Those who do not *approach* — I think that's the word, but I can't be sure — the keyba will sicken and die with the shuddering disease."

The shaman continued, the guttural words pouring out of him as he pointed around the shabono, then he lifted his hands and looked up as if he were describing some wondrous sight.

"Even their children," Delmar translated, "are taught about the disease that lives within them and the importance of approaching the keyba. So from an early age parents train their children to be strong, they teach them how to walk the keyba."

"Walk?" Alex interrupted. "Are you sure that's the right word?"

Delmar asked the shaman a question; the old man grinned as he responded.

"Yes, like a monkey in a tree," Delmar answered. "The children must know how to walk the keyba. And when they are old enough to act for themselves, they approach the keyba, and there they are healed forever."

Something about the word *forever* rankled Michael's nerves. This mysterious ritual might have something to do with halting the destructive activity of prions, but these people were far from indestructible.

Alexandra looked at the shaman with skeptical eyes. "Does this keyba heal only children?"

Delmar repeated the question; the shaman shook his head.

"Adults, too," Delmar explained. "Any woman or man who is willing to approach the keyba will be cured."

Alexandra crooked her finger at Michael, then filled his ear with an angry whisper. "There's no proof of anything here, Kenway. If they cure healthy children, how do we know they were sick in the first place?"

"He said they cure adults, too."

"Adults who can walk the keyba. That doesn't sound like they're curing anyone who is seriously sick."

He shook his head in exasperation. "A while ago you were ready to stay here forever."

"That's before I knew they were curing people who probably aren't even sick."

"Ya-ree was sick. You saw the photo —"

"Your patient might have come here in the early stages and left while he was still ambulatory. This keyba treatment might not have helped him at all."

Leaning back, he considered her words. She had a point — they had no proof that anyone of this village had ever been infected with a prion disease. As far as he could see, Shaman's Wife and Alexandra were the only sick people within miles of this place.

Alex would require more than hearsay evidence to be convinced these people could help her.

He gestured to Delmar. "Does the shaman know Ya-ree?"

The shaman flinched at the question, and Delmar threw Michael a warning glance. "It is taboo to speak another man's name, especially if he is dead."

"Sorry — I keep forgetting about that. So ask him —" Michael hesitated, carefully choosing his words — "if he knows the man with many tattoos — the man who is not here now but once was. Tell him we have come because that man told us about this place."

Delmar translated; the old man's face spread into a wide grin. He clapped his hands as he answered.

Staring into the fire, Delmar translated. "He says the Great Spirit of the keyba told the tattooed man to go to the shabono of the nabas. He suspected that is why we have come." Scratching his head, the guide gave Michael a dubious smile. "It's as if we were expected."

"I don't get it." Alexandra crossed her arms. "Is this keyba their god? Is he a spirit or a totem somewhere out in the jungle?"

Delmar asked the question in a respectful voice, and the shaman looked directly into Alex's eyes as he replied.

"He says," Delmar translated, shifting his weight as the shaman stood, "that if you are not too tired, he will take you to see the keyba. But we must go now, or it will be too dark for us to venture out."

"So it's a tangible thing." Emma, who'd obviously been listening from where she lay by the fire, sat up and brushed sand from her sleeves. "These people are so different from the other tribes. Most indigenous groups in this region are pantheistic; they worship spirits of the trees and animals, but these people —"

"Are genuinely unique — and probably not nomadic." Michael grinned as he stood, savoring this small victory. "Whatever this keyba is, it must be terribly large in order to inspire such awe. So this group remains in one place in order to worship it."

Emma pushed her lower lip forward in thought. "I suppose stability could account for their quality of life, but only to a degree."

"I didn't see anything that looked like an idol when we came in." Alexandra reached out, silently asking for Michael's help as she struggled to stand. "No totems, statues, or rock formations."

Michael bent as he offered his hand, shielding her from Emma's view.

Apparently oblivious to everything but her own thoughts, the anthropologist stared past the opening of the shabono. "It may be located in a sacred grotto. You wouldn't want to lose your god if an enemy tribe came raiding, so you would hide him in a sacred place. You'd want him close, but not too close."

The shaman took two steps, then turned, a watchful expression on his face.

"He's waiting," Delmar said, leading the way.

With Alexandra clinging to his arm, Michael nodded. "We're coming."

As Alex, Emma, and Michael moved through the shabono, Caitlyn, Baklanov, and Olsson rose and joined them.

Michael ducked to clear the low entryway. After passing through the long tunnel — the *alana,* the shaman called it — they stepped out into the field they had crossed after leaving the jungle.

Michael moved carefully through the fruit trees, conscious of Alex's faltering steps at his right side. To any observer they must have looked like two friends walking arm in arm; only he and Alexandra realized how completely she clung to his arm.

"Are you all right?" He kept his voice low so Caitlyn wouldn't hear. The girl moved ahead of them, running through the waist-high grass with a stick, beating out the flying insects that had settled in for the night. "Perhaps you should stay behind and rest."

"I'm tired, that's all." A bright flame of defiance lit her eyes. "I've come a long way to see this . . . thing." She lowered her gaze. "But thank you for the help. I knew . . . I knew I could count on you."

He lowered his gaze, remembering how hostile she had been at their first meeting. He had almost resolved to maintain a safe distance from her, but people weren't always what they appeared to be in first meetings, were they?

Following the shaman, they strode casually through the field and its clusters of fruit trees. Michael noticed the length of their shadows on the grasses; if they did not soon find this keyba, they'd be moving about in darkness — not a pleasant thought, despite the round moon already shining in the eastern sky.

The shaman stopped and lifted his hands, his head snapping back as he stared upward with rapt attention.

"Keyba," he said simply. When Michael reached the old man's side and followed his gaze, the word needed no translation.

The object of the shaman's veneration was not a stone, an idol, or a totem, but a tree — a gigantic specimen towering above a buttressed trunk that sent thick gray tentacles snaking through the earth at their feet. He had noticed the solitary tree when they approached the village, but after so many days in the jungle, the sight of yet another tall tree had not left much of an impression.

Milos Olsson was the first to speak. "Not keyba," he said, his eyes traveling up the length of the enormous tree. "The English word is *kapok,* otherwise known as *Ceiba pentandra.*"

"In Brazil, we call it *sumauma.*" A note of wonder filled Delmar's voice. "We have many such trees, but none like this. Truly, it is the largest I have ever seen."

"The Yagua call it *ceyba.*" Emma walked forward, one hand rising to her hip as she looked up. "And it has long been associated with legends." She shook her head. "I should have known. Shamans have invoked the spirit of the kapok tree for generations. The plant is an important part of indigenous culture, for not only is it used for medicine, but for communication."

Michael turned to look at the anthropologist. "How so?"

The woman's face spread into a wry smile. "We call it the jungle telephone. See those roots? They're hollow, for the most part. And when they are beaten with a club, the sound echoes for miles."

Delmar grinned. "It is true. When I was younger, I once lost my bearings in the jungle. I found a sumauma tree and called for help — men from a nearby village arrived within the hour."

Michael laughed softly. At least he now knew why Ya-ree had referred to his tribe as the "Tree People." They lived in the shadow of this sky-scraping tree.

Alexandra's hand tightened on Michael's arm. "But if our theory is true . . . how does this keyba cure people from prion diseases?" She shifted her attention to Delmar. "Will you ask the shaman if his people eat it?"

The interpreter asked; the old man giggled before responding.

"The animals eat the seeds," Delmar translated, turning back to Alex, "but not the people."

The shaman repeated a phrase he'd said earlier, beating the air with his hands to emphasize his point.

"He keeps saying they walk the tree," Delmar said, his tone dry and weary. "They walk the tree to approach the keyba."

"They climb it?" Alex tipped her head back until her chin jutted toward the darkening sky. "I don't see how they could."

"It would seem they do." Michael gestured toward the west, where the sun was sinking toward a livid purple cloudbank piled deep on the horizon. "If you wish to talk further, I suggest we carry this conversation inside by the fire. In another ten minutes, the mosquitoes will be so numerous we're likely to be carried away."

"And other animals," Caitlyn added in a matter-of-fact voice. "Jaguars are nocturnal, and I think I saw feline tracks in the dirt around the tree —"

"Then by all means, let's get moving." Smiling at the girl, Michael extended his hand, then led her and her mother back to safety.

17 April 2003
6:00 p.m.
They did not talk any more that night. Alex
had a thousand questions to ask the shaman,
but night had settled over the community by
the time they reentered the shabono. Mothers rested with their babies; children dozed
or snored in their hammocks. Looking at the
little ones, Alex felt the pang of nostalgia —
as a young mother, twilight had been one of
her favorite times of the day. Caitlyn had
been an active toddler, and nighttime meant
a few moments of quiet with her sleepy child
followed by an hour or two of silence when
she could collect her thoughts.

She smiled at one young mother, then
moved to the spot her group had claimed as
its temporary quarters. Someone — probably
the women who had remained inside while
they trooped out to see the keyba — had
deposited several woven hammocks by the
fire. She bent and picked one up, then sighed

in relief to see that there were more than enough. No sharing beds on this part of the adventure, thank goodness.

"I'm so tired I could sleep on the sand," Emma murmured, studying the rope at the end of her hammock.

Alex didn't answer, but followed Baklanov to a pair of poles that looked strong enough to support at least a trio of hammocks. She glanced over her shoulder to check on Caitlyn, but her daughter had already strung her hammock beneath Michael Kenway's.

Alex lifted a brow, then quickly looked away. She ought not feel so cynical about the doctor — he was, after all, a good man; she'd seen proof of his kindness on several occasions. And if anything happened to her in the jungle, he'd most likely be the one to escort Caitlyn back to civilization.

Feeling hollow, drained, and utterly lifeless, she hung her hammock between the two poles then lowered herself into it. She had hoped to question Olsson about the kapok tree, but her mind had thickened with fatigue and clouded with confusion.

She lifted her head and leaned out of her hammock long enough to be sure Caitlyn was sleeping soundly and safely, then she dropped into the aromatic bed and let her heavy eyelids fall. Hanging one foot over the edge of the hammock, she let its weight act as a pendulum, rocking her like the proverbial baby in the treetop.

Unfortunately, this baby couldn't go to sleep.

Though her body ached with weariness and her muscles screamed from the strain of the journey, questions haunted her brain, firing a restless cerebrum with adrenaline. She took deep breaths, commanding her body to rest while her neurons fired.

"Twinkle, twinkle, little star . . ."

If the stories she'd heard from Michael and his jungle patient could be trusted, the kapok tree obviously had something to do with the cure for brain diseases. The shaman of the healing tribe had also attested to the story. But how did the curative act? The shaman said they did not eat the seeds, but perhaps they seasoned their food with the bark or some other substance from the tree. Perhaps the cure wasn't ingested orally, but absorbed through the skin. After all, the shaman had said they *walked* the tree, and Olsson's research had proven that canopy leaves were thicker and more potent than those growing in the understory. Plant physiology changed in the awesome heights of the emergent layer, and from what she could tell, the kapok tree was king of the canopy. This specimen stood several meters away from any other sizable tree, but the other kapoks she had observed stretched higher than neighboring trees.

She rolled onto her side and rested her cheek on her hand. The kapok outside this shabono had to be at least as tall as a twenty-story building. The seeds raining from this tree would travel for miles; the wind would take those fluffy balls and fling them far through the jungle.

If that were the case . . . then the seeds must not hold the cure, or other people would have surely discovered it. So the curative agent had to come from the tree itself — this *particular* tree, which differed from all the others in only one observable aspect — it stood alone.

Perhaps the tree's solitude had affected it in some way. Other kapoks might not possess the agent for healing brain diseases because other nearby trees somehow negated it. In one of their talks on the trail, Olsson had mentioned that trees could communicate on some level — certain species seemed to be able to warn each other of an approaching disease so the others could develop resistance. And while trees of differing species fought for every inch of available sunlight in the canopy, crowns of the same tree species at the same height never overlapped each other. Crown shyness, Olsson had called it. Mutual agreement.

But this tree had no companions, no competition. It had grown to a monstrous height and breadth, so perhaps it had managed to manufacture something its kapok cousins lacked.

Then again . . . maybe the answer did not lie in the tree, but in these peculiar people. Emma had already observed how they differed from neighboring tribes. Though they were undoubtedly primitive, their lives possessed a grace and gentility that testified to a more elevated social system. What had her psychology prof always said? *Altruism is a virtue only the well-fed can afford.*

Perhaps these people had discovered a kapok cure for brain diseases because they had more leisure time in which to experiment. Perhaps their discovery sprang from sheer serendipity, the blind luck of some ancient shaman.

On the other hand . . . perhaps the cure she needed was a microscopic entity that had nothing to do with the kapok. Large trees like this one hosted hundreds of other organisms — epiphytes such as bromeliads and orchids, birds, frogs, sloths, and untold numbers of insects. Perhaps the cure for prion diseases came from one of these parasitic life forms. When diseased natives "walked" the tree, their journey inadvertently brought them into contact with the cure.

The curative agent might be microscopic — a spore, perhaps, inhaled as a person climbed through the canopy. After the exertion of climbing two hundred feet, the climber would be breathing deeply, sucking in oxygen and whatever airborne particles existed in the emergent layer.

When she rolled onto her back, she found that her fragmented thoughts had somehow crystallized. Baklanov could help her find an answer. Perhaps the cure was a bacteriophage they'd discover in standing water within the throats of bromeliads high in the tree. Though he no longer had a microscope, they could take away samples for study in a proper lab.

The challenge would be finding a way to transport the fluids.

Energized by the idea, by the time the sun sent its first rays into the opening at the center of the roundhouse, Alex felt as though she'd swallowed five cups of coffee. As soon as the native women began to stir, she rolled out of her hammock, nearly fell on her unsteady legs, then pulled herself up and leaned into the hammock where Baklanov slept.

She shook his shoulder. "Valerik — you awake?"

The man shuddered slightly, then opened his puffy eyes and blinked. "Alex?"

Giving him a weary smile, she massaged her temple, where a headache had begun to pound. "Can you think of a way we could transport soil and water samples from this place? I was thinking the cure for these prion diseases might be a phage found up in the kapok tree."

Brushing his shaggy bangs from his forehead, the scientist sat up. "Do you never sleep, Alex? Such a question, at such an hour —"

"It's important. I've given it a great deal of thought, and it makes sense. What's so different about this tree? People climb it. For whatever reason, people climb it, and they climb it as children. I think that during the climb they might be exposed to something that can arrest the growth of prions and stop the disease in its tracks."

Rising up on one elbow, Baklanov rubbed his nose with the back of his hand, then raked his fingers through his hair. "The liquids might be difficult, especially if we want a pure sample."

"What if we boil some sand, drain it, then saturate it with water from the kapok tree? We could wrap the soil in boiled palm leaves. If we tied them with twine, we might be able to get them out of here before the leaves begin to decompose."

A flicker of respect moved in his eyes. "That might work. Bacteria thrive in moist soil. A little manure will encourage growth —"

"I'll leave you to think on it." She patted his shoulder and turned to leave, but he caught her by the elbow.

"You don't look well, Alex."

She forced a smile. "That's no way to

compliment a woman."

"You are pale — and thin."

"So are you, my friend. Now get up and let's get busy. Today we need to find a way into the top of that tree."

He grunted as she moved away to wake Caitlyn. Before reaching her daughter, though, she saw Michael Kenway bending over the travois and the still form of their patient.

Prickles of unease nipped at the back of her neck. Had Shaman's Wife died during the night?

She breathed a sigh of relief when she saw Michael lift a gourd to the woman's lips. She was still alive, then. For Deborah Simons's sake, they needed Shaman's Wife to survive.

Alex walked to the place where Caitlyn slept, then knelt in the sand. Before waking her daughter, she glanced at the travois and wondered what, if anything, they would be able to do for a woman in the last stages of encephalopathy.

If her theory proved true, an application of the curative agent found in the tree canopy would halt the disease, not restore the patient. Kenway kept insisting that his jungle patient had been completely cured, but she had seen the photograph of Ya-ree's brain tissue, and no one with that many spongiform areas could be considered healthy. Perhaps the al-leged "cure" halted the progress of the man's

447

disease before he had lost the ability to walk and talk.

Still, for Deborah's sake, she hoped something could be done for Shaman's Wife. If they could halt the disease and get the woman to a hospital with access to IV fluids and a feeding tube, the woman might actually live a few more months in relative peace.

Alex looked at her fingers, which struggled these days to fasten the button on her trousers.

She'd give her right arm for a treatment that could halt her disease. She could learn to cope with the muscle weakness, the stuttering, even the tremors that would inevitably arise.

Anything would be better than dreading the inescapable course ahead.

18 April 2003
5:59 a.m.

Michael took his patient's pulse, wiped a dribble of water from her chin, and realized that Shaman's Wife had grown weaker during the night. If some sort of magical curative compound mingled in the air over this place, it had not yet affected this woman.

If a cure actually existed.

He looked up as the sound of children's giggles reached his ear. A mother and two little girls were walking toward him, a bowl of fruit in the woman's hands. She presented the bowl with a grave air and Michael accepted it, hoping he wasn't unwittingly participating in some sort of courting ritual. Nothing happened when he took the bowl; the woman only smiled shyly and led the little girls away.

Unusual, to find generosity in such a primitive culture. They had certainly seen no sign of it among the Angry People.

He picked up a piece of papaya and held it dripping between his fingers, wondering how he was supposed to feed his patient. She could barely swallow, let alone chew, and he risked choking her if he tried to force feed even a small piece. Alexandra had been able to mash bananas to an easily swallowed consistency, but papaya had more substance.

A woman and her toothless infant provided the answer. Michael watched as the young mother slipped a piece of papaya into her own mouth, chewed it up, then spat the nearly liquefied fruit into a gourd and offered it to her child.

Well, when in Rome . . .

Michael bit off a chunk of the papaya and began to chew. Its solid texture reminded him vaguely of cantaloupe — a bad cantaloupe, but a melon nonetheless. When he had chewed so long he feared swallowing the food out of reflex, he picked up the empty water gourd and followed the mother's example.

An hour later, he wasn't sure his patient had actually received any nourishment, but she'd had her mouth well-rinsed with papaya juice.

He looked up as Alexandra approached with Delmar and the shaman. Stopping by the travois, the old man greeted Michael with a smile and a respectful bow of his head.

Alex sank to the ground near Michael, then gestured for Delmar and the shaman to follow suit. "We need to ask him about Shaman's Wife. I knew you'd want to be a part of this conversation."

"Good idea." Propping his hand on one bent knee, Michael looked at Delmar. "He knows we brought this woman to them for healing?"

Delmar nodded. "He knows."

"Will you ask him, then, if the keyba can help her?"

Delmar spoke to the shaman, who answered with many gestures and grimaces, then slowly lowered his hands.

The Brazilian shook his head. "He says she is too sick. She cannot approach the keyba."

"So it doesn't always work." Alexandra uttered the words in a hoarse whisper, as though they were too terrible to speak in a normal voice.

The shaman must have intuited her meaning because he spoke again, repeating certain phrases and gestures. Michael watched in bewilderment as the old man's hands pantomimed reaching upward again and again.

The old man's hands fell into his lap as his eyes rose to meet Michael's. Those hazel eyes were filled with infinite distress . . . and something that looked like pity.

18 April 2003
7:00 a.m.

Alex stared at the ground as discouragement ripped at her heart. She hadn't realized how much she had hoped the healing tribe could help this woman. If they could halt her decline or even set her on the road to recovery, Alex and her team could examine the treatment and extrapolate a protocol that would offer the first glimmer of hope for prion patients.

But the shaman had been emphatic in his opinion, and the man had spent his entire life in service to the keyba. If anyone knew the limits of the treatment, he did.

Excusing himself with a gentle tap on his chest, the old man stood and shuffled away. Alex sighed heavily, then swallowed hard and forced herself to think like a researcher, not a desperate patient. She might be working in a Stone Age village without tools, electricity, or her full strength, but at least she was working in a field ripe for the harvest. Prion diseases were on the rise throughout the world, and out of all the groups on earth, only these people claimed to have met the disease and conquered it . . .

She narrowed her eyes as she looked at her companions. Time was running out. She was traveling with dedicated scientists, but they would want to head back to civilization after a few days, if only to arrange additional trips to this part of the jungle.

So . . . if she had come to the end of her life, at least she was surrounded by other researchers who shared her thirst for knowledge and willingly shared their expertise. She was with her daughter, and she'd found a friend — an opinionated, overly religious male friend, but someone she could trust.

She turned to find Michael's eyes resting on her, alight with speculation. "Are you all right?"

She lowered her gaze. "Right as rain, Doc. Just . . . indulging in a bit of personal assessment."

"Can I help?"

"Tend to your patient, Kenway. I don't think there's anything you can do for me . . . except maybe one thing."

"What do you need?"

A choked, desperate laugh escaped her. "Aside from a cure, at least a dozen drugs, and hope, I don't need much." As tears threatened, she pressed her hand over her face, not willing that the others should see her despair. "You've become a good friend to Caitlyn. I appreciate that."

"She's a delightful girl."

Pressing her lips together, Alex nodded. "If I shouldn't make it out of here . . . or if I'm in a coma . . . will you take her back to Atlanta?"

A tiny flicker of shock widened his eyes. "You'll make it out, Alexandra. If I have to carry you personally, I promise you'll make it out."

She lifted her hand, unwilling to listen. "You can't promise me anything like that. My disease seems to be on a fast track. I don't know if it's been exacerbated by the tropics, a weakened immune system, or my own exposure to prions in the lab, but I'm . . . w-w-weaker than I should be at this stage."

She dredged the admission from a place beyond independence and pride. Looking away in a rictus of embarrassment, she let her eyes follow Caitlyn, who was teaching a group of children how to count on their fingers, numbering their digits in the Indian language.

She laughed. "Know what? I'm actually glad you found out about me. Before we left the States, I thought I might be entering the early stages and that realization only goaded me forward. I thought I had months to keep working, but . . ." She shrugged as words failed. "Sometimes life cheats us. I've done all I can to stay in the game, but it appears we've reached a d-d-dead end."

"No, no, you're so wrong." Crossing his legs, Michael leaned toward her, his face a study in earnestness. "This isn't the end, we don't ever reach the end, don't you see? Even death is not final, for there's heaven after that, and eternity —"

"For you believers."

"Yes." His voice softened. "For believers."

"Say no more, Doc, I know where you think I'll be going. I don't happen to agree, but at the moment I'm not in the mood to discuss fire and brimstone. What I want is your promise to see Caitlyn s-s-safely to Atlanta. I'll give you the name and phone number of my ex-husband's parents — they have agreed to serve as Caitlyn's guardians should anything happen to me. It's all spelled out in my will, but if I go into a coma, I don't want Caitlyn languishing in some hospital waiting room. We can say our good-byes, then I want her to move on with her life."

She pushed stray tendrils of hair away from her cheek, then met his stunned gaze. "Think you can h-h-handle that?"

He nodded. "I can. And I will."

"Thanks." She lowered her hands to the ground, about to push herself up, but he caught her trembling arms. "Not so fast. While I see your reasoning and admire your concern for your daughter, I can't believe you are giving up when we are so close to the answer. It's here, Alexandra, I know there's something here. Look around — there's not a single sign of shuddering disease in this village, and I saw several patients at the other tribe who could have been in the early stages."

"You wouldn't see signs of the disease in a bus stop in Piccadilly Square, either, but that doesn't mean there's a c-c-cure nearby."

"Don't you believe Ya-ree's story?"

She stared at him, her eyes filling with tears. "Didn't you just hear the shaman say there's no hope for this woman? Your patient was delusional. You believe his story because you *want* to believe it. You want to find a cure for the disease that k-killed your wife."

"I want to find a cure for *you.*"

His words hung there, shimmering in the space between them, and Alex didn't know how to respond. Rather than face the emotion in his eyes, she pushed herself up and moved away.

This time he let her go.

Oblivious to her personal drama, the others of her team had apparently been caught up in the spirit of industriousness permeating the village. The men of the shabono were gathering bows and arrows — for a hunt, she presumed. The women were feeding their babies, while older children gathered in small groups and picked up baskets before going out into the field. Following Caitlyn, who had picked up a basket of her own, Alex walked through the alana to the orchard, where a blazing sun threatened to parch the long grasses between the trees.

Baklanov was squatting near the entrance to the shabono, a smear of brown sand on his palm. "This will do," he said, tossing her a quick glance. "As a culture medium, I think it will work."

"Good." She would have said more, but a lump had lodged in her throat. Moving past him on legs as wobbly as a newborn calf's, she walked toward Olsson, who stood at the base of the towering kapok tree.

She couldn't help but notice Bancroft as she tottered across the field. He stood a few feet away from the shabono with his arms crossed, probably scanning the area for signs of the Angry People.

Alex shivered in a momentary panic as her mind brushed against the possibility of an attack. The other tribe certainly had good reason to assemble a war party — the nabas had left with their shaman's woman and six warriors; eventually their scouts would find the dead men's bodies in the brush. That would bring trouble, Emma had assured her, because among indigenous people, revenge followed bloodshed as surely as darkness followed the setting sun.

The wind scissored the grass at Alex's feet, an unexpected and pleasant sensation, for wind rarely penetrated the dense canopy that had covered them for days. Moving with brittle dignity, she crossed the grassy field and stood in the shadow of the giant tree. With her hands on her hips, she lifted her face to the sun, squinting as she looked up through the lacy branches far above her head.

Could these people actually *climb* the tree? It hardly seemed possible that anyone could scale such a towering height, especially when they had no climbing tools. And the tree was far from uninhabited — insect nests hung from its branches, epiphytes grew from crevices in its trunk, and who knew what sort of creatures the knotholes sheltered?

But Delmar had first used the word *approach,* so perhaps they performed some ritual here among the roots . . .

She jumped when Olsson touched her shoulder.

"Sorry." A grin flashed through his beard. "It is fascinating, yes?"

She lifted her chin to stare at the tree again. "Do you think Delmar understood the shaman correctly? Do these people actually c-c-climb this tree?"

He looked at her, his eyes curious, but he was too polite to remark upon her sudden stuttering. "Not terribly likely. It would require a marathon effort."

She wondered if he could tell that merely walking *to* the tree had been a marathon effort on her part.

Looking up, she shaded her eyes with her hand. "What can you tell me about the kapok, Milos?"

The botanist's face brightened at the question. He stepped closer to one of the gigantic roots, then jerked his chin toward the field, where the shaman was mingling with a group of native women. "I don't know how he uses the tree, but a tribe I visited in Africa used the kapok's seeds, leaves, bark, and resin to treat dysentery, fevers, venereal diseases, asthma, and kidney problems." He gripped one of the gnarled roots that rose nearly three feet out of the ground. "The kapok is a beneficial tree. It can also be a lifesaver for a thirsty man who cannot find water."

"How's that?"

Bending down, he tugged on a slender root snaking away from a thicker growth in the soil. "See this?" With a mighty yank, he pulled the smaller root free of the earth, then reached into his pocket and withdrew a knife.

Alex drew in her breath. "I thought we had no —"

"The knife is Kenway's. I asked if I could borrow it to take samples. I had to promise not to let the shaman see it, though."

Instinctively, Alex moved to block the line

of sight between the botanist and the sha-man. Emma had tried to explain why it was dangerous to upset the balance of power between tribes by the introduction of modern weapons, but Alex didn't think the sight of one knife would exacerbate the hostile rela-tionship between the healing tribe and the Angry People. Besides, the Angry People had looted their camp in the attack — they would find all sorts of objects that could serve as weapons once they figured out how to use them.

"Look here." Olsson sliced through the root, then tilted it downward as a stream of clear water spilled onto the soil. "Excellent, yes? Filtered H_2O, straight from Mother Nature's tap."

Alex stared, her mind working. "Has that water ever been analyzed?"

"Why? It's just water."

"But what if it c-c-contains . . . something extra?"

She pressed her hands to her forehead, pushing back her hair as her mind probed the possibilities. Water from this tree, pulled from the soil through the roots, could contain a microscopic organism, an enzyme, or a virus that forced prions to shut down. If these people drank water from the tree regularly, they could climb trees day and night, but the *water* would be keeping them healthy.

She reached into her pocket, then groaned

when she remembered that she'd lost her notebook and pen in the attack. She desperately needed to record these ideas before other thoughts pushed them into a diseased corner of her brain. Remembering was hard enough when one was pushing forty; it was far more difficult when brain cells began to fire only sporadically.

She needed to bounce these theories off Michael. He'd remember what she couldn't, and he might offer other insights.

After thanking Olsson for the demonstration, she began to make her way back to the village. Her knees wobbled atop her calves, and her ankles felt as though the ligaments in them had suddenly gone soft.

"Are you all right?" Olsson's voice followed her.

"F-f-fine," she called, not looking back. "Just a bit weary."

The subject of a previous conversation flooded her mind. The shaman had said that everyone in this village was born with sickness. If this statement was accurate, how had he determined that prion diseases could be transmitted from mother to child? His conclusion agreed with Alex's, but she'd been studying for years and he was an unschooled native.

On the other hand, what if his supposition was incorrect? The children here looked healthy, so he could be completely wrong.

461

Then again, because most prion diseases incubated for years, he could be telling the truth about children whose brains bore the evidence of prion damage even now.

When she altered her course, turning toward Delmar and the shaman instead of the shabono, she saw that a small crowd had gathered in the center of the field. She had planned to ask the old man if anyone in this tribe had ever grown to a healthy old age without approaching the kapok, but the shaman had lifted one hand and was chanting in a singsong voice. His free hand rested on a young boy's shoulder, a pair of smiling parents stood nearby, and for an instant Alex was reminded of the last time she had gone to church. While an American set of parents beamed, the pastor had climbed down from the pulpit to congratulate a young girl on her decision to join the body of Christ.

Alex halted in mid-step, her mind racing. Was this a similar sort of ceremony? She knew most tribes celebrated coming-of-age ceremonies for both boys and girls, so it would be natural for this tribe to work their veneration of the keyba into a similar ritual.

Delmar stood at a respectful distance behind the shaman, and Emma hovered at his side, her ear bent toward the guide's lips as he attempted to translate. Skirting the growing crowd, Alex joined them and said nothing until the shaman had finished speaking to the assembled villagers, the parents, and then the child.

"What's happening?" She looked from Emma to Delmar. "Did the boy kill his first monkey or something?"

Smiling, Delmar yielded to Emma's authority.

"It's quite interesting, actually," Emma said, her eyes shining. "The boy has decided he is ready to approach the keyba. He will do it tonight."

Alex looked at the boy, a thin child of not more than nine or ten years. "Why, he'll kill himself if he tries to climb that tree!"

"He doesn't look worried." Emma gestured toward the young couple by his side. "His parents don't appear overly concerned, either."

"He also doesn't look sick," Michael noted. "I see no signs of tremors or unsteady gait, do you?"

Studying the child, Alex had to agree with Kenway's assessment. She'd love to conduct a thorough examination, but without equipment, the effort would be wasted.

Delmar called a question to the shaman, who slipped his arm around the boy's shoulders and called out his response. Together, the shaman and the boy began to walk toward the tree.

The interpreter lowered his voice as the crowd shifted to follow the pair. "I asked him if the boy was in danger. He says no one has ever died approaching the keyba. The Great Spirit would not allow such a thing."

Emma's mouth pursed in a tiny rosette, then unpuckered enough to ask, "Does this Great Spirit have a name?"

Delmar shook his head. "None they will pronounce to an outsider."

"Right." Emma's voice took on a note of ruefulness. "Names have sacred power, I know."

Alex snorted softly. "This Great Spirit must have quite a bag of tricks."

Delmar squinted in thought. "Perhaps later we shall have the honor of seeing what they are."

The sun was yet an hour from setting, Alex estimated, when the villagers trooped out of the shabono for the final part of the ceremony. After the child's initial request, the shaman and the boy's parents had walked over to look at the massive tree — for inspiration? — before returning to the shabono for feasting, dancing, and the all-important body paint.

As the sun slanted westward, a pair of men stood at the base of the kapok and beat on the drumlike roots, sending the thumping sounds over the fields and deep into the jungle. Alex kept glancing toward the dense forest, wondering if the sound would draw emissaries from the Angry People, but the shaman seemed oblivious to the danger.

The boy, elaborately "dressed" in stripes on his face, chest, arms, and legs, stood between his doting parents while men from the village danced in a wide circle around the tree. As the dancers jumped in joyous ecstasy, the boy lifted his chin and approached the tree dragging a twisted vine that had to be at least twenty feet long.

With one hand resting on Caitlyn's shoulder, Alex caught her breath as she marveled at the boy's ingenuity. Instead of hanging from a rope as she and her companions had in their tree climbing, the boy positioned the vine around the wide tree, then stood at its base holding both ends. Placing his feet flat upon the tree's rough bark, he leaned forward and embraced the tree, then jerked the length of rope upward. As the rope clung to the rough bark, the boy leaned back and used the force of gravity on his body to hold the rope in place.

While Alex watched, the gangly boy continued embracing the tree and moving upward, inch by inch, crying out with the victory of each upward motion. Her arms ached in sympathy as she imagined the effort each movement required. Only sheer strength — and determination — could allow a child to climb a tree in that manner.

A child suffering from a prion disease could

never have managed it.

"That kid must have arms of steel," Olsson quipped, shielding his eyes as he watched the boy maneuver around a wasps' nest. "But I can see how that sort of climb would be easier for children. With their lower body weight, they do not have as much to lift."

"I can see why they call it walking the tree," Emma remarked. "At the beginning, did you see how he braced himself with his feet? It is almost as if he is walking up the side of the trunk."

Alex said nothing as she watched the boy reach the first horizontal branch. Shouting in exultation, he tied his climbing vine onto the branch, then tested several of the hanging lianas until he found one that would hold his weight. He then climbed like Tarzan, disappearing into the foliage of the lower branches.

Alex waited, her stomach clenched tight, and strained her ears for his exultant yelps. Yet the sounds of his voice grew fainter as the shadows lengthened, and by the time the sunset had spread itself like a peacock's tail over the horizon, the boy's cries had faded to a twilight silence.

Alex glanced at Kenway, who was staring up at the tree's crown with disbelief and concern. "Do you think something happened to him?"

His face remained serious, but one corner of his mouth curled in an irrepressible grin.

"By George, I think he's done it."

"But we haven't heard anything. It's much too quiet up there."

He lowered his gaze, and something in his eyes softened. "I shouldn't worry about that boy. They train from a young age, didn't the shaman say so? I imagine the lad's knackered after all that. Probably ready for a bit of a rest."

Alex turned to look at the shaman, who stood with the boy's parents. The men wore expressions of complete confidence, but a flicker of worry moved across the mother's face.

Alex felt her heart twist in sympathy. Mothers were always the first to worry when their children encountered difficult situations.

The villagers remained at the base of the kapok tree until the remaining color bled out of the air, then the shaman lifted his hand and called his people back to the safety of the shabono.

Following the others, Alex looked up at Kenway. "Do they just leave him for the night? What if he f-f-falls asleep and tumbles out of the tree? He's only a little boy."

"I think we have to trust them." He slipped his arm around her waist as she struggled to manage a spot of uneven ground. "But if the shaman's in the mood for conversation tonight, I think we need to ask a few more questions. Something beyond our ken per-

467

vades this place, and it may yet hold the answer we are seeking."

Alex looked at him, wondering if the atmosphere of the place had addled his thoughts, then decided to save her energy and not argue.

18 April 2003
6:00 p.m.

As night fell, once again Michael was astounded by the shaman's generosity. The women brought food to their leader; he shared it with the expedition team members. This time all his fellow travelers save Delmar repaid the shaman's hospitality by returning a portion of the food to his palm leaf, but Michael knew they could not stay in this village many more days. All they needed had been freely offered, and while food and water seemed to be sufficient, he had seen no signs of a surplus. The presence of the research team was draining the village of precious resources, and they had brought nothing to make up the deficit.

They needed to work quickly, Michael realized. Deborah Simons waited in a hostile village, Shaman's Wife was failing rapidly, and Alex's condition worsened with each passing hour. If an answer existed in this place, they needed to find it in a matter of days, not weeks or months.

As he had hoped, the gregarious shaman was willing to talk after dinner. With Delmar interpreting, Michael joined Alexandra and Emma in a conversation with the old man.

"I'd like to know about the boy," Alexandra told Delmar, her eyes shifting to the shaman's lined face. After the Brazilian interpreted her question, the shaman gave her a smile, then lifted his hand to the open sky in the center of the shabono.

As Delmar translated, the old man spoke in a tone filled with awe and respect. "The boy is resting, waiting for the Great Spirit of the keyba. He will wait through the night, until the first light of morning. When we see him again, he will be healed from the shuddering disease."

Michael shot Emma a look. "Almost like an initiation ritual, isn't it?"

The anthropologist jerked her head in a brief nod of agreement. "Many tribes require trials of endurance before a boy can be considered a man. This may be the keyba version of purification." She paused to take a bite of her banana, then swallowed and smiled around their small circle. "In medieval times, squires who had passed the tests of knighthood had to participate in a ritual that included a cleansing bath and a full night of prayer in the chapel. The next morning they took a vow of loyalty to their lord, kissed his cheek, and received a ceremonial blow on the shoulder in return." She shrugged. "Interesting that this jungle version also includes a spiritual aspect."

Alexandra lifted a finger. "But the purpose of the keyba ritual is *healing.*"

"The boy didn't look sick." Michael admitted what he'd been thinking earlier. "He might well be carrying a form of prion disease, but I saw no signs of it."

"And you can't tell me they require that kind of athletic endeavor from everyone." Emma jabbed her finger to the ground to emphasize her point. "What if someone bears a handicapped child who cannot climb? Are they doomed to suffer this alleged disease? What about the girls? Are they supposed to climb the tree, too?"

Michael turned to the shaman. "Does everyone approach the keyba? Even the girls and little ones?"

After Delmar had translated the question, the shaman shook his head. "Everyone walks the keyba," he said through Delmar, "except those who choose not to. And the little ones, the weak ones — the Great Spirit of the keyba sends a mighty hawk to carry their souls to his land."

Alexandra blew out her cheeks. "Everything begins and ends with spirits in this p-p-part of the world," she grumbled. "I would give

471

anything to find a native who can think in terms of practical science. I don't expect them to understand astrophysics, but it'd be *such* a giant step forward if these people could realize that life requires biological answers, not spiritual hocus-pocus —"

"What makes you think the issue being addressed is not spiritual?" Despite a nagging voice that warned him to keep quiet, Michael tossed the question at her. "Perhaps we of the civilized world are at fault for wandering away from basic spiritual truths."

Emma lifted her hand. "Let's postpone the infighting, shall we? We have more important matters to discuss."

"I'm willing to stay on topic," Alexandra answered, her words clipped. Her eyes, trained on Michael, gleamed with defiance. "If the reverend doctor here stops trying to slow our progress with useless suppositions, we might actually learn something tonight."

Sputtering on his indignation, Michael clenched his fist. "You think faith is useless? How can you ignore the myriad medical studies which have proven that prayer leads to quicker recovery from surgery, more rapid growth in premature infants, and has even been shown to help infertile women conceive babies?"

Alexandra flicked a dismissive wave in his direction. "Those studies aren't worth the paper they're printed on. It's not faith that works wonders; it's the blindly optimistic attitude possessed by people who identify themselves as spiritual."

Michael set his jaw, furious at his increasing vulnerability to her. Why did he care what she thought? She was nothing to him but a colleague and a friend — when she felt like being friendly. He shouldn't allow her to rile his temper, but he couldn't help it. He cared. He cared a great deal.

Drawing a deep breath, he forced himself to calm down. "Tell me, Alexandra — do you think that boy in the kapok tree is exhibiting blind optimism?"

She snorted. "Of course! If he doesn't break his neck before morning, he'll come down, the shaman will pronounce him healed, and life here in Stone Age village will go merrily along. Truthfully, I've begun to wonder if these people are sick at all. Perhaps they were once afflicted with prion diseases, but something in the area eradicated the infective agent. Maybe they were like the Fiore in New Guinea, and once they stopped drinking the bones of their dead, the disease disappeared. But these people keep climbing the tree, risking their lives, and believing that it's the tree that heals them."

"*Do* they drink the bones of their dead?" Emma asked the question of Delmar, who murmured a phrase to the shaman. After a moment, the old man replied.

"No," Delmar answered, his voice flat. "They do not."

Alex shot Michael a look of triumph. "Your Ya-ree came from the Angry People, right? He was infected in that tribe. This tribe did nothing to infect him or cure him."

"So you think the tree has no healing powers at all?"

"No more than usual. Olsson said other tribes use the seeds and leaves for other cures, so I have no problem with that. But as far as curing prion damage — that's a stretch, Doc. No, I d-d-don't believe it."

Michael rubbed his jaw as an outlandish idea leaped into his mind. The notion was sheer madness, perhaps even desperate lunacy, but at this point he and his silent patient had nothing to lose.

He turned to the shaman. "Delmar," he said, holding the shaman's gaze, "ask him about Shaman's Wife. He told us the keyba could not help her — was that because the Great Spirit of the keyba is unable to help, or because she's unable to walk the tree?"

After giving Michael an incredulous glance, the interpreter asked the question. Michael felt a moment's pleasure when the shaman didn't answer immediately, but turned toward the woman on the travois. After a long interval, he spoke, his face occupied with a distracted, inward look.

"He says," Delmar translated, "that the

Great Spirit of the keyba can cure anyone. But this woman cannot climb."

Michael glanced at Milos Olsson, who was lounging by the fire and half-listening to the conversation. "What if we could get Shaman's Wife into the canopy? Would the Spirit of keyba heal her then?"

Across the circle, Alexandra groaned. "Now I've heard everything."

The shaman, however, listened to the translation of the question, then lifted his brows. "Could they get the woman into the tree?" he asked through Delmar.

"I think we can." Michael jerked his chin toward Olsson, who had moved closer to the conversation. "If we cut several lengths of vine and devised some sort of harness, could we manage it?"

Olsson glanced from Michael to Alexandra, then tugged at his beard and grinned. "We could use the double rope technique with prusik loops. It would be quite a workout, but yes, we could climb that tree."

"Could we transport my patient?"

Bancroft's deep voice rumbled into the conversation. "I could carry her. If it'll get us back to Deborah Simons quicker, I'd be happy to give it a try."

Taking charge with quiet assurance, Michael looked at the shaman. "If my friends and I take this sick woman into the canopy of the kapok tomorrow, will the Great Spirit of the keyba cure her?"

Once he had heard the translation, the shaman answered with an uplifted hand and a few chanted phrases.

Michael leaned toward the interpreter. "What'd he say, mate?"

"He said," Delmar looked around the group, "that if you can reach the sun and if the woman is willing, the Great Spirit of the keyba will make her well."

As the rising sun pinkened the sky around the kapok tree, Alex stood in the opening of the shabono and clasped her hands, fervently wishing for coffee. Mists covered the empty field outside the village, and she could see no signs of movement in the jungle beyond. But the sounds of life surrounded her — the screech of parrots, the whistle of the toucan, the chatter of monkeys.

She had not slept at all in the just-passed night. Long after the communal fire dimmed and her companions snored, she lay in her hammock and forced herself to breathe deeply, hoping her body could use the period of inactivity to rest. But her brain never ceased to hum with thoughts and random surges of emotion — indignation, worry, wonder, and fear.

Her hands trembled now in odd moments, while words that should have sprung immediately to her lips had begun to play hide-and-seek in her memory. She could walk, once she found her footing, but her legs seemed weak and unable to function after she'd been sitting for long periods. In a few weeks, maybe days, she would be slurring her words and faltering . . . then she would no longer be able to walk at all.

Sadness pooled in her heart, a dark despondency akin to nausea. She'd pushed herself, risked her life and Caitlyn's, and for what? The discovery of a healthy tribe who climbed trees, spoke in riddles, and couldn't help the desperately sick woman they'd brought to them for healing.

Her heart contracted at the thought of her daughter. In a matter of days, Caitlyn would realize how sick her mother was, and one day in the future she would grasp the rest of the truth. If fatal familial insomnia was genetically inherited, Caitlyn would have stood a fifty-fifty chance of not contracting the disease, but in reading Alex's notes, Caitlyn would learn that prions could be passed during pregnancy. The placenta that provided a child with oxygen and nourishment could also bestow a death sentence.

Alex closed her eyes as the shaman's words came back to her on a tide of memory: *The spirit of sickness lives in everyone from birth, and everyone knows this. It lives in the Angry People, and it lives in this people, too.*

Amazing, that such a primitive man could instinctively understand how prion-affiliated diseases were transmitted. Despite his keen understanding, however, the shaman seemed to have missed the fact that something in Keyba Village's environment had eradicated the disease. Alex strongly suspected that their dancing and dangerous tree-climbing were completely unnecessary.

Lifting her face toward the rising sun, she studied the towering kapok in the center of the cleared field. The sunbeams tinted its leaves with gold; parrots fluttered in the midst of the canopy. By August, Olsson had told her, the leaves would fall and the tree would begin to flower. If a child of Keyba Village climbed at that time of year, it might be possible to see a little body perched high in the branches, a tiny figure risking life and limb for the sake of superstition.

She moved aside as someone touched her back, then stammered an apology when she saw an entire line of sleepy-eyed villagers patiently waiting for her to move. Silently stepping to the right, she let them pass through the narrow opening of the alana. No one spoke as they passed, even the babies remained silent on their mother's hips, eyes wide as if curious about why they had risen before the sun to go outside.

When heavier footsteps swished the grass, Alex knew her teammates had also come out to observe this sunrise ceremony. With Kenway, Caitlyn came forward wearing a concerned expression, but her worried look melted when she saw Alex. She slipped an arm around her mother's waist. "I was freaking out, Mom. When did you come out here?"

"Not long ago." Alex pressed a kiss to the top of the girl's head. "I'd have waited if I'd known the people had planned a parade."

Michael slipped his hands into his pockets as their eyes met. "Glad you found your mum, Cait." He lifted a brow. "Everything all right?"

"Right as rain." Injecting a cheery note into her voice, Alex gestured toward the field. "Shall we join the others?"

They walked behind the villagers, who had assembled in a semicircle around the base of the tree. Every head lifted toward the canopy while the shaman moved forward, raising his arms as he sang out a chant in nasal tones.

Standing with her arms looped around her daughter's shoulders, Alex thought of the little boy and realized this would be an apt time for prayer to GODWITS . . . if one were desperate enough to place hope in such silly efforts.

Idly, she raked her fingertips through Caitlyn's tangled hair. "I hope the kid makes it down in one piece."

Michael crossed his arms. "For once, Dr. Pace, I find myself agreeing with you."

One of the villagers shouted and pointed to a bit of greenery bobbing at the midpoint of the crown. The entire group began to yell, punctuating the air with uplifted fists.

Alex called to Delmar. "Can you tell us what is happening?"

"They've spotted him," he answered, "and now they're calling encouragement."

Alex snorted softly. "They'd be better off keeping their ch-ch-children on the ground. I think we should tell the shaman that all this is ridiculous, that they have obviously managed to eradicate the disease through some other means —"

"Patience, Doctor," Michael chided. "Remember your Hippocratic oath? First, do no harm."

"What harm? I'd be helping them take a giant step forward."

"You don't know that. We're the outsiders here, and we haven't the foggiest notion of what this keyba thing is really all about. Until we know, we will do nothing but learn."

Alex lowered her voice. "In case you've forgotten, your patient hasn't time for us to sit around doing nothing."

"Which is why we're planning to do something today. Olsson and I have already worked it out."

Alex felt a shock run through her as their eyes met. "You're not honestly planning to climb that tree?"

"We are. And I'd suggest you come with us . . . if you're still interested in finding a cure." His eyes added *if you're able,* and Alex knew only Caitlyn's presence had prevented him from tossing the words at her as a challenge.

She opened her mouth, about to snap that she could manage anything he could, but a sudden whooping sound stopped her in mid-breath. They both turned as a cry came from the kapok, then the boy appeared in the understory. Moving in the rhythm established by the people's chants and his own answering whoops, he used his vine to good effect, sliding swiftly down the liana.

When the boy's feet touched the ground, he released the vine and lifted both hands in the universal gesture for victory.

The villagers surged forward, surrounding him in celebration. Hands slapped his back and patted his head. Children squealed. His mother and father stood proudly apart from the others, awaiting his progression from the tree to the shaman. Walking in the midst of the jubilant mob, the boy came forward, a broad smile wreathing his face.

Silence fell over the assembly as the boy planted his bare feet firmly in the grass before the shaman, then lifted his hands and boldly uttered a proclamation.

Delmar lifted his head as the boy's words floated on the heavy air.

Alex caught his eye and mouthed a question: "What'd he say?"

Delmar waited for the shaman's answer, then shouted over the crowd's joyous reply. "The boy said, 'I have been touched by the light of keyba, and the Great Spirit has healed me of the disease that kills.' "

"And the shaman?" Michael asked. "What did he say?"

Delmar shrugged. "The shaman replied, 'May you see with new eyes and honor the Spirit of keyba in all you do.' "

Emma Whitmore, who had come closer to listen to Delmar's translation, fisted her hands. "What I would give for a notebook! I've never seen anything quite like this."

"I have." Kenway's voice vibrated with sudden resonance.

"Where?"

A half-smile curved his mouth. "A baptism at a little church in Chingford. There was no tree climbing involved, but the same sort of sentiments were expressed."

Couldn't the man put religion out of his mind even for a moment? Snorting in exasperation, Alex took her daughter's hand and led her in search of fruit for breakfast.

19 April 2003
10:00 a.m.

After again attempting to feed and hydrate his patient, Michael tended the woman's bedsores with juice from an aloe plant, then left Shaman's Wife to rest by the fire. Exiting the shabono, he found Olsson, Bancroft, and Baklanov in the clearing by the kapok tree. Heaps of leafy vine lay tangled on the ground before them, and Baklanov was smoking what appeared to be a colossal cigar.

"Had to find something to smoke." He gave Michael a wry grin. "Nasty habit, I know."

Michael stared at the bits of grass protruding from the rolled leaves between his teeth. "Is that . . . doing the job?"

"Tastes terrible," Baklanov admitted. "Maybe it'll cure me from my addiction."

Michael laughed, then gestured toward the foliage on the ground. "I hope you haven't enlisted these men to make cigars for you."

"We're making rope," Baklanov answered.

"For your grand experiment."

"The children have become enthusiastic helpers." Olsson grinned as he tied one section of vine to another. "They've been collecting vines all morning. Emma has the women helping us strip the leaves."

Michael glanced toward the field, where Emma and Caitlyn sat with a group of women and young girls. Caitlyn was singing, and though the natives couldn't understand a word of the song, they giggled whenever she finished with "Pop! Goes the weasel!"

Picking up a strand of vine, Michael tested its strength, then glanced around for any other sign of villagers. After the sunrise ceremony this morning, the men had gathered their weapons and gone out to hunt; only a few remained in the village for defense. Several of the women were picking fruit from the trees in the field, but most of them had gathered to help the nabas.

They had complete faith . . . which was more than Michael could say of himself at the moment.

"Can we really do it?" Michael shifted to face the botanist. "You'll have enough vines?"

The flat line of Olsson's mouth relaxed. "Sometimes I think the jungle is nothing *but* vines. This liana grows everywhere, and at the right thickness, it is quite pliable. Climbing might be a little slow because the vines will not be as smooth as a rope, but I can think of no reason why the liana would not work. The prusik loops should slide right over them."

Bancroft grunted as he pulled a knot tight. "I don't know much about climbing trees, but I can't stand the thought of what might be happening to Deb in that other village. So if something in this tree will help Shaman's Wife, I say we take her up there and get it."

Michael ran his hand over his jaw to hide his smile. It was true, then — Bancroft had strong feelings for Deborah Simons. He would never have predicted that the burly ex-SEAL would fancy a scholarly entomologist, but one never knew what emotions resided in the secret places of a man's soul.

Stepping directly in front of Olsson, Michael lowered his voice to a confidential tone. "You know we have to do this tonight. Our patient is fading quickly. Though they've been quite generous, this tribe can't afford to have us living with them many more days. The shaman has been sharing his food and the families their hammocks, but you know the old saying — fish and visitors reek in three days."

A brief smile twitched in and out of the tangles of Olsson's beard. "I understand. In any case, the lack of equipment limits our options. We will attempt this climb tonight and consider leaving tomorrow." He glanced toward Bancroft. "Getting us out of here will be your job, I suppose."

Bancroft jerked his head in a grim nod. "Happy to do it. I'd like to find our way back to our base camp before we approach the other village — we could use any supplies we can find. We might locate one of the GPS devices, and if we can even pick up a couple of the weapons or machetes —"

Michael shook his head. "I wouldn't count on ever seeing those machetes again. I've a hunch we've inadvertently done our bit to bring the Angry People out of the Stone Age. They'll probably be searching for other nabas now, in hopes of obtaining more weapons."

"They might be looking for us." Bancroft verbalized an unspoken thought that had been hovering at the edge of Michael's mind. "Think about it. We left with six of their warriors and their shaman's woman. When we return without any of them . . ."

Michael watched as the burly soldier struggled to get a grip on his emotions. "Do you think we're wasting our time going up this tree?"

"Do you?"

Michael recoiled from the man's worried eyes and tried on a smile that felt a size too small. "I'm not sure the keyba can help her — she may be past the point of recovery. But we've come all this way, we've made sacrifices, and we've got to try." He hesitated as Bancroft's eyes seemed to focus on something far away. "Do you agree?"

The guard's throat worked. "I don't know, Doc. I figure I've done more illogical things than this in my lifetime. For Deb's sake, we've got to try something, and if this works, it'd be a sight easier than putting one of the other women on the travois and trying to bluff the enemy before we attack." A trace of unexpected vulnerability shone in the man's eyes as he met Michael's gaze. "I think it's crazy to carry a sick woman up a tree, but the shaman of the Angry People sure thought it would work. So I've been praying it will."

Michael fingered a length of vine. "I didn't know you were a praying man."

"Born and raised Catholic. I guess some things you never really outgrow." Bancroft cleared his throat. "I haven't been to Mass in years, but some of our recent conversations started me thinking. Maybe I've been a little too forgetful of God, but I know he hasn't forgotten about me. He's pulled me out of too many scrapes I never should have escaped —"

"Kenway!" Alexandra yelled from the entrance to the shabono, interrupting the conversation. "The shaman needs to talk to you!"

A broad smile found its way through Bancroft's mask of uncertainty. "She's calling you."

Michael grunted. "So I hear."

"She likes you, you know."

"Surely you jest."

Grinning, the soldier stripped a section of vine with his closed fist, then opened his hand and watched the shredded leaves flutter from his palm. "I call it like I see it, Kenway, and I know what I see. She's crazy about you. And I figure the feeling's mutual."

Excusing himself with a roll of his eyes, Michael squared his shoulders and strode toward the shabono.

Surprising, what emotions could awaken in the secret places of a man's soul.

Crossing her arms, Alex tried to disguise her irritation as the doctor came into the round-house, sunlight glinting off his dark hair. Though the native women were now more accustomed to his presence, they actually twittered when he passed by. The doctor ignored them, but Alex knew he had to notice — and was arrogant enough to pretend he didn't.

What quality about him fluttered feminine hearts? The long hair? None of the native men wore anything longer than an ear-length bowl cut, and not many men in the States or England wore their hair long these days, either. Kenway's collar-length mane, while suiting him perfectly, did seem a little dashing and avant-garde.

Her thoughts came to an abrupt halt, like hitting a wall. Why was she thinking about a *man* when her mind should have been occupied with more important issues? She had to be experiencing a sort of dementia. Delusion, maybe. She'd be hallucinating next.

Raking her hand through her hair, she joined Delmar, the shaman, and Kenway at the sick woman's bedside.

Sinking to the ground, Michael looked at the shaman with an uplifted brow.

Alex drew an irritated breath. "The shaman says he has to talk to her," she snapped, "before you can take her into the tree."

Michael shifted to meet her eyes. "So he asked *me* for permission?"

"Apparently he thinks you have authority over her — maybe he thinks she's your woman."

Kenway gaped in surprise, then turned to Delmar. "Please tell him he may speak directly to her. And if you wouldn't mind translating, I'd like to hear what he has to say."

Heedless of the eavesdroppers, the shaman took the woman's limp hand and began to stroke it with gentle fingers. Slowly and softly he spoke while Delmar translated: "Great mercy is given to you, sister. The nabas have agreed to do what you cannot. They will carry you into the keyba where others have walked, and when the sun rises again you will be touched by the rays of first light. If your spirit is willing, the Great Spirit of the keyba will speak to you, filling your shabono with light

491

and healing."

Alex crooked a brow. *Her shabono?* Was he referring to this roundhouse? There'd be trouble if the tribe planned to adopt this woman as they had adopted Michael's patient.

The mute woman did not speak, but a tide of fear washed through her eyes.

"If you let the light touch you," the shaman finished, lowering the woman's hand to her chest. "You will see with new eyes and honor the Spirit of the keyba in all you do."

The woman did not answer, but a tear slipped from one drooping eye and slid down a shrunken cheek.

Glancing toward the sunlit center of the shabono, Alex saw that the sun had begun its climb toward the center of the sky. Clearing her throat, she stood and wiped sand from her palms. "Are the vines nearly ready?"

"Very nearly." Michael nodded his appreciation to the shaman as he stood. "It's going to be an arduous climb, so if we're going to set out, we'd best go as soon as possible."

"I'll be ready." She turned to find Caitlyn, but Michael caught and held her arm. When she turned, his face had darkened with unreadable emotions.

"Are you sure you ought to go? It's a hard climb, and you're not well."

"I'm well enough."

"Are you?" He hesitated, then released her arm and swiped his wrist across his perspiring forehead. "I could look around up there for you. I could take samples. You needn't risk this venture."

"Worried, Kenway?" She allowed a smile to creep across her face. "I thought you believed in the keyba. I could have sworn that earlier you were daring me to make the climb."

"Maybe I was — I mean, I do believe there's something up there. But I'm not sure I'd advise you to risk your life climbing two hundred feet on a few jungle vines in order to find it."

She stood, watching him, and could not stop herself from pondering what had motivated this expression of concern. Could he be doubting his own faith in the story that had brought them to this place?

She lowered her voice. "Have you forgotten that I risk my life by *not* climbing that tree? If there's a cure and I find it, I'll halt my disease sooner." She caught his eye to give emphasis to her words. "I'm at the point where every d-d-day counts."

"What if you climb and find nothing? Or what if you fall?" His voice, like her nerves, was in tatters.

She closed her eyes and looked away, simultaneously pleased and irritated by his concern. He cared . . . she knew it as surely she knew the sun would rise on the morrow, because no man would risk getting close to a dying woman unless his feelings were genuine and strong.

But he was also wavering in his conviction and she needed him to be strong. For once in her life, she needed someone to offer something inviolate and immutable, something that would not fail.

"I appreciate your concern more than you can know." She placed her hand on his arm. "But in remembering that I am weak and exhausted, you have forgotten that I am also desperate. I can make the climb. I *will* make the climb."

A short silence followed, in which her words seemed to hang in the emptiness as if for inspection, then he nodded.

And as he walked away, her thoughts turned to the God of Desperate Women in Tropical Straits . . .

On occasions like this, she needed something bigger than GODWITS. She needed someone who could heal her brain, restore her body, and refresh her weary soul, but she had no idea where to find him.

Moreover, she was almost positive he didn't dwell in the top of a kapok tree.

According to Alex's calculations, the climbing party began their ascent three hours before the sunset. The plan was simple — four climbers — Alex, Michael, Olsson, and

Bancroft — would climb up the tree and spend the night in the canopy of the kapok.

Because he was the most experienced climber, Olsson would ascend first. Once he reached the canopy, he would attempt to fashion some sort of platform where they could sit throughout the night. Alex would climb next, burdened only by pocketfuls of sterile soil wrapped in palm fronds. Bancroft would follow with the sick woman strapped to his back, while Michael brought up the rear. While they were aloft, Baklanov, Delmar, and Emma would finish their research with the Keyba tribe and prepare for the journey home.

Alex had privately drawn Baklanov aside a few moments before venturing out of the shabono. "I asked Kenway to take Caitlyn back to the States if anything should happen to me in the jungle," she'd whispered. "But if anything should happen to us while we're up in that tree —"

"I will see to your sweet daughter's safety." Baklanov slipped a fatherly arm around her shoulders. "One should offer no less to a friend."

After saying good-bye to Caitlyn, whose eyes shone bright with unshed tears despite an attempt at nonchalant bravery, Alex waited with a length of liana in her hand. Olsson had worked out an ingenious method of scaling the tree. Using a slingshot he'd fashioned from elastic and a forked branch, he had propelled a vine-wrapped rock over the first accessible branch.

"It's a simple process," he'd told Alex as he reminded her how to tie a prusik knot. "When you reach that branch, I'll have another vine waiting. Just untie your prusik knots from the first vine and attach them to the second. Slow, yes, but it will work."

"Ready, Alex?" Olsson's voice startled her from her reverie. "All clear."

Releasing the liana that served as the main climbing rope, she picked up the slender lengths of vine Olsson had set aside for the prusik knots. She tied one around the rope for her left foot, then another for her right. When she was set, she grasped the line with her free hand.

"Good luck, Alex," Bancroft called. "You can do it."

She couldn't look back. If she did, she'd see Caitlyn and Baklanov and Kenway, the man who had an answer for everything except what they might find in the canopy of this tree.

She slipped her right sneaker into the first loop, stepped into it, and felt the knots tighten around her foot. When she knew it would hold her weight, she slid the left loop several inches up the rope. "Here goes nothing."

The world fell away as she swung into

space. She had climbed before, but this felt different, more foreign. She clung to the vine as the wind whipped it, spinning her around and making the world below shift dizzily before her wide eyes.

She closed her eyes, then forced herself to look up. She would keep her eyes on the canopy and not allow herself to be distracted by the villagers, her companions, or the buffeting wind. Her life depended upon simple, single-minded concentration.

As the ragged sounds of her own breathing filled her ears, Alex wormed her way up the vine, only half-hearing the villagers' admiring cries. She took her eyes from the lead rope once and realized she was climbing past a wasps' nest bigger than a bear — after that, she kept her eyes on the vine, feeling her way upward. Her back ached between her shoulder blades, her eyes felt gritty, and her mouth had gone as dry as a desert.

She wanted to whoop in relief when she reached the first branch, but settled for a hoarse, "Finally!" Clambering aboard the wide limb, she let her trembling arms and legs hang over the edge while she flattened herself along its length. She could have closed her eyes and remained in that position all afternoon, but the sight of a determined line of ants spurred her to move again. Leaving the old prusik knots on the lower vine, she tied fresh ones to the second rope Olsson had left dangling, then began to climb again.

She took her time, knowing the others would also move slowly and cautiously. Parrots chattered in the foliage around her while a tarantula hung motionless, blending almost perfectly into the mottled brown bark. Sleeping fruit bats dotted one section of the mighty trunk, and the sight of them spurred her to pick up her pace — once night fell, the bats would wake and begin to hunt. While Caitlyn had assured her they didn't often bite people, the thought of a blind bat tangling in her hair gave her the willies.

Down below her, she heard the villagers begin the rhythmic chant they'd picked up when they welcomed the boy after his night in the tree. Encouragement, Delmar had called it. Alex listened, trying to pick out words and phrases, but from this distance the vocal sounds escaped her. The rhythm, however, vibrated through the tree, and soon her arms and legs began to move in a coordinated fashion, steadily propelling her upward despite the tendency of her exhausted nerve endings to snap at each other.

By the time she reached the canopy, where the branches narrowed and climbing grew riskier, she heard Olsson's welcoming voice. "Over here, Alex. You've almost made it."

Looking up, she saw him above and to the west of her position, standing on a branch while he pointed to a trio of horizontal vines he had rigged between vertical limbs. "Walk on the lower rope, and hold tight to the other two."

Alex gulped, forcing down the sudden lurch of her stomach. "You expect me to walk a *tightrope?*"

Olsson laughed. "It's easy."

"Easy for y-y-you." Determined not to look down, she kept her eyes on the bearded face among the leaves and pulled her feet out of the prusik loops. To her astonishment, once she gripped the "handrails" and established her balance, walking on the rope was not as dizzying as she'd feared. Olsson's strong voice urged her forward, and by the time she reached him, she discovered that he'd led her to the very heart of the tree, where someone had built a sort of platform.

Relieved at the thought of resting in anything solid, Alex dropped into the stick-and-straw structure, then snatched at the edges when it rocked slightly. "Don't tell me," she said, swallowing the panic in her throat, "you just happened to discover a prehistoric pterodactyl nest."

"It does look a bit birdlike, doesn't it?" Olsson took an admiring look at the odd formation. "For a split second I wondered if perhaps this could have been the home of a gigantic bird, but I don't think so. The center has been padded with grasses, and I found a few banana peels around the edges. This is definitely man-made."

"I don't care. I'm just grateful it's here."

Olsson grinned at her as he wound a length of vine between his thumb and elbow. "This nest will be a bit cozy for the five of us, but someone did a good job of constructing it. It's been well maintained, too. Those banana peels are only a few days old."

Sitting up, Alex fingered the grass beneath her and found it fresh, still green in spots.

"The grass." She looked at Olsson, her jaw dropping. "Why, those patches of grass between the fruit trees aren't a fluke, they're crops. They grow the grass to maintain this tree house."

Olsson lifted a brow. "You may be right; such fields do not occur naturally anywhere else in the forest. You'd probably be surprised how much work is required to keep the forest from taking over those little patches."

"No wonder the women and children work in the fields every day! They're not only gathering food, they're tending this . . . thing." She shook her head. "Such wasted effort. Energy they could spend on hunting or weaving is going into the maintenance of a useless bird's nest —"

She paused as Bancroft's voice floated from beneath them. "Alex? Olsson?"

"Keep coming," Alex called. "You've almost made it."

A few moments later, Bancroft's red face

appeared through a tapestry of green leaves. Though drenched in perspiration and breathing heavily, the former soldier seemed in good spirits.

"Great heavens," he panted, squinting up at them. "What are you sitting in?"

Alex managed a weak laugh. "Come on over. You'll see soon enough."

After walking the tightrope, his biceps clenching as he gripped the vines, Bancroft climbed into the nest and scrambled toward the grassy center, bending forward until Alex and Olsson could unstrap the native woman who hung like a corpse from the soldier's back.

For a moment Alex feared their patient had died during the climb, but though her eyelids hung heavy and her pulse was weak and thready, Shaman's Wife still breathed. Speaking in a soothing voice, Alex helped Bancroft settle the woman in the most heavily padded section of the nest, then she tugged on a spray of leaves from an overhanging branch to provide their patient with some shade.

After snapping the slender limb from the branch, she rubbed the broken end over her palm. When a thin smear of wetness appeared on her skin, she brought her hand to her nostrils and sniffed. Might the cure be found in sap formed only in the canopy? Was it possible that others with the shuddering disease had climbed up here and broken off a branch in the same way, seeking shade from the blast of the setting sun?

After jamming the leafy branch into the woven nest so that it provided a margin of shade for Shaman's Wife, she plucked other leaves, then rubbed and tasted them. Olsson gave her an indulgent smile, like a parent amused by the antics of his child. "I have already gathered samples," he assured her. "Leaves from the canopy as well as the understory. If an unusual element exists in this layer of growth, we will find it."

"The curative agent may be something quite ordinary," Alex thrust another broken stem into the woven nest, "but something we've never applied to cellular physiology." She twisted the branch, adjusting it until the shade speckled the sick woman's face. Sighing, she looked at Olsson. "Like looking for a needle in a haystack, isn't it?"

"That is the nature of research," he answered. "But when we find the answer — ah! Then the work is worthwhile."

Yes . . . but sometimes the answer came too late. Field trials proving the effectiveness of Salk's polio vaccine weren't conducted until 1954, but during the epidemic of 1916, that disease struck nine thousand children in New York City alone. And how many lives were lost before medical researchers produced the "AIDS cocktail" that effectively slowed the destruction of the deadly HIV virus?

"Here comes the doctor," Bancroft announced. He and Olsson shifted positions to make room for one more.

Leaning back into the nest, Alex hugged her knees and closed her eyes. She had to admire Kenway's tenacity. He no longer had any personal stake in prion research, yet curiosity and commitment to a single patient had brought him to this precarious predicament . . .

Grudgingly, she admitted the man had courage.

19 April 2003
5:30 p.m.

From a huge woven basket two hundred feet above the floor of the Amazon basin, Michael marveled at the sunset on the western horizon. Brilliant red rays spangled the heavens and the jungle canopy beyond, streaking the heavens white and purple and gold.

He shot a quick glance at Olsson, whose heavy eyes were half-closed. "Do you ever get used to it?"

The botanist's eyes widened. "To what?"

"The . . . majesty of it all. The simple wonder of sitting on top of the world."

"Oh, that." Olsson folded his hands over the receding paunch at his belly, then wriggled his shoulders into the grass lining. "When you have climbed into as many canopies as I have, Doctor, your body tends to appreciate rest more than wonder."

"I don't think I could ever get used to it." Michael glanced at his companions. Bancroft studied the sunset, too, though he kept scowling as he slapped at mosquitoes. Alexandra appeared to be watching the horizon. He waved his hand before her empty eyes, then smiled when her expression shifted into a scowl.

"What?"

"Just checking to be sure you were still with us."

"Where else would I be?"

Leaving her to her thoughts, Michael studied the sky and inhaled deeply as his spirit soared. Surely even Alexandra had to realize that the loveliness unfolding before them had to spring from something other than the evolution of nature.

As the sun dropped behind the western rim and stars appeared in the periwinkle sky, something rustled the leaves a few meters to the south of their perch. Michael felt Alexandra tense beside him. Bancroft muttered a low curse and rose up on one knee to investigate. A moment later the intruder appeared, bathed in the silver light of the rising moon: a sloth.

"Oh, my." Bancroft chuckled. "We've disturbed him."

Alexandra edged closer to Michael. "I'm more concerned about him disturbing us."

Bancroft dropped back into his place. "Don't worry — they are complete vegetarians, and the world's laziest mammals.

Deb told me all about them on the trail. She likes them because she says moths and spiders live in sloths' fur. She is . . . fascinating."

As Bancroft's voice fell, Michael knew the man was surrendering to melancholy. If this night did not hold a cure for Shaman's Wife, they would almost certainly have to resort to violence if they were to rescue Deborah Simons. And an attack, however well planned, might cost them dearly.

Michael ran his hand across his grizzled jaw line. If this were a Hollywood movie, they'd sneak up on the village of the Angry People and take out the enemy warriors with weapons formed of vines and twigs. They'd rescue Deborah and discover the cure of the century conveniently hidden somewhere, all without shedding a drop of blood.

But this was no movie. They'd already lost Fortier, Carlton, Hayworth, and Chavez. If a group of unarmed civilians and one soldier went up against experienced warriors equipped with poison darts, spears, and arrows, they'd be lucky if anyone survived.

He glanced at his teammates. The climb had stamped a look of tired sadness onto Alexandra's delicate features, and the pale rays of the rising moon had bleached all signs of color from her cheeks. Olsson lay on his back, his eyes closed in weariness, and Bancroft's depression was almost palpable, a laboring, hulking presence among them. Shaman's Wife lay propped up against the curve of the nest, her eyes glazed and her mouth slack. Death was almost certainly only hours away.

Michael gave himself a stern mental shake. If he were not careful, he'd slide into the abyss of despair with the others. They actually had reasons to celebrate — they had brought a sick woman into the kapok canopy, the shaman had promised to ask the Great Spirit for help, and though Michael had no idea which spirit the shaman meant, he believed in God, with whom all things were possible . . .

Closing his eyes, he began to recite a poem he had memorized at some troubled time of his life: "The heavens tell of the glory of God. The skies display his marvelous craftsmanship."

His voice wasn't much above a whisper, but the effect was as great as if he'd shouted from the treetop. The chittering of insects shifted to a lower hum and Bancroft stopped slapping at mosquitoes. Even the wind, which had been sighing amid the leaves, seemed to pause and listen.

"Day after day they continue to speak;
night after night they make him known.
They speak without a sound or a word;
their voice is silent in the skies;

507

yet their message has gone out to all the
   earth,
and their words to all the world.
The sun lives in the heavens
where God placed it.
It bursts forth like a radiant bridegroom
after his wedding.
It rejoices like a great athlete
eager to run the race.
The sun rises at one end of the heavens
and follows its course to the other end."

Silence sifted down like a snowfall, then insects once again filled the air with a warm, ambient chirr.

"That is beautiful," Olsson said, his voice thick.

"Roger that," Bancroft agreed.

Alexandra, Michael noticed, said nothing.

Bancroft leaned forward, rubbing his palms against his arms. "Sounded familiar to me. Who wrote it?"

"David, I think." With an effort, Michael pulled his tingling right leg out from under his left. "It's part of the Nineteenth Psalm. I wish I knew the rest, but I'm afraid I haven't studied the Scripture as well as I should."

"Sheesh, can we just put a lid on the true confessions?" Alex glared at him, her tone as frosty as the moonlight. "You guys are talking like we're going to die up here or something."

A flash of teeth gleamed through Olsson's

tangled beard. "A good storm would bring us down, I think. Winds of thirty, perhaps forty knots could knock us out of this tree —"

"No storms will arise tonight." Michael lifted his hand in a gesture of truce, then rubbed the back of his neck and grinned. "We're up here to exude positive thoughts, right, Alexandra? If you are so convinced faith is nothing more than optimism, you must believe that happy thoughts have the power to save our patient."

"I never said that." He didn't have to look her way to know she was glaring at him again. "I came up here because I'm desperately hoping to find something in this canopy that can help prion patients. If by some remote chance Shaman's Wife is even a little improved in the morning, I'll know I have witnessed all the variables that might have initiated her cure."

Frowning, she plucked a handful of dried grass from the lining of the nest, then sniffed at it. "This grass — we didn't see it growing anywhere else in the jungle, did we?"

"Grass won't grow in the rainforest," Olsson muttered. "Not enough sunlight."

"Maybe this is the answer." She held the dried bits aloft, examining them in the moonlight. "The women and children gather it, don't they? And the men are exposed every time they walk to the shabono —"

Michael watched as the beginning of a

smile tipped the corners of her mouth. She would place her hopes in grass, then. Despite Ya-ree's story, despite the fact that she had been walking in that grass for three days with no visible signs of improvement, she would rather believe in grass than in a Spirit with the power to heal.

He looked away as a wave of guilt slapped at his soul. If he were more skilled, he could explain things better, make her see how unreasonable she was to place her faith in only observable things. He should have been stronger, more vocal, more adept at answering Alexandra, Emma, all of them.

He had studied medicine at university, not theology. But a theology course would have served him well, considering that several diseases seemed to spring from troubles of the soul . . .

Crossing his arms over his bent knees, he gave Alexandra an apologetic smile. "Whatever you say, Doctor."

Olsson pushed himself up from the floor and leaned back into the curve of the woven structure. Looking thoughtful, he laced his fingers together, then touched his fingertips to his lips. "You seem to be forgetting, doctors, that the shaman's story involved more than the kapok tree. Didn't you say, Dr. Kenway, that your Iquitos patient spoke of lights guiding him through the forest?"

Michael nodded, but Alex spoke before he

could answer.

"Hallucinations, undoubtedly. Anyone with neuroencephalopathy might be prone to hallucinations, even aural and auditory illusions. When so many brain cells are destroyed, all of the sensory functions are affected."

"I saw no signs of neurological impairment in Ya-ree." Michael met Alexandra's direct eyes. "Nor did he exhibit any signs of tremor."

"Come on, Doctor, didn't you say he was febrile? People shiver with fever. Perhaps what you interpreted as a fever chill was actually an athetoid tremor."

"But he walked out of the jungle. He said he'd been running for a day and a night."

A look of smug satisfaction crept over her features. "Did *you* see him run? Did you even see him walk?"

Would the woman not even accept the word of witnesses? Slowly, he looked out into the dark, his eyes hungry for more light.

"You see?" A triumphant note filled her voice. "You cannot be certain he was not experiencing the symptoms associated with an encephalopathy —"

"Yes, I can." Turning, he held her in his gaze. "I have sat by the bedsides of Creutzfeldt-Jakob patients, and I know the symptoms of the last stages. This man had none of them."

"And I," she countered, "have held a vigil with an FFI patient, whose symptoms were

511

quite similar to those of your wife." Her eyes narrowed. "We have both tended Shaman's Wife, who probably suffers from some variation of kuru, and I daresay her symptoms are exactly like those of the man you treated in Iquitos. Face it, Reverend Doctor — your Iquitos patient may have lived here, his disease may have even gone into remission, but if you found prions in his brain cells, then prions killed him. Or would have, if peritonitis hadn't done him in first."

Michael threw up his hand, weary of the argument. On some other occasion, he might have found Alexandra Pace's tenacity quite admirable. Tonight he found the woman's dogged determination dispiriting.

"Your patient," Bancroft asked. "Was he talking at the end?"

"Except for the very end, yes. He spoke coherently for some time." Michael glanced at Shaman's Wife. "He was not insentient. Furthermore, he was calm as he faced death . . . not at all anxious."

Olsson plucked a stalk of grass from the basket lining and stuck it between his teeth. "Then this religion of the keyba was good for him, yes?"

"I'm not sure," Michael answered. "But I wish we had time to explore it further."

Leaning his head back on the edge of the woven basket, Bancroft crossed his hands over his barreled chest and lifted his face to the expansive sky. "I'd forgotten how bright the stars are," he spoke in a bedside voice, "when no city lights are around to compete with them."

Michael did not reply, but as he crossed his arms and settled in for a bit of rest, he wondered what sort of lights crowded Alexandra's brain. Something filled her mind and heart, falsely bright agonies that prevented her from seeing any other truths.

20 April 2003
5:30 a.m.

Shifting her stiff muscles in the nest, Alex labored to pass the few remaining minutes of darkness by identifying constellations in the diamond-dusted sky. She had never been particularly drawn to any of the earth sciences, but in the last couple of hours she had begun to wish she had taken a course or two in astronomy.

Most of her companions had been sleeping since just after sunset. Within five minutes of the onset of darkness Bancroft had been snoring like a proud Texan with a new chain saw. Olsson slept silently, curled in the grass, and in the center of the nest, Shaman's Wife remained limp and quiet, occasionally moaning in her sleep.

Next to Alex, Kenway rested his head on the edge of the nest. For once he wasn't arguing or debating with her, and she welcomed his silence.

Only two days past full, the moon poured a river of silver light into the canopy, turning her surroundings into surreal black-and-white art pieces. Running her fingertip over the raised veins on the kapok leaves at the edge of their bower, she wondered if the keyba cure lay in the tracks lining the tree's foliage. They were black now, as blood would be black in this light, but the nourishment moving through them served as the lifeblood of the tree . . .

Turning to drink in other bizarre images, she flinched at the sight of Kenway's open eyes and froze as an odd sense of guilt surged through her blood. "What?"

"Can't you sleep?" His voice, soft enough not to disturb the others, vibrated with a note of tenderness.

She waved away his concern. "I haven't slept in d-d-days. I can't seem to stop thinking."

"Would you like company . . . while you think?"

She managed a choking laugh. "You need your sleep, Kenway."

"So do you."

"Yeah . . . but I'm superwoman, haven't you noticed? FFI patients are able to carry a sleep debt far greater than the average person's. If the military could b-b-bottle my energy and isolate the side effects, they'd be —" she faltered before the serious look in his eyes — "invincible."

"I could stay awake with you. We could talk . . . and watch the sun come up."

Inexplicably, tears stung her eyes. Grateful that her face lay in shadows, she shook her head. "We'd only argue and end up waking the others. Go to sleep, Kenway, and save your strength." She forced the next words over a sudden constriction in her throat. "You might have to help them carry me down."

The moonlight shone full on his face as he leaned forward. "Aren't you feeling well?"

Biting her lip, she lowered her eyes. She *hated* to admit weakness; even as a child she had been a poor loser. But someone needed to know the full truth, and Kenway already knew more than the others.

"I'm not sure I'll m-m-make it," she stammered. Tears began to course down her cheeks, but she was not weeping; this was merely an overflow of pent-up emotion.

"Symptoms?" His voice became clinical, detached.

"Muscle weakness. My strength is gone."

"Anything else?"

Shaking her head, she coughed softly as Bancroft stirred. Half-asleep, he looked at her. She wriggled her fingers in a stiff wave, then he grunted and closed his eyes.

"I think I overexerted myself on the climb," she whispered. "I'll try my best to make it down tomorrow, but I'm not sure I can do it."

His concerned expression relaxed into a smile. "I'll help. Never fear, Alexandra, we'll get you down."

He had slipped an arm around her then, probably thinking that the tactile comfort would encourage her to rest, but even though he dozed after a few minutes, Alex remained awake and alert.

She took several samples of leaves, bird droppings, and tree sap, smearing the sand in her palm-leaf pouches. At one point, desperate for something else to do, she had chewed several kapok leaves, half-hoping that a mega dose of whatever curative chemicals they might contain would leach into her bloodstream and work the miracle Kenway seemed to expect. But the leaves had a bitter taste, and Olsson had once warned her that bitterness was nature's way of saying *don't eat.*

By the time the glowing dials on her watch reached 5:30, the birds had begun to chorus and the bats had flapped their way home. Alex crouched low as those warm-blooded creatures flew in to roost, then flinched as a silvery Amazon parrot swooped down to perch on the rim of the nest. Tilting his head at her, he released a tentative squawk, then spread his wide wings and flew off to another branch.

"Sorry if we took your spot," she murmured, a little fascinated by the thought of displacing a bird. "We'll be gone soon."

The parrot's squawk must have penetrated the others' consciousness, for Kenway, Olsson, and Bancroft began to stir.

Raking his hand through his hair, Kenway squinted into the brightening horizon. "Is that the sun?"

"What else?"

Olsson scratched at his chest, then pushed himself upright. "We'd better tend to Shaman's Wife, then. Didn't the old man say something about her having to touch the morning light?"

Were they serious?

Though she believed the men were taking the situation far too literally, Alex moved out of the way as Kenway and Bancroft placed their hands behind the sick woman's head and shoulders, then gently lifted her into an upright position. The sheltering leaves Alex had draped over the woman's body fell away, revealing a shrunken chest and a body so thin she could count every rib —

She'd look like that in a few weeks if they didn't find a cure.

Olsson folded his long legs, moving them out of the way.

"We cannot assume the cure comes from the sun, the atmosphere, or the tree," Kenway said, his broad hand holding the woman's head upright. "So we must expose her to everything she would have encountered had she climbed up here on her own."

Leaning her elbow on the nest, Alex propped her cheek on her hand, silently watching as the men supported the desperately sick woman. Shaman's Wife was awake and groaning in earnest now, vainly trying to communicate — what? A frantic desire to be left alone?

The eastern horizon brightened as beams of sunlight shot past the canopy's border and illuminated a cloudless sky. The black-and-gray landscape bloomed with color; the parrot Alex had glimpsed a moment before flew by again, now clothed in brilliant shades of crimson and blue.

While they waited, the sun ascended like a blazing fire, chasing a blanket of mist from the eastern jungle canopy. Its rays shot up to the sky and ricocheted into the kapok nest, banishing the shadows from the fluttering emerald sea. Her friends' features flushed to the healthy hues of life, colors flashed, warmth enveloped them, and Alex felt a sudden tear roll down her cheek.

If only for this moment . . . the climb had been worth the effort. She couldn't say why the sight moved her, but perhaps such experiences weren't meant to be dissected.

She wasn't the only one affected by the extraordinary sight. Their patient's continuous moan crested and exploded in a guttural sob, then the woman's lips parted and a word spewed from her lips: *"Tck!"* When her body began to tremble, Alex tensed, afraid the woman was seizing. Then those hazel eyes widened, her mouth dropped, and the arms that had hung limp for days twitched and lifted, fingers splayed, toward the sky.

Alex choked back a cry.

As the sun pushed its way over the horizon, the woman's body calmed. The tremors stopped jarring her frame, her arms relaxed, her bent, useless legs straightened and separated to support the woman's weight as she stood. Kenway and Bancroft, who had held her upright during the sunrise, pulled away as the woman took a tiny half-step, then sank to a kneeling position. The unintelligible sounds she had begun to form shifted into words, still unfamiliar, but words nonetheless.

Peering around the woman's shoulder, Alex stared at her face. The sagging skin under the eyes had lifted, the hollow cheeks had plumped, the slack mouth now curved in a smile.

Alex sat in a paralysis of astonishment as the woman began to sing a tuneless chant that seemed strangely appropriate for the situation.

By the time the sun had crested the forest canopy, the woman stood on her feet, thin and weary, but living. Staring at her patient,

Alex struggled to absorb one undeniable, unbelievable fact: The decline of Shaman's Wife had not only been halted, the woman had been *restored.*

"I'm looking at a bloomin' miracle," Kenway murmured.

Alex could not disagree. Something in the tree — or in the combination of tree and grass and sunrise — had apparently healed a fatal, incurable disease.

20 April 2003
6:00 a.m.

Though he knew he looked like a grinning simpleton, Michael couldn't keep a smile off his face. The inhabitants of Keyba Village had welcomed Shaman's Wife with the same enthusiasm they had exhibited the day before in the boy's tree ritual. Now they were bent on celebrating one of their enemy's miraculous encounters with the Spirit of the keyba.

He and the others had begun the descent shortly after sunrise, and Michael had found that descending the huge tree was far easier than ascending. Bancroft had carried Shaman's Wife, and Michael had descended with Alexandra, joined to her by a length of vine tied from her waist to his as a safety support. By resting at intervals, they'd made it safely down without mishap.

Now moving throughout the excited crowd, he stopped when he caught a glimpse of wonder on the shaman's face. Reaching out to catch Delmar's attention, he asked if the woman's healing had surprised the shaman.

"No," Delmar answered, "but he was astounded that you nabas could get the woman safely into the keyba."

Michael had to admit the old man had a point. Each time he had to slip his prusik loops from one vine and tie them on to another, he had wondered if he had taken leave of his senses. The search for a cure had driven Alexandra up that tree, and Olsson was eager for any botanical adventure. Bancroft's strong drive to serve had compelled him to join them, but he, Michael Kenway, had climbed the monster specimen out of concern for two terminal patients . . . only one of whom had been healed.

Now he could admit the truth. At the hospital he routinely signed DNR orders for patients who weren't nearly as close to death as Shaman's Wife had been last night. And while he cared for her as any man ought to care for a fellow human being, his concern for Alexandra had been the motivating force that compelled him to climb that tree.

He looked toward the place where the women of Keyba Village had gathered around Alexandra and Shaman's Wife, their questing hands fingering the Indian woman's hair and Alex's cotton blouse. While Alexandra smiled blandly in confusion, Shaman's Wife spoke freely, her eyes wide and her voice lilting.

Michael elbowed Delmar. "What are they asking her?"

Cocking his head, the guide listened for a moment. "They want to know if she wants to stay in this village or go back to the Angry People."

"And her answer?"

"She wants to stay, of course." The interpreter's eyes darkened and shone with an unpleasant light. "You must convince her to leave. If you want to see Deborah again, the shaman's woman must return to her tribe."

Michael winced under a sharp sting of guilt. The miracle he had just witnessed had so completely filled his thoughts that he had nearly forgotten about their promise to return Shaman's Wife to her people.

Looking at her now, though, he knew they had made a promise they should not keep. The woman fairly glowed with joy, and the gentle ministrations of the other women had evoked a smile that lifted years of suffering from the woman's countenance. He could no more send her back to that primitive, hate-filled tribe than he could give a sweet to a starving child and return it to a barren desert.

He stole a glance at Alexandra, who staggered among the women like a sleepwalker. She looked at them with vacant eyes and nodded automatically while the morning sun highlighted the lines and dark shadows around her eyes and gaunt cheeks.

Reality swept over Michael in a terrible wave — Alex couldn't understand why whatever had miraculously cured Shaman's Wife had done nothing for her.

Grappling with questions, he moved to the shady solitude offered by a banana tree. He had just taken a seat and begun to evaluate the morning's experience when Olsson, Bancroft, Delmar, and Baklanov approached.

The hulking soldier came right to the point. "We need to leave," he said, kneeling in the grass. "We can't risk having Deborah stay in that awful village another night."

Michael leaned back, momentarily distracted from his troubling thoughts. "You're right, of course."

"Baklanov and I have all the samples we need for now." Olsson patted his pockets. "Our data-gathering methods have been laughable, but we can always return with proper equipment."

"I, too, am eager to return." Baklanov smiled as his eyes drifted to the still-celebrating villagers. "But with the proper provisions, I could happily spend a month in this village. These people have joy."

"Gentlemen," Michael gestured toward the women around his glowing patient, "do you honestly think we should send Shaman's Wife back to that horrible place? Look at her — that is not the face of a woman who wants to return to a village of sickness and starvation."

Turning, Baklanov's jaw dropped. "I would have sworn she was at least fifty years old."

"She's more likely twenty," Michael answered. "The illness put those lines on her face."

Bancroft's squint tightened. "But we gave our word."

"But do we owe honor to a dishonorable enemy?" Baklanov posed the question. "Perhaps we can approach the camp, create a distraction, and steal Deborah away. We may not have weapons, but we are five civilized men."

"We are not five soldiers," Olsson pointed out. "And we are traveling with two women and a child."

Baklanov lifted a brow. "We could even the odds if some of the warriors from Keyba Village came with us. They are expert with these primitive weapons —"

"Absolutely not." Michael crossed his arms. "You know these are peaceful people. We do not have the right to involve them in our struggle."

"Why did we make that promise in the first place?" Bancroft's question snapped like a whip, making them all flinch.

"It was the only way," Olsson muttered. "They wouldn't have let us go otherwise."

Michael hung his head as the truth rose up to mock him. Why had they agreed so easily? To save their necks — and because they thought they'd be returning the same woman. Though he had earnestly believed in the existence of the healing tribe, he had not believed they could heal anyone as desperately ill as Shaman's Wife. Help her, perhaps. Heal her? Never.

His words came out hoarse, forced through a tight throat. "The bargain seemed . . . reasonable at the time. And Deborah was willing —"

"Because she believed we'd come back for her as soon as possible." Bancroft's broad-carved face twisted in anger. "Why are we even debating this? Deb needs us, and we need to go get her. If we have to take Shaman's Wife back to her people, then that's part of the deal. If she wants to leave after we've gone, that's her business."

"You think they would let her leave?" Michael met Bancroft's angry gaze straight on. "They'll kill her before they let her go. We all saw how they treat their women."

"I think we should return to our base camp at the lake, then go back to the river." Every eye swiveled in Delmar's direction as he spoke for the first time. "How do we know Dr. Simons is still alive? She may not be." His face darkened. "You do not know these tribes like I do. If she resisted any of their commands, they would punish her. If she is still alive, she is probably wishing for death."

"We are not going back to the river until

we have attempted to rescue Deb Simons." Bancroft spoke in a flat authoritative tone, probably the one he had used to command his SEALs. The tone proved effective with civilians as well, for no one argued.

Scratching at his chin, Delmar shrugged. "Whatever you say. But if you want to avoid bloodshed, you will have to convince the shaman's wife to come with us."

Escaping the scene of celebration, Alex retreated to the shadows of the shabono, then found a quiet space under a hammock. Leaning against the bumpy wall of woven saplings, she pressed her hands to her face and closed her eyes.

Every nerve in her body was screaming, and her brain crackled with the need to rest. During one semester in college she had taken amphetamines to stay awake during finals week; the drugs had made her brain hum with alarming efficiency for a few hours, then she had crashed into the sleep of the dead.

Her mind was no longer humming — she could almost feel the crack and snap of misfiring neurons. Like an overheated engine, portions of her brain were on the verge of explosion. Visions of dead cells, clumped together with spatters of glial material, floated across the backs of her eyelids. Her brain had become a messy minefield, her thalamus a certain disaster. She would have freely surrendered her right hand in exchange for the ability to drop into a coma, but her body would not cooperate. Too many thoughts raced through her head, too many visions rolled like a movie in her mind.

And to further fuel her frantic thoughts, this morning she had witnessed a miracle.

The healing of Shaman's Wife had to be an illusion, a hallucination resulting from her disease. She could have dismissed the entire treetop experience — and would have, without a qualm — but the others had witnessed it, too. Furthermore, unless she had completely misread their faces, they had been as stunned by the experience as she.

Even the reverend doctor had been unable to explain what had happened.

Pressing her fingertips to her temple, Alex felt the slow throb of dilated blood vessels beneath her skin. Since descending the tree, her senses had become overly acute — every sound echoed like a gunshot; every scent threatened to turn her stomach. Perhaps this hypersensitivity had exaggerated her perceptions of Shaman's Wife's healing; perhaps the woman did not really glow with health and happiness.

Somehow — through some trick of her disease or some otherworldly aspect of the jungle — she and her companions had stepped through the equivalent of Alice's looking glass. Perhaps they were not in the village at all, but still in the treetop, drugged by the scent of some exotic vine that induced a creepy virtual reality and played tricks on the mind.

Her questing fingers pinched the skin at her cheek until she winced. She registered pain, all right. And scents from the unidentified roasting creature over the fire did fill her nostrils, as did the stale scent of perspiration from the overhead hammock. Caitlyn had embraced her with arms that felt substantial, and the water someone had offered in a gourd had splashed over her lips and tasted delicious on her tongue . . .

If this wasn't reality, it was a pretty clever counterfeit. But if these things were real — if she really had descended the tree with a mysteriously healed patient — then something had skewed reality and defied the laws of nature and science.

If Shaman's Wife had experienced a genuine cure through the perfect mix of sunlight, elevation, biological elements, and whatever else her cursed disease demanded, Alex should have been cured, too.

"Why w-w-wasn't I?"

Hugging her knees, she curled into a tight ball, then knocked her fist against her head. Why hadn't the cure affected her? Kenway swore it had healed Ya-ree, the natives of this village declared that it worked even for their children, and it had rejuvenated a woman only hours away from death. Yet Alex was far weaker than she had been, for the exertion of the climb had severely taxed her remaining strength.

She didn't need to examine the waistband of her trousers to know she had lost three inches of badly needed fat reserves from her waistline. Her illness was eating her alive, just like . . . Shakespeare's sailor.

She dipped into the well of memory and came up with a scene from *Macbeth,* quoted from the lips of Janice Williams, the spectacled professor who had captivated her in English Literature. Closing her eyes, Alex could hear Professor Williams's crackling voice as she recited the curse Shakespeare's three witches placed upon a sailor:

> I will drain him dry as hay:
> Sleep shall neither night nor day
> Hang upon his pent-house lid;
> He shall live a man forbid:
> Weary se'nnights nine times nine
> Shall he dwindle, peak and pine . . .

If Kenway was right and God did control the universe, then the Almighty had cursed her, denying her sleep and condemning her to dwindle, peak, and pine until nothing but a spent shell remained. But that same God had chosen to heal a primitive, illiterate woman who had probably done nothing more significant in her lifetime than bear a couple of children.

"Why did she d-d-deserve healing," Alex asked the air, "while I didn't?"

The question brought a hushed silence to the shabono. The children playing nearby stopped laughing; an old woman who had wandered in to tend the fire lifted her head and looked in Alex's direction. She might have spoken, but her attention was distracted by a sharp cry from the field outside.

Paralyzed by weariness, Alex watched as the woman tensed, then hurried toward the exit.

An impulse of alarm shot up Alex's spine as the silence filled with women's screams and the cry of angry men. A primal instinct propelled her to her feet and compelled her to follow the woman who had fled the round-house.

Where was Caitlyn?

After stumbling through the alana in a blind panic, Alex reached the opening and stared in horror at the scene beyond. White-painted warriors fringed the fields, bows and arrows and clubs in hand. The shaman of the Angry People stood in the center of the advancing warriors, his fist wound in the hair of a native child who hung lifeless from his grip. Thumping his free hand against his painted chest, he

533

lifted his face to the sky and cried out a challenge.

Alex glanced left and right, but Caitlyn was nowhere in sight. "Oh God, help!" Dropping to her hands and knees, she crawled through the grasses toward a group of children who had taken refuge behind a stand of banana trees.

Peering through the long, drooping leaves, Alex watched as Alejandro Delmar stepped into the field to answer the chief's challenge. His iron hand encircled the wrist of Shaman's Wife, who wept with every step, digging her heels into the ground and flailing uselessly as she resisted.

Alex lifted her head as high as she dared, searching for the other members of her team. Corpses littered the field, the brown bodies of a woman and children who had been dancing only moments before. The woman seemed to be leaning on nothing but air; then Alex realized that six or seven arrows had pincushioned her chest and now held her partially aloft.

She could see no one else from her group — perhaps they had all fled at the first sign of attack. The warriors of Keyba Village had disappeared like shadows, but she knew they had to be watching and waiting nearby.

Delmar called to the enemy, then the vengeful shaman lifted his arm. The green wall of foliage parted and Deborah Simons appeared, her clothing torn and her hands bound together. She stumbled as if she had been pushed, then blinked in the strong sunlight and lifted her head.

"Come," Delmar called. "It has been arranged."

Alex's heart twisted as Deborah limped forward with stiff dignity. Bruising had mottled the woman's clear complexion; one eyelid sagged over a purple cheekbone. One sleeve of her blouse had been ripped away; the exposed arm glistened wetly with blood.

Though she radiated bleakness, Deborah's tormented face seemed to soften as she approached Shaman's Wife. Her trembling lips parted in what might have been the beginning of a smile had she not winced and closed her mouth around bloody gums.

When Deborah reached Delmar, the guide touched her shoulder, then strode forward, dragging the shaman's woman toward the invaders. The shaman came forward to take his protesting wife, then held her while two warriors bound her wrists. Finally he brandished his fist at Delmar, then turned to lead his weeping wife away.

"Deborah!" Emboldened by the exchange, Alex lifted her head. "Over here!"

Sobbing in relief, Deborah stumbled forward. As Bancroft and Kenway materialized from behind a stand of plantains and rushed toward her, an arrow sailed out of the jungle.

Alex tilted her head as she heard the sound of a knife entering a ripe melon, then realized she had heard the arrow strike.

Deborah fell to her knees, her mouth opening. For an instant her forehead knit in puzzlement, then she pitched forward into the grass. Kenway cried out; Bancroft shouted a bloodcurdling oath, and the Angry People vanished into the rainforest.

"Mom!"

Alex turned to see Caitlyn leap up from her hiding place in the grass. "Cait?"

She reached out and pulled her weeping daughter into a close embrace, patting her back and murmuring the only phrase that came immediately to mind: "Don't cry. We're all right."

Caitlyn's grip was like iron, her arms locked against Alex's spine. "Mom, I want to go home."

"So do I, sweetie. S-s-so do I."

The carnage had not ended with the departure of the Angry People. As the natives of Keyba Village gathered their dead, a group of warriors returned with another body they had discovered on the trail. They laid the corpse at Michael Kenway's feet.

Shaman's Wife.

Delmar snorted when he recognized the face. "Stupid thing wouldn't cooperate," he said, propping his hands on his hips. "No man wants a woman who doesn't want him. She brought dishonor to her man by resisting."

Feeling as though her knees had turned to water, Alex sank to the ground as Kenway knelt by the woman's body. She had not been cut, but bruises marked her neck.

Somehow Alex found her voice. "Strangulation?"

Pinching the bridge of his nose, Kenway nodded. "I've seen this type of marking once before, in Iquitos. A drunken man came home and threw his wife to the ground, then placed a broom across her throat and stood on it."

He sat in silence for a moment, then drew a deep breath and turned to Emma Whitmore, who had approached with a look of shock on her face. "You know their burial customs?"

She nodded. "I think so."

"Will you help me tend to her? She has no family in this tribe."

Alex pushed herself up from the ground. "I'll h-h-help, too."

Emma nodded toward Bancroft. "I think someone needs to help him. Kenway, if you and Olsson can construct the funeral biers, we'll prepare the bodies."

Following the example of the Keyba villagers, Kenway, Olsson, and Baklanov constructed elevated burial platforms from vines and branches. As Emma helped the distraught Bancroft tend to Deborah Simons, Alex washed mud from the native woman's face, then finger-combed her long, tangled hair. Caitlyn wanted to help, but Alex sent her away to comfort the children who wandered through the scene of carnage. Their mothers were helping with the funeral biers, pausing occasionally to scoop up handfuls of sand and drizzle them over their heads and shoulders as they keened the dreadful ululation of mourning.

The natives' grief was difficult to witness, but Alex had to particularly steel herself to the heart-rending sound of Bancroft's weeping. Odd, that a former Navy SEAL could feel so much and so deeply for a woman he'd known only a few days. Then again, love was a strange little monster . . .

A few moments later she looked up to see Bancroft crossing the field with large strides, his jaw set in determination. He walked directly toward the shaman, who was kneeling in the grass as he helped the men lash poles together for the funeral biers.

"Why?" Bancroft shouted, apparently thinking he could penetrate the shaman's understanding by the sheer volume of his voice. "Where were your sentinels? How did the Angry People slip by your guards?"

The shaman blinked at Bancroft as Delmar hurried to intervene in what had the potential to become a messy altercation.

As Bancroft threw back his head and jacked his fists to his hips, the Indian tracker stuttered out a translation.

The shaman stood, his head bowed, then spoke slowly and clearly, his voice carrying to the edge of the field. Alex caught Emma's eye, hoping for some clue as to what he was saying, but the anthropologist only shook her head.

"He said there were no guards because all the people were celebrating," Delmar answered. "To honor the Spirit of keyba, they must all celebrate when someone is healed."

"The Spirit is flat-out stupid, then," Bancroft muttered. "Why would he have them celebrate when an enemy is practically upon them?"

Delmar cast Bancroft an uncertain look, then interpreted the question. The shaman closed his eyes and nodded slightly, then spoke, his hands lifting as he looked to the kapok tree.

"He understands your sorrow," Delmar said, "but he says the Angry People are no more threat than annoying gnats. The greater danger lies in not celebrating the Spirit of keyba's goodness."

The Brazilian tracker placed his hand on Bancroft's arm. "Let it go, Bancroft. It is finished."

Bancroft turned and walked toward Alex,

his eyes red. Sensing his discomfort, she shifted her gaze to the grass, granting the man a measure of privacy. It would be hard for a man of action to accept that he had been helpless and unprepared during a moment of attack, but Delmar was right. They could not undo the past.

Kenway and Baklanov had just finished elevating the funeral biers when Alex's mind, numbed by the day's horror and her own weariness, exploded into sharp awareness. "Emma," she said, tugging at the anthropologist's sleeve, "when will they light the f-f-funeral fires?"

Emma glanced around, then shook her head. "I can't say, Alex. Probably near sunset."

Biting her lip, Alex followed Kenway, who had gone for water.

"Kenway," she said, watching him fill a gourd from a clay pot, "we're m-m-missing the obvious."

He hesitated, the gourd halfway to his lips. "What do you mean?"

"Brain tissue from Shaman's Wife. If we could examine it, we would know for certain if what she had was kuru or some other prion disease. Knowing that, we'd know if her cure was genuine."

He sipped from the dipper, keeping his eyes on her, then lowered it. "I can't believe you, Alexandra. First you doubt her cure; now you doubt her disease."

"One night in a tree fort can't cure a prion disease."

"But it did. You saw the evidence yourself."

"It can't. So she must have been suffering from something else, maybe even some psychosomatic disorder. She was cured because she *believed* she'd be cured."

Kenway gave her a hard eye, and from his expression she gathered that he thought she'd taken leave of her senses. "That's a load of codswallop."

"No, it's not."

"Dr. Pace," he crossed his arms, "may I remind you of what you said to me not so many days ago? Consider the principle of Occam's razor — when two theories compete, the simpler is more likely to be correct. The simplest explanation for what happened in the tree is that Shaman's Wife was healed, just as the natives said she would be."

Alex clenched her fingers, resisting the urge to throttle him. "But that's scientifically impossible. If the result we witnessed was a genuine restoration of health, I should have been affected, too. So we need a sample of the woman's brain tissues —"

"No." He dropped the gourd back into the pot, then crossed his arms. "I'd love to humor you, but we haven't the tools necessary for an autopsy."

"Couldn't we —"

"Absolutely not. You are not taking this woman's head, nor her brain, nor any part of her. She deserves a decent rest among people who appreciated her." His tone softened as he looked into her eyes. "We failed her, Alex — she was a person, not a case study, and we used her as a pawn in our experiment. Even if we could get a sample — which we can't, not in these conditions — I'll not use her as a specimen."

"You used Ya-ree."

"He had no family. These people have adopted this woman, and they wouldn't understand."

Alex swallowed hard, her cheeks blazing as though a flame had seared them. He was right, of course. Perhaps they did owe Shaman's Wife a measure of dignity. Besides, any brain tissue they might collect would deteriorate long before they reached civilization.

Still . . . the researcher in her could not help regretting an opportunity lost.

Several hours later, all of the dead — seven, by Alex's count — had been arranged in a circle in the center of the field. As the shaman chanted and the women keened, somber warriors set fires beneath each pyre.

Within their group, a red-eyed Bancroft clasped his hands and stared straight ahead at nothing while Kenway led their team in a memorial prayer for Deborah Simons. Because it would have been rude to ignore him,

Alex bowed her head and tried to hold a positive thought for the woman who should have listened to her brain, not her heart. Deborah had sacrificed herself, and for what? She was dead, the shaman's woman was dead, and so many innocents had been murdered, including some of the children Caitlyn had entertained.

Wrapped in dire thoughts, Alex watched silently as the flames consumed the bodies. What if the healing they all witnessed had been entirely psychosomatic? Eventually the disease would have triumphed, but after exposure to the sun and whatever biological elements existed in the canopy, Shaman's Wife's brain might have produced psychotropic agents that somehow compensated for the effects of the disease. Kenway's Iquitos patient might have experienced the same effect. These genuinely-diseased natives could "walk the tree" and experience natural euphoria at the sight of a sunrise over the rim of the earth. This remarkable rapture, combined with their religion, cosmology, and naturally-occurring elements found in the kapok canopy, might provoke a psychosomatic effect that enabled them to transcend the disease for a few hours or even days . . .

Her nerves tightened as imponderables shifted in her brain like an uncooperative Rubik's cube. Why hadn't the canopy experience affected *her?* Because she knew a canopy sunrise, while extraordinary, resulted from the earth spinning on its axis and not the arrival of a great spirit. Though the beauty of the sun's advent had moved her — perhaps biochemicals in the tree *had* affected her to some extent — her thought processes were too advanced to be influenced as Shaman's Wife had been.

She rested her chin on her fist, biting her knuckle as she considered the theory. As a scientific hypothesis, it would hold little merit without supporting data, but for now this latest premise seemed downright logical. The stuffy researchers who published papers for the leading scientific journals might scoff to think something as basic as a sunrise could induce hysterical healing, but they had not walked in this jungle, witnessed the fervency of these people, or spent an eternal night in a nest that served to make a human feel small and insignificant.

Her eyes sought and found Kenway, who stood with Caitlyn among the villagers watching the fires. Closing her eyes, Alex breathed in the searing scent of burning flesh and knew she would never forget this day or this odor.

She *hated* knowing that her daughter would share this memory.

As Michael watched the shadows stretch across what had become a burial ground, he realized that he had never experienced such a range of emotions in a single day. The morning had begun with wonder and celebration; evening would fall on a people shattered by violence and grief.

Caitlyn Pace held his hand as they stood with the other villagers around the funeral pyres. The shaman, still chanting, dropped an armload of dry twigs and leaves on one reluctant fire, sending a volcano of sparks into the deepening sky.

"Will they come back, do you think?" Caitlyn's voice had gone thin and reedy.

"I think not." He tightened his grip on her hand. "They got what they came for."

Her chin quivered. "Shaman's Wife, you mean?"

He nodded.

545

"I wouldn't have wanted to go with them, either. So I guess I'd be dead, too."

"Caitlyn." Turning, he pressed his hands to her shoulders, then knelt to look her in the eye. "You don't know what sort of plan God has for your life. You can't waste time worrying about things that may never happen. You are special. And you can rest knowing your mum would never let anything like that happen to you. She'd give up her own life first."

The girl considered his answer, then cast him a look of helpless appeal. "My mom is sick, you know. She tries to pretend she isn't, but I know how bad off she is." She stared steadily at Michael, with only a single quiver of her chin to suggest the depth of her fear. "It's the same disease that took my grandmother, I think. The disease Mom is working to stop."

The shock of surprise held Michael immobile. He lifted his gaze, searching the sky for some bit of inspiration that might suggest words to comfort the girl, but everything that sprang to mind seemed trite and hollow.

Caitlyn Pace was young, but she was no child. She had been masquerading behind a brave front for days, perhaps weeks.

He swallowed hard, then rubbed his thumb over her thin shoulders. "How long have you known?"

She lifted one shoulder in a shrug. "Ever since we came to the jungle and Mom started acting strange. But she's getting bad, really bad. She pretends she's fine, but she's not."

Michael nodded. "Your mum doesn't want to upset you. She's working hard to find a cure, and we may be on to something. Shaman's Wife was healed up in that tree."

"But what about my mom? She looks worse than ever."

The dreadful music of mourning seeped into the silence between them. Not knowing what else to say, Michael squeezed Caitlyn's shoulders again, then released her. Before he could stand, she startled him with a question: "Was Shaman's Wife special to God?"

Michael lowered his eyes. "I'm sure she was."

"Then why didn't he help her?"

Blowing out his cheeks, Michael rubbed his hands on his thighs and tried to think. Behind him he could hear the whispering, crackling of the fire that rose above the grieving mourners, as though the flames were laughing. Sometimes he thought the entire jungle was mocking him.

"I don't know, Caitlyn. Perhaps he did help her, but in a way we cannot understand."

"I don't get it." Bending her head, she studied her dirt-encrusted hands. "Why would God heal her just to let her die?"

Michael's thoughts came to an abrupt halt. *Why would God heal her . . .*

Why hadn't that thought occurred to him?

Tenderly, he pressed his hand to Caitlyn's soot-smeared cheek. "There are many things about God I don't understand, but I have learned to trust him. And I must thank you, Cait, for helping me understand something else."

She crinkled her nose. "What'd I say?"

"Come." He stood and extended his hand. "Let's go share some leftover monkey meat with the shaman. I have a feeling he'll be able to answer our questions — now that I know the sort I should be asking."

Though his empty stomach would have welcomed meat of any sort, Michael wasn't surprised to discover that the evening meal was scanter than usual. With most of the day taken up in caring for the dead, no one had fished or hunted. If not for the capybara a woman had hung over the fire in early morning, there would have been nothing to eat.

The women of the shabono split the large rodent into several pieces and shared it with their families. As was his custom, the shaman divided his portion among the expedition members who, in turn, shared their meager portions with him. Bancroft alone refused to eat, but sat against the wall, his bent head resting on his knees.

Caitlyn didn't even ask what they were eating, but nibbled daintily at the meat. The other villagers sat around their individual

548

fires and stared into the flames or hunkered in their hammocks, waiting for sleep to ease their sorrow.

The village dead included one man, one woman, and three children. Now one husband had no wife to care for his children and a wife had no husband to bring food for their little ones. Michael suspected that in time the two mourning families would merge, but not before time had partially healed the pain of loss.

The shaman seemed particularly burdened with grief. He sat cross-legged by the fire, his eyes large and filled with shadows. Michael sat as close to him as he dared, then caught Delmar's eye.

"Do you think it's proper . . . may I ask him a few questions?"

Delmar waited a moment, then murmured something to the shaman. The old man closed his eyes, then inclined his head.

"I'd like to know more about the Great Spirit of the keyba," Michael said. "Does he have a name . . . and can this name be spoken without a loss of respect?"

Delmar asked the question and a moment later the shaman replied in a string of syllables.

"He says he would not have told you the Great Spirit's name before today. But you have walked the keyba, and you have met the Spirit yourself. Your souls have been bound

549

with these people because you have all shared sorrow on this day. So yes, he will tell you the Spirit's name, though he is surprised you do not already know it."

Michael leaned forward as his blood quickened with adrenaline. "Tell him, please, that I do know the Great Spirit. But because I speak another language, I know him by another name. Might I know what he is called among those of Keyba Village?"

Delmar asked the question. The shaman replied with one phrase: "Yai Pada."

The interpreter jerked in surprise. After staring at the shaman for a moment, he asked another question, a sharp one, and the shaman lifted his head to answer. Apparently not liking the answer, Delmar looked away, a cloud settling over his features.

"What?" Michael prodded. "What did he say?"

Delmar did not respond at first, but swiped at his forehead, where sweat had beaded in dozens of tiny pearls upon his skin. "The Spirit who dwells above the kapok is called Yai Pada," Delmar finally answered. "The Angry People also know him, but they call him Yai Wana Naba Laywa. He is the Great Spirit, the one who created everything, including all the other spirits."

"I know this legend." Emma Whitmore, who had been reclining in the sand with her eyes half-closed, sat up. "The Yanomamo speak of a spirit called Yai Wana Naba Laywa. They fear him."

Michael lifted a brow. "Does this spirit visit the Angry People, too?"

A livid hue overspread Delmar's face. "No. They know him as the unfriendly one, the unknowable spirit who eats the souls of children and steals them from their families."

"He eats children?" Caitlyn's voice squeaked through the silence.

"Don't worry, honey." From the dark corner where she had been resting, Alexandra spoke in a rough whisper. "It's all imaginary. Mind games."

Ignoring Alex's comment, Delmar narrowed his eyes at Caitlyn. "When a child dies, Yai Wana Naba Laywa sends a hawk to carry the child to his land. I know many shamans whose spirits have chased that hawk, but the land where Yai Wana Naba Laywa lives is bright and too hot to enter. It is a noisy place, they say, people are always singing there. They celebrate whenever they get new children to eat."

Struggling to hold his temper, Michael gave Caitlyn's shoulder a reassuring squeeze.

"I have heard much about this unfriendly god." Emma brushed sand from her sleeves. "The Yanomamo say he created a big fire pit where all stingy people go when they die." She chuckled. "Even the Yanomamo who refuse to follow Yai Wana Naba Laywa are

551

generous with their food and shelter. No one wants to be thrown into the fire pit."

"Surely these are relatively new concepts to these people," Alexandra said. "I mean, hell is a thoroughly Christian invention —"

"Afraid not." Emma's gaze shifted to Caitlyn, then her eyes thawed slightly. "The Yanomamo believed in the fire pit and Yai Wana Naba Laywa long before their first contact with the white man. These ideas are as old as the jungle, and originated with the shamans who learned the ancient stories from the spirits who guided them."

Turning to see Emma better, Michael propped his elbow on a bent knee. "Have you had experience with these jungle spirits?"

A sly smile curved her mouth. "So what if I have? I devoutly believe in the spirit world, Dr. Kenway, and have found it to be a place of beauty and delight."

"What sort of beauty can you find in a burning field?" Lifting his head, Bancroft wagged a belligerent finger in the anthropologist's direction. "If these people are following jungle spirits who command them to abuse and murder each other, I fail to see the beauty in them."

Emma's eyes went cold. "A strange comment, coming from a professional soldier."

Bancroft jerked his chin. "War is one thing — this was a massacre."

"What you saw today was an act of war,"

Emma continued, "the war for survival. Women are necessary for the propagation of a tribe. Our friend Deborah was obviously not willing to cooperate with the Angry People, so they returned her, hoping to trade her for the shaman's woman. But that woman was also unwilling to cooperate." She spread her hands. "As in all indigenous populations, a delicate balance exists between these tribes. One way to maintain that balance is through warfare. The people of Keyba Village killed six warriors from the Angry People when we arrived here. Today the Angry People killed five members of Keyba Village and Deborah . . . which, I believe, almost evens the score."

Alexandra had gone deathly pale except for the dark circles around her eyes. "They killed little children!" she objected. "This is not a game of tit for tat; it is sheer brutality!"

"It is the way of the jungle." Emma sighed heavily, then raked her hand through her white curls. "I don't expect you to understand; sometimes you must accept these things. But if you don't object when a jungle cat kills a turkey, you must also accept that neighboring tribes frequently kill to maintain the appropriate balance of power."

Having heard all he could stomach, Michael lifted his head. "These natives are not animals. And *this* village —" he lifted his hand, indicating the villagers around them — "is nothing like the Angry People."

"They are better off, obviously, and healthier, but they share the same traits and social structure —"

"You're absolutely mistaken."

"Am I?" Emma stiffened. "And what would you know about anthropology?"

"A person doesn't have to be an anthropologist to understand that a healthy society is built on more than animalistic urges. These people have built a civilization — a crude one, to be sure, but it's a civilization nonetheless — upon higher ideals."

"Prove it." Emma's voice had cooled.

"I think I can." Turning from the chilly anthropologist, Michael bowed his head in a gesture of respect for the shaman, then looked at Delmar. "Will you ask him to tell us more about Yai Pada?"

Emma released an icy laugh. "If you're trying to establish that they worship a spirit, that's no proof at all. The Angry People probably worship an entire pantheon of spirits, as do almost all indigenous tribes."

Ignoring her, Michael waited on an answer from the shaman. After a pause, Delmar asked the question in an offhanded manner. The shaman looked at Michael for a moment, his eyes narrow and black in the fire-tinted darkness, then lifted his hand and spoke in even, measured tones. When he had finished, he returned his gaze to Michael's face.

Delmar tossed a twig into the fire. "He repeated what he said earlier — Yai Pada lives in the sky. He is the creator Spirit, the Spirit above all. He sends a hawk to carry the spirits of children to his land. Everyone, even the jungle spirits know about him, but the people of this village are the only ones who meet him in the keyba."

Michael's stomach lurched upward. "*How,* exactly, do they meet him?"

When Delmar repeated the question, the shaman regarded Michael with an expression of surprise.

"He says you should know — you met him this morning."

Michael glanced at Alex, who was watching with undisguised curiosity.

Rubbing the bristly beard at his jaw, Michael considered his answer, then nodded at Delmar. "Tell him yes, I know the creator Spirit — for many years I have known him. And yes, I felt the Great Spirit's glory in the sunrise while I waited in the kapok canopy. I saw him heal the other shaman's woman."

As Delmar translated; the old man's face creased in a smile that banished the shadows in his eyes. When Delmar had finished, the shaman lifted his hands, speaking faster and with more enthusiasm than he had exhibited since their arrival at Keyba Village.

"He says," Delmar began, struggling to keep up, "that for many days they have been asking the Great Spirit to send one of his people to teach them about him. The one with many tattoos —"

Ya-ree, of course. Michael nodded. "I know him."

"He walked the keyba to ask Yai Pada what he should do. Yai Pada told him to go to the great river and find the nabas who could help. The man left us, and now you are here."

When Michael inclined his head to indicate his understanding, the shaman spoke again.

"We have waited for you to speak of Yai Pada," Delmar translated, "and now you have. But we thought you would come to give us light and teach us. Instead we have suffered sorrow and death since you came."

Delmar paused as a tear coursed down the old man's cheek. "He asks — have you light to give us?"

"Indeed." Folding his hands, Michael gave the shaman a careful smile. "I believe I do."

Alex gaped at Michael Kenway as he spread his hands and began to speak to the shaman. His cultured voice simmered with barely-checked passion, and the others couldn't help but hear. As Delmar translated, men, women, and children from around the shabono halted their activities and came near to listen.

"Long ago, before the jungle existed," Michael paused between phrases for Delmar's translation, "Yai Pada yearned for companionship. So he created a great host of spirits, beautiful creatures with wings and the ability to change their shape."

The Indians looked at each other, their eyes dark and unreadable in the firelight, but no one interrupted or voiced an objection. From her time in the jungle, Alex knew the concept of a spirit world was neither unfamiliar nor surprising to them.

"One day," Michael continued, "one of the

winged spirits grew tired of obeying Yai Pada. He wanted to be the greatest spirit, the one whose voice would be instantly obeyed. So he convinced many of the other spirits to leave Yai Pada's bright land and come with him."

Though Delmar translated in a flat monotone, from the murmur of wonder that fluttered throughout the assembly, Alex knew Michael's words had struck a chord.

"When Yai Pada created the world, he placed a man and a woman in the center of a beautiful orchard. He filled it with gentle animals; the snakes did not bite, the jaguar did not attack. Everything was perfect, and everything in the land enjoyed peace. Then the rebellious spirit decided to speak to the people."

"Omawa," the shaman interrupted.

Michael lifted a brow at this, and Emma explained. "The leader of the evil spirits is called Omawa. The Yanomamo also know about him."

Michael gave Emma a perfunctory nod and turned his attention back to the shaman. "Omawa spoke to the woman and tricked her into disobeying a command of Yai Pada. By obeying Omawa and not Yai Pada, she proved herself unwilling to live in peace with Yai Pada. Though it pained his heart, Yai Pada sent the man and woman out of his perfect orchard and into a jungle where animals attack and vines sting."

After hearing the translation, the shaman crossed his arms and sniffed with satisfaction at this evidence of jungle justice.

"Many, many seasons passed. The people had children, and their children had children. Some of them loved Yai Pada and tried to hear his voice; others listened to the lies of Omawa and the spirits who had followed him. Those who obeyed Omawa killed each other, took revenge, and asked the spirits to kill their enemies. The spirits were happy to do this because Omawa delighted in death and destruction. His greatest pleasure was bringing pain to the people Yai Pada had created for joy. He taught the people how to kill, to rape, to twist the truth into lies. Because of this, all people after the first two were born with a sickness. It is not a sickness of the body like the shuddering disease, but a sickness —" Michael thumped his chest — "of the spirit."

In dazed exasperation, Alex looked around the circle. The guileless natives were eating from Michael's hand, absorbing every word. Even Emma Whitmore seemed fascinated by Michael's retelling of the creation story, though her expression was more analytical than rapt.

"Because Omawa had tricked the people so completely, Yai Pada put his spirit in flesh and came to earth. This one — you could

559

call him Yai Pada Son — he alone was not born with the spirit-sickness, because his father was not a man, but Yai Pada. He came as a baby, he grew to be a shaman, and he suffered all the sorrows other men suffer. Even though he knew he would die a shameful death, still he chose to live among us . . . until Omawa tricked the people and told them Yai Pada Son was evil. The people believed this, and they killed him."

The natives' faces took on an inward look as they absorbed the translation. In order of age, a frown appeared on each countenance as its owner comprehended the significance of divine death.

"But the Son of the Great Spirit cannot die. The fires of the pit could not hold him; his body healed itself. Yai Pada Son walked among men many more days, then he flew back up to heaven. Now he sends his Spirit out to anyone who will choose him instead of obeying the spirits of Omawa."

Michael folded his hands and looked directly at the shaman. "You and your people know about the Great Spirit. He has blessed you with healing and showered you with joy. But he wants to send his Spirit to live inside you so you do not have to walk the keyba to speak to him."

The old man blinked several times, then a rush of color flooded his face, as though the story had caused younger blood to fill his veins. Curling his hands into the sand by the fire, he picked up a handful, then slowly, methodically rained the dust over his head.

"We have done much evil." The shaman dropped his sandy hands into his lap. "We are not like the babies who can fly into Yai Pada's land when they die."

"Yes, you are right," Michael agreed. "But after a killing, do you not hang your weapons on a tree to rid yourselves of shame? The tree takes your killing weapons and makes your hands clean. Yai Pada Son does the same thing. As a man, Yai Pada Son committed no evil, yet he died on a tree to take your shame. He accepted your evil deeds so you can be clean, yes, as clean as a baby who flies to Yai Pada's bright land."

Question filled the shaman's eyes as Delmar interpreted: "So — when we die, are we like the babies?"

Michael smiled. "Yes. When Yai Pada Son lived on earth, he cut a trail for you to follow. When the time comes for your body to die, the hawk will carry your spirit to Yai Pada's beautiful land."

As Delmar translated, the shaman stared into the fire, his face shifting to the look of a man who has just walked into a surprise party. A moment later the lines of heartsick weariness faded from his face. Raising both hands, he cried out, "Yai Pada Son!" and no translation was required.

Following their leader's example, every man, woman, and child lifted their hands. Chanting "Yai Pada Son" again and again, they danced for joy, arms and legs and bodies jumping in a melee of celebration. Having made a communal decision to embrace the Son of Yai Pada, they congratulated themselves with warm hugs, wide smiles, and more whooping than Alex had heard in her life.

Irritable and confused, she drew back from the fire, pulling in her legs lest she be trampled in the merriment. Caitlyn sat next to her, her face rapt with interest, and Olsson and Baklanov leaned against the wall and watched in amusement. Between the two men, Emma wore a frown the size of Atlanta.

She caught Alex's eye, then leaned toward her. "He has no right to meddle in their religion!" She yelled to be heard above the din. "More harm has been done to native people groups in the name of God than anything else."

Bancroft cast Emma a scornful glance. "Why don't you stick a sock in it? They're happy. And they believed in God long before we got here. They just didn't have the full story."

"The full story as *you* know it," Emma countered.

"The full story," Bancroft insisted. "They deserve to know the entire truth. What they do with it is up to them."

Sighing heavily, Alex lowered her head. She intended to bring her hands up to block the sight of Kenway's overactive new converts, but a cold sweat prickled on her jaws when her arms trembled and did not obey. She flexed her arms, trying to stop the trembling, but they continued to . . . shudder.

The truth crashed into her consciousness like a jet disintegrating on the ocean surface. Athetoid tremors resulted from the destruction of brain fibers responsible for the inhibition of muscle movement.

Her disease had just taken a giant step forward.

20 April 2003
5:45 p.m.

Rising from the midst of the happy hubbub, Michael stood and made his way to the water skin that hung from a branch near the entrance. He hesitated, however, when he saw Alex sitting against the wall, her arms trembling and her face ashen.

Caitlyn hovered over her mother. "Mom? Are you okay?"

Alex bared her teeth in an expression that was not a smile. "I'm f-fine."

"You don't look so good."

Michael crossed to Alex's side in broad strides, then knelt by her side and lifted her arm. The sheer lightness of the limb surprised him — she had lost an alarming amount of weight, though it was hard to tell how much in the long pants and long-sleeved shirt she wore.

He smiled up at Caitlyn. "Be a dear, would you, and see if you can find some fruit for your mum? I think I saw a bowl of bananas near the woman who has the twins."

Alex glared at him. "I'm not hungry."

"You need to eat." Michael caught Caitlyn's eye and gave her a "please humor me" look. When she reluctantly moved away, he frowned at Alexandra. "Why didn't you tell me how far the symptoms had progressed?"

Her disease had not diminished the fire in her eyes. "I'm not your patient."

"I'm not your doctor. I hoped I was your friend."

She grimaced at the word. "Are we friends? Sometimes I think we are mortal combatants."

"Then I must apologize for leading you astray." Slipping his arm around her waist, Michael helped her to her feet. He had intended to walk her to her hammock, but once she found her balance, she pulled away.

"I'll be fine now."

"How long have you been experiencing tremors?"

She shrugged. "This is a fluke. The stress of the day, probably." Tossing her head, she took a step forward, then swayed on her feet. "Oh."

He caught her arms before she could fall. "Let me help you."

"I don't need your help."

"You are the personification of stubbornness." He spoke with a creditable attempt at coolness, marred only by the thickness in his voice. "You're going to need my help and everyone else's to get out of the jungle. Bancroft and I can fashion another travois if necessary, and —"

"Leave me alone, w-w-will you?" Her voice had gone ragged, torn by the threat of tears that now sprang to her eyes.

Floundering in an agonizing maelstrom of emotion, Michael pulled her into a darkened spot behind a hanging hammock, then placed his hands on her shoulders and forced her to look at him.

"Alex, I know you're brave; Cait knows you're brave. You don't have to put on a front for either of us."

Tears were rolling down her face, leaving dusty tracks over her sallow skin. "I . . . don't . . . want her to know."

"Good heavens, woman, the child is a budding genius! Do you really believe she can't see how sick you are?"

He felt a sharp stab of regret as Alex's face went slack.

"She knows, dear heart." He whispered the words as he stroked her face, her tears burning his fingers. "We all know, and we want to help."

"Oh, God!" She rolled her eyes toward the ceiling, then slid between his hands to land in a heap on the ground. He followed her, kneeling in the dirt, and heard the words she spat into her hands: "There is no help for me. I've found no cure here."

"Others did." He waited, desperately hoping she would look up and understand the faith that lived in him and within these people. "Don't you see? Caitlyn gave me the key this afternoon. She said *God* healed Shaman's Wife, and in that moment I realized we were wrong to look for bacteria and proteins and biochemicals. We should have been looking for God."

Her hands lowered then, but the look she gave him was anything but gentle.

"They were all cured," he continued, pressing on before she could completely harden her heart, "when they climbed the tree in faith. The kapok didn't hold the cure — God did. The tree is God's gift to them, and their faith in him healed their diseases."

"Faith?" she asked, her voice soft with disbelief. "And how on earth am I supposed to manufacture that?"

20 April 2003
6:40 p.m.

Alex drew a long, quivering breath, barely mastering the anger that shook her to the core. When it came to matters of science, sometimes Kenway made no more sense than one of these simpleminded natives.

"You talk about faith as though it were something I could reach out and snatch from thin air." Her hands, wet with her tears, curled into fists. "I can't do that, Michael. I can't lower myself to the level of superstition and folklore."

"Not even to save your life?"

She released a hoarse and bitter laugh. "Not even. Don't you see? We've already tried that. I wore myself out climbing that cursed tree, and your mysterious keyba didn't work for me. Because I don't believe. I can't believe in hocus-pocus."

She pressed her hand to her head as a train of new thoughts roared through her brain.

Could his argument be valid on a purely chemical level? Every neurologist knew the neurotransmitter serotonin could induce feelings of happiness and well-being. In the same way, could some other chemical neurotransmitter lead a patient to a childlike belief in spirits and healing trees? The brain created serotonin from the amino acid tryptophan, derived from high-protein foods. If she had more time and the proper equipment, she might discover that something in the diet of these native people produced a neurotransmitter for faith, and that same chemical had something to do with healing prion diseases. Why not? Neurotransmitters originated in the brain, where prions did their deadly work.

Groaning, she pounded her head. Her ideas, which should have been clear and logical, felt muddy and complicated. This puzzle held too much to contemplate and too many variables to cloud her thought processes. She couldn't think in this condition. Nothing made sense, especially the events of the last twelve hours.

Kenway took a deep breath, then bent to catch her eye. "There are more things in heaven and earth than are dreamed of in your philosophy . . ."

Her lower lip trembled as she returned his stare. "Don't quote the B-B-Bible to me, Doctor."

"That's Shakespeare, not Scripture."

She flushed. Now he knew how badly she was floundering.

"Listen, Alexandra, and try to follow my reasoning."

"I thought you wanted me to cast reason aside."

"Faith requires reason, too. Since God gave us brains, I'm certain he expects us to use them."

Snorting softly, she pressed her fingertips to her pounding temple.

"You went up that kapok tree as a researcher, not a seeker." His brittle smile softened slightly. "If you had gone as a supplicant instead of a scientist —"

She couldn't stop a laugh. "This village may be primitive, Kenway, but these are not the dark ages. I haven't met a sackclothed supplicant in ages."

"Perhaps it's the wrong word, but it's the right meaning. I meant supplicant in the sense of someone who is truly seeking God." He looked past her with an intense but guarded expression. "I was a supplicant after my wife's death. I could find no answers for what had happened to us, no comfort in the world. So I went to God for explanations."

Alex swallowed hard, trying to dislodge the scream of frustration irritating the back of her throat. "Let me get this straight — your wife died, you couldn't understand why, and you went to God. You said a prayer, Jesus waved some sort of magic wand, and suddenly everything became clear?"

A look of inward intentness grew in his eyes, then he shook his head, sending wisps of black hair flickering past his face. "I still don't have all the answers, but I have faith enough to believe God does. He created us, he loves us, and he hurts when we suffer the effects of evil. He loves you, Alexandra, despite what you may think of him."

An unexpected weed of jealousy sprang up in Alex's heart, stinging like nettles. She didn't understand Kenway's faith, couldn't accept it, and didn't want it, but oh how lucky he was to have found something that made life make sense. She'd give anything to be able to drop her burdens and rest in the certainty that someone else would carry them.

Grief welled within her, black and cold, forcing words over her stammering tongue. "H-how can God know what I'm suffering? And if he loves me so much, why did he give me this disease? Why —" she choked on a sob that rose from somewhere deep in her chest — "w-why is he going to take me from my little girl and leave her alone in the world? If God exists, and if he is all-powerful like you say he is, then he took my mother, my husband, and now he's going to take my life. How can you look at all he's done and say he loves me?"

"God didn't take your husband — from what Caitlyn's told me, he ran off because he didn't want to be a father. That's his fault, not God's. And your mother died from a disease, and disease is a corruption of God's design. Don't you see? Sin is corruption; we are all born into it —"

She threw up her hand. "If I wanted to hear this, I'd have stayed home and watched a televangelist."

"Why don't you want to hear truth, Alex? Why won't you consider the simple facts in evidence? You know God exists — with your own eyes you saw him heal Shaman's Wife."

"I saw . . . a sick woman convince herself that she'd been healed."

"You know that's not true."

Alex gritted her teeth. "Okay — suppose we do p-p-postulate that Shaman's Wife received some kind of supernatural healing. If so, then why did God k-k-kill her only a few hours later? And what about Deborah Simons? The woman claimed to be a Christian. She sacrificed herself for all of us —"

"For you, Alexandra. She sacrificed herself so you could find the healing tribe."

Alex took a wincing breath. Not true. Deborah couldn't have — wouldn't have known.

As if he'd read her mind, Michael nodded. "She may not have known of your need, but God knew. And Deborah was obedient, so when the Spirit nudged her to stay, she agreed. Her death, as hard as it is for us to understand, was a victory — at least, it could be."

Unable to focus, Alex pushed his words aside. "That's crazy." Her throat tightened. "God shouldn't have allowed so many deaths today. They were all innocents."

His mouth shifted just enough to bristle the whiskers on his cheek. "God didn't kill those people. Evil did."

"And *that* I can't accept." She tossed her head and eyed him with cold triumph. "If God is all-powerful, he could have saved every one of those people today, but he didn't. Why not?"

"God *is* all powerful," Kenway answered, speaking in a low baritone that was both commanding and gentle. "His thoughts are higher than our thoughts, and his ways far above our ways. He is greater than evil, and not at its mercy, but he has created men and angels with free will. When men choose evil, suffering always results."

He spoke hesitantly, as if about to say something he knew she would dislike. "God's gift to us is that he takes the suffering we endure and uses it for our good. It's sort of a spiritual alchemy, if you will — lead becomes gold."

"Sickness," she whispered, thinking of Shaman's Wife, "becomes healing?"

"And death," his gaze came to rest on her

questioning eyes, "becomes life." He hesitated a moment, then reached out to grip her trembling hand. "The others want to leave tomorrow, so there's little time remaining. If you want to spend tonight in the kapok tree, I'll help you climb, and so will Olsson. We'll devise some way to hoist you up —"

"Haven't you heard a w-w-word I've said?" She snatched her hand from his, then struggled to stand. Leaving him alone in the shadows, she shouldered her way through the celebrating villagers, then moved into the quiet of the curving alana. The air was cooler here, the atmosphere less irritating.

The man was as dense as a London fog. She'd rebuffed his religious ideas a hundred times, yet still he dangled them before her, doubtless expecting her to snatch at them out of sheer desperation.

How could she believe in something that defied everything she'd ever been taught? Tonight he'd told the natives that God created the world, and everyone knew the Big Bang had led to evolutionary processes that had been creating the world for millions of years. Tonight he had spoken of spirits, good and evil, when everyone knew that life existed on one physical plane. Spirits and ghosts and demons belonged to the realm of folklore, not modern science.

And yet —

She pressed her hands to her head as the

events of the day tumbled in her brain like bits of glass in a kaleidoscope.

This morning she'd witnessed something she couldn't explain, but early man couldn't explain the sun or the seasons, either. Inexplicable mysteries were nothing but logical occurrences that had yet to be explored and understood, so maybe she could admit that Shaman's Wife had apparently been healed in the kapok tree.

"Okay, yes!" She hissed in the silence of the alana. "All right! The woman was healed. She was sick, ready to die, and by the time we left, she had been restored!"

Nothing answered in the narrow tunnel, but nothing was present to answer — no demons, no God, no spirits. Just Alex and the echo of her illogical confession.

She snorted as she considered the ramifications of this trip. If they made it out of the jungle, Kenway would undoubtedly take his observations of the incident back to England where he'd publish a paper that would be hotly disputed for years to come. Then some bright young researcher would look beyond the religious explanation for a rational reason and *that* scientist would discover a link between a chemical neurotransmitter and prions. His work would provide a cure just in time for Caitlyn . . .

But not for Alex. Because she would not be around.

Blinking, she looked up. She hadn't meant to follow the alana to its entrance, but she found herself standing at the edge of the field, where seven charred mounds marked the circle that had earlier held funeral biers.

Breathing in the scents of ashes, despair, and desolation, she moved through the trampled field with shaky strides, then broke into a hobbling run as she neared the papaya trees at the edge of the forest.

She had risked everything to find this village and she was about to lose everything she had gambled. If she remained, she'd only become a burden to her daughter and her companions. If by some miracle she made it back to Atlanta, she'd lie in a limp and helpless body for weeks while her brain frantically formulated theories no one would ever be able to capture.

Better to die here, now, than to drag out the inevitable. Better to let Caitlyn deal with a tragic accident than to suffer the horror of watching a death caused by FFI.

Gathering all that remained of her ebbing strength, Alex pushed her way into the jungle.

20 April 2003
7:02 p.m.

"Dr. Mike?" Michael looked down to see Caitlyn by his side, a pair of bananas in her hand. "Have you seen my mom?"

He glanced toward the alana, where Alexandra had disappeared. "I think she needed some peace and quiet. I'm sure she'll be back soon."

"I hope so." A frown knit the girl's forehead. "I know the alana's supposed to be safe, but it creeps me out after dark." She offered him a banana. "Want one?"

"Sure."

They sat together and ate, sharing a few bites with the village twins, a pair of round-bellied boys who couldn't have been more than three or four. Michael listened with fascination as Caitlyn alternated between making the boys laugh with native words and talking about how strange it would feel to sleep on a flat bed under sheets and blankets.

Yet as the moon peered over the rim of the shabono and lit the center fire, his uneasiness swelled into alarm. Alexandra had not re-appeared, so she might have fallen outside or encountered some kind of trouble . . .

"Excuse me, Cait, but I think I need to stretch my legs."

Leaving her to entertain the twins, he stood and gestured to Bancroft and Delmar. When they met him in the center of the shabono, he lowered his voice. "Alexandra ran outside some time ago." He glanced from the security chief to the guide, knowing both of them would realize the danger. "She is not well, and she was upset when she left. I'm think-ing a search party might be in order."

"Lover's quarrel, aye?" Delmar indulged in a lecherous wink. "I think the lady would ap-preciate it if you went after her yourself."

Michael scowled. "You are out of line, friend. I'll thank you to mind your tongue."

"I'll light a torch and have a look around outside," Bancroft said. "You're right to be careful. I doubt those murderers are out there, but just this morning the shaman showed me a pair of jaguar tracks in the dirt."

Michael nodded. "I'll go with you."

"Dr. Mike?" Like a lost puppy that would not go home, Caitlyn stood by his side again, her hand on his arm.

"Yes, dear?"

A faint line appeared between the child's

brows. "Are you going to look for my mom?"

"Quite right. Mr. Bancroft and I are going to take a look around outside. I'm sure we'll be back with her in a few minutes."

"That's good. Because it isn't like her to leave me." Caitlyn's voice had gone loud and rough, a bulldozer bravely straining to push panic aside.

Seeing the anxiety in her eyes, Michael decided to do something that felt more than a little odd in this place. Mindful of the natives' curious eyes, he placed his hand on Caitlyn's light brown hair, then bowed his head. "Father in heaven," he prayed, "please bring peace to this child's heart . . . and help us find her mother. Keep Alexandra safe, Lord, and guard her from danger and the forces of evil in this place. I ask these things in the name of our Lord."

When he opened his eyes, he discovered that a curious knot of villagers had gathered around him. Like him, they had felt the need for connection; their hands now rested upon the girl's back and shoulders. Several little ones had crowded into the circle, reaching out to grip Caitlyn's hands and arms with their small hands.

When she lifted her head, her brown eyes were wet. "Thank you, Dr. Mike."

"It's going to be all right."

A slow smile crossed her face as the murmuring natives reluctantly removed their hands. "They want to know what you were doing."

"Well —" He searched for the word. "Can you tell them I was praying? Talking to Yai Pada?"

"They thought you were talking in your sleep." She giggled, then said something to a child standing next to her. Amazing how much of the language she had picked up in only three days.

"I don't think they have a word for *praying,*" she told him. "But they will."

"Good. You can teach them all about it while we go look for your mum."

Michael patted Caitlyn's shoulder and sent her back to the hammocks. As he followed Bancroft and Delmar through the alana, he reflected on her comments. Alexandra would never leave her daughter unprotected unless she'd met with an accident . . . or thought the girl would be better off without her.

Had she given up?

20 April 2003
7:10 p.m.

Moving as quickly as her unsteady legs would allow, Alex followed a path into the jungle, then plunged through a thicket of leaves, trudging blindly ahead and stumbling over roots, palms, and mounds of unidentified insects. Tears flowed freely, obscuring her vision, and the sound of her own sobbing filled her ears. She moved through what seemed like yards and yards of foliage, then felt her feet sink in muck.

Swiping tears from her eyes, she realized she was standing in a stagnant pool. She tried to lift her feet, but the strong pull of the mud held her sneakers.

So this was a dead end — just like her work, her motherhood, and her life. Everything she had striven for would vanish into thin air, and she had no power to stop it. She would die in this bog, and who would care? Her friends in Atlanta would forget about her as easily as Alex and her teammates had pushed thoughts of Carlton, Hayworth, Chavez, and Fortier from their minds.

Engulfed in weariness, she squatted in the mud, not caring if she sat on a tarantula, an ants' nest, or an anaconda. Let it end here then. Just let it end.

Michael Kenway would see Caitlyn safely back to civilization — with a little coaxing, he might even be persuaded to adopt her.

The thought resonated within Alex . . . why couldn't he adopt her daughter? Caitlyn's father had never wanted a child, and even though Kenway's religious predilections troubled her, those same convictions would incline him to be a kind and caring father.

He liked Caitlyn . . . far better than he liked Alex, probably. And after losing his wife, it might do him good to have someone else to care for.

Dropping her head onto her hand, she considered the idea. The authorities would not surrender an American child to a British citizen without some sort of authorization, and Alex's will, safely on file in an Atlanta lawyer's office, stated that her ex-husband's parents would serve as guardian in the event of Alex's death.

So her darling daughter could either go with a doughy old pair who wanted her even less than their self-centered son did, or into the foster care system . . . or she could go with Michael Kenway.

Seized by a compulsion to complete one last task, Alex widened her eyes to search for something, anything, she would use to leave a message. Groping along the muddy bank for several minutes, her fingers finally encountered a sharp thorn. After breaking off the thorn — and piercing her fingers in the process — she pulled a wide leaf from a bush.

Surrendering her shoes to the mud, she slipped over the bank and spread the leaf on the ground. Gripping the thorn between her thumb and index finger, she spread the leaf with her left hand and began to blindly scratch out a message:

20 April, 2003.

I, Alexandra Pace, want my daughter, Caitlyn Grace, to be the ward of Michael Kenway if I predecease either of them.

As she worked, her eyes grew more accustomed to the darkness. Though virtually no moonlight penetrated the deep jungle, it did light the tops of the trees overhead, creating sumptuous swags of shadows that hung like deep blue bunting on the plants around her. The forest whispered to itself, the faint patter of rain on leaves blending with the crackle of the night crawlers that came out to devour leaves and branches.

When she had finished, she rolled the broad leaf, careful not to crease the living material, then slipped it into her shirt. They'd find this on her body, probably within a day or two, so the message should still be legible. Then Kenway would comfort Caitlyn and take her back to Iquitos, which was no place for a young American girl. When he realized this, he'd return to England, where Cait would grow up in London and attend the best schools . . .

Sniffing, Alex used the back of her damp wrist to smear tears from her cheek. She had done all she could do; this was the best ending she could devise.

Her thoughts skittered toward Joe Slowinski, the young man who'd died in the Himalayas after being bitten by a krait. Poisonous snakes abounded in the Amazon region, including kraits, pit vipers, bushmasters, and mambas. Back at the lodge, Lazaro had told them that the natives called the fer-de-lance a "ten step," because once a man had been bitten, he could not manage more than ten steps before dying.

Why not lay down here and wait for the paralyzing bite of a viper or carnivore ants? Delmar said the ants' bite had a numbing effect, so perhaps this wouldn't be such a terrible way to die. Horrible for the natives who discovered her body, perhaps, but her friends would shield Caitlyn from that sight. The natives would cover her in leaves and lift her on a burial pyre, safely destroying her body and the prions that contaminated her brain.

She would lie down and wait — but she'd have to find a better place than this. Moving forward on her hands and knees, she bumped into a huge gnarled root that demonstrated its power by pushing up the earth by the pool. Curling into one of its curves, she leaned against its strength, then used her hands to pull her trembling legs into a bent position. She wanted to look as if she had gone for a walk, sat down for a rest, and fallen asleep . . . only Kenway would realize the implausibility of that scenario. Yet out of concern for Caitlyn, he wouldn't dispute it.

Exhaling a deep breath, she closed her eyes and allowed her thoughts to drift back to the happiest day of her life. She had been a grad student, studying in the library, when the first labor pain had struck. Not wanting anyone to think she was some kind of hysterical female, she remained at the study carrel until her water broke, then her screech of surprise brought half a dozen men running — men who promptly turned and fled when they realized they were dealing with a heavily-pregnant woman in labor and not an anguished coed.

After six hours of panting, pushing, and struggling in the safe confines of the Atlanta Medical Center, she wept with joy when the doctor held up a squalling eight-pound, six-ounce blood-smeared baby. She had lifted her weak arms, reaching to take hold of that precious life —

"Dr. Pace?"

Her eyes flew open as light slammed against her eyelids.

Blinking, she struggled to lift her hand to shield her eyes. "Who's th-there?"

"It's Alejandro." The light lowered, splashing over brown mud at her feet and revealing Delmar's silhouette. Alex tilted her head, wondering where he had found a flashlight, then realized something was wrong with the image before her eyes. Delmar stood before her, straight and erect, but his bare feet did not touch the ground, and his outline shone with a faint luminescence.

She rubbed her hand over her eyes, then looked again. Her disease was manifesting another symptom; this had to be a hallucination. "Alejandro?" She peered into the shadows. "You're not really there, are you?"

"But of course I am." Soft laughter tickled her ear. "Your Dr. Kenway asked me to look for you."

A hallucination with a cynical sense of humor. Deciding to indulge her subconscious, she lowered her unreliable eyes. "Can I trust you, Delmar?"

"Implicitly."

"I don't want to go back. So you can leave

me now."

She had expected some token sort of protest, but undiluted laughter floated up from the man's throat. "Michael and the villagers were actually praying for you. Can you believe it?"

Snorting, Alex let her head fall back to the tree trunk. "At this moment, I could believe almost anything." She squinted at the hazy image. "You wouldn't believe what I'm seeing now. You're floating. And glowing. Sort of like the ghost of Christmas past."

A smile flitted across the man's features. "So you've decided to die here?"

Alex stared at the image her brain had conjured as an unformed thought teased her mind. Hallucinations, yes. Auditory changes? Perhaps. But why would her mind completely alter Delmar's personality?

It wouldn't . . . unless, of course, some still-functioning part of her brain had conjured up this vision to talk her out of suicide. If so, the will could overrule reason. If this figment was nothing but inchoate fragments of memories and thoughts, she could safely ignore it . . . if she could tear her eyes away.

"Delmar," she whispered drowsily, "when did you become so awesomely beautiful?"

Glowing like a luminescent firefly, the native guide crossed his legs in a sitting posture and hovered above the ground near her hiding place. "I didn't think you wanted to come back. Jaguar spirit said he has been watching you. He told me you had decided to die."

A chill settled onto her bones — a coldness that had nothing to do with the damp darkness.

She closed her eyes for a long moment, then opened them again. The vision of Delmar — if that's what it was — now stood in front of her, faintly glowing in the dark. Inhaling sharply, she tasted the odors of flesh and sweat and the dried herbs he always carried in his pouch.

She extended her hand, attempting to touch him, but Delmar laughed. "Do not trouble yourself, Dr. Pace. Things are not as complicated as they seem."

"They seem real . . . but I am s-s-sick." She looked away, then studied the outline of her fingers on her thigh. A few moments ago she had been unable to see anything, now she could see her hand in the light reflecting off the guide's image.

"You are sick, yes." Tremors of mirth fractured his voice. "You have tried to keep it a secret, but my spirits told me about you the moment we met at Yarupapa. Yet you are fortunate — tonight you will die here, far away from the others." He tilted his head and gave her a careful smile. "Tell me, is this really what you want?"

"Y-yes." Alex's voice broke in a horrible, rattling gurgle. "It's what I want."

"Good. Because the others will die, too, before they reach the great river again. I will have to kill them."

She lifted her head, but a sudden blow slammed it backward, knocking her skull against the root with such force she saw stars.

Delmar laughed again. "Do not be alarmed, Dr. Pace. If you do not fear death for yourself, why should you fear it for the others? You are all destined to die. As a *sertanista*, I cannot have you bringing other *nabas* to this part of the jungle."

Ignoring the pain beginning to blaze a trail around the base of her skull, Alex gritted her teeth and forced herself to focus. The thing-that-might-not-be-Delmar certainly smelled and looked like Delmar, and that last blow had convinced her he was more than an apparition manufactured by her subconscious. Furious questions raged within her, but the best her stuttering tongue could manage was one word: "Wh-why?"

"Your Mr. Carlton did not do his homework. Yes, I am an Indian tracker in Brazil, but I do not search for natives in order to exploit them — I search so they might remain hidden. The old ways have been entrusted to me, including the safeguarding of our spirit world. This Yai Pada the shaman mentioned is not good — he is unfriendly, he is cruel, he frightens the spirits who care for our people." Smiling, he crossed his arms, and Alex thought she could hear the microwhispers of his shirt fabric as it bent and folded. "Like you, I was eager to find these lost tribes. But now I will make certain no one ever finds them again."

Alex struggled to voice her objection, but Delmar continued without pause. "Yes, the Keyba village has chosen Yai Pada Son. But no one will come to teach them, and soon the children will forget all that happened this night. The old spirits will call to their children — Jaguar spirit and Howashi spirit and Deer spirit. The spirits will remind the people of the murders done this day, and then the people of Keyba Village will go and make war against the Angry People so the old ways will continue." He cocked his head. "Those who survive will starve. If the spirits drive the animals away, this village will die within one year. It will not take long to rid this land of Yai Pada and his Son. Not long at all."

"I — I don't believe you." Alex spat out the words. "You . . . are as crazy . . . as M-Michael."

He shot her a sideward look of cunning that did nothing to quell the panic rising in her breast. "You think I am crazy? Would a bite from Jaguar spirit convince you that I wield his power?"

After doing no more than lifting his index finger a scant inch, a hot, sharp pain scissored through Alex's middle. Locking her jaws, she made a noise that sounded like all the vowels spoken at once, then wrapped her arms around her stomach and writhed in agony.

No, her brain insisted. This was not possible. This had to be part of her illness, some variety of phantom pain triggered by deteriorating neurons, just as the vision of Delmar was the product of her deteriorating brain.

But never in all her research had she read about symptoms like these.

The pain eased, leaving her as limp as a dishrag. She struggled to push herself up to a sitting position.

"Convinced?" Delmar called, floating like a cross-legged maharishi only a few inches from her head. "Or would you like him to nip at your feet?"

As she opened her mouth to beg for mercy, a sharp stab sliced through her foot, followed by a crushing pain. Gasping, she stared at her legs, unable to believe that a caiman or some other creature did not have her foot locked between its jaws.

"I have been a shaman many years," Delmar said, apparently oblivious to her agony. "I have other spirits I could call. They are quick to do my bidding; they are desperate lest I throw them away. But I will not throw them away to follow this foolish Yai Pada. Why should I lose my powers? I have met shamans like the old man of Keyba Village —

the shabonos inside their bodies are empty, for the spirits departed when they began to speak with Yai Pada." He grinned down at her again. "Would you like to feel something from Howashi spirit? He is the spirit of the monkey, and he is mischievous."

The words had no sooner left Delmar's lips when something began to yank at Alex's hair. Six or seven tiny pairs of hands clawed at her scalp, tugging at her hair, pulling out hanks by the roots. Her ears filled with the deafening, high-pitched squeal of monkeys in an uproar while the musty scent of animals invaded her nostrils.

"Do you like my spirit friends?" Delmar's voice now buzzed in her ears. "Would you like to feel them all at once?"

She slapped at her head and screamed, beating off incorporeal assailants, then covered her stomach with her hands and tasted bitter tears. She could not bear this surreal agony. Death was a formidable foe, but this was an encounter with something far worse and far more significant.

The old shaman had said she encountered God this morning. Maybe she had, but she had not acknowledged him. Through her rejection, had she unwittingly chosen his adversary?

Compressed into an ever-shrinking space between the weight of reality and her own stubbornness, she brought her hands to her face. Why had she found it so hard to acknowledge the fact that healing occurred when believers sought it? Why had she been foolish enough to create the God of Desperate Women in Tropical Straits when *the* God had revealed himself in the sunset, in Michael Kenway, and in the healing of Shaman's Wife?

The answer rose like a bubble from the fountain of her soul — because she blamed God for the death of her mother, her husband's desertion, and, most of all, for the disease that had brought her to this dire place. Yet Kenway claimed that God could take even the tragedies of a life and bend them toward good.

If so, God was not a cosmic joker, determined to beat her down at every encounter. He was a patient and compassionate physician, tending to wounds of the heart as well as the body.

"Y-Yai Pada Son!" Broken and desperate, she screamed the name. "Oh, God, h-h-help me!"

The monkeys fell silent, followed by a quiet so thick the only sound was the sobbing whistle of her panicked breathing. The impish hands flew away, the agony at her foot ceased, the pain in her stomach stopped as if it had been on a switch. When she opened her eyes and looked into the darkness, she saw no sign of Delmar, not even a footprint on the muddy bank.

But there was light . . . glowing, sparkling, loving light.

A hallucination?

No . . . a presence. She sensed it in the silence, felt its warmth through the chill of her sweat. The blessed light surrounding her chased away the paralyzing fear and spoke peace to her heart.

Do not be afraid.

The voice held no trace of intimidation, but power pulsed through it, power enough to make Delmar's magic seem like parlor tricks. Alex relaxed, content to die in the light, then she heard a sound on the path and turned to look. The shaman of Keyba Village stood in the light, and when he extended his hand and she took it, she found him flesh and bone.

His smile glimmered in the gloom as he pulled her to her feet. Finding her footing, Alex leaned against the tree. The shaman gestured toward the path, obviously intending to lead her back to safety.

She shook her head. "I can't walk." She lowered her hands and slapped them against her trembling legs. "I'm sick."

The shaman's gaze traveled over her form, then, without a word, the man who barely came up to Alex's shoulder walked forward, turned, and pointed to his back.

Alex coughed rather than release the wry

laughter that bubbled to her lips. Did he actually intend to carry her? She hadn't ridden piggyback since childhood.

The shaman stood there, bent and waiting.

Alex clung to the tree a moment more, then shivered as another truth hit like an electric tingle in her stomach. If her encounter with Delmar had been real — and she now believed that on some plane it had been — then her teammates were in danger. He would kill them all on the journey away from this place.

Inhaling a deep breath, she released the tree and toppled forward, falling helplessly onto the shaman's bony back.

21 April 2003
5:00 a.m.
Alexandra was . . . gone.

The thought slashed into Michael's sleep like a knife. He sat up and stared into the darkness, trying to focus as the world shifted dizzily before his eyes. A thin gray gloom covered the interior of the shabono, draping every hammock and inhabitant in shadows, but the simple fact he could see meant sunrise was not far away.

A film of dirt itched at the back of his neck. As he lifted his hand to swipe his skin, he felt bits of grass and leaves, the detritus of last night's frantic search, clinging to his collar.

Alex had gone into the jungle after dark; he, Bancroft, and Delmar set out after her. They carried torches to search the field and the area around the kapok tree, but after an hour Delmar pointed to a broken branch near the fringe of the jungle. "If she went in here," his brow creased, "we will never find her. We should continue in the morning, when the sun is up and the jaguars have gone to bed."

Michael wanted to continue the search, but even Bancroft warned against it. "We'll get lost if we go in now," he told Michael. "Better to let her take her chances than risk all our lives out there."

Michael drew a breath, about to protest, but Bancroft gave him a look that said, *Now do you understand why I wanted to rescue Deborah?*

Michael snapped his mouth shut and returned to the shabono with a heavy heart. Caitlyn was waiting, exuding terror like a scent. Michael drew the frantic girl into his arms and whispered words that brought neither comfort nor assurance.

"Your mum's clever. She'll be all right," he had murmured, knowing all the while that Alex would not have gone into the forest unless she wanted to cut herself off from her life and loved ones. Like a swimmer who commits suicide by swimming toward the horizon, she had waded into the jungle knowing that each step brought her nearer to some sort of fatal encounter. Even if she did not meet a jaguar, a poisonous snake, or warriors from the Angry People, exhaustion, illness, and dehydration would claim her before too many days had passed.

She had often remarked that finding a cure for her disease would be like finding a needle in a haystack. Finding her in this vast, uncharted jungle would be no easier.

Leaning to peer at the hammock above him, Michael saw Caitlyn's shadowed form curled into a ball. She had fallen asleep beneath his arm hours after the shabono had quieted. After putting her to bed, Michael had paced by the fire for what felt like an eternity before seeking his own rest.

He glanced at the hammock next to Caitlyn's. It still hung empty, so Alex had not come in during the night.

Swinging his legs to the ground, he stood, then silently swatted a mosquito on the back of his hand. Moving quietly to avoid disturbing the sleeping natives, he walked through the shabono, his movements stiff and awkward. His body felt thick and unresponsive due to a lack of sleep. How must Alexandra feel after not sleeping for days?

After moving to the communal fire in the center of the shabono, he bent to pick up a log that had rolled away from the center. Holding it so the embers on the burnt end served as a glowing torch, he walked past the family compartments and squinted into the red-tinted darkness, trying to see if Alexandra had wandered into the wrong hammock during the night.

His heart leaped into his throat when a living thing no higher than his thigh pushed its way through the darkness at his feet, then he saw the outline of a toddling child and heard the sound of streaming water at the pile of sand the children used for a toilet.

"Only a boy," he whispered, "wandering about in the night like any ordinary lad."

Feeling foolish, Michael leaned against one of the supporting poles and forced himself to take steady breaths. The little boy toddled past Michael again, then rolled into his mother's hammock. Save for the buzz of muffled snoring, silence reigned in the shabono until another foot snapped a twig someone had dropped onto the ground. Michael jerked to attention, then recognized the shaman's son. Though he wore a troubled expression, the young man said nothing, but crossed to his hammock and lay down, crossing his arms over his chest.

Michael rubbed the wiry beard at his chin. The shaman's son had probably been drawn out of bed for the same reasons as the toddler. Even when calamity struck, the rhythms of ordinary life had to continue.

After his search, Michael had found three empty hammocks — Alexandra's, one in the shaman's enclosure, and another on the pole above Bancroft. As far as he could see, Alex had not come back.

He'd wait, then. A few more moments of darkness, then the sun would rise and chase away the dangers of the night. He would rouse the others, and together they'd follow the trails and search for any tracks Alex might have made. For Caitlyn's sake, he would expend every effort to find the AWOL neurologist.

He slid down the pole, grimacing as the stern voice of reason mocked his rationalization. Who was he kidding? The woman whose name had awakened him from sleep like a sharp spur meant a great deal to him, too.

"Father," he whispered, lifting his eyes to the socked-in darkness above, "for the sake of those of us who love her, bring Alexandra back."

21 April 2003
5:15 a.m.

Countless sleepless nights were bearing down on Alex with an irresistible warm and delicious weight. Her grip on reality, which had been weakening over the last several hours, finally loosened. Releasing herself to the inevitable, she felt herself falling, soaring through a yawning emptiness that held neither sights nor sounds.

So this is what coma feels like.

She had known her brain could not continue much longer. In the moment she draped herself over the shaman's wiry back, she had known she would not walk again. This was how the disease worked, sapping the patient's strength, draining the patient's energy, muting the patient's speech.

At least the shaman had brought her to a good place. No one would find her here; none of her companions would think to look in this most obvious of locations. They would

601

scour the fields and some of the native trails, then they would reluctantly depart Keyba Village. By the time any of them returned to continue their research, her bones would have been bleached by the sun and scoured by the wind.

The sounds of insects and birds faded along with the raspy sounds of the shaman's breathing as the muffling walls of coma closed around her senses.

Alex wasn't surprised to find that though she could no longer hear, see, or feel, her brain kept firing up thoughts, some seemingly random, others immediately connected to the situation she had just abandoned.

Caitlyn would be terribly hurt — *remember how adorable she looked as a pumpkin in her nursery school class?* — but Michael would comfort her. Michael himself would be dreadfully annoyed with her sudden departure, but he might have done the same thing if the situation were reversed. Both of them knew how unpleasant the end stage of a prion disease would be.

Mother, did you feel this? Did you know I sat by your side until the end?

Odd, that in this coma, cut off from the world, she could feel blissfully happy and fully alive. She had never known such contentment, but it had not begun with the coma. It had begun the moment she cried out to Yai Pada Son and surrendered to his light, giving up her struggles and her arguments. In that moment, while suffering the agonies of the path she had chosen when she refused to acknowledge the God who held sway even in this remote place, she had come face to face with her own inadequacies.

Armed with her knowledge, her intellect, and her practicality, she had substituted science for the God who created it. What a lousy bargain she had made . . .

Alex's thoughts slowed as she sensed a familiar presence. *He* was here, even in her coma, and he would remain with her until the end. But there was no end, was there? Even the people of Keyba Village knew about the bright land where people sang and celebrated. She had always considered such tales mental placebos invented to take the edge off human suffering, but that was before she met Yai Pada in the fullness of his power and glory.

She was drifting, imagining her heavenly reunion with Caitlyn and Michael, when her thoughts skittered toward an unfamiliar sensation. Was that warmth she felt? She should not be feeling in a coma; the sense of touch was one of the first to fade . . . but undeniably, heat caressed her face. Another feeling accompanied it, the texture of dried grass beneath her hands and leaves that crackled when she moved her fingers —

She *moved* her fingers! She *heard* the crackle!

With an effort, Alex commanded her eyes to open. When they obeyed, a noisy, fragrant, tactile world edged back into her consciousness. She breathed in the scents of sweet grass, felt the stubble of prickly twigs beneath her bones, heard the cacophony of parrots vying to see who could best herald the Creator of the rising sun. The warmth of the sun flushed her skin, urging her to rise like a sleeping flower and greet it with strong arms, sturdy legs, and lips that parted in a shout of joy.

Pulling herself upright, Alex stood in the woven nest and laughed aloud as the morning's first rays bathed her restored body in a golden glow.

Some primitive flee-or-fight instinct tightened Michael's nerves when he heard the sound of footsteps swishing through the grass in the alana. He stood, hoping he would be able to escort Alexandra to her daughter before Caitlyn awoke, but Delmar appeared in the entry, his trousers wet to the knees with morning dew.

He nodded when he caught Michael's eye, then held up a large leaf and jerked his head toward the fire. When Michael joined him there, Delmar squatted and spread the leaf on the sand. "I found this in the grass outside. No other trace of her, I'm afraid."

Kneeling, Michael winced as the age-old instinct seized him by the guts and yanked for his attention. "What is it?"

"I think she tried to leave us a note." Delmar lowered his voice. "Not a very encouraging message, I daresay."

Michael stared at the huge leaf. In an uneven, primitive script, his friend had written:

I, Alexandra Pace, want my daughter, Caitlyn Grace, to be the ward of Michael Kenway if I predecease either of them.

Groaning, he sank onto the ground and dropped his head onto his hand. His heart kept telling him that Alexandra wouldn't do this, but the message before him seemed to indicate otherwise.

Beside him, Delmar cleared his throat. "We need to make preparations for leaving, Doc. You said it yourself — our presence here is taxing these people."

Lifting his head, Michael looked at the guide through bleary eyes. *This is how Bancroft felt when we left Deborah Simons with the other tribe.*

"Now that the sun is up, we need to search again." His voice scraped like sandpaper against his own ears.

"I've already looked. I was out there before sunrise with a torch, and I found this leaf after the sun came up."

"I didn't hear you go. Where did you search?"

"Everywhere. I walked all through the field and followed fifty yards of the nearest trails. If Dr. Pace spent the night walking through the jungle . . . well, I am afraid she is beyond our reach." A regretful smile flitted across the guide's face. "Sorry, Doctor, I know you liked her a lot. But she was sick, and I think this may have been her escape."

Michael looked away, lest Delmar read agreement in his eyes. Alexandra had been upset last night, but if she had decided to flee, surely her common sense and logic would compel her to return this morning. The old saying about things looking better in the bright light of day held a lot of truth. If Alex would only come back, she would certainly see that suicide was not the answer.

Standing, Delmar moved to the communal water jug. "Some of the tribes have a practice — when food is scarce, they take their old ones into the jungle, settle them into their hammocks, and walk away. You nabas think that is harsh, but it is really better for everyone. Apparently Dr. Pace thought so."

Michael stared at the guide. "I can't believe Alex would do that to Caitlyn. When the others wake, I'd like to form search parties and spread out over the area. It's entirely possible she survived the night and got lost while trying to return —"

Delmar shook his head. "She had no hammock. The ants would have gotten her if she fell asleep."

"*She wouldn't fall asleep,* don't you understand? She *can't* sleep! That's what's killing her!"

"She is gone, I tell you." Delmar splashed water into a gourd, then lifted it. "Still, we will look. But only for a short while. Then we are leaving, because we need to make good progress before the sun sets."

A suffocating sensation tightened Michael's throat as the native tracker moved away. He could plead Alex's case with Bancroft, but with Deborah's death weighing on the guard's heart, he would probably not do more than a perfunctory search. Like Delmar, he would look at this leaf and assume Alex meant to die, though for Caitlyn's sake he would never voice that thought. Baklanov, Olsson, and Emma would be sympathetic, but they were ready to leave. They'd probably join in the search for an hour, then pack up their samples and happily say farewell to Keyba Village.

Caitlyn, however — he swallowed hard and leaned forward, wrapping his arms around himself. How could he, a man who had never had a daughter, look into that little girl's eyes and soothe an agony like this? Caitlyn had known about her mother's illness, but she had not expected to be abandoned in the jungle. She'd be traumatized, and when the feeling of numbness passed, she'd be furious at Alex for leaving and at Michael for not moving heaven and earth to find her mum.

Several of the women and children had

608

risen by the time Michael stood and made his way toward the place where Caitlyn slept. She looked so vulnerable in the hammock, so much like a child, that his resolve rushed away like water going a drain.

He was praying for strength and wisdom when a woman's cry drifted into the shabono through the open roof. "Hey! Anybody awake down there?"

The voice was clear, female . . . and American.

Caitlyn sat straight up in her hammock, her eyes wide as saucers. "That's Mom!"

"Alexandra?" Michael cupped his hands to his mouth and yelled, but the sound didn't seem to travel beyond the circle of sleepy villagers. After reaching for Caitlyn's hand, Michael hurried through the alana and into the open field.

"Alex?" Yelling at the top of his lungs, he shielded his eyes from the blinding sun and peered toward the forest.

"Mom?" Caitlyn joined him. "Where are you?"

"Look up!"

Slowly, Michael turned to see Alex descending from the kapok, her bare feet wrapped in prusik knots, her arms strong and steady on one of the vines Olsson had left behind. Without pausing to think, Michael ran toward the gnarled tree.

He had just hurdled one of the largest roots

when Alexandra jumped from the vine, ripped the prusik loops from her feet, and ran to meet them. She threw her arms around her daughter, squeezed her tightly, then leaned back and gripped the girl's narrow shoulders. "I've never been so glad to see anybody in my life!"

"Mom?" Caitlyn's voice came out as a feeble squeak.

"What, honey?"

"Don't ever go climbing trees in the dark again."

A glow rose in Alexandra's face, as though she contained a candle that had just been lit.

"I'm so sorry, sweetie, if I scared you. But I'm okay. I'm really okay."

Stunned by the health and happiness glowing on Alexandra's face, Michael stared at her without speaking.

With one hand still holding her daughter's, she turned to face him. "Thank God you're here. I was afraid I'd miss you."

"Miss us?" He could manage nothing more; his mind had gone idiotic with surprise.

"Yes." She bit her lip as she glanced at her daughter. "I fell asleep. In the nest, I'm fairly sure I fell into a coma. Yet the sun woke me up, and though I knew what would happen and how it would happen, I didn't know what day it was. For a moment, I was afraid Delmar had already led you out."

"We're still here."

Her thin cheek curved in a smile. "Thank God you're still here."

Caught up in a wave of some emotion Michael hadn't expected, Alexandra pressed her hand to the back of his neck. Her touch sent shooting stars down his spine, and when she kissed him, his hands slipped up her arms, bringing her closer.

"Go, Mom!" Caitlyn cheered from the sidelines.

Almost embarrassed at the surge of happiness jetting through him, Michael pulled away and stared at the miracle in his arms.

"Thank you," she whispered, her gaze as soft as a caress. "You were right. About everything."

"Just a moment, please." Unwilling to release her, Michael kept a firm grip on her arm as he tipped his head back to study the tree canopy. "Last night you could barely walk. How in the world —"

"I'll tell you in a minute." She bent to kiss the top of her daughter's head, then squeezed Caitlyn's shoulder. "Run into the shabono, honey, and tell Mr. Bancroft I need to speak to him. It's important."

"Okay." As the grinning girl sprinted away, Michael turned to face Alex. "Answers, please. I feel like a complete wally."

She blinked. "I beg your pardon?"

"An idiot. Please, Alexandra, explain yourself."

Her happy expression faded to calm sobriety. "Last night, the shaman found me in the jungle. I don't know how he managed it, but that wiry old man tied me onto his back and carried me up the tree — you must have given him the idea. Somehow he knew I was sick . . . and he knew I was ready for healing."

Unnerved by the sudden change in the woman, Michael stared at her for a moment, then broke eye contact, his gaze drifting off to safer territory. "How'd he know how to find you?"

A shy smile crept into her voice. "I met Yai Pada last night. I went into the jungle to die, and I would have died there if not for Yai Pada. I was lying in the jungle, unable to move and in all kinds of pain from the evil spirits —"

"What evil spirits?"

"From Alejandro Delmar." Her dark, earnest eyes sought his. "He intends to kill all of us in the jungle, Michael. We've got to stop him."

He took a half step back. "Surely you're mistaken."

"I'm not."

"How do you know this?"

"He told me himself."

"When?"

"Last night."

"Alex," Michael drew a deep breath, "last

night Delmar was with me and Bancroft, searching for you. We never ventured more than a few feet into the trees."

"He was with me, in spirit form. I know it sounds unscientific, but I saw him, smelled him, *felt* him." Her voice scraped as if she were laboring to speak, but her words began to come faster. "He's a shaman, but he's nothing like the shaman of this village. He has power — I saw it, I experienced it. And he wants to kill all of us so no one will ever come to this village again. He's afraid of missionaries; he's afraid someone will teach the people more about Yai Pada."

For an instant he feared she had suffered some sort of mental breakdown in the night, but the woman he held in his grip was nothing like the weakened patient he had argued with only hours before. Like Shaman's Wife, she was still thin, but health had been restored to that emaciated frame. And if God could heal her body through the miracle of faith, surely he could heal her mind and spirit.

"Okay," he whispered, drawing her into the circle of his arms. "Relax. We're not going to say anything now; Delmar would only deny it. But we'll watch him on the trail. We'll warn Bancroft. We'll be fine, Alex. We'll be ready."

She tipped her head back to study his face. What she saw in his eyes must have convinced her he spoke the truth, because a moment later she lowered her head in a sober nod.

"There's one other thing."

"Yes?"

"The old shaman. I'm almost positive the exertion of the climb brought on a heart attack. When I woke up this morning, he was sitting beside me in the nest . . . but he had no pulse."

She lowered her eyes. "I'm so sorry, Michael. If I had known what would happen, I would never have let him make the climb."

Pain squeezed Michael's heart as he thought of the wise old man who had done so much for his people . . . and his uninvited guests. "He did what he wanted to do, Alexandra . . . for you."

Raking his hand through his hair, Michael squinted at the shabono and wondered how he would explain a dead shaman to the people of Keyba Village.

Alex's cheeks burned under the pressure of dozens of pairs of eyes. After greeting her at the base of the kapok, Michael had escorted her into the shabono, where he approached the shaman's enclosure and spoke to the shaman's son. Delmar had approached, his eyes narrowed, and though the sight of him sent ghost spiders crawling along the back of Alex's neck, she said nothing as he translated Michael's horrible news.

The old shaman was dead. His body rested in the keyba.

The shaman's son issued orders; a few moments later several men approached the tree with climbing ropes. Alex, Emma, and Caitlyn joined the quiet villagers who waited while the men scaled the tree, then lowered the old man's lifeless body by means of a twisted vine.

The shaman's body now lay next to the fire,

where weeping women were bathing the corpse and preparing it for burial. The men of the tribe sat in a circle around the women while the shaman's son sat in the place his father had once occupied.

Unfortunately, Delmar sat at his right hand. When the tracker looked directly at Alex for the first time that morning, hatred flickered in his eyes like heat lightning.

The shaman's son sat without speaking, his face stony and blank. Michael had delivered the hard news about the man's death, now Alex had to provide an explanation.

She stepped forward, distancing herself from her companions, for she alone bore the responsibility for what had happened.

Though she had been perspiring all day in the tropical heat, her hands suddenly felt damper, slick with the cool, sour sweat of fear.

She swallowed hard, lifted her chin, and met the young man's gaze. "Your father," she said, speaking slowly so Delmar could translate without her having to look at him, "was a very great man. When I was sick, he took pity on me and carried me into the keyba. Though he was strong, the climb was hard, and he had lived many seasons. When I opened my eyes in the healing light this morning, the shaman . . . was dead."

The younger man closed his eyes, squeezing them so tight his face seemed to collapse on itself. Alex looked away, unable to bear the sight of his forced stoicism. She knew very little about these people, and had no idea how — or if — they would hold her responsible for what had happened.

No longer translating, Delmar continued to whisper into the young man's ear. The shaman's son recoiled, then he glanced at Delmar with suspicion in his eyes.

Increasingly uneasy, Alex glanced at Emma. "Can you guess what he's saying?"

"He didn't translate accurately." Caitlyn spoke up, glaring at Delmar. "He said you bewitched the shaman and killed him. He says you have an evil spirit, and everyone knows this. Last night you did not rejoice with the others when they called on Yai Pada Son. He says you went up the keyba to steal the shaman's life, for you were the one about to die."

"He lies!" Alex looked around the circle of natives, searching for an ally, but nearly every face mirrored the expression of distrust worn by the shaman's son.

Alex reached for Caitlyn's hand. "Speak for me, Cait. Tell them what I said — they have to know what really happened."

"A child has no right to speak." Delmar barked the objection, and something like smugness entered his face as he stared at Alex. "You must take her and leave this place at once. We must all go and leave these people in peace."

Michael stepped to Alex's side. "We're not going yet. Let Alexandra have her say."

Delmar tossed a smirk in Caitlyn's direction. "Children do not speak in tribal council. And this is only a girl —"

"She is a very gifted young lady." Michael's hands fell on Caitlyn's shoulders. "What do you think she's been doing during our time here? She's been learning the language. So if she wants to speak for her mother, I think you should let her."

Olsson gestured toward Emma. "You speak some Yagua. Can you interpret?"

Slowly, the older woman shook her head. "I don't pick up things as easily as I used to. But from what I can tell, Caitlyn's telling the absolute truth."

"Then it's settled," Bancroft growled, crossing his beefy arms as he glared down at Delmar. "Let the kid talk."

Speaking slowly in her lilting voice, Caitlyn uttered a string of words in the tongue of Keyba Village. The natives looked at one another as she continued, and when their eyes filled with amazement, Alex couldn't tell if they had been surprised by Caitlyn's gift with language or with the content of her speech.

When she had finished, the shaman's son turned to murmur to the native sitting next to him, then he lifted his voice and addressed the gathering.

All noise ceased as a balloon of quiet but intense attention centered on Alex. She looked to Caitlyn for the translation. "He says," she whispered, "that everyone can see that you now honor Yai Pada. You were sick and now you are well. The Great Spirit of the keyba does not allow one person to steal health from another; that is not his way. He is not like Omawa, who lies and kills."

Feeling the sting of tears in her eyes, Alex lifted her eyes to address the shaman's son. "Last night my body was sick, my spirit was dark. I went in the jungle to die. When I could no longer bear the pain, I cried out to Yai Pada Son —" she avoided Delmar's gaze — "and he came to me in light and warmth."

She paused, looking around the circle of expectant faces as Caitlyn translated. "After that, your shaman came to me and offered his help. Though my spirit had light, my body was still weak. So your shaman tied me to his back and walked up the tree with me."

She hesitated as the next words filled her mind. Though they felt undeniably *right,* they contained a mystery she had not yet begun to understand.

Perhaps she was not meant to understand everything . . . yet. But God had spared her, and she would learn. She had a lifetime to learn.

"Just like Yai Pada," she continued, "who

became a man and died to remove our shame, your shaman carried me to the keyba and gave his life to heal my sickness. Now I am well, and his spirit is with Yai Pada." She looked at the fire, gazing beyond it into the future. "One day I will see your shaman in Yai Pada's bright land, and I will honor him for his sacrifice."

The shaman's son had not moved during her answer, but at the conclusion of Caitlyn's translation his chin quivered and his eyes went glassy with tears. Inclining his head in a curt nod, he spoke again. At the conclusion of his speech the warriors turned to pluck bows, arrows, and spears from the walls of the shabono.

Alex drew a deep breath to still her storming heart. "Cait, what are they doing?"

A sly smile curved Caitlyn's mouth as Alejandro Delmar stood and stalked out of the shabono. "They are preparing to enforce the shaman's order. He told Delmar to leave at once because he is an enemy of Keyba Village."

The young shaman's hazel eyes found and locked on Alex's. "You speak truth," he said through Caitlyn's interpretation, "because last night the spirit of Yai Pada came to me in a dream. I saw the hawk taking my father's spirit to the land of Yai Pada. When I awakened, I stepped outside to see the shining men in white guarding the base of the keyba."

"Shining men?" Alex glanced at Michael. "Are they from some other tribe?"

Smiling, Michael reached out and took her hand. "I'll explain later."

Cursing Keyba Village with every breath, Delmar pressed into the jungle, occasionally glancing upward to gauge the rays of the sun. He would walk northward, skirting the lands of the Angry People, and he would reach the black water lake before the ignorant nabas. He would send his spirits to act as scouts, and he would lie in wait for them. When they finally came, in two days or three or four, he would kill them with bows he would fashion out of vines and green wood.

He would make paralyzing darts from the inayuga palm and a knife from a sharp fish fin. When the nabas lay helpless at his feet, he would find Alexandra Pace and cut out her heart, sending her to the faraway land of the one she called Yai Pada.

Moving with a stealthy step, he called on Jaguar spirit to speed his journey. He would need time to set his traps for the nabas, time to think about how he would kill them in order to send the most graphic message to other outsiders who might invade this territory.

He increased his pace, moving through the jungle like a shadow, dodging limbs and leaping over tangled roots. Jaguar spirit gave him speed, and the spirit of the hawk helped his feet take flight.

His mouth twisted in irritated humor. The nabas probably thought they had defeated him, but this unexpected turn of events would actually work in his favor. Killing them on the journey back would have been difficult — he might have managed to make one or two of the killings look like accidents, but they were clever people. They wouldn't have been fooled for long.

Now, however, he would have the advantage of surprise . . . and time to plan.

Content in the thought of his coming victory, he summoned Deer spirit, one of the slyest and most charming spirits he had ever entertained. She came to him on a ray of light, dancing before his eyes as he loped through the jungle.

"My beloved friend," she crooned, a smile lighting her narrow face. "You think you have done well?"

"I have." He ran faster to demonstrate how relaxed and invincible he felt. "I will kill the outsiders at the lake and drag their bodies to a well-traveled spot. Then everyone will know it is not safe to venture onto this island."

Deer spirit's smile lit her brown eyes, glowing beneath long silken fringes. "You think this will stop nabas from visiting the Angry People?"

"I do."

"You think these killings will stop the people of Keyba Village from seeking Yai Wana Naba Laywa?"

"It will. They will forget what the nabas have told them about the one they call Yai Pada."

Her mouth curved in a smile, and something moved in her velvet eyes. "You are a foolish, stupid man."

Before Delmar could react, something smacked him from behind, cracking against his skull and filling his ears with the dull thump of a hand against a drum. He pitched forward and landed on his wrist.

For a moment all color ran out of the jungle and the screech of the parrots faded, then indignation fired his blood. What had happened? Why would Deer spirit turn on him?

He pushed himself up, then winced as a screaming sort of pain shot from the inside of his right wrist all the way up his arm. Looking down, he saw that his hand bent at an unnatural angle — he had broken it in the fall.

Pulling his wounded arm to his chest, he

looked up to address the spirits around him. "What have I done?"

"You have led the outsiders to our place," Deer spirit hissed.

Jaguar spirit growled deep in his throat. "You have let the woman find healing."

"You have allowed them to speak of Yai Wana Naba Laywa."

"You have opened the doors to the land. Others will come."

A murky red mist churned across the floor of the jungle, obliterating the moss and carpet of wet leaves. Somewhere in the distance, a thunderclap exploded, its baritone rumble fading slowly in the distance.

Delmar sat still as rain began to tap against the leaves, whispering through the jungle. "They will not come, I promise," he called. "Help me trap them, and we can make sure they will not come again. They will fear you, and they will stay away."

"The people who follow Yai Wana Naba Laywa fear nothing." Deer spirit spoke in a voice filled with quiet menace. "You were a fool to bring them here."

"I wasn't!"

"We are finished with you."

"No!" Delmar shrieked, but the slashing rain muffled his voice. Blinking against the water in his eyes, he struggled to stand.

"Watch me! Give me speed, and I will run to set a trap. Give me strength and I will kill all of them, I will —"

Something smacked him in the face, sending a shower of lights sparking through his head like a swarm of fireflies. Tasting blood in his mouth, he lifted his head and stumbled backward into a tree.

"You love me!" Lifting his good hand, he curled it into a fist and shook it at the spirits whirling around him. "For years you have begged me to keep you close, and I have been good to you! How can you do this now?"

The only answer was another blow, one that slammed into the side of his head and sent a spray of darkness across the backs of his eyes. He leaned sideways, pressing his uninjured hand to his face as something clubbed the back of his neck.

He would have fallen if he had not decided to run. Sheer momentum carried him forward, but there was no escaping the voices buzzing in his ear, the horrific visions flitting before his blurry eyes.

"You are finished!"

"You are weak!"

"You are old and foolish!"

"You are a stupid excuse for a shaman!"

Still he ran, sweat and blood soaking the hair of his chest and staining his T-shirt. Something moved the air at his right. He ducked in time to avoid another blow, this one aimed at his eyes. "I have not failed you!"

"Liar!"

"Stupid!"

Gasping in panic and disbelief, he raced ahead, squirming through the wet foliage, until a low hiss filled his ear and turned his blood to ice.

The Serpent spirit.

Heated silver fangs sliced through the air and entered his eyes, sending blinding white pain through his head. As a scream clawed at the back of his throat, Delmar pressed his hands to his face, stumbling backward as a series of new thoughts entered his wounded brain:

Liars. Murderers. Thieves.

His spirits had been false all along.

He would have screamed this opinion, but Deer spirit, the charming one who had entered his heart as a small boy and had been his best friend ever since, chose that moment to idly tap his chest, knocking him off balance and sending him backward into a nest of carnivore ants.

In the moment before his writhing body stilled into paralysis, Delmar shrieked a curse upon the spirits of the jungle.

17 October 2003
10:00 a.m.

Bracing himself for the heat, Michael stepped through the double doors of the hospital and turned north to walk up Calle Ricardo Palma. Walking through the heavy, humid air often felt like pressing one's way through wet wool, but the locals were right — in time, you did get used to it.

Slipping his hands into his pockets, he whistled a tune as he strode over the cracked sidewalks of Iquitos, nodding to several passersby who shot curious glances in his direction. The constant putt-putt and honking of the motor *karros* filled his ears, and within two minutes a shoeshine boy was dogging his steps. *"Limpio los zapatos, señor?"*

"Ahora no, *gracias."* He gave the kid a sole and moved on.

After reaching the Hotel Victoria Regia, he stepped into the lobby and shivered in the air conditioning. The Victoria Regia, the crown jewel of Iquitos, even offered air conditioning in its guest rooms.

He nodded to the pretty brunette behind the desk. *"Señora Pace, por favor."*

Smiling, the young woman turned to ring Alexandra's room. A few moments later Caitlyn raced into the lobby, then jumped up to throw her arms around his neck.

"Hello, Cait! I think you're two inches taller!"

The girl immediately dropped her arms and smoothed her blouse, settling down to a more ladylike demeanor. "Not quite. But I have been doing more than growing."

"Like what?"

"I've been studying Portuguese."

Michael glanced toward the elevator, saw no sign of Alexandra, then gave the girl a smile. "Lovely. We'll have to take you to Brazil sometime."

"Can we go there on the honeymoon? Please?"

He lifted a brow. "Um, no. The honeymoon is in London, where my mother is dying to spoil you with biscuits and scones. Your mother and I will be in Scotland, which is right around —"

His thought dissolved into nothingness as the elevator doors slid open and Alex stepped into the lobby. Though only two weeks had passed since he'd last seen her, the sudden sight of her still stole his breath away. Her sleeveless white cotton dress flattered her endlessly, and he could see that health had restored the curve to her cheek and . . . well, all the proper places.

Smiling, she came forward and slid into his arms, then kissed him. When she pulled away, Michael cleared his throat, pretending that her touch didn't affect every atom of his being. "Sorry," he began, unable to stop one hand from reaching out to stroke her arm, "that I wasn't able to meet you at the airport."

"Don't worry about it." Even her voice was stronger now, fuller and more alluring. "I think I'm beginning to feel quite at home in Iquitos."

Stepping back to look at her, he found himself at a loss for words.

"What's the matter, Doc?" She gave him a perfect smile. "Cat got your tongue?"

"Something like that." Smiling, he nodded toward the street. "Shall we go? Everyone at the hospital is desperate to meet you, and Fortuna will have my head if we don't go there first —"

Alex caught his arm, her fascinating smile crinkling the corners of her eyes. "Before we go, I wanted you to see this." Reaching into the leather bag at her shoulder, she pulled out a stapled document and presented it to him.

He scanned the title: *An Analysis of Variant Kuru (VK-TSE), a transmissible spongiform en-*

630

cephalopathy discovered in the native population of northeastern Amazonia, by Dr. Michael Kenway and Dr. Alexandra Pace.

He shook his head. "You didn't have to put my name first."

"Yes, I did. If not for you, I wouldn't be here."

Taking the manuscript, he flipped through the pages, then paused at the abstract on page one:

After significant study and months of research, the authors have discovered that indigenous populations in the vicinity were infected with prions through oral ingestion and/or placental migration at birth. The original source of the infection is unknown, but animals that are no longer common in the area are possible suspects.

The alarming rate of infection — nearly 100 percent of the local population — resulted in the near decimation of a tribe known as the Angry People. A neighboring tribe, however, Keyba Village, found a cure in *Ceiba pentandra,* commonly known as the kapok tree. The method of implementation remains an area of some dispute, for treatment does not prove effective with every patient.

This research project opens new windows into prevailing philosophies regarding whole-patient treatment. For patients who agree with the kapok cure in mind, body, and spirit, the success rate is 100 percent. Successful treatment not only results in a halt of the disease's symptoms, but a complete restoration of health.

Conclusion: One particular *Ceiba pentandra* heals infected natives who climb it in faith. Science alone does not hold the answer to the cure's effectiveness, and more work in the field is needed, particularly regarding the importance of undeniable links between the mind, spirit, and body. It is the authors' opinion that this work will teach physicians and researchers to think of patients not as bodies to be treated, but as complete persons with mental, emotional, and spiritual needs.

Lowering the pages, Michael met Alexandra's gaze. "So . . . is there a Nobel prize in this for us?"

She chuckled softly as she linked her arm through his. "Not likely. Though it would make a nice wedding present."

A knot rose in his throat as he lost himself in her gaze. In the weeks following their initial canopy experience, the frostiness and fear that had so often occupied her eyes completely melted away. They had even climbed into the canopy again, with Caitlyn, and the following morning the three of them greeted the sunrise together.

And as he watched Cait thrill to the Creator's moving, molten sky, he realized that he could no longer imagine living without the American woman and her daughter.

Now he squeezed Alex's shoulder. "Are you sure of what we're about to do?"

"I've never been more sure of anything in my life." Without looking away, she called, "Cait? You ready to go get married?"

"Right-o," Caitlyn called, nicely managing a British accent. "I think that'd be quite lovely."

"Right, then." They stood together, barely touching, breathing each other's breath, until Caitlyn tugged on Michael's elbow.

"Are we going to get married today or not?" she asked, exaggerating her exasperation. "I'm growing older by the minute, you know."

Michael kissed the tip of Alexandra's nose, then extended his hand to the girl who would soon be his daughter. "Let's go, you cheeky thing. First we stop at the hospital, then it's on to the church."

Caitlyn did not complain, but grasped his hand and grinned as he led the two loves of his life out of the hotel lobby.

AUTHOR'S NOTE

Like most of my novels, *The Canopy* is a blend of fact and fiction.

The Angry People and Keyba Village are fictional, but their language, religious beliefs, and spiritual practices are based on the beliefs and practices of the Yanomamo tribe in Brazil as described in Mark Ritchie's *Spirit of the Rainforest.* As I read Ritchie's book, the nonfiction account of the Yanomamo shaman's experience, I was stunned to learn about the tribe's encounters with nabas (outsiders), angelic visitors in white, and the spirit they now call Yai Pada.

The information about prion diseases is almost accurate, the exceptions being: (1) the timeline of Alex's progression of symptoms and (2) the fact that fatal familial insomnia is presently considered to be genetically inherited. No evidence yet suggest that it is passed from mother to child as Alexandra theorizes. Prion infections, however, have been transmitted from mother to offspring in animals, so I think Alexandra's hypothesis is reasonably valid.

I need to make one other correction — though my research led me to believe bleach reliably killed the infective agent behind scrapie, in May 2003, only weeks away from this novel's printing, I discovered a more recent source which states that since prions are not living organisms like bacteria or viruses, antibiotics and other drugs have no effect upon them. "You could put pure bleach or pure formaldehyde in a test tube with them and it wouldn't destroy them," says Arthur Caplain, chairman of the department of medical ethics at the University of Pennsylvania (*The New York Times Magazine,* May 11, 2003, p. 39).

At the time of this writing, there is no cure for prion diseases, though in January 2003 *The New York Times* reported that researchers have found a way to treat two deadly heart ailments caused by misfolded proteins. Scientists are hoping that this treatment, consisting of a "small molecule" drug that halts the misfolding process, will eventually be used to treat other prion diseases.

We have not heard much about transmissible spongiform encephalopathies in the United States, but in September 2002, I stumbled across an article in *People* magazine about three hunters who died from Creutzfeldt-Jakob disease, most likely contracted from eating venison. CJD, as it is commonly called, is a prion disease. A December 16, 2002, *Newsweek* contained an article about herds of deer infected with chronic wasting disease (another prion disease) in the American midwest. While I do not believe there is a reason to panic, I do believe these diseases are among us and should be closely monitored.

I, for one, am not going vegan . . . yet.

DISCUSSION QUESTIONS FOR READING GROUPS

1. This book can be read as an adventure story and an allegory, a work in which the characters and events are to be understood as representing other things and symbolically expressing a deeper, often spiritual meaning. What elements in this book represent other things? What do you think the author is trying to say by this use of allegory?

2. With which character in the story did you most identify? Why?

3. What "disease" are all humans born with? Hint: It's not a disease of the body (though our bodies certainly feel its effects), but rather a disease of the soul. What is the "treatment" for a sick soul?

4. Why do you think the natives' brains were not transformed when they were healed in the tree? If they had diseased brains, how

were they able to function in the physical world?

5. In order to come to complete faith, Alex goes through three stages of belief. Can you identify them?

6. The first stage involves mental agreement. At what point does she see proof of Michael's story and mentally agree that he is onto something?

7. The second stage involves emotional agreement. At what point does Alexandra bend her emotions to the point where she is willing to believe?

8. The final stage of faith involves a surrender, an act of placing trust in someone else. At what point does Alex experience this kind of surrendering belief?

9. At one point in the story, Michael wishes he were better equipped to handle the religious skepticism of his fellow travelers. What could he do to equip himself?

10. Why do so many physicians concentrate on the healing of the body while they ignore the soul?

11. Consider the strangler fig — the tree that

grows down from another tree, gradually covering it until it dies. If this tree were a metaphor, how are we like the strangler fig? How are we like the host tree?

12. To the Romans, Paul wrote: "But God shows his anger from heaven against all sinful, wicked people who push the truth away from themselves. For the truth about God is known to them instinctively. God has put this knowledge in their hearts. From the time the world was created, people have seen the earth and sky and all that God made. They can clearly see his invisible qualities — his eternal power and divine nature. So they have no excuse whatsoever for not knowing God" (1:18–20). How does this passage relate to the plot of the book?

REFERENCE LIST

I owe thanks to the staff of Yacumama Lodge in Peru for providing comfortable lodging, a fabulous education, and a truly unforgettable Amazon experience.

I also owe many thanks for medical advice to Dr. Harry Kraus Jr., novelist, friend, and surgeon, as well as Dr. Mel Hodde and his wife, Cheryl, who make up the writing team known as "Hannah Alexander." Any medical mistakes are my responsibility, not theirs.

Bushels of thanks to Susan Richardson for test-driving the manuscript more times than I can remember.

Thanks to Gaynel Wilt for traveling with me to the Amazon jungle and for sharing her memorable photos. Thanks to my husband, Gary, who let me go to the jungle while he stayed behind to manage our home. Thank you, Bill Myers, for saying, "You really ought to go."

Among my many sources for research (including a weeklong trip to the jungle and too many magazine articles and Web pages to list), I found the following books useful:

John Boorman, *The Emerald Forest Diary* (New York: Farrar, Straus Giroux), 1985.

Stanley Coren, *Sleep Thieves: An Eye-Opening Exploration into the Science and Mysteries of Sleep* (New York: Free Press), 1996.

Roger Harris and Peter Hutchison, *The Amazon* (Old Saybrook, Conn.: Globe Pequot Press), 1998.

Margaret D. Lowman, *Life in the Treetops: Adventures of a Woman in Field Biology* (New Haven, Conn.: Yale University Press), 1999.

Geoffrey O'Connor, *Amazon Journal: Dispatches from a Vanishing Frontier* (New York: Dutton), 1997.

Richard Rhodes, *Deadly Feasts: The Prion Controversy and the Public's Health* (New York: Simon and Schuster), 1997.

Mark Andrew Ritchie, *Spirit of the Rainforest: A Yanomamo Shaman's Story* (Chicago: Island Lake Press), 1996.

Richard Evans Schultes and Robert F. Raffauf, *The Healing Forest: Medicinal and Toxic Plants of the Northwest Amazonia* (Portland, Oreg.: Dioscorides Press), 1990.

Linnea Smith, M.D., *La Doctora: The Journal of an American Doctor Practicing Medicine on the Amazon River* (Duluth, Minn.: Pfiefer-Hamilton Publishers), 1999.

Patrick Tierney, *Darkness in El Dorado: How Scientists and Journalists Devastated the Amazon* (New York: W.W. Norton & Company), 2000.

The employees of Thorndike Press hope you have enjoyed this Large Print book. All our Thorndike and Wheeler Large Print titles are designed for easy reading, and all our books are made to last. Other Thorndike Press Large Print books are available at your library, through selected bookstores, or directly from us.

For information about titles, please call:

(800) 223-1244

or visit our Web site at:

www.gale.com/thorndike
www.gale.com/wheeler

To share your comments, please write:

Publisher
Thorndike Press
295 Kennedy Memorial Drive
Waterville, ME 04901